6x 5/05

Deadline

for a Critic

For Javan

Acknowledgments

Gratitude for technical advice to:

Sgt. Roy Awe, Homicide, Detroit Police Department

Ramon Betanzos, Professor of Humanities,
    Wayne State University

Detroit Free Press:
        Lawrence DeVine, Theater Critic
        John Guinn, Music Critic
        Neal Shine, Senior Managing Editor

Detroit Symphony Orchestra:
        Cathy Compton, Viola
        Oliver Green, Personnel Manager
        Gunther Herbig, Music Director

Jim Grace, Detective, Kalamazoo Police Department

Sister Bernadelle Grimm, R.S.M.,
    Samaritan Health Care Center, Detroit

Timothy Kenny, Deputy Chief of the Criminal Division,
    Wayne County Prosecutor's Office

Walter D. Pool, M.D., Medical Consultant

Wendy Schulte, Modeling Consultant

Hal Youngblood, Host of "Hal Youngblood's Nighttime Report"

Any technical error is the author's.

Part One

Preparation of the Body

1

There is something special about an execution.

Ordinarily, the condemned is suffering from no fatal disease. No mortal wound has been inflicted. At least not yet. All the vital forces of the body tell it to go on living. It is not time to slow down. It is not time to die.

But some outside force, some external element—authority—decrees that it is, indeed, time to die. And so, by fiat, it is.

That is what is so special about an execution, whether it be legal by way of capital punishment or illegal as in an act of murder. A life is taken before its apparent due course has been completed. One faces eternity prematurely. The ultimate trauma, as it were.

Often, some sort of quasi ceremony is observed. Sometimes the condemned is permitted to pray, to put his or her soul in order. Sometimes the morbid curiosity of the executioner must be satisfied: How will the condemned face death? Sometimes invitations are issued and a procession to the death chamber is formed.

Traditionally, the condemned is given the choice of a final meal. Such was the case with Ridley C. Groendal. Except that he was not aware that this was to be his last supper.

"Ramon," Groendal said, tucking the napkin over his tummy, "what would you suggest?"

"Monsieur would enjoy the pâté tonight, I am sure." The waiter exuded a poise that went with his job. After all, the London Chop House was the consensus prestige scene of Detroit restaurants. And its prices reflected that eminence.

Groendal nodded. "Yes, yes, yes. And I think some of your beluga caviar."

"No . . ." Groendal's dinner partner murmured to no one in particular.

". . . and perhaps some Brie," Groendal continued.

"Incredible," Peter Harison murmured again.

"Excellent," Ramon said. "And you, Monsieur Harison?"

"Nothing. If anything, I'll help Mr. Groendal with his hors d'oeuvres."

"Of course." Ramon's right eyebrow lifted almost imperceptibly. "And something from the bar?"

"A double martini, up—chill the gin—with a twist," Groendal said.

"Ah, the usual. Very good. And Monsieur Harison?"

"Nothing."

Ramon left them.

"Would you mind telling me whatinhell you're trying to do?" Harison's fury was intensified by frustration.

"Not at all, m'dear. Just having a decent meal."

"Decent meal! With all that fat and salt and cholesterol? You can't have forgotten you've got a heart condition!"

"That's not the only condition I've got."

"That can't be helped."

Ramon brought the drink and hors d'oeuvres.

Groendal took a long sip of the martini. He wanted the drink to provide a mellow glow before its power was diminished by food. "That's precisely the point, dear Peter: It can't be helped. So—eat, drink and be merry. For tomorrow . . ."

"That's precisely the point." Harison spread some Brie on a portion of matzo. "We want as many tomorrows as we can possibly have. But we're not going to have many if you let your diet go to hell like this."

"Patience, Peter. After all, tonight is a special night."

Ramon returned. "Would the gentlemen care to order? I know you have a performance to attend."

"Thoughtful, Ramon," Groendal acknowledged. "Care to join me in the Caesar salad?" he asked Harison.

His companion simply shook his head.

"Very well," Groendal continued, "I'll have the Mediterranean salad. And . . . how's the Yorkshire pudding?"

"Perfect."

"Of course. Then the pudding with the prime rib, and cottage fries."

"And for dessert?"

"The coconut cream pie?"

"Excellent as always."

"Perfect."

"And Monsieur Harison?"

"Dover sole and baked potato." His voice was barely audible.

"I beg pardon?"

"The sole and a baked potato."

"No salad or dessert for Monsieur?"

"That will be all, thanks."

Ramon left.

"Suicide!" said Harison.

"Hmmmm?"

"You know you're going to make yourself ill, Rid. But worse than that, you're flirting with another coronary. And you know the doctor said you can't take another one."

"Life is a mystery, Peter. Death is a mystery. We never know what we will die from or when. We live each day to the fullest, no?" As he spoke, Groendal continued to heap portions of matzo alternately with pâté, cheese, and caviar.

"That's not you, Rid. You were never that way before. This fatalism has taken over your personality. It's not healthy."

"Life is not healthy . . . at least mine isn't."

Ramon brought the entrées, and Groendal's salad as well. It was his custom to take salad and entrée in the same course.

Before tasting either beef or potatoes, Groendal sprinkled salt generously on both. Harison winced and shook his head.

After servicing several other tables, Ramon returned to his station, from which vantage he could oversee the progress of his diners. He was joined by Vera, a waitress garbed, as was he, in black tie.

"Slow night," Vera commented.

"Should pick up. It's early," said Ramon.

She nodded toward Groendal and Harison. "I see you've got the bastard."

Ramon shrugged. "Rub kitty wrong, kitty scratches. Rub kitty right, kitty purrs. He's not so bad."

"He's not so bad as long as he's eating exactly what he wants. And from what I can see, he's eating exactly what he wants. You should have seen him a couple of weeks ago when he was observing some kind of diet. I thought he was going to have me served with an apple in my mouth."

Ramon suppressed a smile. "Have no fear: Harison keeps him on the straight and narrow."

"Hmmph." She pondered for a moment. "When was the last time anyone saw Groendal without Harison?"

Ramon winked. "Don't be so coy. There are no closets anymore."

"Don't get me wrong. I don't care who's screwing whom in this town. It's just that there's something to be said for discretion. As far as Groendal and Harison are concerned, flaunting their relationship doesn't exactly show tact."

"Don't be so hard on them, Vera. As a matter of fact, it must be doing them some good: Look at all the weight Monsieur Groendal has lost in just the past few months . . . one of the fringe benefits of a *mariage d'amour.* One tends to try to improve one's appearance for one's beloved, n'est-ce pas?"

"There's another name for it."

Ramon waited.

"AIDS."

"Oh, come now, Vera. That's not nice."

"Not nice, but probably true. Don't tell me those surgical gloves you've been wearing are so transparent nobody's noticed them."

"No notice is taken when one is discreet."

"So why do you wear them?"

"One cannot be too careful."

"Well, if he does croak I can think of a lot of local artists who will not be at all sorry."

Ramon smirked. "That's not at all like you, Vera." He noted that Groendal and Harison had finished. As he hastened to bring dessert and coffee while the table was being cleared, he pulled taut his thin rubber gloves.

Ramon's habit of wearing gloves while serving at table had originated with the relatively recent proliferation of AIDS. He washed his hands so often that his skin was rough and raw, a condition which fostered the introduction of infection. Yet it was impossible to avoid handling used dinner utensils bearing diners' saliva. And saliva, reportedly, might be one of the vehicles for the transmission of AIDS. One could not be too careful.

He had articulated that thought to Vera in seeming jest. But he was concerned. Especially when serving someone such as Ridley C. Groendal. Ramon would never forget the specter of Rock Hudson, a sometime visitor to the Chop House, in the later stages of what seemed then a newly discovered disease, Acquired Immune Deficiency Syndrome. That substantial, rugged, handsome man reduced to a skeletal shadow of himself. One look at the ravaged Hudson had convinced Ramon he must take every precaution against AIDS. This was not something amenable to the so-called miracle drugs. This was a fatal illness that weakened and ravaged the body unmercifully.

So, while he wore the surgical gloves as a matter of routine, it was specifically from one such as Groendal that Ramon felt he needed protection. None of the diners ever had complained about the gloves, or even seemed to notice them. Whether or not any of the diners had actually contracted this dread disease, all understood the nature of the illness and the need for self-protection for one in Ramon's position.

"You're not going to do that too!" Harison said as Groendal lit a cigar.

Groendal tilted his head back and blew a series of smoke rings. "Peter, either I am having an unaccustomed problem making myself clear or you simply refuse to believe me. The fact is, in what time I have left I intend to enjoy myself to the fullest . . . that can't be so difficult to understand."

"But Rid, enjoying yourself to the fullest is shortening the time you have left." His voice held a hint of desperation.

Groendal swirled the cognac in his snifter and appeared to study its amber smoothness. "We must not forget, Peter, that God—or somebody—has decided to drop the final curtain on my life somewhat prematurely. So I am going for quality rather than quantity. Peter, the last thing in this world I want is to go out as a cripple. We've talked about this. Why is it so difficult for you to accept? After all, it's my life, not yours."

Harison had no response.

"Peter, let me live my life my way. And let me end my life my way."

Harison winced inwardly, but tried not to show how deeply his friend's words had distressed him.

Groendal finished the pie, the cigar, coffee, and cognac almost simultaneously. He signed the bill with a flourish, including a generous tip.

A valet brought the car. Harison, as was his role, climbed into the driver's seat. They traveled up Woodward Avenue in silence. Harison was conscious of Groendal's labored breathing. Several times, Harison stole a glance at his companion. Groendal's complexion was sallow and his face seemed somewhat stretched. It was not actually elongated; the illusion was caused by his dramatic weight loss and the resulting sunken cheeks and recent lines in his face. Groendal should not be working tonight, Harison knew. He should be home resting. But then, neither should he have ingested the dinner he'd just eaten.

It came down to the fact that nobody told Ridley C. Groendal what to do. Not even the management at the *New York Herald,* from which publication Groendal had recently retired, had dictated to him. Certainly no one at the *Suburban Reporter* to whom Groendal contributed his regular column and periodic reviews, dared challenge an arts critic with his credentials. For Groendal, this was much more than a second career (which, financially, he did not need); it was more an outlet for criticism that he had to vent.

The expression of this criticism—which many claimed was harsh, persistently negative, self-serving, even cruel, vindictive, and unjust— earned Groendal many enemies. In his former vantage at the *Herald,* these enemies had been a cosmopolitan, international group of artists.

Since his retirement—a bit early and, as it turned out, forced—most of his more famous victims had been able to forget if not forgive him. It vexed Groendal that he was no longer in the power chair of the *Herald.* He tried to compensate by blasting away at hapless local talent as well as the headliners who passed through town.

* * *

It was early enough so that Harison was able to find a parking space on Woodward, across from Orchestra Hall, site of tonight's concert.

Groendal strode through the lobby as if he owned the Hall. Harison, following closely in his wake, presented the tickets—two on the aisle— as had been the case these many years they had been attending first-nights.

The two men immediately became the center of attention of the few patrons who had arrived early.

Harison, of moderate height and build, was distinguishable by a nearly completely bald pate from which erupted two significant side tufts of hair, making him most resemble Clarabelle the Clown, of "Howdy-Doody" fame.

Groendal, still impressive and distinguished, despite his ominous weight loss that gave him a haggard appearance, was tall, with a heavy head of salt-and-pepper hair. A dark blue suit fit him rather well since it had been recently purchased. He slipped off his black overcoat and draped it over one arm as he advanced to his down-front seat.

Groendal was easily and readily recognized because, unlike most other critics, his self-promotion machine was always well-oiled. His flamboyance in word and deed, along with his photo, was (at his insistence) well-publicized.

As the two men settled in, Groendal began studying his program. "Look at this, will you?" He did not bother lowering his voice.

Harison paged through his program. He glanced at the offerings, but said nothing, waiting for Groendal's inevitable comment.

"Octets by Schubert and Mendelssohn and a quintet by Beethoven," Groendal noted quite loudly. "Can you imagine that? Schubert, Mendelssohn, and Beethoven! Romantics! Romantics! Romantics! It just goes to prove the point I've been making over and over: David Palmer has not yet entered the twentieth century!"

The thought crossed Harison's mind that it was possible that the Schubert, Mendelssohn, and Beethoven would be well performed. But he did not bother saying so. He knew that his friend had selected his target for the evening and was already composing his review.

However, Harison knew he was expected to play a docile devil's advocate. Over the years, the role he played opposite Groendal had become so defined as to be routine.

"Now, Rid, you know how difficult it is to get audiences to accept some of the modern composers. Maybe Palmer doesn't think Detroit is ready for Schönberg and Ives. After all, he's got to try to fill this place."

"Nonsense! The way to do it is to tuck them in. All right, have your Mendelssohn and Beethoven, or your Schubert and Mendelssohn, but drop Bartók in there. The reason the expressionists, the atonals, the minimalists, haven't caught on is that cowards like Palmer shy away from them. Detroit will never grow up until people like Palmer are driven out of positions of leadership!"

That was enough. Harison had played his part in this oft-repeated scenario. He knew he was right. This was the first century in which, with rare exception, the composers of that century were not performed. In Mozart's day, they played Mozart. In Beethoven's era, they played Beethoven. And of course the masters were still extremely popular. But avant-garde composers of varying degrees of daring—such as Schönberg, Cage, Bartók, and Ives—seemed to appeal mainly to other modern composers. It was as if today's composers of serious music were writing for each other. Certainly not for the general public, which largely shunned them.

So it was a form of artistic suicide to schedule the moderns, particularly in a program of already limited appeal such as tonight's chamber concert.

No doubt about it: David Palmer, leader of the Midwest Chamber Players, was in for it. Harison knew Palmer would be blasted for, among more basic reasons, daring to offer three Romantic composers on the same program with nary a bow to the twentieth century.

But it didn't really matter what the provocation might have been. Maestro Palmer would have gotten a nasty notice in any case. That was Ridley C. Groendal. To know him was not necessarily to love him. That was an accomplishment of Peter Harison—and few others.

*　*　*

"Uh-oh . . . take a look out there!" Cellist Roberta Schwartz beckoned David Palmer to the peephole.

"Who is it?" Palmer asked. "Oh, never mind; I can tell from your tone: It's the gargoyle, isn't it?"

"And early, too."

"Naturally. He wouldn't want anyone to miss the fact that he's arrived. Groendal—either early or a late grand entrance—you can depend on it . . . the *News* or *Free Press* here yet?"

Roberta moved her head from side to side to scan the panorama of the hall. "No, not yet. But why should they be: They're normal."

She moved away from the peephole so Palmer could use it.

"Uh-huh." Palmer squinted through the small opening. "There he is, the old fart, already making notes in his program. I mean, how can you review a concert before the damn thing begins?"

"I wonder how we did."

Despite his foreboding, Palmer smiled. "Not well. On that you can depend. I wonder what we did wrong this time?"

"This is only a guess—God knows Groendal could write anything as long as it's so filled with jargon that no one can comprehend it—but if he's writing before we begin, I'll bet he doesn't like the program."

"That sounds a little too logical for Groendal."

"Just for safety's sake, you wanna tuck in a little Stravinsky?"

"Not unless you want everyone to leave at intermission and not come back—ever!"

"Just asking."

"Let's just give it our best shot. At least we can hope the two dailies will be honest and maybe even objective. Besides, I'm afraid I insured us a really rotten review from Groendal."

"That couldn't have been hard. Most people can get a really rotten notice from him without trying at all. What could you have done besides become leader of this group?"

"I sent him a note . . . a letter."

"Conciliatory, I hope."

" 'Fraid not. I really told him what I think of him and his so-called expertise. And I added a little personal message that should have set his teeth to grinding."

"I guess it wouldn't matter; in the final analysis we're all going to get it eventually. Oh, well, maybe we'll get lucky: Maybe your note will upset Groendal so much that he'll just up and drop dead. He does have high blood pressure, you know."

"And heart problems too." Palmer seemed uncomfortable. "I must admit the thought has crossed my mind. What a service to humanity if someone could eliminate him! Maybe it could be done by making him so damn mad he'd explode."

He wrinkled his nose. "I don't think my note worked though. I sent it quite a few days ago and . . . well, there he is: ready to stick his stiletto into us and twist it."

"Oh, don't give up hope. You know how backed up the mail gets at Christmastime. Maybe the post office hasn't delivered your message yet. So maybe Groendal hasn't read it yet." She grinned. "Maybe you'll kill him yet."

The very real possibility that he might be able to bring about Groendal's death, or at very least his removal from the artistic scene, had occurred more than once to Palmer. The prospect made him almost giddy. There was little doubt that eliminating Groendal from the critic's chair would be hailed as a noble deed.

Well, in any case, it had not worked. For there he was—or rather, there they were, Batman and Robin. The Midwest Chamber Players would perform Beethoven, Mendelssohn, and Schubert, and would perform them very well. After which the group would be massacred by Ridley C. Groendal. It was foreordained.

"Let's get limbered up," Palmer said. "Just fifteen minutes till showtime."

Palmer and Schwartz joined the other strings in exercising fingers and flirting with some of the melodies they would be playing in just a few minutes.

*   *   *

"God, I wish they wouldn't play so loudly when they warm up," Harison remarked.

"It's Palmer, that showboat! It's his way of dominating the other musicians. Don't worry, Peter; I'll take care of him."

Harison was certain Palmer would be cared for unto critical death. He turned slightly to see who else might be arriving a bit early. "I think that's Mitchell a few rows back."

"Who?"

"Carroll Mitchell—the playwright."

"You do him too much honor. He doesn't deserve the title."

*   *   *

"For some reason, this always seems to be the most exciting moment at a concert." Lynn Mitchell had just settled into her mid-main floor seat.

Carroll Mitchell smiled. "You mean all that noise? That's cacophony."

"No, Mitch, listen: The musicians are tuning their instruments and warming up. And in between, you can catch snatches of the melodies they're going to play . . . hear that one?"

"What one?"

"There: the violin. It's the loudest. That's David Palmer. It's sort of a trademark with him. No matter whether it's a small chamber group like tonight or the Detroit Symphony, you can always hear him above everyone else."

"Yeah, okay, I can hear him. Isn't that kind of distracting to the other players?"

"I don't know. It's just the way he is. But isn't that a lovely melody? It's the Mendelssohn. Don't you get a thrill, Mitch? Behind those curtains are eight professionals getting ready to recreate some of the most beautiful music ever composed."

"Don't get me wrong, honey. I know I'll enjoy the performance. I just don't get much out of warm-ups. But then we're even: You don't get much out of the calisthenics before a football game."

"Oh, come on!" She grimaced in mock anger. "What do your actors do before one of your plays?"

He cleared his throat. "Limber up, lose their cookies . . . things like that. But that's different."

"Oh?"

"The audience doesn't hear any of that. They do their make-up and warm-ups in their dressing rooms. Even if they did do it backstage, they'd never be heard by the audience. So it's not the same as all that racket we're hearing now . . . although the feeling must be the same. Getting ready for any audience is a nerve-wracking experience. You never know what to expect. Each audience has its own character and no two are exactly alike. And if you don't grab them at the opening curtain, you may never get them. At least that's the way it is in theater. I assume it's the same with a concert."

"I suppose so," said Lynn. "Except that a concert like tonight's has three chances to catch or lose you."

"Three?"

"Um-hmmm. If you don't like the Beethoven, then how about the Schubert or the Mendelssohn? Speaking of those three old faithfuls, I don't guess the situation makes him very happy." She nodded toward the front of the hall.

"Who's that?" Mitchell craned to see.

"Down front, second row, on the aisle . . . see?"

"Damn! Groendal! Did you have to point him out? All he has to do is show up and an evening is shot. I think his motto must be, 'Help Stamp Out Fun.' I hope those poor souls backstage don't know he's here."

Lynn shook her head. "If they don't know now, they certainly will after his review is printed."

"What was it you said . . . something about old faithfuls?"

"The program. It's three composers from the same general era. And worse, there's nobody from this century represented."

"Well! A sin that cries to heaven for vengeance, I assume. You know, probably a whole bunch of these people came tonight just to enjoy some beautiful music. But just seeing Groendal and knowing the kind of review he's bound to write, they're going to be hypercritical themselves —see if they can guess what he's going to find wrong and try to agree with him."

Lynn sank down in her seat so Groendal was no longer in her line of vision. "I don't know how he keeps getting away with it. Just because he used to be with the *New York Herald!* Now he's a big fish in a little pond. I swear, somebody ought to tell him where to get off."

Mitchell shifted nervously. "Uh, honey . . . I haven't mentioned it to you . . . but . . . I did."

"Did what?"

"Told him where to get off."

Lynn turned to face her husband. "You did *what?* To Ridley Groendal! When? How?"

"About a week ago. I sent him a letter. I'm afraid I really let him have it. It may have been foolish . . . but I don't regret it. Besides, I can't take it back. He must have gotten it by now. I haven't heard a word . . . but undoubtedly he's mentally composing a killer review for my next play."

"He won't have to wait that long; isn't Marygrove going to do *New Hope* next month?"

"Yeah. But that's been around awhile; he bashed that all over the place a couple of years ago."

Lynn shook her head. "Doesn't matter. He's done it before. Knocked the performance and kicked hell out of the play. Well, dammit, I'm proud of you! It's about time someone had the guts to let him have it. I'm glad you did it. I can just see him when he got your letter. He must have been furious. I doubt that anybody ever had the guts to do that before. Matter of fact, the shape he's in, I'm surprised it didn't kill him."

"Tell you the truth, I wouldn't have minded one damn bit if we had read that he'd been carted off to the hospital. I guess I just didn't quite reach the old boy's notoriously short fuse. I feel sort of like somebody in an old Western who takes on a hired gun. I drew and fired—and missed. Now he can shoot me down at his leisure."

"Never mind." Lynn patted his arm and snuggled close. "I'm proud of you no matter what happens."

*   *   *

"Isn't that Carroll Mitchell and his wife up ahead?" Valerie Walsh asked.

"Where? Oh, yeah, I think so."

Bill "Red" Walsh was much better qualified than his wife to verify the presence of the Mitchells. A professional basketball player, at six-feet-eight he was sixteen inches taller than his wife—a petite and beautiful local actress.

The usher showed them to their seats near the rear of the main floor. There was a stir among nearby patrons. Some recognized Valerie. But from his size alone, not to mention the frequency of his appearances on the local sports pages, more people identified her husband.

Valerie paged through her program.

"Now, that's a coincidence, isn't it?" Walsh did not bother with a program. He was present only because his wife wanted his company. "I mean Mitchell's being here just a few rows ahead of us. Aren't you supposed to be in one of his plays soon?"

"*New Hope.*" She did not look up.

"Yeah, you did that one before, didn't you?"

"Um-hmmm; a couple of years ago, when it first opened."

"Was it that long ago . . . God!" Walsh squirmed, attempting to find comfort in a space definitely not meant for a large person. It was by no means an uncommon challenge. "Hey, isn't that the guy you're always talking about?"

"Who?" Valerie looked up.

"There . . . down front, near the aisle . . . you know the guy." Walsh seldom adverted to the fact that others' sight-lines did not give them the same view that his aerie gave.

Finally, by half-standing, Valerie was able to spot him. "Groendal! Well, you're wrong about one thing, Red. I don't 'always' talk about the bastard. Only when I've been fouled and the referee refuses to call it."

"Gotcha!" And he did. "If he weren't so old, I'd pop him for you."

Valerie smiled. "That's sweet of you, love. But it wouldn't solve anything. He'd just come back needlessly hurting people twice as much as before . . . if that's possible."

"Well, we know you can't get his attention by batting him around, eh? Any of you people ever think of putting out a contract on him?"

Valerie looked up, startled.

"Just kidding."

"Well, I should hope so."

"Seriously . . . he sure seems to be making life rough for a lot of nice people. I wonder how long he's gonna go on doing that?"

She sighed. "I don't know." She shook her head. "Ordinarily, we don't get so worked up over criticism, even when it's negative. After all, I'm in a field where everything is pretty much subjective. Either you like a person's performance or you don't. It's not like you and basket-ball. There you can measure a performance by some pretty objective standards—points scored, percentages, assists, shots blocked, rebounds, things like that. With me, I can deliver my lines perfectly, make no mistakes in performance; the audience may love me . . . and still a critic can blast me just because he didn't like what I did . . . or maybe just because he's got something against me personally."

"Yeah. There's some sportswriters that are like that. No pleasing 'em."

"Well, that's the way it is, I guess. You're right; there's an element of subjective evaluation even in sports, I suppose . . . though not as much as in the arts. But a jerk like Ridley Groendal goes beyond that. He's vindictive and mean. He's the type of critic who needs to feel more significant than the artist he's critiquing." She paused. "You know, I didn't think I could get more angry at him, or loathe him any more than I do. But his latest review of the Detroit Symphony really reached me. He even singled out Dave Palmer for individual blame."

"That's bad?"

"There's really no way, from the vantage of the audience, to tell if one specific musician in the entire first violin section has made a mis-take. God, even the conductor can't do that! But Ridley C. Groendal can!

"He's really got it in for Dave Palmer, along with just about everyone else, and he's going to nail him every chance he gets. You watch: When he reviews tonight's concert, odds are he'll single out Palmer and blast him."

"But from what you tell me, he does things like that all the time. How come *this* reached you?"

"I don't know; I guess it was just the final straw. Anyway, I sent him a nasty letter."

"Uh-oh. What's that gonna do to your career?"

Valerie smiled briefly. "Honey, my 'career' is taking care of you and our kids. Oh, I know once upon a time, Groendal had a shot at my career and hit it dead center. He can't hurt me anymore, much as he still tries. But I can reach him. I mean really reach him: scare the hell out of him."

"You mean like old Scrooge in *A Christmas Carol?*"

"That's the ticket. It's about time somebody let that rotten creep know that, to some extent, we all live in glass houses. And some of us have some pretty big rocks to throw."

"Uh-oh, there go the lights. The concert's about to start."

       *   *   *

"Finally!" Harison said. "We're about to get started. About time."

"I can hardly wait." Groendal's voice dripped sarcasm.

Harison turned one final time to view the near-capacity audience. "Uh-oh! They're just coming in now. In the balcony."

"Who?"

"Charlie and Lil Hogan."

"That piece of trash. He'd be better off staying home and working on a novel. Not that it would do any good. No matter what he tries, it's still going to be a sow's ear."

       *   *   *

"Hurry up! The lights are dimming; the concert's about to start." Lil Hogan looked about frantically, trying to locate their seats.

"It's all right," Charlie assured her, "we've still got a couple of minutes." He handed their stubs to an usherette, who led them down the aisle and indicated two empty seats toward the middle of the row.

"Excuse me," Lil said repeatedly as she led the way around and past a series of legs. "Well, here we are," she remarked as she sat down.

"Lil, you're just going to have to get more organized. We can't keep arriving places at the last minute. My heart won't take the strain." He was kidding and she knew it.

"Your heart's okay, Charlie. And nobody knows that better than I. Unfortunately," she nodded toward the main floor of the gradually darkening hall, "Ridley Groendal's heart seems to be every bit as good as yours."

"What's that? Oh, my God, there he is!" Hogan hesitated in lowering himself into his seat. Directed by his wife's gaze, he identified Groendal in the diminished light.

"He seems to have survived your letter," Lil said.

"If truth be known, I don't give a damn whether he survived or not. The thing is, I feel better. I've been keeping a whole bunch of things bottled up for so many years. It just felt good to get them off my chest. But I'm not done with that bastard yet." .

"Well, for what it's worth, I thought it was high time somebody told him off—for all the good it'll do. I think he's one of those people who are so nasty to the core that they can't be reached."

"There goes the curtain, Lil."

"Right. Let's enjoy the concert until we read Ridley C. Groendal and find out how lousy it was."

"Damn!"

2

It was an unpretentious building, a squat, two-story gray structure near the corner of Jefferson and the Chrysler Freeway. It was particularly unprepossessing considering the enormous influence of the *Suburban Reporter,* for which the little building was headquarters.

It had not always been thus.

The *Reporter* had begun in the mid-twentieth century as an advertisers' and buyers' guide. The brainchild of Jonathan Dunn, it was, in the beginning, a shoestring operation—literally. Shoelaces were used to hold together cigar boxes that contained the monthly receipts.

As it turned out, the *Reporter*'s very survival was attributable to the determination, tenacity, and talent of Jonathan Dunn. He, almost alone, nursed it through its vicissitudes and growing pains as well as the insults and derogations directed at it. "Legitimate" journalists, i.e., editors and staff writers at Detroit's daily metropolitan newspapers, invariably referred to the *Reporter,* if at all, as the "Shoppers' Guide."

Generally, those in the editorial section of almost any publication tend to think that anyone can sell advertising while it takes rare talent to "write." So there is a tendency on the part of reporters, editors, and columnists to look down pseudoaristocratic noses at a publication composed almost entirely of ads.

Thus, while the "big" papers were snickering at the *Suburban Reporter,* this modest "shoppers' guide" was growing, imperceptibly at first, then like Topsy.

It expanded from a monthly to a weekly (more bad jokes, puns on weekly vs. weakly) to twice weekly.

Then, over the years, many heavy local advertisers left Detroit for the suburbs. There they found an indigenous publication geared precisely to their desires.

Now, positions were nearly reversed. The big dailies began to scramble for ads in direct competition with the maligned *Suburban Reporter.* Once a week, the *News* and the *Free Press* published special regional sections. But an impartial observer would have to conclude that the *Reporter* had been there first.

And as the *Reporter* grew fat, its editorial sections began to increase both in size and influence. While the pay scale and fringe benefits did not compare favorably with all that the unions had won at the dailies over the years, the impact of reportage and opinion was in a similar, if not the same, ballpark.

An ideal vehicle then, for a Ridley C. Groendal.

Groendal's career at the *New York Herald* had been terminated somewhat prematurely. He could have retired at age sixty-five. By mutual agreement he might have continued virtually interminably. As it happened, management forced him into retirement at age fifty-seven. It was not a happy parting but it was one whose details were carefully worked out if not to everyone's delight, at least to everyone's minimal satisfaction.

The *Herald* had grown most unhappy with Groendal's work over the years. In the beginning, he had seemed to possess all the erudition of which he was prone to boast. As time passed, it became evident to informed readers as well as to management at the paper that what Groendal possessed was the appropriate jargon required for criticism of the various art forms. He also manifested a disgust, at times an outright loathing, for most artists, writers, and performers.

In the early days it was the acid flowing from his pen that had attracted both his editors and readers; he may have caused great pain among the fine arts community but he was seldom dull.

As he did battle with the years, however, he grew predictable and effete. Eventually, the complaints and protests of the fine arts community—and its moneyed patrons—touched a chord with management. It was both the quantity and quality of protest that did the trick.

Management determined that Groendal must go. That decision was followed by weeks of meetings dedicated to the question of how to get rid of him. For one, his position was protected by contract. And two, a knockdown, drag-out war was an unseemly sort of wrangle for the staid *Herald* to get into with any of its employees. Finally, no way did the *Herald* wish to, in effect, admit that its principal critic was by and large a fraud.

However, management has ways of inducing employees, even those protected by contract, to leave. While employed at the same publication and receiving the same pay, writers can be given rotten assignments.

They can be put on the graveyard shift. They can be shunted to inferior work space. There are countless ways of prompting resignation or retirement, with neither an admission of administrative blunder nor the payment of enormous severance.

Ridley Groendal was as aware as anyone else in the business of the myriad avenues of coercion open to management. When the writing on the wall became crystal clear, Groendal wisely decided to cut his losses. He entered into a prolonged bargaining position. This resulted in his early and seemingly honorable retirement garnished with a formal, seemingly sincere statement of regret from management.

At which point, Groendal and his inseparable companion Peter Harison decided to return to what had once been home for Groendal— the Detroit area. And so, the previous year, the two had moved into a most adequate house in Dearborn Heights.

With the generous retirement settlement from the *Herald,* along with his considerable savings, Groendal—as well as Harison—could have lived out his years comfortably. And that, from a critical standpoint, would have been that.

Had not Jonathan Dunn entered the picture.

Of course there were rumors throughout the industry of what had really happened between the *Herald* and Ridley Groendal. But the scuttlebutt, by and large, did not filter down to the general public. Any publication that would employ Groendal at this stage would have been a laughing stock due to these inside rumors . . . a fate that couldn't have disturbed Dunn less. He'd survived all the stages of disrepute; names would never hurt him.

Thus, when Dunn learned that a writer with Groendal's fame (or notoriety, depending on one's viewpoint) was now living in the area and was idle, the grand idea struck.

It did not take Groendal long to take the bait.

At the outset, he knew it was near perfect. Granted, the pay was a joke, and the platform, compared with his former stage at the *Herald,* was inconsequential. But he was itching for a pulpit—of whatever kind —and, pound for pound, the *Suburban Reporter* was not all that bad. Naturally, if he had to condescend to some sort of provincial podium, he would have preferred the *News* or the *Free Press* with their massive circulations. Short of that, he was satisfied with the *Reporter.* The right people were reading it. Its reputation and clout were mushrooming. And he had carte blanche.

So, much to the chagrin and downright anger of the local fine arts community, the deal was struck. Groendal had his pulpit.

* * *

It was almost midnight when Groendal let himself and Harison into the now otherwise deserted building. They would have arrived sooner had not Groendal—over Harison's fruitless protest—insisted on stopping for another dessert and liqueur.

Groendal went directly to the editorial room where three word processors waited. Considering all the alcohol he'd had this evening, he walked very steadily. Harison followed, stopping only to gather Groendal's mail, which he placed on the desk at which Ridley chose to work. Then Harison sat at a neighboring desk, to leaf through news releases.

Groendal wasted no time. After programming the VDT, he began feeding it immediately. This confirmed Harison's hunch that Groendal had mentally written this review long before . . . likely before the concert had even begun.

As he typed, Groendal gave vent to self-satisfied little cluckings, as he always did when writing a review. Harison, used to the sounds, paid little attention.

In short order, the review was finished. The ritual, peculiar to the two, proceeded. Groendal pushed himself from the machine and Harison moved in to read the copy on the display terminal.

Harison had to adjust his vision to discern the small white characters on the green background. Groendal moved around the desk and began going through his accumulated mail.

Groendal's style was so familiar to Harison that it was easy to skim the copy. He looked for the telltale phrases, clauses, that were the hallmark of a Groendal review. After all these years, they were not difficult to spot. ". . . wrestling running passages strenuously to the stage floor and pushing uncomfortably the strident tones of a violin, which, in David Palmer's hands, became a deadly weapon . . ."

Ah, yes. Clearly—had there been any doubt?—this was not destined to be a favorable notice. ". . . Palmer's tendency to be treacly . . ."

Another.

"After an uncertain beginning, Palmer led the tremolando strings through a tangled maze of fragmented phrases and passingly inhibited emotions."

This might be one of Ridley's better efforts.

"The Midwest Chamber Players might be directed back to the drawing board. The Schubert and Mendelssohn did not work together. The Beethoven, for example, was tame and humorless as a result of being sandwiched between these two majestic and stentorian pieces. His chaste little quintet almost died of suffocation. The entire performance contained passages that were lost in amorphous rhapsody and, with it all, the players missed a needed sense of intuitive mania."

While Harison continued to read—or, more actually, scan—the review, Groendal created a steady tattoo of pieces of junk mail hitting the metal wastebasket. Publicity releases and promotional pieces followed one another to the trash.

Harison scanned on.

"Palmer's interpretation was tainted by Mendelssohn's neuroticism, aided and abetted by the ensemble's aberrant phrasing."

The tattoo had let up. Harison glanced at his friend. Groendal, having disposed of the junk mail, was starting on the first class mail. Harison returned to the review.

"The Beethoven might have been better had it not been for Palmer's quivering hypersensitivity to the most minute whines of the score. Thus the audience was subjected to almost shockingly bland odd gobblings which, in no time at all"—Groendal was in rare form—"became a little amorphous."

"Why that pompous son of a bitch!"

Harison looked at Groendal. His mouth was working, but nothing coherent was escaping. His outburst apparently had been occasioned by the letter he was reading. As he slammed the page down, his fist hit the table. The impact must have hurt, but his obvious anger seemed to sublimate the pain. He picked up another letter. Harison returned his attention to the review.

"Palmer seems determined to cement his reputation as Lord High Commissioner of all that is declamatory, bombastic, and pretentious in music. His is the stolid, detached, and uninspired attitude that so often infects leaders of chamber groups. This evening's offerings produced nothing so much as a potpourri of embarrassments."

Groendal uttered something, Harison had difficulty making out what. Something like, "She can't get away with this! She won't get away with this!"

"Were you talking to me?"

"What? No! No!" Groendal slammed the second letter on the desk and with the opener quite literally attacked a third envelope.

Harison read on. Mercifully for David Palmer and the Midwest Chamber Players, there wasn't much more. "Overall, the string sound was overwhelmingly undernourished, entirely and unfortunately due to Mr. Palmer's utter lack of music substance. Not that Palmer was inventive enough to take any chances with his program. Tonight's performance was analogous to a trapeze artist trying to insure the safety of his act by refusing to let go of the bar. To carry this torturous metaphor to its fatal conclusion, Palmer had better never try to perform without a net."

"Say," Harison commented, "this is rather good, Rid."

"Who does he think he is, God Almighty?" Groendal quite obviously was not responding to Harison. Rather, the critic was focusing his total concentration on a letter he was now crumpling into a small wad. "By God, I'll show him who's God!"

Harison grew attentive. It was difficult to see clearly by the soft fluorescent glow of the desk lamp, the sole light they had turned on. But it appeared that Groendal's face was becoming flushed. Harison was only too well aware of how very far Groendal had strayed from a sensible diet this evening.

"Rid, are you all right?"

Groendal now seemed oblivious to Harison's presence. He bounced the crumpled letter against the desk top and selected yet a fourth envelope.

"Of course! This one had to be from him! Four of a kind! All present and accounted for! All ganging up against me, are they? Well, we'll just see who gets the last laugh!"

Groendal tore the envelope away from the letter, spread the two pages on the desk and quickly, furiously read through it, pausing only to spit out invective.

"That's . . . that's ancient history!" He clutched at his tie, jerking it loose from his neck. "He wouldn't dare bring that up! Why, it was as much his fault as it was mine!" Suddenly, he turned frantic. He first fumbled with, then tore at his shirt, popping off the top buttons.

"Rid! Calm down!" Harison moved to Groendal's side. "Calm down! You're only upsetting yourself! Get hold of yourself!"

"Peter!" Groendal's eyes bulged. Rising from his chair, he clutched Harison's jacket with both hands, shaking the smaller man like a doll.

"Peter! None of them could do it alone! I could beat them one by one! I've done it before! Lots of times! They could never get away with this otherwise! But . . . Peter! But . . . Peter!" Groendal pulled Harison so close their noses almost touched. Now desperately concerned, Harison was unable to move. He could not escape Groendal's clutch.

"Peter . . . Peter . . . I . . . Peter! Oh, God . . . this can't be! I need . . . more time! Peter! Peter! Stay!"

Abruptly, Groendal released his grip, made a clutching gesture toward his chest and pitched forward, burying Harison beneath him.

It was Harison's turn to experience fear. He was pinned beneath what he was certain was literally dead weight. But in times of terror, some people's strength becomes as the strength of ten, whether or not their hearts are pure. With such unexpected strength, Harison pushed Groendal up and off him.

Still close to uncontrollable panic, he examined Groendal. He could detect no signs of life. But what did he know? Not only was he not at home with dead bodies, he was repelled by them.

Harison backed away from Groendal's still form. Could Ridley yet be alive? Was he just unconscious?

Harison wasn't sure what he should do next. CPR—any form of resuscitative aid—was beyond his capability. Help—he must call for help! 911. 911, the all-purpose emergency line. He turned and hurried through the door to the switchboard room, running into desks and overturning chairs on his way.

The board, as usual, was shut down for the night. How to activate it? Which buttons? He picked up the headset and with his other hand began to push switches. Nothing seemed to work.

Finally, despairing of getting a dial tone, he dropped the headset and ran toward the exit. Maybe he could find a public phone. Maybe it would not be out of order. Maybe he could avoid a heart attack himself.

3

Getting scooped in one's own newsroom is a bitter pill indeed. Such was the lot of *Suburban Reporter* staffers who responded to their editor's frantic phone calls in the wee hours of the morning. The general feeling was that they should do something. But what?

Most of the surface questions had already been asked by the television reporters: "With me is Detective Charles Papkin. Sergeant, have you found any signs of foul play in the death of Ridley Groendal?"

"We're not ruling out anything."

Or: "With me is Jonathan Dunn, publisher of the *Suburban Reporter*. Mr. Dunn, what will be the effect of Ridley Groendal's death on the print journalism field?"

"Ridley Groendal was an institution, a legend in his own time. He's going to be missed, there's no doubt about that."

A statement of the fact of Groendal's death, along with the taped interviews, would be included in the morning news programs. The story, as far as television was concerned, either would die at this point, or—if there were further developments—there would be more interviews for the noon, six and/or eleven o'clock news. Since most people got their news from television, most people would learn that a critic had died under somewhat questionable circumstances and that he would be missed by, among a few others, his publisher.

Reporters from the *News* and the *Free Press* were next in line, demanding considerably more background information than the TV people. Some were milling about in search of provocative quotes or any other angle to the story no matter how seemingly insignificant.

Reporter staffers had their questions too. But they knew that everyone else would be in print long before they would. They had to go for a second-day story. So far, they had accomplished little more than returning to stare at the still unmoved corpse of the late Ridley C. Groendal. And Groendal was now history.

"You say that Mr. Groendal didn't complain about anything this evening? No pain?" Ray Ewing, now questioning Harison, was by far the more affable of the two detectives present.

"No," Peter Harison answered. "He seemed to be feeling fine. The review he finished just before he died was one of his better efforts. And I don't think he could have done that if he'd been feeling ill. Rid was not the sort to work over great discomfort."

"But you mentioned something to Sergeant Papkin about what Mr. Groendal had to eat tonight . . ."

"Yes, I did." Harison was getting a bit testy. This was the second time he'd gone over the evening's events. "Do I have to do this again?"

"If you don't mind." Ewing's manner made it clear that it didn't matter whether or not Harison minded. He was going to do it again. The implication was not lost on Harison. "You never know when some detail will come to mind. Could be a big help."

"Oh, well, Rid really indulged himself tonight . . . uh, last night now, I guess. Anyway, he ate and drank all the wrong things. Bad for his heart, which was not all that strong."

"Why would he do that? I mean, if he knew it was bad for him."

Harison shrugged. "It certainly wasn't the first time Rid did something foolish like this. He was not the abstemious type. He liked his food and drink and he didn't, let us say, regularly deny himself. So tonight's dining and libations were not in any way unique. It's just that they happened to happen on a night when there would be a . . . a complication."

"Now that's one of the things I wanted to ask you about, Mr. Harison. We've heard from several sources, some of his fellow workers here, that Mr. Groendal was, well, a rather heavy eater. But he doesn't look like one . . . I mean, he could not be described as obese. As a matter of fact," Ewing's inclined head indicated the corpse stretched out on the floor nearby, "he seems to be pretty thin."

Harison shuddered. He had been trying assiduously to avoid again viewing his friend's body. Now that his attention was directed to the corpse, Harison noticed abstractedly that Groendal was now blue—at least the exposed skin of his face and neck were a bluish hue. "Well," he commented, "he wasn't always."

"I'm afraid I don't get it. If he had a weight problem and he was currently eating the way you've described, how come he wasn't a heavy man?"

Harison hesitated. "I guess you'd find out anyway. There'll be an autopsy, won't there?"

Ewing nodded.

"Rid had AIDS. That contributed to, if not caused, his somewhat emaciated appearance."

"I see." *I wonder,* thought Ewing, *if he got it from you?* It was not a certainty that Groendal had contracted the disease from Harison, but it was an hypothesis until something better came along.

Ewing had put this possibility—that theirs was a homosexual relationship—on hold in his mind shortly after he had arrived on the scene. It was not merely that the two men were together when Groendal died; a number of other factors contributed to the premise. The two were not journalistic colleagues. The deceased, the detectives were told, was a critic. The other stated he was not employed but was living in retirement. But he would not say from what he had retired. Then too, Harison had a slightly effeminate air.

That, along with the fact that they shared the same address and that neither was married, added to the suspicion that they were a homosexual couple. That Groendal had AIDS was about all Ewing needed to spell out his probable sexual preference. Short, of course, of coming right out and demanding the information from Harison. Which Ewing was prepared to do should such become relevant.

"I found it," said Papkin, returning to Ewing and Harison.

Ewing looked at the other detective inquiringly.

"The other letter Harison says Groendal was reading just before he keeled over. It's all crumpled into a ball." Papkin was carefully unfolding and smoothing a piece of paper.

"Where'd you find it?"

"Over there . . . on the floor." Papkin indicated a spot under a desk several yards from the desk at which Groendal and Harison had sat. "He must have been pretty goddam mad to have slammed it down hard enough to bounce it all the way over there. And it's crushed so tight it's tough straightening it out without tearing it."

"Oh, he was mad, all right," Harison said. "I've never seen him so angry."

"I found something else," Papkin said. He held up an object he had enclosed in a plastic bag, protecting possible latent fingerprints.

"Oh?" Ewing studied it without reaching for it. It appeared to be an empty syringe. "Where was it?"

"On the floor under the desk—next to that letter."

Ewing turned to Harison. "Do you know anything about this?"

Harison seemed startled. "It's a syringe."

"We know that. Do you know of any reason we should find it close to Groendal's desk and near a letter he had discarded?"

Harison appeared to have recovered from his initial shock. He shrugged. "It's probably Rid's. He is—was—a diabetic. He had to take regular insulin injections. It's the same size and type that Ridley used."

"Then we should find traces of insulin—and nothing else—in the syringe."

"I . . . I suppose so. Of course."

"One more thing: Do you have any idea how the syringe got on the floor?"

Harison shook his head. "Not really. I guess he must have missed the wastebasket. Or, maybe the cleaning lady was careless when she emptied the basket."

Wordlessly, Papkin placed the plastic bag with the four letters, apparently the last ones Groendal had read. These letters by themselves constituted more than enough to initiate a homicide investigation. But it was always nice to have a possible weapon as evidence—the proverbial smoking gun. In this case, a syringe that had been used by somebody— Groendal, or, perhaps, his killer.

"We'll have it checked out," Papkin said. "Are you done with Harison?"

"For the moment, yes." Ewing turned back to Harison. "We'll undoubtedly have more questions. We'd appreciate your keeping yourself available."

Harison left the detectives with some reluctance, though he had no singularly attractive option. A few reporters were still waiting to ask more questions, most of which would undoubtedly be impertinent. Eventually he would have to make funeral arrangements. He was not looking forward to that. And, inevitably, he would have to go home— by himself. He knew that would be wrenchingly lonely.

All in all, he minded least talking to the detectives, especially Ewing. He, for one, did not ask some of the more embarrassing questions. But now the detectives had sent him away. So there was nothing to do but face the unpleasant tasks that lay ahead.

*   *   *

In wordless agreement, Ewing and Papkin moved to an otherwise empty section of the newsroom so they could compare notes uninterrupted.

So far, all had gone by the book. The EMS had been first to respond to Harison's emergency call. That emergency medical squad had been followed by uniformed police and then by the medical technicians. Then Homicide had been summoned, and the routine investigation into an unexplained death had begun.

It was routine procedure. In the wake of a sudden, unexplained death, when there was any question whatsoever, the homicide department was summoned. Homicide detectives spent much of their time in the fruitless investigation of what often turned out to be very natural deaths. The theory was: Take every precaution; don't let a big one get away just because, on the surface, it appeared to be a natural death.

In answer to Papkin's question as to what might have directly precipitated this apparent heart failure, Harison had mentioned the letters Groendal had been both reading and reacting to just before he had collapsed.

Both plainclothes officers and the uniforms had then begun a search of the desk and wastebasket. They found all the third and fourth class mail in the basket; as well as three letters and four first class envelopes (together with some unopened first class) on the desk. It was not until Sergeant Papkin found the fourth letter crumpled into a wad on the floor—and picked up the syringe next to it—that they felt they had everything. Now, each read the letter that Papkin had done his best to smooth out.

"Well, what d'ya think?" Papkin asked.

"I'm not sure. These letters are dynamite. They'd be enough to get a rise out of just about anybody."

"I agree. So, suppose these people knew that Groendal had a history of high blood pressure and a bad heart . . ."

"Yeah, suppose."

"Seems to me they'd be creating a degree of risk so high they could figure that Groendal would get so worked up about them that he'd croak."

"Uh-huh." Ewing nodded. "And I get the impression almost everybody knew about Groendal's condition—his heart condition."

"Not everybody." Papkin smiled crookedly. *We* didn't know."

Ewing's answering grin evidenced a more genuine amusement.

"Charlie, I've been telling you for years you ought to be reading the fine arts section of the paper. Ain't no use both of us knowing just the box scores and the major league standings."

"So why should I have to sacrifice myself just so's we can be a well-rounded team?"

"Now that you mention it, no reason. Not as long as there's other people we can ask. And I did. And it turns out that, at least among the crowd that pays attention to the stage and books and the like, Groendal is very well known and so is his delicate condition."

"So," Papkin concluded, "what you're saying is that we've got a collection of four people, each presumably aware that Groendal had a bad ticker—and each of them sends the guy a letter so threatening and so filled with hate that any one of them could drive him up a wall." Papkin looked sharply at his partner. "Are you implying something like murder by remote control?"

"On top of that," Ewing continued to pursue his own line of thought, "we've got all four letters landing on him at the same time. So we could have not only the possibility of remote control murder, but a nice case of conspiracy on top of it all."

"You've got a suspicious mind, Ray. Have you considered that with all his health problems, maybe it was just time for this guy to go—period?" He reached for the letters and riffled through them. "See—" he looked triumphantly at his partner, "these letters aren't even all dated the same day. One is dated Sunday, one Wednesday, and two Thursday."

Ewing waved a hand as if chasing a mosquito from in front of his face. "There's one more thing."

"What's that?"

"These four letters Groendal read before he keeled over: Each of them was geared to drive him up a wall, but one of them stands out above the others. Did you notice? It would have put the fear of God into a normal healthy person, let alone a guy with a bad heart."

"Yeah, I know the one you mean. But even assuming you're right—and that's a pretty far-fetched assumption—how could we prove that one particular letter did the trick?"

"I don't know. Maybe the internal evidence. The content of the letter itself. We've got either the amazing coincidence of four letters just happening to get here about the same time. Or, it was no coincidence; it was a conspiracy. Or, one of the four really knew how to reach Groendal.

And that one letter deliberately written did it . . . and the other three letters just happened to arrive at the same time . . . what do you think?"

Papkin cocked an eyebrow. "How about this Harison character? Were he and Groendal fags?"

"I don't think there's much doubt about that. They lived together. Neither one's ever married. As far as I can tell, Harison lived off Groendal. Harison's a little swishy. And—the bottom line—Groendal had AIDS."

Papkin nodded. "That should do it."

"I think the only reason Harison admitted it is that he knew the M.E. would find it. I guess he figured we would really think something was fishy if we had to discover that for ourselves."

Papkin shook his head. "That sort of opens up the book on Harison."

"How's that?"

"Maybe he doesn't figure into all this, but it does put a new light on him."

"Huh?"

"Assume that Harison is the one who infected Groendal: How did Groendal feel—well, how would you feel about someone who gave you AIDS? Say Harison is a carrier—some guys are, you know, without having symptoms themselves—I mean if you sexually transmitted a fatal disease to somebody, what does that say about your feelings for him? It's hardly a loving gesture. And if you did give AIDS to somebody and he wasn't dying fast enough, maybe, just maybe, you could scare him to death."

"That's stretching, Charlie. For all we know, Groendal got AIDS from somebody else, not from Harison. Hell, for all we know, Groendal got it and gave it to Harison . . . if you want a motive for Harison, that makes more sense.

"So," Ewing concluded, after a moment's silence, "What've we got?"

Papkin glanced at his notes. "What we've got is one very sick guy. Jeez! He's got AIDS, he's a diabetic, and God knows what else. He has one hell of an evening for himself. He eats all the wrong things, he drinks way too much. He gets mad as hell, he has a stroke or a heart attack or whatever—the M.E. will tell us—and he croaks."

"Or?" The twinkle in Ewing's eye made it clear that he didn't believe a word of it.

"Or," Papkin continued, "we got a guy who managed to make quite a few dedicated enemies. Any one of those four letter writers could—and probably did—want him dead. Each one knew him well enough to know that his health was in an iffy state. What if each one decides to let it all hang out and see if some pretty definite threats can push him over the edge? It wouldn't be the first time someone scared somebody to death."

"Only, in this case, they would have angered him to death."

"Yeah . . ." Papkin stroked his chin. ". . . nice twist." He pondered. "But . . . what if the four of 'em get together and decide there's strength in numbers? And all four agree to send their letters at roughly the same time?"

"Why not at exactly the same time?"

"To throw us off. I don't know—just a guess for now. But they get together on it to zap him. Now that's conspiracy!" Papkin sounded downright exhilarated.

"Possible," Ewing acknowledged.

"Seems all Groendal had was enemies . . . 'cept of course for Harison. But Harison probably gave him AIDS. With friends like that, what would Groendal need with enemies?"

"Harison again! How would Harison have done it?" Ewing turned devil's advocate. Someone had to.

"I don't know. We've just started . . . wait a minute: Groendal was a diabetic. He needed insulin. Harison lived with him. He could've monkeyed with the insulin. He could have seen that Groendal got too much—or too little—of the stuff. Or, he lived with the guy, maybe he added something to the insulin."

"Why would he do that?"

"Why'd he give him AIDS?"

"Who says he did?"

"Okay, say he didn't. Say he's clean. Maybe he was mad as hell because he knew that if Groendal had AIDS that had to mean that Groendal had sex with somebody else. He couldn't have been happy about *that*—"

"Unhappy, okay. But mad enough to kill?"

"Why not?"

"And you claim *I've* got a suspicious mind! But if Harison did it, what about the letters?"

Papkin shrugged. "Just a coincidence . . . or"—he grinned—"maybe not." He made ready to leave. "Either way, we may need every suspicion in your suspicious mind. Right now, we've got a dead man. It could be accidental or it could be death by natural causes. But if I had a last buck—"

"I know: You'd put it on homicide. So would I."

4

Looks like a full house, thought Father Robert Koesler as he searched for a parking space. Thanks to some thoughtless and inconsiderate parking, there was no room in the mortuary lot. At least it was appropriate, the priest mused. We have just finished with the feast commemorating a night when the Holy Family found no room at the inn. Almost blasphemous, since Koesler was cruising in his small but well-heated car.

There was nothing for it but to park on one of the neighboring streets. The bad news was that it hadn't snowed quite enough yet to have had the secondary streets plowed. The good news was very much like the bad; it hadn't snowed enough to render driving and parking next to impossible.

He had to park a couple of blocks from the Morand Funeral Home. As he automatically locked his car, he had to admit he shouldn't have been surprised by the number of people who had come to pay their respects. Ridley C. Groendal had been a Very Important Person: a onetime columnist for a prestigious New York paper, a critic whose opinion had been known to contribute to the premature closing of plays and an occasional concert. And a writer whose reviews were feared by authors.

Now that Koesler had phrased the career of Ridley Groendal in just those thoughts, the conclusion seemed inevitable that Groendal might not be remembered for anything very positive. Just for creating depression and dread in the hearts of writers and performers.

Because Groendal had been very much a Catholic as well as a Very Important Person, he was, by corollary, a Very Important Catholic. That meant that Koesler could expect a bumper crop of priests at tomorrow's funeral. Which was no problem; it merely entailed the reservation of a few pews for the visiting clergy. None of whom, undoubtedly, would be attending tonight's farewell rosary.

Koesler, stamping snow from his rubbers, was greeted by the mortuary owner.

"Hi, Lou. Looks like an SRO crowd."

"Right, Father." Morand took Koesler's coat and hat. "And almost all for the Groendal wake."

"Uh-huh."

"He's in there." Morand indicated a room out of which spilled an overflow crowd. By opening several sliding panels, Morand had made this the largest slumber room in the home. Still it was not large enough.

"I sort of figured that."

"Want me to escort you to the bier?"

"No, no, Lou. I can make it okay."

Morand headed for his office with Koesler's hat and coat, leaving the priest, by his own choice, to fend for himself.

Koesler, at some inches over six feet, was able to get a better than average perspective of the crowd. It was like old home week. He recognized quite a few parishioners. That was to be expected. Koesler was pastor of St. Anselm's parish in the Detroit suburb of Dearborn Heights. And Ridley Groendal had been a parishioner for the past year or so.

But there were quite a few others whom Koesler recognized from the old days at Holy Redeemer parish on Detroit's near west side. Koesler was pleased they had remembered. It had been many long years since he and Groendal, among many others, had grown up in that venerable neighborhood. It was good to see the familiar faces, although many of them remained no more than familiar—at present no names came readily to mind.

He began to make his way through the crowd, something he had done many times before. Two ceremonies that regularly bid for the services of a priest are weddings and funerals. For Koesler, after some thirty years as a priest, all the weddings and funerals at which he had presided seemed to blend into one massive hodgepodge.

Only a few such occasions stood out individually and clearly in his memory. Koesler, like many of his confreres, was forever being greeted, often effusively, by seeming strangers who took it for granted that he remembered their wedding or the funeral of a loved one. There were just too many to keep them all distinct in his mind.

Of course the funeral of Ridley C. Groendal, for many reasons, was one of the few he would remember.

Getting through this crowd was not unlike swimming upstream. Koesler had to struggle against a current that kept everyone cheek by

jowl. As he tapped shoulders and excused himself, he was greeted first
by hostility that resisted relinquishing hard-won and established space.
But as soon as his clerical collar was recognized, he was graciously
ushered on. Old friends from Holy Redeemer days or present parishioners would exchange a few words with him as he resolutely made his
way toward the bier. He recognized his parishioners, of course, but did
not fare so well with the Redeemerites. Most he could not identify until
they introduced themselves. Then, usually, he remembered them.

At long last, he reached the remains of Ridley C. Groendal. Here at
least, as at all such gatherings, there was room to breathe. No matter
how many mourners attended a wake, the deceased was always ac-
corded some breathing room. The deceased, of course, needed it least.
However, the prime beneficiaries of this ample space were the chief
mourners who invested the most time in this vigil.

In the case of Ridley Groendal there was only one chief mourner.
Among those aware of the situation, it was no surprise that Peter
Harison evidently was the one and only bereaved.

Harison, at Father Koesler's approach, rose immediately. "Good of
you to come, Father."

"Sorry for your loss, Peter." The priest knew that neither greeting
had any genuine meaning. In reality, he had to attend the wake, so
there was no need to thank him for coming. In another sense, he was
there quite willingly for a great number of reasons, not the least of
which was the fact that Ridley Groendal and Robert Koesler went back
a long way together. On the other hand, Koesler's salutation had been
empty—a response not unlike the traditional "Fine" when someone
automatically asks, "How are you?"

Now came that familiar void that so often occurs at funerals when no
one, neither the visitor nor the bereaved, knows quite what to say.

After some moments, Harison broke the awkward silence. "Appropriate, don't you think?" He was pointing upward.

Koesler reflexively looked up. What was "appropriate"? The ceiling?
Heaven? "Appropriate?"

"Why, the music." Harison seemed surprised that Koesler was unaware of the music.

"Ah, the music." Koesler had been vaguely conscious that there was
something "extra" going on. Until his attention had been directed to it,
he had paid no mind. Something like many of the movies of the forties
whose inane musical score never quit. Once one became conscious of it,

one became painfully conscious of it. So it was now. The piped-in music had blended in with the conversational murmur throughout the room. Now that he heard the music, he didn't like it. "What is it, Peter?"

"*Portals,* by Carl Ruggles."

"Sort of strange, isn't it?"

Harison looked offended. "Ruggles was a champion—an early one, I might say—of contrapuntal sound and dissonance. He employed the ten-tone serial technique."

It was Greek to Koesler. He knew only that he did not like it. "Interesting." A comment befitting a strange hairstyle, bizarre clothing, an ugly baby—or aberrant music.

The ambiguous remark seemed to mollify Harison. "Rid would have liked it. He enjoyed fearless creativity. I gave the tape to Mr. Morand and asked him to play it." Harison seemed pleased with his choice. "But, I suppose we shouldn't be talking about that now."

"We can talk about whatever you'd like."

Harison tilted his head slightly as if understanding something that should have been obvious. "This is what you ordinarily do at wakes, isn't it, Father? You get the mourners to talk about the deceased so you will have relevant material for your eulogy."

Koesler smiled briefly. "I'm afraid you're right."

Harison smiled more broadly. "Well, you certainly don't have to quiz me. You knew Rid as well as anyone."

"Not really." This was getting into dangerous territory. It was true that for quite a few years, as youthful contemporaries, Groendal and Koesler had been classmates and, if not the best of friends, friends nonetheless. Groendal had indeed confided some very personal secrets to Koesler. But their paths had parted shortly after college.

Koesler had chosen the local Catholic seminaries for his education. He'd gone through the seminary high school, college, and theologate and been ordained a priest for service in the Archdiocese of Detroit. He'd been assigned to several parishes before being named editor of the local diocesan newspaper. Later, he was named pastor of St. Anselm's parish. And that, in his rather prosaic curriculum vitae, brought him up-to-date.

Groendal too had entered the seminary in the ninth grade. But he had left, just before graduation from college. Thereafter, with only three early exceptions, he had had no connection with Koesler until moving into St. Anselm's parish a little more than a year before his death.

Koesler knew, mostly from mutual acquaintances, that Ridley had earned a doctoral degree from the University of Minnesota. Later, he'd worked at a series of newspapers until he'd landed that prestigious job with the *New York Herald.* Thereafter, since he'd become a celebrity, it had been rather easy to follow his career.

"What do you mean, 'not really'?" Harison pressed. "You knew him during his most vulnerable years, when he was growing up. And now you've known him during the last years of his life."

Koesler was unsure how to reply. It was more a challenge than a question. Fortunately, at that very moment, another visitor demanded Harison's attention. Excusing himself, Harison rose to greet the newcomer, leaving Father Koesler to ponder a response, as much to satisfy his own curiosity as Harison's.

Could Harison be jealous? Of what? Of no more than a passing adolescent friendship. True, during the past year, Groendal had made it a point to visit Koesler with some regularity. But that was on more of a casual than a friendship basis. The problem was not Koesler's relationship with Groendal. The problem was the connection between Groendal and Harison. The tie between them had complicated Koesler's life during the past year and continued to do so even now.

During the past year, Rid Groendal had come by appointment to see Koesler about two or three times a month. They had been unconventional visits in that they involved neither confession, instruction, counseling, repartee, or even reminiscences of the good old days. Mostly, the evenings were spent with Koesler listening to the "Gospel According to Groendal."

Koesler put up with it because, on the one hand, on Sundays Groendal joined himself to the captive audience in St. Anselm's church and turnabout was fair play; and, on the other hand, while the Gospel According to Groendal had little to do with that of Jesus Christ, it was at least provocative.

Perhaps the most startling thing disclosed in these visits was that Groendal's Catholicism was of the rock-ribbed traditional variety. Curious for one whose avowed artistic tastes ran to avant-garde music, bizarre stage productions, and unconventional literature. But when it came to religion, Groendal favored the Latin liturgy—with the Tridentine, rather than the modern Mass. His theology had not advanced much beyond the basic *Baltimore Catechism.* And the Church was not the People-of-God, but the Pope, who would let everyone know of the slight possibility that there might be a doctrinal change.

Groendal assured Koesler that this entire theological viewpoint was shared by Peter Harison, boon companion.

However, Groendal and Harison were a homosexual couple. It was the only chink Koesler could find in their otherwise conservative theology. Both men were well aware of the official Church teaching that, while preaching tolerance of the people involved, condemned homosexual acts as sins against nature. A classic interpretation of the principle —hate the sin, love the sinner. They were aware of the teaching. They chose to ignore it.

While their rationale on this subject was extremely unorthodox, it was by no means unique. As happened so frequently, it all depended on whose ox was being gored. Koesler knew many liberals who themselves demanded freedom from authority while demanding that all others conform to their views. And conservatives who insisted on absolute unanimity with the Pope in all things—except for those issues on which they disagreed with the Pope.

So, in the course of the past year, Koesler had become quite familiar with the Gospel According to Groendal and Harison. There had been times when the priest had tried to insert a divergent word; but, finding that fruitless, eventually he just sat back, relaxed, and listened.

One thing he had wondered about all those months was whether Groendal ever shared with Harison what had been told to Koesler. From Harison's comment a few minutes ago, Koesler now guessed that Groendal had kept Harison in the dark as to what had been discussed in the rectory. In one unguarded moment, Harison had given the unmistakable impression that he envied Koesler's relationship with Groendal —whatever it might have been.

But since Koesler was not one to needlessly chance betraying a confidence, Harison's curiosity would have to remain unsatisfied.

The priest's musings were terminated when Harison returned and resumed his adjacent chair. "So, Father, what will you talk about in your eulogy tomorrow?"

Koesler rubbed his chin. "To be frank, I don't know yet. There are so many things . . ."

"But to be specific . . . ?"

"I truly don't know, Peter. I even thought of asking someone else to give the homily. I'm afraid I'm a little too close to be as objective as I'd want to be."

"Oh, no, Father! Believe me, Rid would want you to speak over him. You've got to do it!"

Koesler smiled. "Peter, I only said I'd thought about asking someone else. I wouldn't, really. It's my place to do it. It's just that I'm not sure what tack I'll take. But don't worry: I've had enough experience so that something will come to mind."

Harison seemed apprehensive. He placed his hand on Koesler's arm. "Father, there's something you may not know. It may have a bearing on the whole funeral. It'll probably be in the paper tomorrow anyway. But you should know beforehand. It's only fair."

"Peter, what are you getting at?"

"Father, Rid had AIDS."

"He did!" Koesler shook his head. "I guess that explains that weight loss. I'll be darned."

"But he didn't get it from me."

"He didn't?" Koesler did not succeed in keeping the surprise out of his voice.

"No. It was the only time he was ever unfaithful. He had to go back to New York—something about settling details of his pension. There was a lot of pressure . . . stress. It was a weak moment. Can you imagine that, Father? One unfaithful moment and then . . . that!"

Koesler thought for a minute. "Peter, why are you telling me this?"

"Because once they publish the results of the autopsy, everyone will know. You might get in trouble with the Church . . . having his funeral."

"Peter, do you think the Church would deny Christian burial just because someone contracted AIDS?"

"One never knows what the Church might do these days."

"Well, at least that one is not on the books. There won't be any difficulty in having Rid's funeral."

"Thank God!" Harison's great relief was evident. "I've been wrestling with my conscience for days wondering whether to tell you. Rid told me he confessed his unfaithfulness—oh, not here . . . not to you. In another parish."

That must have been some confession; Koesler wondered which priest got that one.

"Rid just wasn't himself lately, since it happened—the thing in New

York, I mean." Now that he had broken the ice, Harison seemed intent on unburdening himself. "Have you dined with him lately?"

Koesler shook his head.

"He's been killing himself. Deliberately. Eating all the wrong things. Drinking all the wrong things. It was remorse. I'm sure of it. I think he was just never able to forgive himself for what happened. And then with AIDS . . . well, it was just a matter of time. Watching him punish himself was killing me too. It was such a tragedy, Father. One time . . . one time! It's so unfair!"

Harison began to sob. Bystanders shuffled and moved away. Most found it awkward to stand helpless in the face of such grief, let alone seeing a grown man cry.

Koesler placed an arm across Harison's quivering shoulders.

How very odd, thought the priest. Two men whose very lifestyle has been roundly and consistently condemned by the Church—the Church that they fervently believe in. Yet they simply deny the condemnation and go on acting as—so far as they are concerned—devout and practicing Catholics. Then, when one of them contracts a disease associated with the lifestyle, they're sure all hell is about to break loose. None of it made any sense.

Harison's sobbing had caused a hush to fall over the large room.

Koesler wished someone would turn off that damn music.

Part Two

Greeting the Body

5

"Happy New Year."

"Yeah. Same to you." Koesler returned the greeting even though there was still a full day before New Year's Eve. "How's the new job?"

Raising his eyes as if in supplication, Father Jerry Marvin breathed a sigh of anxiety. "Jeez, I don't know, Bob. It was a straight player trade but I think there should have been some cash involved."

Marvin, one of Koesler's priest-classmates, had just assumed his new assignment as rector of Sacred Heart Seminary. The former rector had become pastor of Marvin's former parish, St. René Goupil. The switch was the choicest bit of clerical gossip making the rounds. In obedience to his bishop's will, Marvin had left a thriving suburban parish to take a post that was a mere shadow of its former self. In the early to mid-sixties, Sacred Heart had bulged with seminarians. Now there were so few students that every movable archdiocesan department had been pushed into the seminary building just to keep as much of the edifice as possible open and operating.

"Look at it this way," Koesler kidded, "you are no longer merely Father Marvin. You're a rector. You are the Very Reverend F. Gerald Marvin."

"A consoling thought," Marvin replied. "I'll have that stitched on my underwear. That way I'll be sure to get it back from the laundry."

"You moved in yet?"

"Uh-huh. Just in time for the second semester. It's like Sklarski said when he got old St. Vincent's: 'Yeah, boys, a plum . . . a little wrinkled, but a plum.' I had Mass a few times with the kids. I can't quite decide whether to tell them about the Good Old Days or not."

"Tell them. By all means, tell them. There was nothing like it. But try not to sound too much like Inspector Frank Luger, NYPD."

Marvin, a fellow devotee of the old "Barney Miller" TV series, laughed. "I'd better get out of here and let you get ready for the funeral. Talk to you after." Marvin, already vested in cassock and surplice, left the sacristy to take his place in one of the pews reserved for the visiting clergy.

Koesler had guessed correctly that Ridley C. Groendal would be recognized as a Very Important Catholic and would thus draw quite a few priests to his funeral. It had been wise to reserve several of the front pews on the "Gospel side" of the church. It was 9:45 A.M., fifteen minutes before the cortege was expected, and already the reserved pews were almost filled.

Looking out the door of the sacristy into the body of the church, Koesler was engrossed by the difference in demeanor between the laity and the priests.

Lay people, arriving singly, in couples, and groups in advance of the cortege, entered the church, generally awkwardly. Non-Catholics usually gave themselves away immediately. They were out of their element and showed it. Ill at ease, they glanced about awkwardly, trying to pick up some acceptable liturgical action from those who might be Catholic. Even then, few attempted a genuflection before entering a pew. And though most Catholics knelt for at least a few moments before seating themselves, Protestants regarded kneelers as, perhaps, the instrument that caused the Reformation.

Catholics, on the other hand, entered with assurance and familiarity. But also with a reverence that was more habit than conviction. Genuflections were abortive. Signs of the Cross were truncated. And the hands: What to do with the hands? For some reason, Catholics in church could not let hands dangle at the side as was natural in any other sphere of life. So, usually, hands were carried folded over the pubic area for no other reason than that Catholics were accustomed to joining their hands in prayer with elbows propped on the pew ahead. Since this was a place of prayer, and while walking there was no place to prop one's elbows, hands joined in front fulfilled the happy medium of hands both dangling and folded.

In contrast, it was a joy to watch priests gather. Like fish returning to water, church was home for priests. They entered casually, genuflected fully, knelt naturally, and had no problem whatsoever with their hands. Not infrequently, priests carried something. With some of the older priests, that might well be a breviary, the almost extinct special monastic prayer book. If they carried nothing, their hands hung quite naturally. They were, after all, home.

Most gratifying was the way priests greeted each other. Almost every priest knew almost all the others. As they gathered, there were smiles of recognition, nods, nudges, a few words, but mostly the nonverbal communication that marks a uniquely shared life and experience.

Koesler glanced at the wall clock. One minute past ten. Not unusual. Funerals had a habit of tardiness. So did weddings. Weddings were much worse.

Activity in the vestibule. The outside doors propped open, letting out a healthy chunk of heat. It was all so familiar. Ridley C. Groendal was arriving for his last visit to church, a little late and literally breathless.

Koesler nodded to the Mass servers, altar boys and girls, and in silence the small altar procession moved through the sanctuary, down the middle aisle, to the rear of the church.

The burnished metal casket containing the mortal remains of Ridley Groendal was placed on its carrier. The morticians in attendance stood impassively at the head and foot of the casket. Six pallbearers stamped snow from their shoes. Breath was exhaled in visible vapors as cold air invaded the church. Only the first few mourners stood in the church. The others would have to wait until the procession moved forward. Peter Harison, of course, was first among the mourners.

Koesler opened the ritual and read, *"The grace and peace of God our Father and the Lord Jesus Christ be with you."*

"And also with you." Everyone was supposed to respond. Only the servers and Peter Harison did.

Koesler sprinkled the casket with holy water as he read, *"I bless the body of Ridley with holy water that recalls his baptism of which St. Paul writes: All of us who were baptized into Christ Jesus were baptized into His death. By baptism into His death we were buried together with Him, so that just as Christ was raised from the dead by the glory of the Father, we too might live a new life. For if we have been united with Him by likeness to His death, so shall we be united with Him by likeness to His resurrection."*

As a white ornamented cloth was spread over the coffin, Koesler read aloud, *"On the day of his baptism, Ridley put on Christ. In the day of Christ's coming, may he be clothed with glory."*

He continued, *"Let us pray. Lord, hear our prayers and be merciful to your son, Ridley, whom you have called from this life. Welcome him into the company of your saints, in the kingdom of light and peace. We ask this through Christ our Lord. Amen."*

Koesler nodded to the server carrying the processional cross and the group began retracing its path through the church. As they slowly walked up the aisle, the organist and choir—the choir because a Very Important Catholic was being buried—began the hymn, "I Will Raise Him Up." Most of the priests joined in the refrain. In all, this was a much grander greeting of the body than in a common garden variety Mass of Resurrection.

While processing down the middle aisle and managing to maintain custody of the eyes, Koesler did glance from side to side occasionally.

He was very surprised to see one of them. He was astonished to see the second. At that point, he decided to put the remainder of his amazement on hold until he checked out the rest of the congregation. Sure enough, he spied the third and then the fourth. All four of the original suspects in the investigation of the death of Ridley C. Groendal were present. Five, if one counted Peter Harison among the original suspects. That all were able to attend this funeral was due entirely to a decision of the Deputy Chief of the Criminal Division of the Wayne County Prosecutor's Office.

For the past couple of days there had been considerable speculation in the media over Groendal's death. All that was certain was that there was an ongoing investigation. The police had been extremely secretive. Left with little detail, the press had been constrained to come up with some fairly wild conjecture.

The case had been solved last night, although the media were just now being briefed, so it would be surprising if anyone here but the principals would know that. It was almost miraculous what could be accomplished between the 7:30 P.M. recitation of a rosary for the deceased and bedtime.

Father Koesler would be the last to claim that he had solved the mystery. And, in strict truth, he probably had not. But he certainly had brought the puzzle to such a point that the solution needed only a finishing touch by the authorities.

This was by no means the first time Koesler had been involved in a Detroit homicide investigation. It had happened several times. But generally he had been dragged into these situations quite beyond his will. Sometimes he had simply happened to be on the scene when the murder was perpetrated or when the investigation had begun. Almost always there was something "religious," or specifically "Catholic" involved.

In any case, the police had been able to utilize his expertise in the solution.

However, in the matter of Ridley C. Groendal, Koesler for the first time had come aboard neither reluctantly nor out of the blue. He had, indeed, volunteered his assistance. He did so because he was in the singular position of having known not only the deceased but also each and every one of those suspected of involvement in his death. Koesler not only knew them all; he was privy to the personal conflicts that marked and scarred their lives.

It would not cross Koesler's mind that he had come on like a white knight or a fictional detective and singlehandedly solved this case. Far from it. He was no more than a simple parish priest. And happy and fulfilled in being that. The homicide department had done its usual thorough and painstaking job of building the case. In all probability, they would have closed the matter unaided by any outside agency. But Koesler had been able to contribute some information that proved helpful. Well, perhaps something more than that. Koesler's information, when presented, proved to be the crowning touch of the brief investigation. Koesler had been able to provide the elusive ingredient needed to tie up all the loose ends.

But the presence of all the suspects at the victim's funeral struck Koesler as peculiar, to say the least. He wondered if it might be unique. So few things were.

Well, time enough after the funeral for the law to exact punishment. For now, there was a liturgy to celebrate.

What an odd word to describe this function, thought Koesler. Nevertheless, he resolved to do his best with the celebration of a Mass of Resurrection. The main block—Koesler knew himself well—would be that ever-present stream of consciousness that was sure to provide him with one distraction after another.

All had entered and been shown to their places. The church was almost filled. The undertaker placed the lighted Paschal candle at the head of the casket. The congregation was attentive. All was ready.

Koesler intoned: *"In the name of the Father, and of the Son, and of the Holy Spirit."*

"Amen." Most of the congregation responded.

"The grace and peace of our Lord Jesus Christ and the love of God and the fellowship of the Holy Spirit be with you all."

"And also with you," was the response.

Koesler continued. *"My friends, to prepare ourselves to celebrate these sacred mysteries, let us call to mind our sins."*

In the silence that followed, Koesler's gaze fell on David Palmer. David Palmer, the musician. Unbidden, memories flooded back.

The vaulted ceilings and hardwood floors of Holy Redeemer grade school.

Boards creaking as children walked, rapidly perhaps but never running lest one of the nuns was sure to whack you. Silence, as simultaneously throughout the building, classes began. Then the only sound, Sister raising her voice at a slow, lazy, or disobedient student. Or, as nuns glided down a hallway, the rattle of the fifteen-decade rosary wound through their belts.

These were the 1930s and all was as it had been for a century or more. Catholic children attended Catholic schools or the breadwinner heard about it after he confessed his sin of omission to the priest of a Saturday evening.

Nuns, without whom a parochial school system never could have been attempted, were swathed from head to toe in distinctive religious habit. The garb of the Sisters Servants of the Immaculate Heart of Mary, the teachers at Holy Redeemer, was a color that became identified as IHM Blue. They also wore a black scapular that slipped over their shoulders and draped to the floor fore and aft. This was capped by a stiff bonnet that pinched the cheeks and eventually wore an almost permanent ridge in the forehead.

They began each day with Mass in the convent at an ungodly early hour. Breakfast was followed by another Mass with the children in attendance. They taught school all day. Prayed, dined, prepared lesson plans, and retired. Only to do the selfsame thing the next day. And the next and the next. During summers they usually returned to college to pile up more hours toward another academic degree.

* * *

In an office just large enough for a small desk and chair and a spinet piano, Sister Mary George, IHM, is conducting a music lesson.

Seated at the piano is Robert Koesler, undergoing his weekly humiliation.

"No, no, Robert . . ." Sister vigorously taps a baton against the piano. ". . . you have a left hand. It's not just for waving at the keys. It's supposed to play the correct notes."

"Yes, Sister."

"It's not that you don't have talent, Robert. It's that you don't practice, isn't it?"

"Yes, Sister."

"How many hours did you practice this week?"

"Uh . . . I don't know, Sister."

"Not many, I'll wager. Robert, you don't like Czerny, do you?"

"Uh . . . no, Sister." Actually, Koesler had nothing against the composer personally. He just did not enjoy scales and arpeggios that had no tunes worth mentioning. But whether or not Koesler liked Czerny, his answer would have been the same. To small obedient Catholic children of that day, nuns' questions, like that just posed by Sister Mary George, were rhetorical.

"That's another one of your problems, Robert: You don't build foundations. All you want to do is put in windows."

"Sister?"

"I know you want to play beautiful music, lyric music, Robert. But you can't do that unless you practice these fundamentals. First you build the foundations, then you can put in the beautiful ornaments. Do you see, Robert?"

"Yes, Sister."

"Do you have any questions?"

"Uh . . ." There was one question Koesler had been wrestling with for a very long time: Why did all nuns smell exactly the same? Something like Fels Naphtha or Ivory soap. But he would never have the boldness to ask it. Or rather, by the time he would have the courage to ask, it no longer mattered. "No, Sister."

"Very well, then, Robert. Next week do the same Czerny exercises. And this time pay attention to your left hand. Then, only after you master that, you can go on to that little Mozart prelude. Now, don't forget orchestra practice this afternoon."

"No, Sister." Koesler would have much preferred a quick game of baseball after school. But he would be there for orchestra practice. For starters, he would be killed if he didn't show up. First blood would go to Sister. The coup de grâce would be delivered by his parents.

Music lessons cost one dollar an hour, a laughably low price even then. But Koesler's hard-pressed parents found it difficult to produce that extra dollar. And they had emphatically impressed upon their son that they expected some results for their investment. He might not practice what he considered "the dull stuff" assiduously, but neither would he skip a lesson nor miss orchestra practice.

Another family in Koesler's neighborhood could afford money for lessons even less than the Koeslers. But the other family had even more reason to invest whatever they could in their son's musical career. They were the Palmers and their son, David, was a prodigy.

Both Fred and Agnes Palmer were musicians. Both played in chamber ensembles regularly. Agnes gave lessons. But her instrument was not the violin, and David's was. Besides, there was that peculiar impediment that makes it problematical for a parent to undertake the formal education of one's own child.

The first inkling the Palmers had of their son's gift was when he was three years old. Agnes Palmer had just completed playing Debussy's "Clair de lune." As she walked away from the piano, she heard a small high sound. It was her son, humming perfectly what she had just performed. Soon thereafter, David began repeating on the piano the melodic lines of works his parents played. At the age of five, he found a violin and the violin found him. In no time, he convinced his parents that it would be through the violin that he would most perfectly express his God-given talent.

With one thing and another, the Palmers concluded it would be a crime not to do everything in their power to advance the boy's musical education. So, for a hard-earned dollar a week, they sent him to Sister Mary George.

Sister, for her part, was painfully aware that David's talent far surpassed her ability to challenge it. But she knew the Palmers could not afford anything beyond her. So she began to make plans with regard to David and a relatively new musical camp in northern Michigan called Interlochen Arts Academy.

There was one other boy in that neighborhood, and in the same class with Koesler and Palmer, who showed some considerable musical talent. Ridley Groendal.

Koesler could be mentioned in this threesome only because he was a classmate and took lessons from the same teacher as the other two. Outside of that superficial connection, he was simply not in their class and he and everyone else knew it.

Actually, Groendal was not in Palmer's class either. Groendal was an adequate pianist for a young student. But he was not especially gifted. Palmer was the one and only wonder child of the group.

Unfortunately, while almost everyone was in awe of David Palmer's musical gift, no one was paying enough attention to the rest of Palmer's personality. As a result, few people realized that all this special attention had gone straight to Palmer's head. He was becoming a first-class brat. Those adults who were aware of David's bumptiousness tended to overlook it as the natural eccentricity of a budding genius.

*　　*　　*

The memory fades as Father Koesler becomes aware of an altar girl standing before him, holding an open ritual.

Koesler read aloud: *"Lord, hear our prayers. By raising your son from the dead, you have given us faith. Strengthen our hope that Ridley, our brother, will share in His resurrection. Who lives and reigns together with the Holy Spirit, one God forever and ever. Amen."*

As he looked up from the book, Koesler once again noticed Palmer, as isolated as if in a telescope. This time their eyes locked. David Palmer, musician extraordinaire. At least an extraordinary musician for a parochial setting such as Holy Redeemer.

The memory gains strength.

*　　*　　*

It is orchestra practice.

Robert Koesler has had a difficult day. He had been poorly prepared not only for the piano lesson but for most of the rest of his classes as well. And, worse luck, he had been called on for recitation frequently and fruitlessly.

But now this practice is important. It is a rehearsal for the annual recital wherein Sister Mary George is able to showcase the progress her music students have made. The recital is mostly for the benefit of proud and hopeful parents.

Over the past several years, there has been no doubt which of her pupils Sister has wanted to star. In a parochial setting, a David Palmer comes along once in a lifetime, if then.

As far as the orchestra is concerned, Robert Koesler plays the drums. That thinking is as follows: Koesler could have been the orchestra's pianist, except that Ridley Groendal is a better pianist—much better. But Koesler did play the piano on special occasions, such as the annual recital. Thus, to keep him around, he was given the drums—bass and snare—to play. (This under the amateur assumption that anyone—at least anyone with a sense of rhythm—can play the drums, an assumption that would definitely not be shared by a professional.)

Rehearsal began with the orchestra performing Kettelby's "In a Persian Market." Even Koesler could tell that this performance would, if Kettelby were not already dead, kill him. Only two exceptions mitigated this: the piano and what in a professional orchestra would be the concertmaster—Ridley Groendal and David Palmer. Groendal was correct and accurate. Palmer's tone soared.

Sister finally dismissed the orchestra with the hope that "we can get away with that." It was not to be. But in the inner recesses of her heart, she was allowed to hope.

Instruments, chairs, and music stands were removed noisily to prepare for the special numbers in the recital.

Robert Koesler waited in the wings while a series of extremely nervous younger children blundered through solos, duets, and trios. Most of them left—some in tears—immediately after their respective performances.

Koesler was scheduled to play a duet with David Palmer near the end of the program. When their turn came, the two took to the stage, bowed to an imaginary audience, and began. Their number was Bach's simple but tender "Air for the G-String." Palmer's interpretation was so virtuosic that Koesler found himself playing beyond his ordinary ability.

As the last note died away, the hush was almost reverential. Then a burst of applause from the few remaining students as well as from Sister Mary George herself.

Koesler had to admit that this was pretty heady stuff. He might like doing this more often . . . as long as he could accompany David Palmer.

So inspired was Koesler that he resolved to stay for the final few compositions, rather than to seek out that inevitable baseball game.

After the remainder of the more talented students performed—Sister always kept the best wine till last—the final duo was ready. The finale was to feature Palmer and his violin, accompanied by Groendal on the piano. They were to perform Rimski-Korsakov's "The Flight of the Bumblebee," a demanding piece that could spell frustration or be a tour de force for violin, trumpet, piano—whichever chose to carry the theme.

The two young musicians appeared on stage. They, as had each previous performer, bowed to a nearly empty house. It would be filled on the following day for the actual performance.

Something was going on. Koesler could feel the vibes. They were not good. Groendal struck an "A"; Palmer checked his instrument for tuning. There was a pause as the two collected themselves. Palmer's right foot tapped out the third and fourth beat of a measure, setting the tempo.

They began. Or, rather, Groendal began. He was playing "Bumble Boogie," a popular parody of the famed "Flight." Palmer, taken completely by surprise, had clearly been tricked. He stood as if he were a still photo mounted on stage.

Sister Mary George leaped from her seat as if catapulted. "No! No! Now, stop!" she shrieked.

With a smirk, Groendal lifted his hands from the keyboard.

"Ridley! Whatever possessed you, boy?" Sister was both bewildered and quite angry. "Is this all you think of our concert? That you should fool around like this? Honestly! You could have Job chewing carpets! What is the matter with you, young man?"

"I'm sorry, Sister." It was not even a good pretense.

"Now you settle down! This is the finale of the whole concert. Perhaps you don't think you could be replaced. Well, think again, young man! It's true that this is short notice. But nobody is irreplaceable! Nobody! I could have Robert Koesler, here, take your place. It would require all-night practice, practically. But you could do it, Robert." She was now looking at Koesler, who slouched even further down in his seat. Please God, not me!

"Now, you start again from the beginning. David? Are you all right?"

Palmer, still frozen in the same position, nodded.

"Then," Sister ordered, "set the tempo and begin."

"The Flight of the Bumblebee" began in the tempo in which Rimski-Korsakov had written it. But the tension was deep. Groendal punched out the staccato chords too loudly. Palmer's rendition of the melody was not unlike that of an angry bee.

They finished at last to cautious applause. Not that the performance was not good. Indeed, it could have been described as inspired. But there was concern for Sister Mary George and her temperament. However, she seemed somewhat mollified by the reading Groendal and

Palmer had finally given the work. So, with a few additional warnings, she dismissed the remaining students.

Koesler sensed that this was not the end of the matter. He lingered until everything had been packed away, then followed Groendal and Palmer as they left the auditorium. Palmer left first, but waited just outside the side door. Once Ridley was down the steps, Palmer was on him.

Shortly they were three as Koesler joined the scuffle. There was a lot of rolling around, threats, mild curses, even a tear or two. Since all three were roughly of the same slight build, not much damage was being done. No one was getting mauled by the others. Nevertheless, Koesler's participation—intended to bring peace—was not altogether successful.

"Wait a minute! Wait a minute!" Koesler shouted. "Come on! Break it up!"

They rolled around a bit more. Eventually, all three were standing, with Koesler somehow between the other two.

"That's better," Koesler pronounced. Though it wasn't much better.

"What was the idea, anyway, you jerk?" Palmer said.

"There wasn't any idea, smart guy," Groendal replied. "It was a joke, just a joke. Can't you take a joke? Or is the great genius too high and mighty for a joke!"

"Some joke!" Palmer shoved Groendal, nearly restarting the fracas.

"Wait a minute!" Koesler stepped more firmly between them.

"What's this to you, anyway, Koesler? This isn't your fight," Palmer protested.

Koesler had more altruistic reasons than either Palmer or Groendal would comprehend. So Robert alleged a more mundane, if no less true, motive. "Cause I've got a stake in this thing, too. "If you," to Groendal, "injure him, I'm out one-half of my duet and I won't get to perform. And if you," speaking to Palmer, "injure him, I'm gonna have to learn 'The Flight of the Bumblebee' overnight. You heard Sister!"

Both Palmer and Groendal found Koesler's reasons too laughable to pursue a fight neither of them really wanted. But they were in no way over their ill feelings toward each other.

"Okay . . . but this isn't the end of this, Ridley," Palmer said. "You can bet your bottom dollar on that! We're not done!"

"Suit yourself, hotshot. Any time!"

And thus they parted.

After an uneasy evening and a night filled with portentous dreams, Koesler began the next day in an exhausted state. His parochial morning Mass was marked by the sort of prayer one expected from the trenches. Still, there was nothing he could pinpoint. Just a general feeling that this day might well see an event that would have lasting and horrible consequences. He went through morning classes in a kind of trance.

The students who were to perform in the orchestra and/or one of the recital numbers were excused from afternoon classes.

Koesler's apprehension was not alleviated when Sister Mary George announced that representatives from Interlochen Arts Academy would attend the recital. She said it with a glint in her eye that was meant for David Palmer.

Unfortunately, her ambiguous statement was intercepted by Ridley Groendal. He considered himself easily qualified and deserving of a scholarship to Interlochen. This was his chance, his golden opportunity. He had anticipated this moment. He would not let it slip by. As far as he was concerned, his entire future hung on his performance today. He was ready. His overwhelming craving for this scholarship completely emptied his mind even of all thoughts of David Palmer.

Koesler, seated near Groendal, somehow sensed Ridley's reaction to Sister's announcement. Koesler's forebodings intensified. He knew for whom the scouts came. In a sense, he was happy for Palmer. David deserved the best possible musical training and his parents certainly needed the aid of a scholarship. In that, their financial situation was no different from nearly all the families of that lower middle-class section of the city.

The Groendals could have used a scholarship too. Ridley came so close to qualifying. But close was as near as he would come. Tragically, Groendal's proximity to an Interlochen free ride put him, at least in his own mind, in competition with Palmer. It was a competition Ridley was doomed to lose.

In all, Koesler was grateful that his small talents did not qualify him for Interlochen, not even as a paying student. Not the type who was driven to win at any cost, he was better off out of the competition.

Gradually, the audience—mostly mothers, occasionally a father, of the performers—gathered in the auditorium. There were quite a few guests no one could place. More than likely, they were just interested parishioners responding to the notice of the recital in the previous Sunday's parish bulletin. But somewhere among those strangers were the Interlochen scouts.

Their presence had different effects on different people. Nervous amateurs became more apprehensive. The more talented performers became a bit more keyed-up. But none more-so than Groendal and Palmer. If there is a single moment that dictates the remainder of one's life, this was that moment for each of them.

The orchestra opened the program. It was as Koesler had suspected: They did not "get away" with "In a Persian Market." Never had the beggars of that piece been more in need of help.

The recital began at the bottom with the youngest students. Some few forgot their memorized sections midway through and fled the stage in tears. Others, particularly considering their tender ages, did quite well.

"Which ones do you think they are, Bob?"

Koesler was startled. Peeking at the audience from the backstage wing, he had not heard Ridley come up behind him. "Which ones do I think who are?"

"The scouts! The scouts from Interlochen," Groendal whispered.

"Oh, I don't know. Probably some of the people who keep going out and coming back."

Groendal thought that made sense. As the afternoon wore on, the performers played to a radically changing audience. Some of the adults exited as soon as their children had finished performing. Others arrived in approximate time to hear their children, scheduled for later in the program. Still others, if one cared to note, returned periodically as if to hear selected individuals.

"Nervous?" Koesler asked.

"Butterflies in my stomach," Groendal confessed. "But I don't think nervous. I know what I've got to do."

"Too early for you to get nervous anyway. I'm the one who's on soon; you got a while to wait yet."

"Huh? Oh, yeah."

It was evident that Groendal had nothing on his mind but his own performance.

The time came for Koesler and Palmer to take the stage. As far as Koesler could tell, those in the audience who had been going in and out all were settled in their seats. In all truth, Koesler knew it was not to hear him.

They played "Air for the G-String" beautifully. Or, more specifically,

Palmer performed it expressively, caressingly. Koesler accompanied him adequately. They concluded to enthusiastic applause. Koesler basked in the acclaim, while realizing it was his only in very small measure.

After a few more performers, it came Groendal's time.

He exuded great presence as he came onstage, bowed confidently and spent a few moments collecting himself before beginning Rachmaninoff's "Prelude in C-Sharp Minor." He managed to capture the initial sound—three notes with their corresponding chords—of church bells. In the second section, he accelerated with near abandon. He brought the piece to a close in power and dignity, and received a justified ovation at the conclusion.

Groendal returned to bow for a curtain call, all but unheard-of in a parochial school recital. He came off the stage beaming with Moses-like incandescence. Whatever it was—adrenalin, the power of prayer—he had played well beyond his natural ability. He could not have picked a better time to do so. As of this moment, his future as a professional musician seemed assured.

"Congratulations, Rid!" Koesler greeted him enthusiastically. "You did it! That was great!"

"Yeah, I did! That was terrific. I don't think I ever played it better. Wow!"

Others backstage gathered around, congratulating him. Sister Mary George was forced to shush them so the recital could continue undisturbed. But it was evident she was pleased with his performance.

It was obvious to Koesler that Groendal had completely forgotten that his time on stage was not yet over. As far as Ridley was concerned, the climax had been reached; there was nothing to follow.

But Koesler was acutely aware that the end had not come. Indeed, it was precisely the coming moment that had been the cause of all his foreboding. Strange that it seemed to so trouble Koesler while Groendal, whose moment of truth this might well be, was so unconcerned that he appeared to have forgotten entirely his engagement on stage with Palmer.

It came. After the rest of Sister's other prize pupils had finished, the showplace of the recital was at hand.

Koesler began to wonder if he was alone in his premonition of disaster. Maybe he was. Sure, that's the way he was. He tended to be pessimistic about things. Nothing would go wrong. Rid Groendal certainly would not pull another dumb stunt like his "Bumble Boogie" rehearsal. For one thing, he'd had his little joke. And for another, presumably he had garnered quite a few credits with the Rachmaninoff "Prelude." There was no doubt he'd done extremely well. The assumption was that the Interlochen scouts had heard him. From all appearances, a pretty safe assumption.

Finally, Palmer would do nothing to foul up the performance. This was his big chance. Outside of playing it beautifully, Palmer had proved little in his "Air for the G-String." But "Flight of the Bumblebee!" Great artists could demonstrate virtuosity with that.

Groendal and Palmer entered from opposite sides of the stage. Groendal seated himself at the piano, arranged the music, and sounded an "A" as Palmer gave his violin one final tuning. Palmer fixed his instrument between chin and shoulder and glanced at Groendal. Both nodded: they were ready.

Here they go.

Palmer tapped his right foot against the floor. Koesler's eyes popped wide. It was too fast—way too fast, impossibly fast! But Palmer cut into the melody at just that impossible pace.

The tempo was much more demanding on Palmer than it was on Groendal, who was merely playing accompaniment. Still, Palmer was the one who had established this speed. And it was he who was maintaining it.

After the first several measures, he left Groendal floundering. At first, Ridley tried to keep up. Finding that impossible, he tried playing on the first beat of each measure. But that was foreign to his practice of the piece.

Finally, shoulders sagging, he surrendered and played no more.

It became a solo.

And what a solo! The audience—those who could block out Groendal's humiliation—sat mesmerized by Palmer's merciless attack. If anyone had any doubt that this was a certified prodigy, all hesitation was erased by this singular presentation.

Especially at the speed he had set, it was no wonder that Palmer completed "Flight" in near-record time. The conclusion, executed with a flair, drew a standing ovation.

Few were even aware of Groendal slinking from the stage. Koesler was. "It's not the end of the world!" Koesler put both hands on Groendal's shoulders, halting his progress toward the exit.

"Yes it is!" Groendal tried, but was unable to get by Koesler.

"Don't leave! You can't leave! You've got to stick it out! If you just leave now, you'll never live it down."

"You don't understand! You don't understand!" Tears were streaming down Groendal's cheeks. "It's the end of everything! I had it. It was mine. If it hadn't been for that damn Palmer!"

"Don't let him see what he did to you. Come on over here and get yourself together." Koesler led, or rather forced, Groendal into a recess of the wings.

No one else paid much attention; they clustered around the stage as David Palmer made his triumphant exit. Inspired mainly by Sister Mary George's ebullience, everyone was congratulating Palmer.

"Excellent, David!" Sister enthused. "Even I had no idea you could play that well. I'm sure our special visitors were impressed. Oh, my, yes." And then, as if giving a fleeting thought to the accompanist Palmer had left behind, "It's really my fault. I should have scheduled 'The Flight' as a solo." She looked about. "Where is Ridley? Has anyone seen Ridley?"

It was a command performance. Koesler was glad he had kept Ridley from running off in humiliation. He pushed Groendal into the group that encircled Sister and Palmer. At least, thought Koesler, Ridley's tears were dried. Maybe nobody would notice the red eyes.

"Oh, there you are," Sister said. "Now don't feel bad, Ridley. You did your best. Nobody could have known that David would have been so inspired. It was my fault. I should have scheduled that as a solo. It's not your fault. None of my other students could have kept up with David. Not today!" She could not disguise her pride in David Palmer. "Besides, Ridley, you did very well with the 'Prelude.' Very well, indeed, Ridley."

"Yes, Sister."

After several more minutes of nearly unrestrained adulation, the group dissolved, leaving Palmer, Groendal, and Koesler wordless but high in emotion.

In a moment's fury, Groendal swung out at Palmer, who easily stepped back and away from the wild blow. Before anything could develop, Koesler grabbed Ridley, pinning his arms from behind.

"Just let me put this down," Palmer gestured with his violin, "then let him go. I can handle him."

"Don't be idiots!" Koesler said in a low tone. A few stragglers were glancing back. He did not want them to return. It would only spur the combatants on.

"Palmer," Groendal said through clenched teeth, "you've ruined me! You've destroyed my life before I could live!"

"Don't be an asshole, Rid," Palmer replied. "This will teach you not to fool around like you did at rehearsal. You shouldn't try something like that with your betters. Next time you're supposed to play accompaniment, play it. Don't try to embarrass me."

"That's why you did this to me? You ruined me, you ruined my musical career because of one joke? You did this! For that?"

Palmer grunted. "Your musical career! What musical career? You're a hack piano player! You won't ever be more than that! Hell, Ridley, I did you a favor. I let everybody see that you're no musician. It saved the guys from Interlochen a lot of time. And hell, Rid, it saved you a lot of silly hope. You couldn't have cut it at Interlochen—if that's where you thought you were heading—and it's better for you that you know it now. Hell, that's right, I did you a favor, Rid!"

Palmer, by his own monologue, seemed to have convinced himself of what he claimed.

"Who are you to say I couldn't have made it?" Groendal seemed again close to tears. "I was terrific with the Rachmaninoff. Sister even said so. And if you hadn't tried to be Paganini—"

"You're complaining about the tempo. It was too fast."

"Of course. And you did it on purpose!"

"But don't you see? If you were as good as you think, you could have kept up. Yeah, I stepped up the tempo. And I did it on purpose. I did it to teach you a lesson about fooling around with me. But it also taught you your place. And your place isn't with me or where I'm going. I'm going to Interlochen and I'm going to the top. And you don't belong in either place. Got it, stupid?"

"We'll see about that." Groendal was doing his best to choke back tears. He knew he could not succeed much longer. "But just remember, Palmer: I'll get you for this! Somehow I'll get you. If it takes the rest of my life. And it doesn't matter what happens to you, the score will never be even as far as I'm concerned."

He turned and ran, stumbling, to the stairs.

Palmer yelled after him. "When you try to get even, just remember what happened here today. I'm always going to have the last laugh. Do you hear that, Groendal? I'm always going to have the last laugh!"

Nearly two months later, it was announced that David Palmer had been awarded a scholarship to the National Music Camp at Interlochen. A school assembly was held in his honor and congratulations poured in from nearly everyone but Ridley Groendal.

From the recital until the end of the school year, not a word would pass between Groendal and Palmer. After that, as they entered high school, their paths would diverge until many years later, when Groendal would have become a professional critic and Palmer a professional musician.

Palmer attended Holy Redeemer for the first two years of high school. Then, as part of an augmented scholarship, he was able to become a full-time student at the Interlochen Arts Academy, whence he then graduated.

Groendal, mostly as a result of frustration over his scuttled musical ambition, decided to become a priest. So he, along with Robert Koesler, attended Sacred Heart, Detroit's high school and college seminary.

One incident before the end of that fateful final year in primary school would have serious repercussions many years later.

It was a fire that threatened to burn down Redeemer auditorium. The fire department termed it arson. The culprit was never identified. It was started on the stage of the auditorium but destroyed only the grand piano and a relatively small portion of the hardwood flooring.

Shortly after the fire, David Palmer approached Robert Koesler. "I've got something to show you." Palmer handed Koesler a photograph.

Koesler studied the indistinct picture, "Okay, I give up; what is it?"

Palmer ran his finger over the photo. "This is the stage of our auditorium . . . see, there's the Redeemer shield on the back curtain. And there are the two chairs that we usually use when we need them for props."

"Uh-huh," Koesler agreed. The landmarks were clear only after identification.

"Okay. Then here is the grand piano. It's on fire . . . that's why it's hard to see what's on the picture: because of all the smoke."

"Uh-huh."

"And this," in a tone of triumph, "is your pal, Ridley C. Groendal, starting a fire at the other end of the piano."

"What? Wait a minute! You can't tell that; there's too much smoke. It's somebody, but you can't tell who."

"Oh, no? Who else do you know who looks exactly like this?" He assisted Koesler's inspection with a magnifying glass. "The baggy pants with a hole in the knee. But now, look! See on the tennis shoes: 'R. C. Groendal.' Oh, it's Ridley, all right. He set the fire!" Again the triumphant tone.

"He didn't see you take the picture?"

"I didn't care whether he did or not. But he didn't. He was behind the worst of the smoke. See: You can barely make out his head. It's all covered with smoke."

"He doesn't know you've got this?"

"Nope. You're the only one who knows."

"So . . . why are you showing it to me?"

" 'Cause you're the only one I can trust to keep the secret. And I wanted somebody besides me to know."

"Well . . . what of it? They put out the fire before it did any really serious damage. And Ridley probably was doing nothing but taking out revenge on the piano he thinks failed him. What are you going to do with this?"

"Nothing."

"Nothing?"

"Nothing . . . for now."

"What do you mean, 'for now'?"

"I'm going to save it."

"Save the picture? What in heaven's name for?"

"For someday."

"Someday? What do you mean someday?"

"I don't even know when that'll be. I sure as hell don't need it now. I've got the poor bastard where I want him right now. I don't need to drop this on him. I'm just going to hold onto it. Maybe someday I'll need it. Maybe someday I'll have to settle the score with him once and for all. Then I'll use it. Maybe someday it'll drive him nuts for everybody to know he's nothing but a sneaky firebug."

Koesler said no more. His mind was swimming in these revelations. He had never before known an arsonist. He was devastated that one of his friends was a firebug. But he could not deny Palmer's proof.

Koesler was even more disconcerted that another of his friends could be so mean-spirited. He would not have thought David Palmer capable of blackmail.

Koesler's premonition that a horrendous evil would evolve from an otherwise innocent music recital had proven accurate.

Part Three

———

Liturgy of the Word

6

Father Koesler hoped his mouth was not hanging open. It often did when he was lost in thought. And he had, indeed, been lost in the memory of Robert Koesler, the musical hack; David Palmer, the gifted musician; and poor Ridley Groendal, talented, but not quite up to his own or others' aspirations and expectations.

By simply bringing his eyes into focus once more, he saw David Palmer seated in the congregation. He appeared to be musically evaluating the motet just rendered by the choir. There seemed no other thought or concern on his mind.

There should have been.

Koesler forced his attention back to the Mass of Resurrection. It was time for the Liturgy of the Word. There would be three readings from the Bible: one from the Old Testament, one from the Epistles, and one from the Gospels. Since the Second Vatican Council, there had been a reemphasis on the importance of Scripture in the Mass. Before Vatican II, Scripture readings had been more or less perfunctory. Nor had much importance been made of drawing upon the Scriptures for homiletic purposes.

All that had been changed. Now, Catholics were encouraged to find the living presence of God in "God's Word."

William Doran, one of St. Anselm's lectors, stepped to the podium to read from the Second Book of Samuel.

"The king was shaken and went up to the room over the city gate to weep. He said as he wept, 'My son Absalom! My son, my son Absalom! If only I had died instead of you. Absalom, my son, my son!' Joab was told that the king was weeping and mourning for Absalom; and that day's victory was turned into mourning for the whole army when they heard that the king was grieving for his son. The soldiers stole into the city that day like men shamed by flight in battle."

Doran closed the lectionary and held it high, saying, *"This is the word of the Lord."*

To which the congregation replied, *"Thanks be to God."*

Koesler reflected that while Doran read well, there was one in the congregation who would have read even better. That would be Carroll Mitchell. Although he was a playwright and a screenwriter, his earliest training and experience on stage had been as an actor. And he had the actor's finely trained voice and presence. He would have read the Scripture excerpt magnificently. But that, of course, was out of the question under the circumstances.

The sight of Carroll Mitchell brought Koesler's memory back to his earliest days at Sacred Heart Seminary. When he had first entered that specialized high school in the early forties, he had known no one but his fellow Redeemerite, Ridley Groendal.

In those days, seminaries were well supplied with candidates for the priesthood. They would become steadily more crowded until the dramatic drop of the seventies.

Seminary faculties of that era liked to think that they conscientiously promoted only the best and brightest. In reality, as time would tell, it was a buyer's market. Because there was such a record number of students, the administration had the luxury of being very selective in their choice of who would move on to the priesthood. The weeding-out process went on inexorably from year to year. While great numbers of students were dropped for intellectual, moral, or medical reasons during high school and college, it was not rare for some to be asked to leave even during the final four years of theology.

Koesler and Groendal quickly blended into that group of young men who had a common vision and goal. As high school freshmen, they were hazed by sophomores. They bought tickets to nonexistent swimming pools. They were sent on missions to off-limits sections of the buildings. Eventually, they became upper classmen.

Quite a few students were musically inclined. But there were no David Palmers with whom to contend. Early on, Groendal resolved that he would dominate the musical scene. And so he did. He became the principal organist, frequent accompanist for others, and regular performer whenever concerts were held.

Koesler continued to play the piano mostly for his own amusement. He was in competition with no one. While Groendal competed, or at least tried to compete, with almost everyone. It was, Koesler had often thought, as if Ridley were obsessed. With the exception of sports—Groendal had never been very well coordinated—he seemed compelled to challenge nearly everyone.

This tendency led to disaster when Groendal collided with Carroll Mitchell. Mitch, as everyone called him, was to the theater what David Palmer was to the violin—a natural. Tall and freckled, with thick red hair and brows, Mitch, with his chiseled features, was one of the seminary's most handsome students.

But he wasn't just a pretty face. He had a powerful, affecting, and pleasing voice, great presence, and the ability to involve an audience with genuinely moving performances.

To top it off, Mitch was a playwright—albeit an amateur. None of his plays had been published; all of them had been performed in the seminary, without charge and on a shoestring. Many were no more than skits, sometimes pulled together for a full-length performance. Though most of his work was comedy, he had also done serious drama, particularly on Lenten themes.

Though Ridley did perform from time to time, he knew he could not keep up with Mitch on stage. But he did consider himself a playwright and he had worked out some fairly entertaining stage pieces. Of course in that setting one could be fooled. A captive audience, the students were astonishingly easy to please.

And so the rivalry between Mitch and Ridley went on. But the only one conscious of the combat was Groendal. As David Palmer before him, Mitchell never considered Groendal a competitor.

Enter the subject of girls.

Koesler and Groendal had, in a manner of speaking, been without them virtually all their lives. While they attended Holy Redeemer School, boys and girls were separated from the first through the twelfth grades. Thus, through the first eight grades, neither boy had ever been in class with a girl. Girls, of course, could, under ordinary circumstances, nowhere be found within a seminary building. This would seem at best strange to almost anyone but a strict Catholic and/or a seminarian of that time.

Strange but true.

Over the centuries, the Church had formed a system that mass-produced priests, who were at the same time asexual and macho. It achieved the macho image by emphasizing "masculine" pursuits. Sports were not only encouraged, there was an insistence on at least minimal participation. The more violent the physical contact the better.

At the same time, a brotherly camaraderie was nurtured. But this good fellowship had to be completely free of any sexual feeling. Even the hint of anything remotely sexual between seminarians was branded a "personal friendship" and was grounds for expulsion.

Women, in the abstract, were easier to exclude from the future celibate's life. As Tertullian once remarked about women: "The judgment of God upon your sex endures even today; and with it endures inevitably your position of criminal at the bar of justice. You are the gateway of the devil."

If that were not strong enough medicine, a little more than a hundred years later, St. Augustine wrote: "I consider that nothing so casts down the manly mind from its height as the fondling of a woman, and those bodily contacts."

So, instead of *"those* bodily contacts," seminarians were encouraged to dust each other off in baseball, elbow each other in basketball, flatten each other in football and maim each other in hockey. "Particular friendships" scarcely ever sprang from such violent contacts. Before vacations—Christmas, Easter, summer—the seminary rector would ramble on to the effect that, "Take it for granted, boys, that you'd like girls if you tried them. So, don't try them."

At one point in high school, Koesler and a few others decided they would like to spend a profitable summer as lifeguards. So they took the Red Cross safety course, only to discover that seminary rules forbade them to be lifeguards at a public beach or pool. They could be lifeguards only at a summer camp for boys.

It took only a modicum of thought to realize there was something one might well expect to find on a public beach that would never be found at boys' camps. Girls.

What the seminary seemed to be teaching was that while it was all right to save girls' souls, it was very definitely not all right to save their bodies.

Or, as St. Alphonsus Liguori once noted (replying to his own rhetorical, "Is it then a sin to look at a female?"): "Yes; it is at least a venial sin to look at young females. And when looks are repeated, there is also danger of mortal sin."

He wrote that in the eighteenth century, but the theory was still very much alive in the seminaries of the 1940s and fifties.

Briefly, that was the setting for the formation of the priests of yesteryear. The priest was to be a man's man with no overt or covert sexual expression whatever. To help achieve this goal, the seminary system was replete with some of the strictest discipline imaginable. By and large, it worked.

In the seminary of Groendal and Koesler's day, there was one major exception to this rigorous code: Carroll Mitchell.

Mitchell's attitude toward the seminary's attitude toward women was one of benign neglect. His reaction was somewhat akin to that of Eddie Daugherty, who had entered a seminary several decades earlier. Daugherty, who later became a journalist, wrote in his autobiography that a seminary spiritual director had explained women apparently so attractively that Daugherty decided he wanted one. So he quit the seminary and, as it turned out, found quite a few.

Mitch could see nothing basically wrong with women. He understood that there was a solemn promise to lead the unmarried life expected of a priest. But he wasn't a priest. Not yet. And he hadn't made anyone any promises. He was not unaware of the seminary rules nor of the rigid attitudes behind the rules. He thought they were silly.

His was a most rare reaction. That was a day when rules were not a matter for discussion or dissent.

The love life of Carroll Mitchell, considering his station, was both rich and varied. It was anyone's guess how many and who knew about it. It was not general knowledge, although certainly his closer friends and associates knew.

Koesler, associating through sports and an occasional stage appearance, was close enough to know. Groendal, as a fellow playwright, was close enough to know. As were several others. They did not so much envy him as just not understand.

It was questionable that anyone on the faculty might know. If they did, they should have expelled him . . . unless they were marking time in hopes this talented lad would straighten out before the administration's hand was forced.

It was also reasonable to assume that Mitch felt some of the pressure caused by all these people keeping his secrets.

But pressure was coming from other fronts too.

Easter vacation was almost over. Only a couple of days remained before Mitch would have to return to the seminary and complete the final few months of his junior college year. By his lights, he had been making good use of his time. He had dated Beth Yager practically every night. As far as he was concerned, it was time for vacation to end. The excuses he was giving his parents for his nightly absences from home were growing very thin.

In 1949, drive-in theaters were a relatively new phenomenon. But already, in strict moral circles, they were known as "passion pits." They were just made for the young Carroll Mitchell.

"What's supposed to be showing here tonight, anyway?" Beth Yager asked.

"Who cares?" Carroll Mitchell answered. "We wouldn't be able to see it anyway."

He was correct. The car windows were so fogged over, it was impossible to see out even if either occupant had been interested. The sound track might have provided some clue. But they had not bothered to bring the speaker into the car. There was still a measure of cold in the spring night air, so they had pulled the portable heater in.

Mitchell had the family car. This was taking a bit of a risk; there was always the chance that someone—a neighbor or a fellow parishioner—might recognize the car or the license. But Carroll Mitchell was not above taking chances.

Carroll and Beth were engaged in what was called necking and petting—making out—in that slightly more innocent day. They had been at it for quite a while. So each had probably committed a mortal sin, since, in the traditional version of Catholic theology, sins of the flesh were always serious matter. And mortal sin consisted of serious matter —full knowledge and full consent.

They certainly knew what they were doing and surely had consented. Each would include it in the next confession. As would just about every other Catholic young adult. The priest might be kindly or abrupt. He would assign a penance—an average of about ten Our Fathers and ten Hail Marys. Mitch would be sure to omit from his confession that he was a seminarian. To mention that would be to court a long lecture on jeopardizing one's vocation.

Like a swimmer struggling to the surface, Beth fought her way to a sitting position. "Whew! Let up for a minute, okay?"

With some reluctance, Mitch backed off to his end of the seat. He lit a cigarette, further fogging the windows.

Beth tried to adjust her clothing. Though none of it had been removed, it had been considerably loosened and twisted. "How am I ever going to explain all these wrinkles?"

Mitch exhaled two streams of smoke through his nostrils. "Don't try."

"You've got to be kidding! I look like I've been in a wrestling match. Which is not far from the truth. My folks are going to notice."

"The idea is not to stand around waiting for them to notice. I'll get you home as quietly as possible. Go in the side door, head directly for your bedroom, and change before they get a chance to see you."

Beth shook her head. "You've got an answer for everything, haven't you? How do you do it?"

"An inventive mind." He didn't think it wise to mention that this was by no means the first time he had confronted this problem. It was, after a brief but intense relationship, the first time with Beth.

She looked at him directly, one eyebrow cocked. "Are you sure you want to be a priest?"

He seemed surprised. "Sure. Why not?"

"Won't the presence of women all over the rectory kind of clutter your image of celibacy?" Beth and most of her friends were well aware of Carroll Mitchell's reputation as a restrained Casanova. Someone, versed in Latin, had dubbed him Romanticus Interruptus. He would paw and fondle and hug and French, but he would not "go all the way," as the euphemism had it. The legend grew that if he ever threw caution to the winds, he might just marry that girl.

Mitch chuckled. "Whatever gave you the idea there'd be women in my rectory? Rectories are homes for unmarried fathers, not mothers. And no tunnel to the convent, either."

"Really! And when is this magic transition going to take place? When they ordain you? And what makes you think you can turn yourself off like a light bulb?"

"I can do it . . . or haven't you noticed I go just so far and no farther?"

"I know. It's not natural."

Mitch smiled. "It's supernatural."

"Supernatural! Come on! You mean what we've been doing in the back seat of this car tonight is supernatural?"

"Well, preternatural." In truth, Mitchell had a difficult enough time satisfying his own conscience without trying to explain the rationalization to someone else. "Look, it's this easy: I don't know whether I'm going to be a priest or not. I think I want to be. That's what I'm in the seminary to find out. I'm a little better than halfway down that road. I've been in almost seven years. I've got five to go.

"If, when I get close, it looks like all the lights are green for the priesthood, I'll make the supreme sacrifice. Until then, I don't need to wonder whether I like girls. I love 'em!" He cracked the window open and flicked his cigarette out, then grinned and reached for her. "But enough talk. I'm getting lonesome."

"Hold it!" It was Beth's turn to light a cigarette. "There's more to it than this, you know."

"What?"

"One-night stands."

"Wait a minute! I'm not like that. I don't do that kind of thing."

It was true. Although he had been close to many girls, he had never been the one to put an end to any of the affairs. In each case, the girl became convinced that the relationship was dead-end and had nowhere to go. Of course, Mitch had never done anything to prove them wrong.

"I don't mean 'one-night stands' literally. I mean all these wrestling matches in confined places like the back seat of a car."

"Well, excuse me if I can't afford a limousine."

"I don't mean a limousine."

"Then what?"

"A bed."

Panic seized him. "A bed!"

"Yes. You know: a long, soft thing where you can stretch out and be comfortable instead of being twisted up like a pretzel."

He couldn't put his finger on it. Somehow the back seat of a car meant a momentary fling while a bed conveyed the idea of a commitment. Permanence. Marriage.

He sat bolt upright. He'd been challenged. All thought of resumption of necking and petting was wiped away. This had to be settled first. "Well, you know, Beth, this isn't as easy as saying, 'Your place or mine?' Our parents would not be nuts about the idea of us going to bed."

"There are other beds."

"Can you afford a motel? I can't."

"How about where you live?"

"I told you—"

"I mean the seminary."

"The seminary! You must be out of your—"

"They've got beds there."

"Of course they've got beds there. They just don't allow women in them."

"Why not be a pioneer? Be the first to have a room with a girl instead of a room with a view."

"That's impossible. The place is packed with men. How would you get in there? How could I get you past the guys on duty? There are some rules I can get away with breaking. But this! I'd be out on my ear in a minute."

"Impossible? For you? Afraid to take the chance?"

Afraid to take the chance? Now, there was a gauntlet. His mind raced. Was there a chance in a million of pulling this off? There were many more doors besides the front door. There was the matter of time and timing. The best time of day or night and gauging the amount of time it would take to get from here to there and from there to there. With some cooperation and a barrel of luck, a guy might just pull it off.

Yeah, with scrupulous planning and a lot of luck, it might just work.

The idea was beginning to intrigue him. To the best of his knowledge, it had never been tried before. What a challenge!

And what a risk! In a sense, his entire future in the Church would depend on success or failure in an enterprise like this.

"Okay, let's do it! Just give me time to set it up."

Her eyes flashed. "How much time?"

He thought. "A few weeks . . . a month at most."

She frowned. "That's pretty close to the end of school. You're not trying to put this off till summertime, are you?"

"No, no . . ." He was still thinking. "Not summertime. If anything, that'd be more chancey. There's no tight schedule then. There may be fewer people around but there's no predicting where they may be or when.

"No, it's chancey as hell. But the only time to try it is when everybody's there and on schedule."

She caught his excitement. "You mean you're really going to try it?" She had not planned this. It had just happened. But she couldn't have been more thrilled.

"I couldn't resist."

She crushed out her cigarette in the ashtray, smiled at him with a new, warm welcome, and slid down until she was reclining on the seat.

He flicked up her skirt, placed his hand firmly on her inner thigh and got back to the serious business of heavy breathing.

7

Robert Koesler would never forget the final few months of his junior year in college. Too many traumatic events took place to forget any of them.

This, the third collegiate year, marked the first time seminarians were allowed to have private rooms. Previously, those who boarded at the seminary had slept in huge dormitories where there was a minimum of privacy and a maximum of adolescent horseplay.

Individual rooms were awarded students for the junior and senior years of college. The rooms—very small and spartan—were located in a section of the building called St. Thomas Hall. No conversation or fraternizing was permitted in the Hall, only study and sleep. Leading one wag to suggest that if any student were to die in St. Thomas Hall, when at long last the body was discovered, they would just put handles on the room and bury him in it.

Beginning shortly after Christmas, at the start of the second semester, the faculty announced an open competition for members of the Philosophy Department—third and fourth college. It was a voluntary arts and letters contest with many categories to choose from. Entries and entrants were to be prepared by the final week in May. The competition would be judged the first week in June.

Characteristically, Koesler chose the category of declamation in which to compete. All he had to do was memorize a lengthy speech from Shakespeare, and recite it while acting it out.

Carroll Mitchell was very serious about the competition. He volunteered to write an original play. It would not be performed, but judged as a written work.

When he learned what Mitchell had planned, Groendal of course decided to join in the combat. He too would write a play.

They were now nearing the time of judgment, a unique event in the annals of the seminary. It was an exciting time. Very shortly, winners from the various categories would be announced. The school year was coming to a close. Summer vacation would begin in a matter of weeks.

To cap the climax there was Mitchell's saucy plan to smuggle a girl into his room. To be sure, few knew of this daring project. From the start, Mitchell knew he couldn't complete this caper without some minimal conspiracy. But it would have to be confined to as few trusted friends as possible. Among those let in on the secret were Koesler and Groendal.

Least apprehensive of all involved in this adventure—which had been lightheartedly code-named "Cherchez la Femme"—was Mitchell himself. To him it was no more than a game, a game for which he had carefully prepared and was destined to win.

To the others, it was one gigantic and needless risk. If they were caught, they had no idea what sort of punishment would be meted out. Aiding and abetting fornication, as far as they could discover, was an as-yet uncodified offense against seminary order. But there was no doubt in anyone's mind that the administration would be creative in finding a penalty.

Of course there was no uncertainty as to what lay before Mitchell should he be caught. He would be out on his ear before that day was done. So the principal peril was Mitchell's. But there was enough ancillary hazard to go around for everyone.

The only reason Koesler agreed to collaborate was out of loyalty to Mitchell. It would not by any means be the first time Koesler had been in violation of a seminary rule, only the most serious. Why Groendal was aboard was anyone's guess. Even he was not quite sure. Ridley, a very complex person, was little understood by anyone, including himself.

Now it had come down to the final meeting for "Cherchez la Femme." This was a summit assembly of only the principals. Mitchell, Koesler, and Groendal. Each clad in cassock and Roman collar, a privilege granted from third college on, the three walked briskly in endless wide circles around the seminary grounds, firming up the plot.

"Does it have to be this Sunday?" Koesler asked.

"What's the matter with this Sunday?" Mitchell countered.

"I don't know. It's so soon."

"What do you mean 'soon'? We've been talking about it for almost three weeks. This is the final Visiting Sunday of the year. The place will be lousy with guests. That's what I'm counting on."

"He's right, Bob," Groendal said. "There's always plenty of confusion on Visiting Sunday. Parents, grandparents, sometimes brothers, sisters, cousins, friends . . . all ages. The perfect time to smuggle somebody in, particularly a girl. It's just about the only time there are girls in the building."

"But there aren't any girls in St. Thomas Hall," Koesler insisted. "There aren't *any* visitors permitted in St. Thomas Hall. So what's the good of the crowd as a camouflage?"

Mitchell sighed. "We've been over this before, Bob. The idea is to get her into the building without raising any suspicions. When we get to St. Thomas Hall, that's where you guys come in."

"I don't know . . ."

"Bob," Mitchell said, "if you want out, say so. Nobody's making you do this. I just asked you because first, you can keep a secret. And second, I thought you'd be willing to help me."

"I'm not begging off," Koesler said. "It's just that since I agreed to get involved, I've been doing a lot of thinking. Too much, in fact. It's getting in the way of just about everything—studies, exams. The more I think about it, the more I ask myself, Why? So, why?"

"I told you: I promised her."

"But it's so silly. You, maybe we, are toying with expulsion. And for what?"

"I promised. But, if you want out . . ."

"I can't handle it alone," Groendal protested.

"We can always get somebody else." Even as he said it, Mitchell was not at all sure he could come up with a replacement for Koesler, particularly on such short notice.

"No, no; I'll do it. You promised her. I promised you. I just think we should have been more prudent before any of us did all this promising."

"Relax, will you. Both of you! Nothing's going to go wrong. It's all very simple. What is it? An afternoon. One afternoon out of your whole life?"

Neither Groendal nor Koesler cared to comment on that. For a few moments, they were silent as they broke off their circling pattern and headed for the building.

Perhaps, thought Koesler, Mitchell was right. It was just an afternoon. And Mitch had planned things carefully, as he always did. Nothing could go wrong. It was futile and foolish to worry.

As they entered the building and headed for their rooms in St. Thomas Hall, Mitch began to recapitulate. "Now, Beth will get here right at two o'clock, one hour after visiting time begins. There will be a big crowd here by then. It's always that way. The main bunch gets here right off the bat. By two, more will be coming. But nobody will be leaving yet. Bob meets her at the front door. You got that, Bob?"

"Yeah, okay. But . . . what if she's not the only one wearing a green dress?"

"You forget: She's looking for you, too. How many girls in green dresses will be looking for you?"

"Okay."

"All right," Mitchell continued. "Then what?"

"Then I escort her down the first-floor corridor. We go all the way around the first floor and end up at St. Thomas Hall. Then I check things with Rid."

"And what do you do, Rid?"

"I've already checked out the first floor and made sure there's nobody around. When Bob gets there with Beth, I go through the Hall and make doubly sure there's nobody around. Then I stay at the far end, while Bob lets her in the Hall."

"And Bob?"

"I let her in the Hall. She already knows the number of your room. When she goes in, I stay at my end and make sure nobody enters until she gets to your room and goes in. And . . . that's pretty much it."

"Right. Neither of you will be needed again until four, when she leaves. And the process will be just reversed, with the two of you at either end of the Hall making sure the coast is clear. Then she'll come out and mingle with the crowd that's leaving at the end of visiting hours. And that's it."

They arrived at Mitchell's room. Neither Koesler nor Groendal made any move to enter. After all, it was against the rules for any student to be in any other student's room.

Oddly, it did not seem strange to either of them that they were observing a rule that they would help smash to smithereens in just a few days.

"By the way," Groendal said, "now that all the plans are made, what are you going to do in here for two whole hours on Sunday?"

Mitchell looked at Groendal in amazement. "You mean you actually don't know?"

The superior tone did it. Groendal dissolved in embarrassment.

Mitchell looked knowingly at Koesler, who had a blank expression. Mitchell shook his head. Neither of his confederates had any real idea why they were putting their careers at risk. If truth be known, even Mitchell had no practical knowledge of what might follow necking and petting. But he was more than willing to find out.

In any case, there was nothing more to say. All plans had been made and checked. Everything was prepared. Each was ready to go to his own room.

"By the way. Rid, how did your play go?"

The question took Groendal by surprise.

"My play? Oh, you mean for the arts contest. Okay, I guess."

"I would have helped you with it," Mitchell said, "but I was entered in the same contest. Somehow it just didn't seem kosher."

Groendal recoiled. "I don't need any help from you or anybody."

"Sorry." Mitchell knew he was the better playwright. He also knew he had touched a nerve. "Anyway, it's all over except for the judging. You make a copy of yours?"

"Sure."

"So did I. Let's trade off. We can read each other's play."

"Why?"

"No reason. I'd just like to read your work and I'd like you to read mine. I mean we both really like the stage. It'd be fun to read each other's work. Unless a miracle happens, one of our plays is going to win. Then the school year'll be over and we'll never get to read each other's stuff."

"I don't know . . ." Groendal seemed most reluctant.

"Hey, it's okay, Rid. Just a thought. Forget it."

Groendal's expression changed. "Okay. It might be fun. I'll go get it now and we'll trade."

In the ensuing couple of days, Mitchell found little time for anything other than cramming for final exams. He was able even to keep from thinking about "Cherchez la Femme." On Saturday afternoon, he found a little spare time. He also found Groendal's manuscript and decided, since the exchange had been his idea, he'd better read it.

Mitchell studied the title. "The Biggest Miracle." He smiled. How like Rid to write a religious play. Appropriate too, since the judges would all be priests of the seminary faculty.

Mitchell began to read. As he turned the pages, a frown appeared. The more he read, the deeper the furrows. Several times he put the manuscript aside and sat lost in thought. When he finally finished reading, he went immediately to the library, where he spent nearly an hour in the reserve stacks until he found what he was seeking. He checked out a small black book. Then he went to the recreation rooms in the basement of St. Thomas Hall where, as he had expected, he found Ridley Groendal listening to classical records and smoking a cigarette. There was no one else in the room, so Mitchell took a chair next to Ridley.

Mitchell gazed intently but wordlessly at his classmate.

Groendal finally broke the ice. "Good play. I finished it last night. Sort of a downer, though . . . I didn't think you tied up all the loose ends at the conclusion."

"They weren't supposed to be tied, Rid." Mitchell paused. "Rid, why'd you do it?"

"Do what?" But Groendal's eyes betrayed awareness; he knew.

"You're a creative person, Rid. I know that. You've done some pretty good stuff in the past. You didn't have to steal a play!"

"What?" Groendal did a bad job of stubbing out his cigarette. "I don't know what you're talking about."

"Your play." Mitchell tapped the manuscript in his lap. "It's about a seminary faculty composed of very educated men—as a matter of fact, it's an all-male cast."

"It was written to be performed by a seminary. And they're always looking for all-male casts."

"One faculty member is deathly ill," Mitchell continued as if he'd never been interrupted, "and one is having serious problems with his faith. And there's an agnostic doctor who is taking special care of the sick priest."

Groendal nervously lit another cigarette.

"So there's a miracle. Or at least it seems like a miraculous cure of the sick priest. And this partially restores the faith of the doubting priest. Until the doctor goes to confession and tells the doubter that the cure wasn't a miracle. The sick priest simply responded to the medication. So the doubter is torn up by a knowledge he can share with no one because of the 'seal' of confession. And then at the end there's a real miracle that restores the faith of the doubting priest."

Groendal anxiously tapped a long cigarette ash into a tray. "Sounds like a pretty good plot to me."

"It seemed like a pretty good plot to Emmet Lavery, too." From beneath Groendal's manuscript, Mitchell extracted the small black book he had checked out of the library. "Except that Lavery called it, 'The First Legion.'"

"A coincidence," Groendal murmured.

"Coincidence! Change your seminary faculty to his small Jesuit seminary and everything is pretty much the same. Oh, I'll give you credit for rewriting the ending . . . and I think yours is better, more believable. But the rest of it you stole."

"Oh, come on, Mitch!"

"Sometimes word for word. Look at this . . ." Mitchell indicated parallel passages in the bound play and in Groendal's manuscript. In both versions a character says, 'I . . . begin to see . . . the biggest miracle . . . is faith . . . and to have faith is the miracle!' To which another character responds, 'I have prayed for faith like yours, but it won't come.'

"And that," Mitchell continued, "is only one example, Rid. They're all over the place. And what's more, you know it! You have to know it! You copied them!"

Groendal lit a fresh cigarette from the butt of the previous one. Ordinarily, he did not chain-smoke.

"This is why you were reluctant to exchange manuscripts with me, wasn't it?"

"At first, yes," Groendal admitted. "But then I wanted to see if it could get by you. Obviously, it didn't.

"I knew I was taking a chance—with you and, to a lesser degree, with the faculty." He shrugged. "I figured it was worth the gamble." He looked at Mitchell. "What are you going to do about it?"

"The question, Rid, is what are you going to do about it?"

Groendal exhaled a long stream of smoke. "Nothing."

"Nothing! Rid, don't you understand? This is plagiarism. It's a crime!"

"There's no guarantee that it will be performed even if it wins."

"You submitted it in a contest as if it were yours. And you stole it. Doesn't that mean anything to you?"

"Let him who is without sin cast the first stone!"

"What?" Clearly, Mitchell had not expected that response.

"What about your little adventure tomorrow afternoon?"

"What's that got to do with this?"

"You're not exactly sinless, you know. You're going to fracture a prohibition that is so taken for granted that nobody even took the trouble to make a rule about it."

"Apples and oranges, Rid. I'm going to fool around a bit . . . pay off on a promise I made. What we're talking about here is serious. Rid, we—you and I—respect—reverence—the theater. We've spent a lot of time on stage. We've both written plays. You can't throw all that in the gutter by stealing somebody else's work! For us, especially, it would be like a sacrilege!"

His eloquent plea met with silence.

"Well?" Mitch finally prodded.

"I'm not going to do anything."

"But you'll be discovered. How's it going to be to have plagiarism on your record?"

"They won't discover it. I'm banking on it."

"But I did."

"You're more perceptive than they are. I thought it might get by you. It didn't. But it will get by them."

"What if it does? What if it wins? What happens if you win with a stolen play?"

"I can live with it. Besides, I improved it; even you had to admit that!" Groendal hesitated. "What about you? Are you going to do anything about it?"

Mitchell's eyes widened. Obviously he had not considered this eventuality. He had thought he'd be able to convince Groendal to clean up his own mess. "I don't know, Rid. I'll have to think about it."

Mitchell rose and left. He took with him both the book and the manuscript. At that moment, Ridley Groendal knew what Mitchell would do. After their conversation, it was transparent. Mitch could not see that borrowing an idea was just a normal response to writer's block.

Nothing was more dangerous than a self-righteous person bent on inflicting some sort of justice on a poor soul. If nothing was done about this, Mitchell would surely blow the whistle on him. So, something would have to be done. But what?

8

Robert Koesler stood in the seminary foyer. A very busy place this Sunday as a steady stream of visitors kept entering and gathering here, each bunch meeting their student and then dispersing to various designated visiting parlors.

He had heard that dying people have their lives pass before them. He didn't know about that. But he did feel that his career as a seminarian and potential priest might be grinding to a halt as a result of what he was about to do. And most of his past transgression of seminary rules was marching through his memory.

His infractions ran from the prosaic, such as talking during periods of silence, tardiness, and unexcused absences, to the more exotic, such as playing table tennis during study period and helping to place another student's bed beyond anyone's reach atop a dormitory stall. But nothing approached today's folly: in effect, smuggling human contraband within these sacred walls. And all out of a sense of loyalty to a friend.

When, he wondered, would he learn?

There, coming through the front door: a young lady in green. She seemed to be alone. As she climbed the steps, Koesler, with an expectant look, stepped in front of her. She gazed at him quizzically. Instantly he knew this was not Beth. Awkwardly, he tried to act as if he were moving forward to greet someone else as the young lady dodged by and joined her party.

What an outrageous adventure! Here he was, waiting for someone he didn't know who, in turn, would be looking for someone she didn't know.

For just an instant he wondered whether it might be feasible to simply call the whole thing off. The thought lasted no more than a split second. As foolish as he now considered his participation in this plot, he was indeed committed to it.

"Bob?"

He looked down. How did she get there? He hadn't noticed her. But there she was, very pretty in a bright green dress.

'Y . . . yes," he managed to stammer.

"I'm Beth."

"Uh-huh." How had she found him? Waiting for their visitors to arrive were many underclassmen in civilian clothes. And there were quite a few from the Philosophy Department, dressed as he was, in cassock and Roman collar. "How could you tell it was I?"

"I asked around. Somebody pointed you out."

"You didn't!"

"Yes, I did. How else was I going to find you?"

"I guess you had no choice."

Would her inquiries prove embarrassing for him if this whole plot came unraveled?

"Well, come on; let's go."

After they had walked a considerable distance, Beth remarked, "My, this is a large building!"

It was. But familiarity had artificially shrunken the distance for Koesler. "It helps if you remember that basically it's built in a square. The chapel's in the middle of the square. Then the four corners sprout their own extensions. There's the auditorium in one corner, the convent and infirmary on another, the gymnasium on the third, and St. Thomas Residence Hall on the fourth."

"Ah, St. Thomas Hall. That's where we're going, isn't it?"

"That's right." As far as Koesler was concerned, they couldn't get there too soon.

They walked in silence for a while. Koesler had to admit she certainly was pretty. But, worth the risk? Not as far as he was concerned. Anyway, in a few minutes, if all went as planned, his role would be completed until it was time for her to leave. And that, compared with getting her in, would be duck soup.

"Hmmm . . . I was wondering," Beth said, "why are you wearing that?"

"What?"

"That uniform."

"The cassock?"

"Yes. It's a priest's uniform. But you're not a priest—she looked up at him incredulously—are you?"

Koesler grinned. "No. We're supposed to start wearing the cassock in third-year college. It's sort of the uniform of the day. We wear it just about everywhere, I guess, except for sports and in our rooms."

Her nose crinkled. "Does Mitch wear one of these cassocks?"

"Uh, ordinarily, yes." That was it. That was the reason Mitch did not want to meet her himself: He would have had to be wearing his cassock. He didn't want her to see him in a "priest's suit." It might well cramp both their styles.

They arrived at the double doors leading to St. Thomas Hall. This was it. Koesler took a deep breath. It was considerably reassuring to find Groendal on duty.

"How's the coast, Rid?"

"We're in luck; not a soul in sight," Groendal replied.

"I'm Beth." She extended her hand.

"Ridley Groendal." His hand was in and out of hers in a second.

Koesler felt foolish for not having introduced her. But he would not be able to relax until she was out of his jurisdiction—which, with any luck, would only be a few seconds more.

Wordlessly, Groendal entered the hall and walked deliberately down its length, looking from side to side as he went. At the other end of the hall, he peered up and down the staircase until he was certain no one was around. Then he signaled to Koesler, who looked back down the main corridor. There was still a crowd at the front entrance but no one seemed to be looking down the corridor or paying any attention to them.

"Okay," Koesler said, "go ahead."

"Isn't this a little too complicated?" Beth complained.

"Go!" Koesler almost shouted.

She gave a startled little jump and hurried into the hall.

"Room 12, don't forget!" Koesler stage-whispered after her. He waited until he saw her knock rather timidly at the door of room 12, and enter. Then, as if the weight of the world had slipped from his shoulders, he almost skipped down the corridor toward the rear of the building. Two hours to go and the business would be done.

What to do with two hours on a bright, balmy spring day having just shed a heavy burden of responsibility? Nothing inside the building. He changed into casual clothes and went outside to play a little baseball. He had taken the precaution of advising any potential visitors not to come, thus avoiding any conflict on this trying day.

Pick-up games were in progress at several of the seminary's five diamonds. He joined one. He hadn't a care in the world. Well, one: He would have to be back on duty for this silly caper at four promptly. He consulted his watch. It was exactly three o'clock. Whatever Mitch and Beth were doing, they were right in the middle of it.

*   *   *

It was exactly three o'clock when there was a brief but insistent knocking at the door of room 12 in St. Thomas Hall. Summarily, the door was flung open.

Later, when he tried to recall that moment, Mitchell would say that all he could remember was a long row of red buttons and red piping on the black cassock of Monsignor George Cronyn, rector of Sacred Heart Seminary. Of course, Mitchell went into a state of shock.

Beth, on her part, remembered the Monsignor's face, mostly because it was as red as the trimming on his cassock.

As the door swung open and banged against the wall, Beth instinctively pulled the sheet up so that it pretty well covered both of them to the shoulder level.

For a moment, no one said anything. There was almost nothing to say. Mitch and Beth had been caught *in flagrante delicto*. A most rare, if not unique, instance in the annals of the seminary, at least to that date.

"Mr. Mitchell," Monsignor Cronyn snapped the syllables, "you have betrayed a sacred trust. I want you gone from the seminary by vespers this afternoon. Gone for good! Is that understood?"

Presumably the question was rhetorical; the rector did not wait for a reply. He merely retrieved the door whence it still vibrated near the wall and closed it behind him, again with a resounding bang.

Cronyn stormed along the corridor and up the staircase to his room. All the way he fought mixed emotions. He was furious with Carroll Mitchell, a young man who had shown such great promise. He might have made an impressive priest. His grades were well above average. He showed creative talent on the stage and as a playwright—abilities that promised great success in the pulpit. And he had an attractive, manly personality that easily would have drawn young boys to the seminary to test their vocations.

But what Mitchell had done was patently intolerable. If the seminary faculty had learned that he was even dating steadily, the student would have been warned most forcefully. If it had been proven that he had fornicated, Mitchell's expulsion would have been seriously debated. But to flaunt the affair as Mitchell had done! Bring the girl into the seminary, right into his room! A young man such as this could never again be trusted. But to have thrown away so promising a career so nonchalantly was a crime that very nearly cried to heaven for vengeance.

Nor was Monsignor Cronyn all that happy over how he had learned what was going on in room 12.

The principle of "fraternal correction" had been around a long time. Still, it remained a dangerous tool in the hands of almost anyone, let alone an adolescent with perhaps a personal ax to grind. At the beginning of each scholastic year, when Cronyn would explain the notion of fraternal correction, he would try to emphasize the dangers inherent in such an action. Nevertheless, it was part of seminary policy that a student report to the authorities any other student who was guilty of a flagrant violation of law—God's or the seminary's.

And thus it had been in the stated interest of fraternal correction that Ridley C. Groendal had come to Monsignor Cronyn's office at approximately 2:45 that afternoon to inform on what he thought was happening in Carroll Mitchell's room.

In all probability it had been the proper thing for Groendal to do. Still, it was extremely rare that any student would turn in another. Even though Cronyn understood the importance—historical if none other— of fraternal correction, in his heart the Monsignor was leery of, and indeed disliked, the principle. Nor did he much care, privately, for a student who would—he hesitated to use the word, but, yes—betray a confrere.

In spite of his intellectual acceptance of the procedure, at his core Cronyn found squealing distasteful; he could not help looking upon the informer with a certain amount of loathing.

There were exceptions, of course. It was thoroughly understandable to speak out to save oneself or another innocent party from harm, as in the case of incest or child abuse. But it was quite another thing to cry havoc just because a rule was being violated.

From this day forward, Monsignor Cronyn would have to force himself to try to be objective with regard to Ridley C. Groendal.

* * *

Regularly checking his watch, an action that was second-nature to him anyway, Koesler knew that it was precisely twenty minutes to four when he left the baseball game. He took a quick shower, climbed back into his cassock and returned to the entrance to St. Thomas Hall at exactly four o'clock.

He waited almost five minutes. Trying not to draw too much attention, he kept glancing down the hall. He was impatient and growing a little angry. Visiting hours were over at 4:30. There were just a few more minutes left to get Beth out of St. Thomas Hall and out of the building. A challenge was a challenge, but Mitch was taking unfair advantage of this situation.

At last, patience exhausted, he entered the hall and walked toward Mitchell's room. As he neared it, he saw that the door was ajar. For one confused moment, he wondered if his watch had slowed or stopped. Had he erred and failed Mitchell? He hurried forward to the open door.

Inside the room, Mitchell was throwing clothes into a suitcase.

Koesler was perplexed. "What the hell's going on, Mitch?"

Mitchell looked at him briefly, then returned to packing. "What the hell's it look like?"

"You're packing. But what for?"

"I'm out on my ear, Bobby. Just like you tried to warn me."

"I don't understand. Did something go wrong?"

Mitchell smiled bitterly. "I'd say so. The rector dropped in while Beth and—I were . . . uh . . . in a sort of compromising position. And he took that occasion to fire me."

"But that's impossible. I was very careful when Beth and I were going through the halls. Nobody paid any attention to us. And I certainly would have noticed the rector if he had been in the corridor anywhere."

"How about if somebody told him?"

"But who could . . ." Koesler did not complete the sentence. There was only one who could have told. "Rid." Even as Koesler pronounced the name he had difficulty believing it was true. "Ridley?"

"Rid!"

"Are you sure? How can you be sure?"

Mitchell closed the suitcase and snapped the lock. "We've already had it out. After Cronyn pronounced sentence on me, Beth . . . oh, hell, Beth got dressed and left. Cronyn didn't say who did it, but I was pretty sure. I found Rid in the rec hall listening to his goddam classical music. We had it out. It was Rid, all right."

"But why? Why would he do a thing like that? I can't believe it!"

"Why did he do it?" Mitchell obviously was fighting back tears and, as time passed, having a harder and harder time of it. "Okay. I'll tell you . . . but you have to promise to keep it a secret."

Koesler nodded. Briefly, he reflected that he was becoming the receptacle of a lot of secrets. He knew he would have lots of secrets to keep if he ever became a priest. He hadn't known he would have to warm up in advance so often.

"It's got to do with the contest," Mitchell explained. "You probably know that I entered a play."

"Yeah, I remember."

"And you know that Rid also submitted a play?"

Koesler thought for a moment. "Uh-huh."

"Okay. So we both entered plays. But, the poor slob was afraid he couldn't beat me. So he stole a play that had been written about fifteen years ago. He didn't even bother changing very much of it."

"He plagiarized!"

"Uh-huh. And when we exchanged plays and read each other's I recognized the work he stole. So I confronted him and finally got him to admit it."

"So where's the problem?"

"He wouldn't withdraw it from the competition."

"They'll discover him!"

"He doesn't think so. Anyway he said he was going to go through with it. And I wouldn't promise him I'd keep quiet."

"But he was going to keep your secret today."

"That's the way he looked at it too. But it's not the same thing." He shrugged. "Anyway, he was afraid I was going to turn him in. So he decided to cut me off at the pass: If I were caught this afternoon, I wouldn't be around to turn him in."

"But . . . what's the point? You could still turn him in."

"Maybe yes, maybe no. But he guessed right—at least part right. I'll take my medicine. I gambled—and I knew it was a gamble—and I lost. Of course I wasn't figuring on a betrayal. But you've got to plan for everything." He shook his head. "I was stupid. I should've realized that once I was a threat to him, he might try something. It just never entered my head that . . . well, he's won this round.

"But I'm keeping a copy of his manuscript, his plagiarism. Someday, who knows? Someday it may hurt him as much as this hurts me—to have people know that he stooped to plagiarism to try to beat me in a contest."

"Mitch," Koesler said, "if you don't mind my bringing this up, your plan pretty much lowers you to Rid's level. This sort of thing—where you hold on to revenge for what might be a lot of years—can take a lot out of your character, too. I'd rather see you turn him in now or just forget about it."

Mitchell shook his head. "This is the way it's going to be, Bobby. It's the way Rid wants to play the game. These are practically his rules. I'd like him to spend the rest of his life waiting for the other shoe to fall. And I don't plan to drop the other shoe until or unless it will hurt him the way I've been hurt.

"I know, I know . . ." Mitchell waved away the objection Koesler was about to make. ". . . it's not the Christian thing to do. But sometimes you have to go back to the eye for an eye, tooth for a tooth. This is one of those times.

"Now, Bobby, by official decree, I've got just a few minutes before I've got to get out of here. Cronyn said by vespers. I'll have to come back sometime and pick up my books and the rest of my stuff. But this may be the last time I'll see you for a while."

Mitchell offered his hand and Koesler grasped it. If they had not been schooled in the macho lifestyle they might have wept on each other's shoulder.

It was not the first time, nor would it be the last in Koesler's experience, that a talented young man would leave the seminary. In each case, it would cast grave doubt on his own vocation. But somehow, in some way, he would remain even as others left.

*   *   *

Koesler blinked several times and returned to the present. He looked around the church and again fixed on Carroll Mitchell. Beth had banked on landing him by becoming his first sexual experience. She had been mistaken.

Instead, she had become the personification of his disgrace. For, as far as Mitchell's family was concerned, his expulsion was an unmitigated disgrace.

Ridley Groendal won first place in the contest. He had calculated correctly that no one on the faculty would tumble onto the fact that he had stolen the play. But, until the scholastic year was completed, he figuratively held his breath waiting for Carroll Mitchell to denounce him. It did not happen. But in a certain sense, Groendal never again completely exhaled. Always, somewhere in the wings, Carroll Mitchell held the proof that in the queen of arts, Ridley C. Groendal was a thief.

9

Peter Harison had just begun the second Scripture reading.

In this rather large congregation, he was just about alone in feeling a sense of loss at the death of Ridley Groendal. Thus it was not unexpected that Harison had a difficult time controlling his emotions as he read. It was one thing to sit passively while a loved one was being buried and quite another to, in a sense, have to perform. But, all in all, he was doing rather well in reading an excerpt from the Letter to the Romans.

"At the appointed time, when we were still powerless, Christ died for us godless men. It is rare that anyone should lay down his life for a just man, though it is barely possible that for a good man someone may have the courage to die. It is precisely in this that God proves His love for us: that while we were still sinners, Christ died for us. Now that we have been justified by His blood, it is all the more certain that we shall be saved by Him from God's wrath."

Father Koesler had spent considerable time selecting the three Scripture readings for this service. Brought together, as he would attempt to do in his homily, they should convey exactly the message he wished to leave with this congregation.

He could not bring himself to consider this present group as mourners. Ridley Groendal appeared to have one genuine mourner. Perhaps, counting himself, two. The others? Most of them merely the curious, though some were faithful parishioners with nothing better to do, and a few were victims of Rid's acerbic pen who wanted to make sure their antagonist was truly dead and buried.

Finally, there were the special four, singularly selected by Groendal as targets of his distinctive venom. Koesler wondered about their present state of mind. Koesler wondered about them a lot.

Though she was extremely diminutive, Koesler was able to spot Valerie Walsh seated near the rear of the church. Locating her was really more difficult, since she was not accompanied by her pro basketball-size husband, "Red."

In Ridley Groendal's adolescent and adult life, there had been six pivotal characters. Five of them—Peter Harison, David Palmer, Carroll Mitchell, Charlie Hogan, and Valerie Walsh—were here. Of these, the one who seemed entirely out of place was Valerie.

Harison was what was euphemistically referred to as Groendal's "significant other." Beyond that, the two were fast friends. Between Groendal and the others was a free-flowing stream of enmity. Palmer, Mitchell, and Hogan had clashed with Groendal in their younger lives and ever since had figuratively been at war. But the much younger Valerie had not been a participant in any similar relationship.

The letters the four had sent to Groendal prior to his fatal heart attack explained, at least in part, their ill-fated connections. But only one who was privy to the entire affair could understand everything, including Valerie's involvement. And Robert Koesler was eminently qualified to be that one person.

This facet of Groendal's life had not begun with Valerie, but with her mother. It had happened at the end of the year of the fated altercation between Groendal and Carroll Mitchell. The incident that would radically change several lives occurred during the two-week Christmas vacation.

It was the final year of college for both Groendal and Koesler, their final year at Sacred Heart Seminary. Next school year they were to graduate to the newly opened St. John's Seminary in Plymouth, Michigan.

But this was Christmas and all was well. Two days before the feast itself, vacation began, and the seminarians returned to their homes and, only slightly less importantly, to their home parishes. Monsignor George Cronyn forcefully urged all his wards to report to their respective pastors, who, presumably, had an abiding interest in their potentially future priests. More often than not, starry-eyed seminarians were rudely dashed back to earth when their pastors couldn't for the life of them remember the students.

That surely was the case with Groendal and Koesler. Both were from Holy Redeemer parish, which was staffed by priests of the Redemptorist Order. Through a set of particular circumstances, Groendal and Koesler had not followed the vast majority of their peers to the Redemptorist seminary in Kirkwood, Missouri, but had gone instead to the local diocesan seminary.

Had they become Redemptorists, they could have been assigned to any Redemptorist mission in the world, or, equally likely, they would have developed a series of sermons that they would have delivered from one parish mission to the next. As diocesan priests, they would serve in whichever Detroit parish or position the bishop chose for them.

This Christmas of 1949, both Groendal and Koesler had gone through the formalities with their forgetful Redemptorist pastor. Then, as a kind of sop to their status as seminarians—even if in the wrong seminary—they were invited to serve the glorious Mass of Christmas Eve.

Several days after Christmas, Koesler proposed to Groendal that they take in a movie. The Stratford, their neighborhood theater, was showing *Adam's Rib*, a film about which Koesler had heard good things. Groendal agreed enthusiastically. He was becoming a dedicated devotee of the arts and had read a number of lavishly favorable reviews of *Adam's Rib*. It was set: That night they would meet at the Stratford at 6:45, in plenty of time for the seven o'clock showing.

* * *

They met at the appointed time, bought their tickets and hurried in out of the snow. They eschewed the popcorn concession. Groendal considered munching refreshments beneath the serious student of the art. Koesler concurred most reluctantly; paraphrasing the dictum on wine with a meal, he thought no movie complete without popcorn.

As they handed their tickets to the usherette, something happened. Koesler was not sure what, but something happened. In a later era, it would be referred to as "chemistry." In any case, for no explicable reason, Groendal lingered just a little longer than necessary at the door. He said nothing to the usherette, whose tag identified her as Jane Condon, and she said nothing to him. But something happened.

The theater was only partially filled. They selected seats on the right, on the aisle, about midway down.

Koesler was still trying to comprehend what chimerical sort of magic had happened at the entry a few moments ago. With his brain idling, he barely restrained himself from genuflecting before entering the row.

It wouldn't have been the first time he had slipped into that Catholic ritual in a theater. He had also once made the sign of the cross at the end of a movie, before realizing he was not in church and this was not the end of a religious ceremony. By these mindless modes of ritual could Catholics be picked out of a crowd.

Slowly the lights dimmed and everyone settled back to be entertained. There were coming attractions, followed by a newsreel, followed by a cartoon. At last *Adam's Rib* began.

Koesler was one who chuckled aloud when amused, Groendal was not. The silent amusement of his companion, contrasted with his own laughter, made Koesler more conscious of Groendal's presence. And his awareness of Groendal led to Koesler's heightened awareness of Jane Condon.

Ordinarily, Koesler would have been oblivious to an usher or usherette who made frequent trips up and down the aisle, especially while being absorbed in a good film. But because of the contrast between his and Groendal's outward reaction to a very humorous movie, Koesler became acutely aware of his companion. And Groendal was very much aware of the peripatetic Jane Condon. Each time she passed, going up or down the aisle, Groendal's head turned. For Koesler, it was like watching two performances, one on the big screen, the other in the next seat. It was distracting, yet interesting.

When the movie ended and lights came up, Koesler felt satisfied in having witnessed a deathless comedy. He also felt somewhat disturbed by Groendal's reaction to the usherette. Disturbed because Koesler was unsure what this reaction might bode. He looked about, but could not see the usherette, only patrons smiling at the movie they had seen and struggling into their outer winter clothing.

It was not yet 10:00 P.M., so Koesler and Groendal decided to stop at a nearby drugstore for a snack and a rehash of the movie.

"Who was that blonde, the defendant in the trial?" Koesler asked.

"Judy Holliday."

"I don't think I've ever seen her before."

Groendal shook his head while swallowing some ice cream. "Neither have I. This is her first film. She was terrific, wasn't she?"

"Yeah, very funny. Which reminds me: Outside of Tracy and Hepburn, I didn't recognize any of the other principals."

"You're right. Most of the others were stage actors until now, like David Wayne, Tom Ewell, and Jean Hagen." Groendal seemed to be feeding on his own enthusiasm. "It just shows you how great these legitimate actors are. You know, in the beginning, particularly in the beginning of the talkies, they were pulling people off the stages in New York and shipping them out to Hollywood for the movies. A film like this really makes me proud of the stage."

Koesler sipped his piping hot coffee. He had enjoyed the movie and he had read about it since vacation had begun. But he was amazed at Groendal's familiarity with it. "How did you ever find out so much about this film? I thought I'd read a lot about it. But I didn't find half of what you're talking about. How did you do it? We've been on vacation only a few days. You been spending all your time in the library or something?"

"Tell you a secret," Groendal said.

Not another secret!

"I get reviews smuggled into the seminary."

"You do?"

"My mother, God bless her. She cuts out clippings of reviews of books, stage plays, and concerts. Once in a while she includes reviews of special movies."

"How does she get the clippings to you?"

"In letters. She folds them inside her letters."

"And they never censor your mail?"

"From my mother!"

It was beyond Koesler. While he enjoyed reading reviews, it would never occur to him to go to such an extreme measure to get them. But he wanted to get back to this postmortem. "How about the writing!" he enthused. "Wasn't it good?"

"Especially good. The credit was to Mrs. Garson Kanin. But that really is the actress Ruth Gordon. How's that for talent!"

"Who's Ruth Gordon? No, wait . . . wait! I remember: She's been in a million movies."

"Right. And she came from the stage, too!"

All this talk about the stage brought to Koesler's mind another person who idolized the stage, more, even than Groendal—Carroll Mitchell.

Funny, now that he thought of it, Koesler had never heard Groendal refer to either Mitchell or Dave Palmer after they had passed out of his life. It was as if they had never existed. Or more as if they had been merely stepping stones in Groendal's development. They had been used and then discarded.

Actually, Koesler himself had had considerable difficulty in continuing his friendship with Groendal, particularly after Mitchell's expulsion. Of course, Koesler did not approve of what Groendal had done, especially in informing on Mitch. But Robert Koesler from an early age had always been extremely nonjudgmental, a trait he had inherited from his Bavarian father.

Admittedly, in not sitting in judgment on Groendal, Koesler was stretching the spirit of understanding and forbearance to its breaking point. But it had not snapped—not yet. After all, Ridley was still a fellow seminarian, and, theoretically at least, a future priest.

Fleetingly Koesler wondered whether Palmer and Mitchell, in turn, had forgotten Groendal. After what they had been through, Koesler doubted it. Somewhere out there was proof that Groendal was an arsonist and a plagiarist. Whether or not Groendal ever reflected upon this, still it was so. Somewhere out there were weapons that were loaded and cocked, but not fired. Not yet.

Groendal, pumped up by his own meticulous research, seemingly could not dam his surge of information. "Can you believe," he continued, "that George Cukor, the director, completed this movie in just thirty-seven days? That's a record for a major movie! And that song at the end . . . the one that's dedicated to Katharine Hepburn . . . what was it?" Groendal was piqued that he couldn't think of the title.

" 'Farewell, Amanda." Koesler was self-congratulatory that he could contribute an essential bit of background.

"That's it: 'Farewell, Amanda.' Know who wrote it?" Certain that Koesler didn't, he swept on. "Cole Porter!" Groendal seemed as pleased as if he himself had written it.

"You're pretty worked up about this, aren't you?" Seldom had Koesler seen Ridley this high.

"It's a great movie, Bob. I'm going to go back and see it again tomorrow."

"See it again!"

"God knows if we'll ever get to see it again if we don't take this opportunity . . . want to come?"

"I don't think so, Rid. It's a great movie. They'll probably release it again some year."

"Maybe, maybe not."

It could not have occurred to either that the movie would be shown any number of times on television. At that time, television was barely beginning its collision course with movie houses. And the movie houses were waiting for the TV fad to fade. Movie cassettes and VCRs were no more than a technologist's dream.

They parted, going their separate ways through a light snow shower.

On his way home, Koesler suddenly began to wonder how much Groendal's projected return to the Stratford was predicated on a desire to see the movie again and how much depended on seeing that usherette again. Peculiar. Were they getting into another "Cherchez la Femme" adventure? If so, how odd! Rid was the one who had blown the whistle on Mitch.

On his way home, Groendal's mind was in turmoil. He tried to focus on the movie. He wanted to remember everything, literally everything. But, as if it were a rubber band, his memory kept snapping back to that usherette. Jane Condon. As far as he could recall, he'd never seen her before. Yet, when he gave her his ticket, there was something about the way she looked at him . . . something in the eye contact. He was not sure what.

And all those times she had walked up and down down that aisle! She didn't have to do that. Each time she passed, she had looked at him. And stranger still, he had looked at her.

Maybe it was all just a fluke. Tomorrow evening when he returned to see the movie again, that would tell the tale.

He felt a moment of panic. What if she wasn't there? What if tomorrow was her night off? Oh, what difference did it make? He wanted to see the movie. That's why he was going back: to see the movie.

But, as he climbed the steps of his house, he had to admit that it made a difference.

10

His mother understood. His mother always understood. His father groused about the admission price. It was not like he stood in the way of Ridley's seeing a movie, but my God, Mr. Groendal groused, he's already seen it.

Mrs. Groendal explained the importance, for one whose life is art, of being immersed in that art. She explained it once. She would not do so again. Having been cowed once more by his redoubtable wife, Mr. Groendal coughed up the money.

Ridley, almost at the last minute, decided to attend the 9:30 P.M. showing. A different sort of audience than the early crowd, he commented. His mother understood completely.

She was there. Taking tickets. His heart seemed to skip a beat. He did not understand it. He gave his ticket to Jane Condon. She tore it in half. But when she returned his half, she held on to her end of the ticket. Expecting simply to be presented with a ticket stub, Groendal was startled to be momentarily joined to this young woman by a scrap of cardboard.

"I guess you must have liked the movie." She smiled, a very engaging smile.

"You remember me?" He had let himself doubt that she would.

"Sure! Who wouldn't?" Didn't he realize, she wondered, what a most attractive young man he was?

She released the ticket stub. But he did not leave . . . not immediately. He was aware that a line was forming behind him, a line of people waiting to get in. Although she did not tell him to, he would have to move along.

"I was wondering . . . if . . . I mean, do you get off after the movie . . . I mean after this showing?"

"Uh-huh."

Some in the line were starting to complain and wonder aloud what was causing the holdup. Groendal knew he had to hurry. He was flustered.

"Well . . . would you be willing . . . would you like to have something with me . . . I mean a snack after the show? I mean . . ."

"That'd be nice. I'll meet you back here in the lobby after the show."

It was good that the date had been accepted; the mood of the waiting line was growing ugly.

Groendal had to force himself to concentrate on the screen. His mind kept racing ahead to the date, his first ever with a girl. But, by determined concentration, he did manage to pick up some additional nuances in the direction, lighting, and dialogue.

After the movie, Groendal waited until the theater had nearly emptied. He found Jane, overcoat over her uniform, waiting in the lobby. He held the door for her, then headed in the direction of the drugstore. There was no snow, but a sharp wind made it seem colder than the temperature. Jane put her arm through his. It was the first time anyone had done that to Ridley. It made him feel good. He felt protective.

Jane ordered a Coke; so did Ridley. He was grateful. Money was not abundant.

They talked for a long while about *Adam's Rib*. Jane was duly impressed with Ridley's knowledge of the film and its background. His information was quite comprehensive by almost any standards. But Ridley was running out of data. And he didn't know what to do next. What happened when one got done telling a girl all one knew? What could they find to talk about then? As long as Ridley could expound on one of his favorite subjects, he felt relaxed and at ease. But one could not run on with technical information forever. Then what?

Then a few minutes of silence. Normally, Ridley felt about silence the way nature reacts to a vacuum: he abhorred it. But now, for some reason, it felt comfortable.

"You don't remember me, do you?"

"Remember you?" Ridley clearly did not.

"I was only two years behind you at Holy Redeemer. But there's no reason why you'd remember me."

"Well, the girls were separated from the boys," Ridley needlessly explained.

"I know." She had been there.

"But you remember me?"

She lowered her eyes. "Sure . . . I . . . I had a crush on you."

"You did?" It had never crossed his mind that anyone would.

"Uh-huh. I used to watch you every chance I got. I remember especially how good you could play the piano. I used to go to the recitals just to hear you."

The recitals! Ridley had pretty well blocked out the memory of the recitals, especially after that fiasco years ago with David Palmer. In fact, he had rather effectively blocked out David Palmer. Ridley found it embarrassing that Jane would remember any of that.

"I remember the last year you played in the recital. You played that Rachmaninoff 'Prelude' so well I was thrilled. I never forgot it."

"Really? Then you must remember later in that recital when I didn't do so well as an accompanist." Might just as well face up to it.

"Oh, that was all the fault of that other boy. He was going too fast. I felt so sorry for you."

She knew it was Palmer's fault and she sympathized! Where had she been when he'd needed her? "I never knew any of this."

"I've kept watching you when you come home for vacations. You look so nice when you're serving, especially now that you wear the collar and dress like a priest."

She'd seen him in the Roman collar, knew he was a seminarian, and still kept her crush alive apparently. This was not hanging together. She was a product of parochial school. So she must have known that priests and even seminarians were off-limits. But here she was, talking to him just as if he were an ordinary young man and not a seminarian just a little more than four years short of ordination to the priesthood. Maybe even flirting with him. He couldn't figure it out.

After a slight pause, she continued. "I was sort of wondering what you were doing tomorrow night."

"Tomorrow night? That's New Year's Eve, isn't it? I don't know. I can tell you one thing I won't be doing: I won't be seeing *Adam's Rib*. I'd never be able to talk the old man into the price of another ticket. So, I don't know . . . haven't got any plans."

"You're not going to a party? A New Year's Eve party?"

"Uh-uh." He did not bother adding that he'd never been to a New Year's Eve party.

"Well, would you like to come over to my house? We can have a kind of small party."

Part of Groendal was hearing Monsignor George Cronyn proclaiming that seminarians should take for granted they would like girls if they gave dating a chance, so nip it in the bud. And part of Groendal told him this might be his very last chance to test that theory. But, if he were to go to the party, what would he tell his parents?

Because he had been carefully programmed, it did not strike Ridley as odd that at age twenty he was still asking permission to use the phone at the seminary and still accounting to his parents for every place he went.

His educated guess was that his parents—read his mother—would deny him permission to go to a mixed party on New Year's Eve. His mother and Monsignor Cronyn were of one mind when it came to girls. Somehow he would have to invent a party for and by seminarians at somebody's house. Then pray fervently that neither parent checked. He thought he could carry it off. He seldom if ever lied to his parents. And they seldom if ever checked up on him.

After all this thought, he agreed to go to Jane's party. She would be able to get off duty after the first showing of *Adam's Rib* tomorrow evening. He should come to her house about 9:30 P.M. She gave him directions. It was in the neighborhood; it would be easy to find.

Everything went smoothly the next day. Ridley did all the chores expected of him and then some. His mother readily agreed to the seminarians' party that night, cautioning him only to be very careful because the weather promised to be rather treacherous. His father was grateful the kid didn't need any more money.

At 9:30, he set out for Jane's home. He did not want to be unstylishly early. He, of course, walked all the way. As he neared the house, he looked in vain for clusters of cars parked nearby. He concluded nearly everyone was from the neighborhood and, like him, would be walking.

When he climbed the steps to her front porch, there was no indication of a party of any sort going on. Decidedly odd.

A seemingly breathless Jane answered the bell. She was wearing a green and red floral print dress. She was very pretty and when she looked up at Ridley, her eyes seemed to sparkle.

"Am I early?" As Ridley entered, he looked into the living room. It appeared there was no one but the two of them there.

"No, you're fine." She took his coat and hat and hung them in the hall closet.

"Well, then, where is everybody?"

"We are everybody."

"We are—I don't understand. I thought this was a party."

"You can have a party with two people."

"And your parents?"

"Out. At their own party. They probably won't be back until early in the morning."

"You mean we're the only people in the house . . . no one else is coming?"

Jane shook her head and smiled. "Scared?"

Ridley swallowed. This was a first. He felt that this evening might test Monsignor Cronyn's theory.

"Don't worry." She laughed. "Nothing's going to happen. I just thought this would be a nice time for us to get acquainted. Besides, I hate New Year's parties, don't you?"

"I don't know. I've never been to one." It did not occur to him to cover his inexperience with a lie.

"You have lived a sheltered life, haven't you."

He could not argue the point.

"Come on." She led him into the living room. "I put together a snack."

He looked around. It was a room one could find in almost any home in that neighborhood. Not, in fact, unlike his own. The walls displayed a liberal supply of pictures about equally divided between religious and family; venerable furniture that had belonged to more than one generation; knickknacks owing their continued presence to a family that threw nothing away. An ornate carpet, once thick, now worn thin in spots favored by a series of comfortable feet.

She sat on the couch. He hesitated, then selected a nearby chair. She smiled. The snack, on a tray on the coffee table, was near the couch, not the chair. She brought the tray to him. He took a paper napkin and a plate and selected half a sandwich. It was impossible, at least in those days, to overfeed a seminarian. She seemed to sense that: She pushed the coffee table near Ridley and set the snack tray on it. He was silently grateful.

She returned to the couch and kept what she presumed was the proper clerical distance.

"So," he took a bite of the sandwich—ham and cheese, very adequate, "you work at the Stratford. Full-time?"

She chuckled. "Hardly. Just evenings. Three, maybe four a week. Plus anything else I can get. Right now, during the Christmas rush, I've had a job at Hudson's. That was neat: the Baker streetcar from here right to Hudson's. Some of the jobs are not nearly so convenient."

"But why? Why all these jobs?"

"College. I'm going to the University of Detroit. Someday I'll be a teacher."

Groendal felt guilty. Since last year, his junior year in college, the Archdiocese of Detroit had been picking up most of the costs of his education and would continue to do so all the way through the final four years of theology. Both he and Jane were going to college. She was toiling for nickels and dimes anywhere she could find employment, working her way through college. While, as far as financing his education was concerned, he was coasting.

"Did you ever think of becoming a nun?"

From his perspective it was a perfectly logical question. Most parochial pupils at one time or another consider religious life. And the IHM nuns who had taught them at Redeemer were exclusively a teaching order. If Jane wanted to be a teacher and was short of funds—well, the idea made sense to Groendal.

"I must admit the idea crossed my mind." Jane had a most attractive smile. "But it's not for me . . . too confining."

"Oh." Ridley finished the other half of his ham-and-cheese sandwich. There was a lull in the conversation.

"I was wondering—that is, if I'm not imposing on you—if you would play the piano for me. It's in tune," she added hastily.

Groendal dried his fingers with the napkin. "I'm afraid I haven't kept it up. After what happened at that recital, I lost my enthusiasm." He tried not to recall that humiliation. Whenever the memory resurfaced, so did the bitterness.

"Oh, what a pity! You mean you don't play at all anymore?"

"No, I still play. But rarely. It's just that . . . well, back then, I was aiming at something, something that could have become a concert career. When that didn't . . . work out, I just let the serious side of training slide. Practice, and all that."

"Does that mean you won't play for me?"

"If you want me to, I'll try. But my fingers aren't as supple as they were when I was really working at it. I just want to warn you that in these last seven years I've lost technique instead of gaining it."

Jane hesitated. "Can you still play Rachmaninoff's 'Prelude'?"

"I'm afraid to try. I haven't played it for years. I'd probably just mess it up. And Rachmaninoff doesn't need that."

"Well, then, anything."

"Okay."

Ridley moved to the piano, rubbed his hands together, getting as much warmth as possible into his fingers, and essayed a few exercises. He then selected some popular pieces of the day that were lyric and lazy, giving his reluctant fingers a chance to limber up.

He played "That Lucky Old Sun," "Scarlet Ribbons," and "Tell Me Why." Simple tunes, but he chorded them imaginatively. He could hear Jane humming along. Her voice was pleasing. Frequently, he played for schoolmates' singalongs. He was accustomed to a group of male voices, not universally in tune. Jane's soft soprano was a pleasant change. He played on from a little further back "Everybody Loves Somebody," "Bluebird of Happiness," "Now is the Hour."

His fingers were beginning to respond and to do nearly what he wanted of them. He moved into the classical field, staying in adagio tempo. Mendelssohn's "Consolation," Handel's "Largo," Chopin's "Prelude in A" and "Prelude in C Minor." He decided to take a chance on Liszt's "Liebestraum." While it was far from perfect, he played it better than he'd hoped. Works by Bach, Sibelius, and Grieg followed. He lost track of time. So immersed was he in the music he loved that he even forgot Jane for a while.

He stopped. He'd been playing for almost an hour and a half. He'd begun to sense control of the music. It was, of course, far from what he might have expected if he had been faithfully practicing daily. But it was by no means either clumsy or sloppy playing. He could sense that Jane was more than thrilled at what he could draw from the old upright.

"I think I can play that Rachmaninoff for you now."

Softly but enthusiastically she applauded the idea.

He played it every bit as letter perfect as he had seven years before, with the added maturity and perspective of the intervening years as a bonus. He concluded with the full, crashing chords that for fifty years had brought audiences to their feet in resounding applause.

Jane neither stood nor applauded, but she was deeply moved. "That was beautiful."

He felt drained. And he was perspiring. It was the first he'd noticed that. The house was warm but not excessively so. He had been working hard and he felt it. He stretched, and flexed his back muscles. His shirt was damp and adhesive.

Jane noticed. "Come sit on the couch and let me rub your shoulders. It'll make you feel better."

He thought about that. There were a lot of considerations. On the positive side, it would relax him and it was the least Jane might do in payment for a far better than average concert. On the negative, there was Monsignor Cronyn and his exhortation against girls. In all, the scale swung heavily to the positive. He joined Jane on the couch, back toward her, waiting to absorb the promised massage.

"That was just beautiful . . . gorgeous! The most beautiful concert I ever heard." She kneaded his shoulders and upper back.

"Thanks."

Her surprisingly strong fingers dug into his muscles, generating a medicinal inner heat. "Were you kidding . . . I mean about being out of practice and all?"

He laughed. "No, I wasn't kidding. What I did, in effect, was practice on your time. The pop tunes weren't difficult at all. I just kept working into more demanding stuff until I had warmed up enough to do a decent job with the more complicated pieces. Besides, it wasn't that I haven't played for the past seven years, only that I haven't been practicing every day. It's not all that much of a miracle."

Ridley surmised that Jane was not an habitué of the concert hall. His makeshift presentation probably was one of the outstanding musical events of her limited cultural life.

"Well, I think it was wonderful!"

The steady kneading was growing painful. "I think that's enough." He moved to the opposite end of the couch. "But thanks. It was a very good massage. I feel very relaxed."

"That's good." She glanced at her watch. "Oh, look at the time!"

He consulted his watch. A quarter to twelve. It made no profound impression on him. Only that it was very late. Under ordinary circumstances, way past his bedtime.

"It's almost midnight!"

He could not argue the point.

"We should have something to drink."

"We should?"

"Of course. It's New Year's. Everybody has a drink at midnight on New Year's Eve."

"They do? I'm sorry, I didn't bring anything."

"Oh, that's all right." She got up and walked toward the kitchen. "There must be something in the house."

Ridley began to have qualms. To this point in his life, he'd been a beer and wine man. And not much of that.

"Do you have any preference?" she called from the kitchen.

He knew he should express his known limitations, but, "Not really. Anything will be fine."

She emerged carrying a tray on which were two glasses and a bottle. As she drew nearer, he could see ice in each glass. The bottle bore a not unfamiliar label, though he had no idea what it might taste like. It was Cutty Sark.

She set the tray on the coffee table, which was now no longer near the couch but close to the chair where Ridley had been sitting. She poured a bit of the amber liquid in each glass.

"I couldn't find any champagne. I think champagne is what's called for on New Year's Eve. I guess we'll have to make do with Scotch." She presented him with one of the glasses. "I've never had it myself, but my dad swears by it. He just sips it, so it must be pretty powerful."

Ridley sniffed the drink. He'd seen them do that in movies. The drink was usually brandy, but Scotch could not be far different. He recoiled. The aroma was abrasive. Keeping in mind the example of Jane's father, Ridley took a small sip.

It was repulsive. Which did not necessarily indicate that it should be dismissed out of hand. After all, cigarettes had been a not dissimilar experience. To begin smoking, or to take up the habit after a hiatus, was difficult. It was, indeed, challenging. Cigarettes, initially, were horrible. The nicotine invaded one's bloodstream, made one dizzy, and caused coughing fits. But if one stayed with the weed long enough, smoking became second nature. One could not imagine arising without—coffee without, breakfast without, talking on the phone without, attending a meeting without, etc., without—a cigarette.

Jane seemed to be having the same experience. She took a sip and considered. But, in spite of it all, she took another sip.

So did Ridley. He could not argue that something was happening. But what?

Ridley was guilty of two errors that an experienced drinker would never make. He was hungry. With the exception of that single sandwich, he had had nothing to eat since a light supper hours earlier. And he was thirsty. So the Scotch to some extent was taking the place of water. On a nearly empty stomach, liquor can do awesome things. Already he felt lightheaded. For that matter, so did Jane.

"You know, Ridley," she said wistfully, "I didn't know a single boy in my high school graduating class."

"Neither did I. I mean, I didn't know any of the girls in my graduation class."

"That's different. You didn't have any. You were off in the seminary."

"It's not entirely different. I could tell you about some seminarians who knew lots of girls. Matter of fact, one in particular, about a year ago, got in quite a bit of trouble over a girl."

"Really? How?"

"I shouldn't talk about that. I don't want to talk about that. It will make me angry all over again. And I don't want to get angry tonight . . . this is great stuff, y'know?" Ridley took another sip. It wasn't burning as much now as that first taste. Maybe it *was* like cigarettes. Maybe you *did* get used to it after a while.

Jane poured a little more Scotch over his diminishing ice cubes. She added more to her own glass. She had to walk to and from the table to accomplish this. She was not unsteady. "So, you didn't know any girls in your class?"

"Not a one."

"I'll bet you've known your share since then."

"Not really."

"Oh, come on."

Ridley swirled the liquor in and around the ice. He'd seen them do that in movies too. "Would you believe this is the first date I've ever had in my life?"

"No."

"It's true. It's my first date. And where did I take her? Nowhere. Her house!" Affected by the Scotch, he looked as if he were about to cry.

"You took her just where she wanted to go." A hint of a slur was entering Jane's speech. "She didn't want to go out with all the gang. She wanted to spend a quiet New Year's Eve at home. And you gave her a marvelous concert. I'm the luckiest girl in the world this New Year's Eve . . . wait; let me get some more ice so your drink doesn't bother you."

She walked into the kitchen without once staggering. But she had to concentrate on each step, something she'd never had to do before.

Before returning his glass and letting the liquid already in it dissolve some of the fresh ice, she poured in another splash of Scotch. She "freshened" her own drink likewise.

"What about you?" Ridley looked across and found no one there. Jane had seated herself on the floor in front of the couch. He slid down to the floor. The least he could do was be on the same level as his hostess. "What about you?" he repeated. "I'll bet you've had your share of boyfriends since you started college." He sounded as if he resented the idea of her dating anyone else.

Jane sipped her drink and shook her head. "Been too busy. Working, going to school, doing the required reading, all that. Almost no social life at all. No time."

"No dates?"

"I couldn't say that. I've been out on a few dates, mostly doubles. But not with a boy alone. I mean not with a man, a college senior. Never like this, in a house alone."

His thought processes were getting a bit muddled. There was something about being in a house alone, together. It sounded as if something should follow. If they were in the house alone, together, something should be happening. But what?

A sharp crack sounded outside. It seemed to come from some distance. It was followed by a series of similar noises.

"What was that?" Ridley was almost shocked into sobriety. It was only momentary. The Scotch resumed control.

"Gunshot, I guess. Look, Ridley," Jane showed him her watch. "It's midnight. It's a new year. Happy New Year, Ridley."

He extended his hand and was startled when she leaned forward and kissed him lightly on the lips. Unsure of how to react, he leaned away.

"Happy New Year, Ridley!" she repeated.

"Happy New Year, Jane." His response was more bewildered than heartfelt.

"Don't look at me that way, Ridley. People are supposed to kiss on New Year's Eve. It's the thing to do."

Ridley wasn't thinking too clearly. He did seem to recall a number of movies wherein there was plenty of kissing on New Year's Eve. That much checked out. But in the movies there always seemed to be crowds of people around with a lot of flying confetti and noisemakers.

"Then," he challenged her smartly, "where's the confetti and the noisemakers?"

Her smile was a little crooked. The liquor had taken its toll on her mental processes as well. "You don't have confetti or noisemakers at home, silly. That's just for big parties in restaurants and hotels. At home you just have a private party. It's a special time for being close."

He appeared skeptical. "You're sure about the confetti and noisemakers?"

"Sure. But you could sit closer."

He edged toward her a tentative few inches. She moved likewise until they were touching. She let her head fall back on his shoulder. That, he thought, felt nice. He leaned back against the couch and let his right arm rest over her shoulder. She looked up and kissed him.

"It helps, you know, if you kiss back."

"Oh."

She kissed him again. This time he puckered to receive the kiss and felt something odd . . . as if her tongue was licking his lips. It did not feel unpleasant, but his mouth opened in surprise. Her tongue went further. What was she doing?

He drew back. "Are you sure you haven't had a lot of boyfriends?"

"Just a few. And we never did anything but kiss."

He would have argued the point further but he was by no means in condition for effective argument. "What do you call that? When you use your tongue?"

"French kissing."

"So that's what French kissing is about . . . it seems sort of silly."

"Try it, you may like it." She tilted her head back.

This time, when they met, her mouth was open. Again he was surprised. This must be what she had intended by encouraging participation.

From that point on, liquor, passion, and nature provided an ineluctable drive. Kisses led to embraces. Buttons, zippers, belts, clasps gave way. Finally, nakedness itself became a stimulus.

At one stage, she protested, but her pleadings only goaded him on. It was a frenzied struggle in which, in the end, both consented with what voluntary was left them. Then it was over.

Ridley was exhausted, yet relaxed, and slightly more sober.

He looked at himself. He seemed to be all bloodied. He gave no thought to whose blood; he assumed it was his. He had been hideously deformed by his copulation! He came close to vomiting.

Numb, he gathered his clothing and began to dress.

"This isn't what I planned." Jane seemed to speak without thought. She was as shocked as he by what had happened.

"It was a sin. We have to confess it."

"We can do that."

"I've got to go."

"Stay just a while. Please. I don't want to be alone now."

"I've got to go. I shouldn't have come."

"Please."

"I'm sorry." He struggled into his overcoat and, after fumbling with the door, stepped out into the air. It all but completely cleared his head. With a few mumbled apologies, Ridley walked away.

As he walked, he prayed. He confessed his sin to God. He promised God he would confess to the priest.

When he arrived home, he found his parents had retired. He showered, scrubbing himself again and again. Above all else, he was confused. He had just committed a sin—in the Catholic lexicon, one of the most abominable sins. From what he'd heard and read, of all possible mortal sins, fornication was supposed to be the most nearly worth it. But he had found it abhorrent. He was confused.

After Ridley left, Jane put on a robe and put her clothing in the washer. She was alone at the very moment of her life when she most needed someone to be with her. She had just lost her virginity. Throughout her training in parochial schools, she had been taught that this gift was to be guarded, protected, and saved for the one with whom she would spend her entire life within the bonds of sacred matrimony. But in one drunken evening everything had been irrevocably taken from her.

She was confused, ashamed, embarrassed, and abandoned. She needed to talk but had no one to talk to. She could not tell her parents. She had no friend in whom she could confide such a secret.

She would tell a priest, of course, but that would be in confession. And he would not console her. He would excoriate her.

That night, Jane didn't sleep. She wept. And when, in the early hours of the morning, her parents returned from their more innocent New Year's Eve party, Jane turned her head to the pillow to muffle her sobs.

11

Father Koesler stepped to the lectern and read the Gospel story of Jesus calling Lazarus back from the dead. When he finished, all the priests present sat down. Following their example, the rest of the congregation sat.

At most weddings and funerals it was a safe bet to expect a goodly number of non-Catholics, lapsed Catholics, and infrequent Catholics, many of whom would be unfamiliar with the ritual of the Mass. Under these circumstances, it was common for a priest to tell the congregation to stand, be seated, or to kneel (or, if kneeling were perceived as a form of martyrdom, they might sit). But everyone, Catholic or not, would feel comfortable following the example of a bunch of priests. At least in the matter of protocol at Mass.

There were funerals and there were funerals. In his more than thirty years as a priest, Koesler had officiated at just about every possible variety. Basically, they fell into one of two categories. There were funerals in which there was great and sincere grief. Or funerals in which there was little if any genuine mourning.

On grief-filled occasions, it is difficult to find words of real consolation, so great is the sense of loss. When there is little mourning, it is difficult to find words that can stir feelings unaffected by the presence of death.

Except for the desolate presence of Peter Harison, Ridley C. Groendal's funeral held no sense of mourning, loss or grief. Indeed, some in the congregation seemed to evidence relief, perhaps even elation. It was to this generally uncaring attitude that Koesler addressed himself in his approach to a homily.

Eulogizing Ridley Groendal would have been simple for Koesler. Seldom had the priest known a deceased more personally than he had known Ridley. In the end, it was the extent of Koesler's knowledge of Groendal that argued against a eulogy. Koesler simply knew Ridley too well. If the priest had begun a biographical sketch, it would have been all but impossible to delete inappropriate facts and details. All things considered, it was wiser to go with one of the many standard homilies he had developed over the years.

So he began with a quotation from Benjamin Franklin written just a few weeks before the great statesman's death:

"As to Jesus of Nazareth, my opinion of whom you particularly desire, I think the system of morals and religion, as he left them to us, the best the world ever saw or is likely to see; but I apprehend it has received various corrupting changes, and I have, with most of the present dissenters in England, some doubts as to his divinity, though it is a question I do not dogmatize upon, having never studied it, and think it needless to busy myself with it now, when I expect soon an opportunity of knowing the truth with less trouble. . . ."

The point of the quotation, as Koesler explained, is that it is impossible to prove empirically what happens after death. All we know, with certainty, is that we must die. After that, what? We move into the realm of heaven, hell, or purgatory. Or we are nothing. Or we return to earth in some other form. Benjamin Franklin refused to speculate on the final outcome, anticipating that—as it turned out—in a few weeks he would die. At which time, he would know the truth.

The Christian, Koesler continued, chooses to believe. In what? He returned to the first reading wherein King David expresses his willingness to die in the place of his son Absalom. Even though Absalom proved himself the most ingrate of sons, seeking his father's overthrow and death, still his father loves him so much that even in the face of this hostility, David would die in Absalom's place. It was easy to move from the figures of David and Absalom to God the Father and us His children.

Koesler then went on to the second reading where Paul points out that it is only barely possible to imagine laying down one's life for a very good person, very dear to us: a husband, a wife, a parent, a child. How then can we comprehend the love of God who sends His Son to die for us while we are no better than sinners?

At that point, Koesler usually adapted a lesson once developed by John Henry Cardinal Newman on the tears of Christ at the graveside of Lazarus. The Gospel story records Jesus weeping as he stood outside the tomb. The bystanders were moved to comment, "See how much he loved Lazarus!"

The strange feature of the story is that Jesus must have known that within minutes this scene of mourning would be transformed into one of incredible and incredulous happiness. Because Jesus would command that the large stone blocking the tomb's entrance be rolled back. Then he called to the dead man, "Lazarus, come forth!" And the corpse, entombed three days before, lived again.

The point that Newman made, and Koesler borrowed, was that Jesus must have been moved to tears simply because his friends themselves were inconsolably grief-stricken.

In all, it was a homily emphasizing the love and forgiving power of God.

As he delivered the homily, Koesler made eye-contact with various members of the congregation. Judging from their expressions, Ridley was in desperate need of a good measure of love and forgiveness from someone. And no one is in a better position to give it than God. Perhaps the only one.

As he surveyed the congregation, Koesler intermittently fixed on the five people whose lives had so mingled with Ridley's and, to some extent, with Koesler's.

Peter Harison, David Palmer, Carroll Mitchell, Valerie Walsh, Charles Hogan.

Each had touched—some would say collided with—and changed the others' lives. Their influence continued even unto death.

Valerie Walsh was a beautiful woman. Her garb, considering that she was attending a funeral, was rather defiant: red overcoat and green fur hat. She appeared more to be celebrating the Christmas season than mourning a deceased person. Well, truth in advertising: More than likely, she was celebrating.

It was remarkable how very much Valerie resembled her mother. Yet Jane Condon was pretty rather than beautiful. Whereas Valerie knew far better how to help her natural good looks with just the right makeup and hairstyling.

In fact, if it had not been for what had happened between Groendal and Condon, Koesler would have been hard-pressed to remember what Jane Cordon looked like. Koesler had probably seen her many times in her role as an usherette at the Stratford. He undoubtedly had seen her often as a student at Holy Redeemer. But he'd never really noticed her. He had never paid any attention to her until those few sparks had flown between Jane and Ridley during that Christmas vacation so long ago.

What a profound change that had brought to their lives! Strange how little the time they had had together and yet what an impact those few hours had had on them.

Ridley had told Koesler about it, but not until they had returned to the seminary after Christmas vacation. He told all just as it had happened, sparing almost no detail. Koesler, uncomfortable throughout, had tried to interrupt and bail out several times. But Ridley had insisted that he be heard out. Finally, he got to the part where, after struggling into his overcoat, he had gone home to spend a sleepless remainder of the night.

"And that's it?" Koesler asked.

"That's it."

"Rid, why have you told me all this?"

"I had to tell somebody."

"Well, I can think of one place where it would have been more appropriate."

"Where's that?"

Koesler hesitated.

Ridley thought a moment. "Oh, you mean confession. Well, I went to confession the Saturday before we came back here."

"Then . . . why me?"

"I told you: I had to tell somebody!"

"For the love of Pete, you told a priest!"

"I went to confession to Father Buhler."

"Aha! Good old Father Buhler. And he, of course, didn't hear what you said because he can't hear anybody. So you mumbled, and he didn't understand a word. But he did give you a penance and absolution . . . just for kicks, what kind of penance did you get?"

Ridley smiled self-consciously. "Five Our Fathers and Five Hail Marys."

"For what you did!"

"How would he know? He didn't hear me."

"Okay; but whether he heard you or not, you told him. You told somebody. So, Rid, for the last time: Why me?" As it turned out, Koesler never in his life would be happy that Groendal had picked him to confide in.

"You don't understand. I couldn't go to confession to a priest who would understand me. For one thing, the priest might know or guess that I'm a seminarian and then all hell would break loose. But whether that happened or not, any priest who understood would yell at me."

"And I won't."

Groendal nodded. "And besides, you were there at the beginning, when we sort of met. You knew I was going back to the Stratford. And you knew we weren't invited to any seminarian's New Year's Eve party."

Everything began to fall into place. Koesler could understand Ridley's need to get it off his chest, but Koesler thought him cowardly not to have unburdened himself to a priest more honestly.

Finally, there was the New Year's Eve party Groendal had told his parents about. If push came to shove, Ridley might want Koesler to corroborate his story about that nonexistent party. He hoped it didn't come to that. He was unwilling to lie for Groendal. Listen to his pseudoconfession—all right; lie for him—no.

But no need telling Ridley about that decision. It would only prompt pleas, possibly even some threats. All unnecessary unless Ridley's parents should ask, and there was little chance of that at this late date.

However, something still disturbed Koesler. "How is Jane taking all this?"

"What do you mean?"

"This must have been a bombshell for her, too."

"I don't know."

Koesler stopped. The two had been walking around and around the grounds at the rear of the seminary.

"Come on, come on!" Groendal urged. "If we stop walking, they'll wonder what we're talking about."

Koesler resumed walking. "What do you mean, you don't know! You don't know how Jane is taking all this?"

"What difference does it make? It probably wasn't her first time."

"Wasn't her first time! What are you talking about?"

"It was her idea."

"Huh?"

"Look, the New Year's Eve 'party' was her idea from the start. She's the one who invited me over to her house even though she knew her parents wouldn't be home. And if anyone needed more proof, there's the liquor. Again her idea."

"I don't know, Rid. From the way you told the story, it sounded as if she was as surprised at the way it turned out as you were. Maybe it was just a mistake for both of you. And when it comes to blame, Rid, you weren't exactly following Monsignor Cronyn's advice."

"Come on! You can't believe that stuff: 'Just presume you'd like girls if you tried them, boys. Then, don't try them.' That's hogwash, Bobby!"

"Maybe . . . but I believe you believed it until, for whatever reason —for God-knows-what reason—you 'tried' it."

Quite by common, if unspoken, agreement, they turned to one of the walkways that led back into the building. Recreation period was nearly over; study was about to begin.

"So," Koesler tried to sum up, "feel better?"

Groendal contemplated for a moment. "Yeah, I guess I do. I just wish you hadn't brought up Jane."

"What?"

"How she felt about all this. To be perfectly honest, I hadn't thought about that at all. If I had to consider it, I suppose she would feel about the way I do. Maybe a bit more guilty," he hurried on so Koesler couldn't interrupt, "since it was her idea. But no matter whose idea it was, it ended so badly that I guess we were both ashamed and embarrassed.

"I don't really know how we're going to face each other . . . I mean eventually. We'll have to see each other again sometime, I guess."

"Yeah, that may be rough. At least you'll be tucked away in here until Easter vacation. So you're safe till then. It's poor Jane I'm thinking of."

Groendal shook his head. "No need to be terribly concerned about her. She'll be plenty busy. Working at the Stratford—or any other part-time job she can get. And going to school at U.D."

"That's right, I remember; you did mention school."

They entered the building and stamped the snow from their boots.

"One thing," Koesler added. "Now you can probably sympathize a bit more with Mitch."

"Who?"

"Mitch . . . Carroll Mitchell. He didn't pay any attention to Monsignor Cronyn either. He tried girls and found he liked them . . . boy, did he like them!"

Groendal thought for a moment. "No, not really. I haven't made up my mind on that. For one thing, I seldom think of him. And as far as girls are concerned, why, hell, I've only known one and that encounter was a disaster. Maybe it's just too soon.

"Right now, I think it will be a long time before I 'try' a girl again. If ever."

Part Four

Presentation of Gifts

12

Father Koesler sat down after the homily, as was the custom, so that everyone would have a few moments to reflect on what had been said.

In the silence, he let his gaze drift through the congregation. Predominant in that group were, of course, the two-and-a-half pews of visiting priests. Briefly, Koesler wondered how his sermon had gone over with his confreres. He surmised that most of them held the attitude that they had heard it all. He'd bet a good number had been daydreaming throughout. It didn't matter. He didn't need the approval of his peers. He enjoyed it and welcomed it, but didn't need it.

Seated, it was difficult for Koesler to find the person he was looking for. Then, a rather large man leaned forward to retrieve something from the floor, disclosing, seated behind him, Charlie Hogan.

That made four: Hogan, Valerie Walsh, Carroll Mitchell, and David Palmer. Five, if one included Peter Harison. Strange that all the original four would be here in person—or, in the case of Jane, at least represented.

On the other hand, it would have been unusual, given the interplay between them and the deceased, had they passed up this occasion.

Charlie Hogan was special, at least to Koesler, for Charlie had been a Catholic priest. And while he was no longer functioning as a priest, for ten years he had been an integral part of this amazingly homogeneous fraternity. As such, there existed between him and all other priests, functioning or not, an enduring camaraderie. A silent acknowledgment that "we alone" know the life. Know its secrets, its rewards, its demands. Others may guess at what this life is like, but more often than not, they will be mistaken. Only we know because we have lived it. And lived it together.

Charlie had been ordained in 1958, four years after Koesler. Both had been ordained for service in the Archdiocese of Detroit. But of greater importance to Hogan's relationship with Groendal, Charlie had been a seminary high school senior when Groendal and Koesler were college seniors.

Under other circumstances, Koesler would consider such thoughts distractions from the Mass he was celebrating. But, strangely, when the gifts were brought to the altar, beginning that part of the Mass called the Offertory, he felt momentary impatience that his reminiscences had been interrupted.

The "gifts," of course, were the bread and wine, which would be "consecrated." In Catholic belief, the bread and wine would, at the priest's hands, be changed into the presence of Jesus Christ. For centuries, until the coming of Vatican II, bread and wine were either placed on the altar before Mass or were adjacent to the altar and simply moved there by altar boys.

Now, regularly, they were placed on a table out in the congregation and brought to the priest in a more or less solemn procession. On Sundays, the gifts of bread and wine were accompanied by the more mundane gift of the monetary collection. Collections are not taken up at weddings or funerals. Even among Catholics, some things are not seemly.

Peter Harison, naturally, was one who presented part of the gifts. At almost any other funeral there would be little difficulty finding additional volunteers. But this was not a run-of-the-mill funeral. And it was not all that easy to find the remainder of a retinue to complete the procession.

Fortunately, there were a few actors, authors, and musicians who had been favored by Groendal in life, so they served him as pallbearers in death. They also presented the remaining gifts.

While waiting at the front of the sanctuary for the presentation, Koesler pondered the coffin before him. If not for the white cloth and closed lid, he would be looking at Groendal more or less face to face. Lay people were wheeled into their funerals feet first. Thus, if they could see, they would be looking at the altar just as they had in life.

Priests were carted in headfirst, so that they would be looking at the congregation, just as they had in life.

That bit of trivia reminded Koesler that Ridley might have been a priest. He might well have been a priest, if not for . . .

*　　*　　*

After their talk following the eventful Christmas vacation of 1949, Groendal did not mention Jane Condon to Koesler again. But Ridley changed. Initially, he became more reclusive. Koesler found him in the recreation rooms far less frequently. When he was there, he was usually off in a corner by himself chain-smoking. He played the piano only if coaxed and then not the bright show and pop tunes the guys wanted to hear.

Soon, nearly everyone could not help but notice that some sort of change had come over him. Only Koesler had a clue as to the cause. Of course he said nothing to anyone, including Groendal.

It was not until the last year of Groendal's life, when he and Koesler renewed their relationship, that Ridley hinted at what had happened to him during that period.

Partially due to Koesler's expressed concern for Jane Condon, Groendal could not get her out of his mind. The possibility that he had inflected a massive emotional trauma upon her haunted him. He thought of confessing this possible additional sin. But, on the one hand, it was not a certainty, just a possibility. And, on the other, none of the present priest-faculty was deaf or even slightly hard of hearing.

Added to this was a recurring nightmare. In the dream, Groendal, in one way or another would get involved with some girl. Always it was a puzzling person. The heart of the dreams usually differed one dream from another. But all ended in the same terrifying nightmare.

He and the girl—both nude—would be wrestling. As they fought, Groendal would enter her. Then she would pull away, taking his genitalia with her, leaving him covered with blood.

He would wake with a start, dripping with perspiration, heart pounding.

In time, he grew to fear sleep. After the mandatory lights-out at 10:00 P.M., Groendal would cover the transom with a blanket, turn on a small reading lamp, and read well into the night.

When at last he would topple over from sheer exhaustion, he might be spared the nightmare only because he had somehow driven all dreams away. However, he would then pay the price of achieving no release from tension through dreams. It became a vicious cycle.

All of this he kept carefully locked inside. As a result, he began to suffer from increasingly deep depression.

As the weeks passed, Koesler became more concerned. He had noticed Ridley's decline earlier than anyone else because, knowing what was bothering Groendal, Koesler had been alert to the problem almost from the first manifestations.

Koesler tried to interest Groendal in something, anything, to get his mind off the problem. Very little besides music, literature, and theater interested Ridley. And he was, consciously or not, steeping himself in the gloomiest and most melancholy expressions in each of those arts.

Sports could have been a healthy outlet, especially since it was basketball season. There is little time for introspection or deep thought during a basketball game. Unlike football, wherein there is a good bit of standing around waiting for the action, and baseball, where there is even more of that inactivity, basketball is a game of almost constant motion favoring reflex action more than deliberate activity.

But despite his considerable—for that era—height, Groendal had never been very serious about basketball—or any other sport for that matter.

Koesler, on the other hand, while not one of the seminary's foremost athletes, was actively involved in sports. As a member of the college basketball varsity, he was helping coach the high school varsity. Eventually, he determined that might be his best chance to help Groendal. If Koesler could get Ridley involved in the high school basketball program, maybe that could be the vehicle out of this lethargy into which Ridley seemed to be sinking.

Interesting Groendal in assisting him to coach basketball proved easier than Koesler had anticipated. Inwardly, Groendal remained indifferent to the game. But he thought the exercise forced on him by the commitment might help him get some decent, restful sleep.

The next problem was selling the team on a coach who did not know enough about the game to qualify as a coach. After a few, ineffective starts, Koesler sold them simply on doing him a favor. Ridley Groendal, Koesler explained, was a friend who happened to be in need. He was having a bad time and needed exercise and companionship. And if they weren't interested in helping people in need, whatinhell were they doing in a seminary? That did it. With pronounced reluctance and grudging charity, the consensus was: Bring him on; we may make a jock of him yet—but don't bet on it.

Chief among those who bought the charity angle was Charlie Hogan. It was Hogan who taught Groendal—whose previous expertise was limited to basic dribbling, passing, and layups—niceties such as the difference between a zone and man defense, pick-plays, give-and-go, the butterfly drill, and so forth.

At first, Ridley's participation was predicated entirely on getting the exercise he needed in order to get some troublefree sleep. But as time passed, Hogan's patience and good humor began to have its effect. Groendal began to join in with more spontaneity, even to the point of enjoying the sport and looking forward to practices.

As a fringe benefit, just as he had hoped, he began to get the restful sleep he so wanted and needed.

Not that Groendal would ever be varsity caliber. He had no natural physical coordination. But he did reach the level of being able to assist the other coaches.

Koesler was so pleased he was ready to award himself an honorary doctorate in amateur psychology. Ridley's entire attitude had returned to near normal. Once again, seated at the piano in the rec room, Groendal became the life of the party. Koesler thought nothing of the friendship that was building between Groendal and Hogan. Neither did Groendal and neither did Hogan.

Charlie Hogan was a lithe lad, built perfectly for either dancing or baseball. And there were many similarities between the art and the sport. Despite not being very large, he was an outstanding football player. He excelled at baseball as well. Though the seminary fielded neither a football nor a basketball varsity, the sports were wildly popular on an intramural basis.

At almost any other high school, Charlie Hogan might well have been "Big Man on Campus." But since high school and college at Sacred Heart Seminary were at that time, for all practical purposes, housed in the same building, the two were more or less inseparable.

At other institutions, high school graduation was a major event. At the seminary, one simply passed from "fourth high" to "first college." This peculiarity tended to keep high school seniors "in their place," which was not near the top of any totem pole.

Hogan was interested in much more than athletics. He was an avid reader and enjoyed music. He had written a couple of articles for the *Gothic,* the seminary publication. By no means was he on the same level as Groendal in the arts field. Hogan was, after all, four years younger and nowhere near as broadly talented. But particularly after Groendal was dragged into the sports world, they did have some common interests.

So the friendship grew—cautiously. Almost without exception, everyone in the seminary was extremely sensitized to the pitfalls of a "particular friendship." The rules of conduct made explicit the terminal punishment reserved for that specific infraction. And once each year the rector explained the purpose and meaning of the rule in nonspecific terms.

Charlie Hogan did not consider theirs a "particular friendship." He knew he was not "that way." He was an athlete. He didn't even know how people who were "that way" thought. He and Ridley were friends, good friends. He had to admit he knew no one else in the seminary who had such a good friend who was as much as four years his senior. They just shared common interests, that was all.

Ridley Groendal did not consider theirs a "particular friendship." What could be more innocent than two people teaching each other what each knew best? He realized the seriousness of such a liaison and the penalty attached to it. Besides, to recall for an instant something he was trying very hard to forget, he was heterosexual. He'd certainly proved that with Jane Condon.

Koesler did not consider the relationship between Hogan and Groendal a "particular friendship." In the first place, Koesler himself had virtually introduced them. He had done so only to help Ridley out of the doldrums. And it had worked. In the second place, Koesler did not entirely understand all the implications of a "particular friendship" even though he'd heard it explained eight times now.

So it wasn't a "particular friendship." And it prospered.

Month followed month. Ridley learned more about basketball, though he became no more adept at it. Hogan learned more about music. They enriched each other in their love of literature. They spent many brief recreation periods walking around the back grounds. Frequently they were joined by others of the high school basketball varsity. The fact that they seemed to feel no need to be alone together further reinforced the conviction that this was not a "particular friendship."

Easter was approaching, and with it, spring. And with that, the conclusion of the basketball season and the beginning of baseball.

Hogan brought the matter up. "So, Rid, are you as bad at baseball as you were at basketball?"

"Probably not quite. It is the national pastime, so I know more about it. But I don't suppose I play it any better."

"Wait a minute." Hogan laughed. "We'd better get right on your case. Baseball's right around the corner. If you're going to coach us, we'd better get some practice in."

Groendal was instantly serious. "Charlie, I'm not going to coach baseball. There was a special reason why I got involved in basketball."

"Yeah, because Bob Koesler made you."

Groendal smiled. "More than that. I didn't want to get into it; I just had a special reason for needing a lot of exercise. And that problem's been solved . . . at least it seems to be.

"It's time to be honest with myself. Outside of my friendship with you and the other guys on the varsity, I've got no business hanging around with high schoolers, even if they're seniors. I had a reason. And now I don't."

It was Hogan's turn to be serious. "You mean we won't be friends anymore?"

"I didn't say that. Sure we'll be friends. It's just that I no longer need to coach something I know nothing about."

They were silent for several moments.

"What's the matter?" Groendal asked.

"Nothing. It's just a surprise is all. I just took it for granted that you'd coach. I guess I'll miss you."

"Charlie, it's almost Easter. In a few months I'll graduate. Then it's on to St. John's Seminary in Plymouth. We'll be in different schools. It's not like we're going to be in the same place the rest of our lives."

"Oh, I know. It was just the surprise. I guess I'll be able to pitch without you on the sidelines."

"Who said I wouldn't be on the sidelines? I'm just not going to coach, that's all . . . okay?"

"Sure. We'll go out and win one for the old basketball coach."

"Besides," Groendal's voice took on added animation, "I've got a present for you."

"To celebrate your graduation?"

"To repay a bit for teaching me just about all I know about basketball."

"Judging from what you learned about basketball, this doesn't have to be much of a present."

"The Met's coming to town."

"The what?"

"The Metropolitan Opera Company—New York."

"That's nice . . . so what?"

"It's time you saw your first opera, is what."

"Are you sure?"

"Positive. A week from next Saturday they're doing *Carmen* as a matinee. It's maybe the most popular opera of all time. A great way to begin."

"Jeez, I don't know, Rid. Using up the one and only all-afternoon permission I've got this month on an opera. I don't know. . . ."

"Trust me. You're going to love it. We'll get something to eat afterward. It'll be a great afternoon. Just the right thing to do before we begin Holy Week and then Easter."

"How long's an opera?"

Groendal chuckled. "With intermission, maybe three, four hours."

"That's a lot of sitting, Rid. I'll make a deal with you: We end the day with a couple, three games of handball."

"Handball! You'll kill me!"

"I'll go easy. Just exercise. That's what you wanted in the first place, isn't it?"

Groendal laughed. "You're on."

During the next ten days, as often as they could get together, Groendal explained and demonstrated on the piano the intricacies of *Carmen.*

Secular newspapers, including Detroit's three dailies, were not permitted in the seminary. So Groendal was unable to read the previews and reviews of the various operas the Met presented during its single week in Detroit. But he knew which works were being staged each evening, and he explained the plot of each to Hogan.

Hogan considered the plots ridiculous. Groendal admitted that the plots, generally, were mere props on which the composers hung their unmatched music. Thus Hogan was cajoled into listening to many recordings of many operas.

Finally, Saturday arrived. Hogan could not help being caught up in Groendal's excitement. They arrived early for the matinee at Detroit's mammoth Masonic Temple. As usual during the Met's week in Detroit, there was a nearly full house. Many patrons wore their best finery.

Hogan would have preferred waiting outside to watch the people arrive. But Groendal could hardly wait to get inside and absorb the atmosphere.

Finally, the orchestra filed in, took their seats, and unlimbered their instruments. The house lights dimmed as a warning to latecomers. Then all was darkness except for the small lights of the orchestra's music stands. The maestro arrived at the podium, bowed to applause, shook hands with the concertmaster, raised his arms expectantly, and lowered them to the crash of Spanish chords that usher in the tragic tale of *Carmen.*

Indoctrinated as he had been by Groendal, Hogan understood and appreciated many nuances of this ageless masterpiece. It was a glorious afternoon.

Afterward, they stopped at a department store on the way back to the seminary and had a snack at the lunch counter. It was not much of a meal, nor were the opera seats all that expensive, but the afternoon meant a considerable outlay for Ridley.

There was a déjà vu quality to all of this for Groendal. He had been on only one other date. Both occasions were connected with the theater. Both times he had been strapped for money and had chosen extremely inexpensive places to eat. One had been with a young woman, the other with a young man. He shrugged off the comparison. It was apples and oranges.

It was a violation of rules to return to the seminary later than dinnertime. But Groendal, as a prefect, and thus in charge of law enforcement to some degree, would find the loopholes.

True to his word, Groendal joined Hogan in the handball court. There were eight indoor enclosed courts, only one of which was a singles court.

The rest of the students were finishing dinner, after which they would go to the chapel for the communal rosary. So Groendal and Hogan were alone in the subterranean courts. It was odd not to hear other voices, other handballs ricocheting off other walls. The only sound was their labored breathing, the squeak of their sneakers and the lone ball bouncing from wall to floor to wall, then being slapped again by a gloved hand.

In order to prolong the games, Hogan restrained himself from killing the series of easy setups that Groendal kept lobbing against the front wall. Nevertheless, three games were completed in less than forty-five minutes. Hogan had hardly worked up a sweat.

Not so Groendal. Even with his basketball workouts he still was not anywhere near in shape. So it was impossible for Hogan to talk him into another game. The agreed-upon three games would be it—Hogan, of course, easily winning all three by lopsided scores.

At that time of night, with no one around, that section of the building could be eerie. It was reasonable for Groendal and Hogan to use the same locker room. Ordinarily, Groendal would have used the college facilities and Hogan the high school. Tonight, both used the high school facilities. Actually, it had been Hogan's suggestion. Groendal thought it sensible.

One could always depend on the seminary powerhouse for hot water. Even with hundreds of young men using gallons of hot water daily, the supply seemed infinite.

The question of where all this hot water came from did not cross the minds of either Groendal or Hogan as they stood under the shower's strong jets. It just felt so good and relaxing.

"This has been a really great day." Hogan had to speak very loudly to be heard above the cascading water.

"What? Oh, yeah . . . it has."

"Carmen could have been a little slimmer, though."

"Slimmer?" Groendal wondered what slimness had to do with singing the classic role. He was so used to opera's tendency to cast solely on vocal ability that it never occurred to him that a nondevotee might prefer a heroine who more nearly resembled a seductress.

"Yeah," Hogan went on, "when she did that dance, I thought the table was going to give way under her."

Groendal smiled. "You're supposed to be listening to the tones she produces."

"How can you overlook that both Carmen and Don José were so fat they never could have gotten together? So why did Don José run away from the army? He would have been better off there than trying to get close to Carmen.

"And another thing: That bullfighter—Escamillo—he was really built. When he and Don José had that fight, Jeez, Escamillo could have broken Don José in half. Who's going to believe they fought to a stand-off?"

With all this talk of physiques, for the first time Groendal regarded Hogan's body with more than casual interest. This was the first time they had showered together. The first time Groendal had seen Hogan nude. It was a revelation to Groendal that Hogan had an—yes—attractive body. It resembled Michelangelo's David.

Now that he noticed it, Groendal could not keep his eyes away from Hogan's body. Groendal was beginning to be aroused and there seemed nothing he could do about it. Hogan, intent on showering, did not notice.

There can be too much even of good things, Hogan thought. He felt as if his skin would shrivel if he stayed under the hot water any longer. He turned off the shower. So did Groendal. Hogan grabbed a towel from the shelf and threw another to Groendal. Together they went into the large drying room that separated the showers from the locker room.

Groendal preceded Hogan, who playfully snapped Ridley's rear with the towel. Instantly, Groendal turned and grabbed at Hogan. Their still wet bodies locked in what began as a lighthearted tussle. Later, Groendal could not fix at what point the wrestling bout ceased being playful and became, for him, erotic. But there was no doubt that it did.

When the evolution occurred, Charlie Hogan reacted first in utter disbelief, then in shocked surprise. For a while, he tried to act as if it weren't happening. He tried to kid Groendal out of what was becoming for Ridley very serious business.

At last, when Hogan could no longer pretend that what was happening was not happening, he began to fight in earnest. Although Groendal was considerably larger, he was not the coordinated athlete Hogan was. In no time, Hogan had beaten him off.

But Hogan did not stop after he had effectively ended the affair. He kept pummeling Groendal until the counterattack itself became serious.

Groendal stood, back to the wall, taking blow after blow as just punishment. He did or said nothing to defend himself.

In a fury, Hogan kept hitting, and with every punch, he either sobbed or cried out, "Rid! Why'd you do it? Rid! Goddamit! Why'd you do it?"

At last, Hogan backed away. He was shocked at the damage he had done. Ridley's upper torso was covered with livid marks; his face would be much the worse for wear for a long time. Slowly, Groendal allowed himself to slide down the wall until he was slumped on the floor.

Hogan stood over him, fists still formed. Actually, tears were flowing so freely Hogan could hardly see. Somehow, inert on the floor, Groendal seemed almost an old man.

Hogan retrieved his towel from the floor. Without looking back, he walked from the drying room to the lockers, still mumbling, "Rid, why'd you do it? You ruined everything, Rid; Goddamit, why'd you do it? Why'd you do it?"

Slowly, gradually, Groendal managed to stand. He did so only because in a short while the rest of the students would have completed the rosary and would have a recreation period. Some, undoubtedly, would be coming down to this part of the building. He did not want them to see him like this.

He had to call on every psychic and physical resource he had to get dressed and make it up the back stairs to the infirmary. He hurt so badly he didn't know whether he would live or die. And he didn't care.

13

The infirmary was the particular preserve of Sister Sabina, popularly referred to as the Sabine Woman. As was true of nearly all nuns of that era, completely covered as they were—except for hands and face—by a religious habit, she appeared of indeterminate age. A tree's years are figured by its rings. If Sister Sabina were judged, similarly, by her visible wrinkles, she would have to be in excess of a hundred years old.

Facetiously, it was said that it was almost impossible to be admitted into the infirmary—but that if one did get in, it was almost impossible to be released. That bit of levity held its measure of truth.

Yet when Ridley C. Groendal staggered into the infirmary and rang the bell summoning Sister Sabina, he had no trouble getting admitted. Once she saw his face, she knew where he belonged. When she started tending to his torso, she wondered whether he might not be a candidate for hospitalization.

The damage was sufficiently serious to call in the staff physician, who did ship him off to nearby Providence Hospital for X-rays, which revealed no more than a lot of contusions ranging from mild to fairly serious and a couple of hairline fractures that, in a young body, should heal in time.

So he was sedated, given some medication to alleviate pain, and sent back to the seminary infirmary for the healing process to begin. In keeping with the diagnosis of serious injury and the prognosis of recovery after rest, Groendal was allowed no visitors except medical personnel during the following week.

For Groendal the time passed from tedium to monotony with long periods of dreamless sleep. In the early few days, consciousness was too filled with pain to allow much serious or profound thought.

Later, as it hurt less and less to move about, he began to give some consideration to his predicament.

He had no way of telling what was going on outside the infirmary. He saw no one but Sister Sabina. She brought medication and food and checked his bindings. Few words passed between them.

He did not want to talk about what had happened and, so far, outside of a few cursory questions from the doctor, no one had pressed him for facts or details. Groendal was afraid that anything he might say to the nun might open the door to an investigation. So he said nothing, except to respond to her inquiries about the location and intensity of his pain.

Sometimes he could hear the faint sounds of a radio from somewhere in the far reaches of the infirmary floor, but he could not make out the tune or identify the announcer. He knew something must be going on. No student was ever in sick bay for several days without the rumor mill's grinding out some scuttlebutt. But he had no way of telling what sort of information that might be.

Unbeknownst to Groendal, for once the rumor mill was operating comparatively factually. Enough people had sufficient information to put together a reasonable scenario. Known (generally): Groendal and Hogan had associated with each other with some frequency (most suspended any judgment as to its being a "particular friendship"). Ridley and Charlie had gone to the opera last Saturday. Neither had been at dinner that evening. For all practical purposes, Ridley had disappeared from view that night and it was reliably reported he had been admitted to the infirmary and held there incommunicado ever since.

Charlie, on his part, gave every evidence of having lost a dear friend in death. Though everyone was certain Groendal was in the infirmary, Hogan resolutely refused to address the subject or answer any questions. In short, it seemed a strong probability that Hogan had put Groendal in the infirmary. With that probability, the likelihood grew that the friendship between the two might, indeed, be "particular."

But if Hogan had indeed put Groendal in sick bay in a fit of anger, where was that anger now? Hogan acted more as if he were in mourning than in the aftermath of fury.

Then, too, if they had had such a serious fight in anger, Hogan likely would have been publicly reprimanded, possibly expelled. If, on the other hand, it had been a "lover's quarrel," the administration probably would still be debating how to handle it. This, in that seminary at that time, was not a common enough problem for some routine response to be in effect.

No one knew—at least no one could be sure—that Hogan had been interrogated by Monsignor Cronyn and that decisions had been made.

Least of all did Groendal, isolated in his infirmary bed, have any way of knowing. For him, it was as if Holy Week were going on somewhere far, far away—like the Holy Land—rather than merely in another part of the building.

Of course, he wasn't conscious much of Palm Sunday and Monday and Tuesday of Holy Week. Steady consciousness began for him on Spy Wednesday. On Holy Thursday he was aware that he should be playing the organ for services.

Good Friday he spent in special prayer united to the suffering of Christ. Easter Saturday, he knew that after the early morning service and Mass, the students would be leaving for Easter vacation. He knew it even if he could not hear their joyous voices as they bid each other farewell and jumped into their parents' cars for the ride home.

Then it was Easter Sunday and no one was left. Those few others who had been patients in the infirmary seemed to have miraculously recovered. The panacea, naturally, was vacation, and even Sister Sabina couldn't hold them prisoner.

Groendal was another question. Though a bit unsteady, he was able to move about. He might have gone home had it not been for the unspoken consensus that some vital confrontation was yet to take place. But take place it would.

After he had been injured, his parents had been informed that he'd been admitted to the infirmary, that his condition was not serious, but, however, that there were to be no visitors. Then they were told that he would not be released from sick bay on Easter Saturday, but probably shortly thereafter. They would be called when he was ready to leave. Like all good Catholic parents, they took the priest's word as Gospel; they would not dream of questioning it.

*　　*　　*

Easter Sunday dawned bright with the promise of spring and rebirth.

Robert Koesler was back in the familiar confines of Holy Redeemer, his home parish church. He was acting as master of ceremonies at the solemn-high Easter Sunday Mass. For those parishioners, including Koesler, who had carefully and penitentially observed Lent, Easter was its own reward. They had invested sacrifice and intense prayer and now were reaping joy and fulfillment.

In the church, incense filled the air with its special churchy odor and alleluias were exchanged between priest and choir celebrating this special season.

But Koesler's attention wandered. By now, the ritual and his function as master of ceremonies were so familiar to him that he could function quite adequately even with his attention sharply divided. And it was understandable that he should be thinking about Ridley Groendal and wondering about his absence from this scene. In the rotation these two classmates had established, Groendal should have been master of ceremonies at this Easter Mass. It was his turn. But, as far as Koesler could learn, Ridley was still at the seminary and still in sick bay.

Koesler had heard all the rumors and, in hindsight, could not deny them. From the shreds of evidence the students were able to gather, it was arguably possible that Groendal and Hogan had fought. And that, preceding this, they had formed a "particular friendship." In fact, about the only indication that this might not be so was Ridley's previous liaison with Jane Condon. And Koesler alone knew about that.

That episode to the contrary notwithstanding, Koesler was forced to ponder the consequences if the rumors should be accurate. In which instance, he could not clarify his confusion.

His religion currently taught him that homosexuality was not merely a sin but an abomination. In years to come, that position would be modified to state that the sexual preference for the gay life could be considered as neutral and only the acting out of that preference an abomination. This clarification was of small comfort to the homosexual since it slotted the person in not only a celibate, but a chaste life.

And that was the precise problem presenting itself to Koesler's logical young mind. The Catholic priesthood of the Latin rite demanded nothing less than a chaste celibate life. What difference could it make if one's inclination were homo- or heterosexual? In neither case was one allowed any sexual expression.

Yet, if the seminary authorities were to discover that Groendal had committed sin with Jane Condon, he undoubtedly would be reprimanded and punished.

If they discovered he'd sinned with Charlie Hogan, Groendal likely would get the ax.

True, Carroll Mitchell had been expelled for his sexual escapade with Beth Yager. But that punishment hadn't been inflicted so much for the act itself as for the flagrant flouting of the rule.

So Koesler was left wondering. He could not envision Groendal as an "abomination." No matter what he'd done.

The priest-celebrant turned to the congregation and sang, in Latin,

"Ite, missa est" (Go, the Mass is ended), *"Alleluia! Alleluia!"* The choir responded, in Latin, *Deo Gratias"* (*"Thanks be to God"*), *"Alleluia! Alleluia!"* Koesler's mind turned again to Ridley. Go? Go where?

Which, at that moment, was exactly what Ridley Groendal was wondering. Go? Go where?

There was no longer any compelling reason to remain in the infirmary. He—or rather, his body—was healed. At least enough to function without professional care. On the other hand, there was no possibility of his leaving. Not till the other shoe dropped.

This week's silence had been deafening. Someplace out there, people were talking about him, determining his fate. But not a word had been spoken to him about it. That word would be spoken; of that he was certain. But when? He would go out of the infirmary in the very near future. Of that there was no doubt. But to where?

Monsignor Cronyn appeared at the open door. He wore his black cassock with the red trim, buttons, and sash. He wore his black biretta with its red pompon. Somehow the biretta seemed to formalize the occasion.

"How are you feeling now, Mr. Groendal?" Nothing special was intended by that address. Cronyn always used that title when referring to senior students.

"Hurting a bit."

"Otherwise okay?"

"Yes, Monsignor."

"Sit down, Mr. Groendal." Cronyn gestured toward the bed while he sat on the room's only chair. "Care to discuss how you were injured?"

Groendal thought a moment, then shook his head. A little more than a week had gone by. Impossible that the authorities didn't know what had happened. Better not to volunteer any information. Better to play it by ear.

"Yours were serious injuries, Mr. Groendal."

"Yes, Monsignor."

"They could not have happened by accident, now, could they?"

"No, Monsignor."

"You appeared to have been beaten rather severely. The doctor provided us with that information."

Groendal nodded.

"Are you going to tell me about it?"

Groendal shook his head.

"Are you going to tell me your side of it?"

So, one side of it already had been told. Groendal simply waited. The other side would undoubtedly come out now.

"Very well," said Cronyn. He handed Groendal a manila folder containing two typewritten sheets, the second of which bore a signature. "Read this, Mr. Groendal."

Groendal read carefully. Several times he had to stop to rub his tearing eyes. It was "the other side of it"—Hogan's side. As he read, Groendal had to admit it was a fairly factual, objective account of what had happened between himself and Hogan over the past several months, along with a detailed and again objective narration of what had taken place a-week-ago Saturday.

Missing from the account were the involuntary but compelling feelings Groendal had experienced about Charlie Hogan. Groendal understood there was no way Charlie could have been aware of those feelings. Obviously the feelings had not been reciprocated.

Besides, in a situation such as this, people were interested only in the facts and nothing more. No set of extenuating circumstances could mitigate what Groendal had done—certainly not as far as Monsignor Cronyn was concerned.

Groendal finished reading. The statement had been signed, *Charles Hogan*. Groendal closed the folder and handed it back to the monsignor.

"Well?" said Cronyn.

There was no response.

"Well, is what you read an accurate account of what has happened?"

"Yes, Monsignor." Groendal knew there was no point in going into those intense, driving feelings. Feelings which undoubtedly Cronyn had never experienced toward anyone.

"In the interest of fairness," Cronyn said, "I should point out that Charles Hogan did not offer that statement spontaneously."

It helped that Charlie had not come forward voluntarily.

"However," Cronyn continued, "it was not difficult for us to deduce, at least in general terms, what had happened. From my interrogation of young Hogan, it seemed likely that a 'particular friendship' had been formed not by both of you but by you alone. Therefore, I placed Hogan under the obligation of fraternal correction."

That was it! Suddenly, it was so obvious that it might have been spelled out in neon. It came through in Cronyn's tone and in the hint of a smirk that appeared briefly. It wasn't so much that Cronyn had been patiently waiting and expecting turnabout to become fair play. It was more that he would be glad to see it happen.

It had been almost exactly one year since Groendal had invoked "fraternal correction" as the principle under which he had denounced and exposed—some would say betrayed—Carroll Mitchell. It was, Cronyn had thought at the time, a rather craven use of a device that had originally been intended more as an adjustment for the common good than as a means to satisfy spite.

Granted, Mitchell had flouted a very important rule. Still, it had been one of those boys-will-be-boys things, a sort of sowing-of-wild-oats affair. The seminary system was programmed to produce macho men of asexual behavior. It was also geared to forgive an occasional lapse as long as the fault occurred with someone of the opposite sex. This preserved the image of the macho man and merely revealed a chink in the armor of nonsexual expression.

If Mitchell had not been so brazen, he might have been forgiven. If Groendal had not betrayed Mitchell's confidence under the guise of "fraternal correction," the offense likely would never have been detected.

Mitchell had been one of Cronyn's favorites. The rector had foreseen a great priestly career for that talented young man. All of which had been destroyed by Groendal under the pretext of a warranted denunciation. However, Ridley's disclosure could not have been swept under the rug. It required an official response. As a result of which, Mitchell had been expelled.

Cronyn had resented being manipulated by Groendal; now turnabout had become fair play. And more. It was Cronyn's chance to even the score. Groendal had, in Cronyn's opinion, misused the device of "fraternal correction" once. Now, one year later, it was being used against him.

These thoughts had occupied Groendal's mind all the while the rector was explaining the situation as it affected him and Hogan.

"And so, Mr. Groendal," Cronyn concluded, "the faculty feels that young Hogan was more a victim than a perpetrator in this affair. Nevertheless he was old enough to know better. He should not have become so involved with any other student, 'particular friend' or not. We have decided that Hogan will lose virtually all privileges for the remainder of this scholastic year."

Groendal felt sorry for Hogan. He was miserable at having been the cause of Charlie's punishment. All in all, though, it wasn't cataclysmic. Summer vacation was only two months away. Charlie wouldn't have long to go.

"As for you," Cronyn continued, "you have a choice. You may resign from the seminary or you will be expelled.

"Before you say anything"—Cronyn's gesture silenced Groendal, who gave every sign of wanting to speak—"I should tell you that you are most fortunate to have an option. The majority of the faculty voted for expulsion. But some few made a cogent argument for leniency.

"So, you have a choice. Which will it be?"

Groendal wondered who his friends were. It seemed like a choice between being allowed or not being allowed a blindfold for one's execution. One ended up just as dead either way.

Strange, he thought, that he had not anticipated being sacked. He knew that what he had done was wrong. And that they probably would find out about it. He just hadn't thought it was that bad.

In the brief time he now had to consider his options, it was clear, if painfully so, what he must do.

"I will resign, Monsignor."

"A wise choice. That is what will be noted on your record. This is a week of vacation; none of the students will be here. You may remain in the infirmary if you need to."

"I can function all right, Monsignor. I'll be out of here today."

"Very well."

If he had not already done enough penance, Groendal soon would. He groaned audibly as he dragged himself through the corridors gathering his books and belongings. And the worse was yet to come. He phoned his parents. They would pick him up.

Over the next several days, Groendal learned just how fortunate it was that he had been allowed to quit. He would have preferred death to having to explain the real reason for his leaving the seminary. As it was, he was forced to lie over and over, stating that he had left voluntarily. During his nearly eight years in the seminary, the vocation had sunk its roots into his soul so that by this time, there was nothing in the world he wanted more than to be a priest.

And now it was gone. Finished.

In the following weeks, he seemed to exist in a veritable vacuum. He had contact with almost no one. Bob Koesler had phoned a couple of times during Easter Week, but Groendal had not wanted to talk with anyone who knew the truth. And Groendal was quite sure Koesler knew.

By the time Groendal had gotten over some of the physical and psychological hurt, Koesler was back at school and beyond Ridley's reach.

Not a word from Hogan. In the early days of Easter Week, Charlie Hogan's would have been the only call Groendal would have answered or returned. The need to talk to Hogan was almost physical.

The longer the lack of communication continued, the more bitter Groendal became. No one could deny they had been in this together. But Charlie Hogan was back at the seminary. Charlie's vocation was still alive. Had he no word for someone with whom he had shared so much? Could he pretend Ridley Groendal no longer existed?

In time, Groendal had to put all that behind him and go on with life. It wasn't easy. The conflicts he'd experienced over the past years with David Palmer, then Carroll Mitchell, then Jane Condon, and now Charlie Hogan, had taken their toll. Sometimes he felt as if he were moving through life in slow motion. But he had to go on.

The priesthood was gone. He had to put that out of his mind. But he wasn't dead. He had a long life ahead. One thing was certain: He had to find a new career.

Briefly, he considered Interlochen. But David Palmer was ensconced there; even if he were able to gain admittance to Interlochen, he would be limping artistically and, without doubt, Palmer would shoot him down. No, Interlochen was not feasible. He was sure only that he must finish college and do postgraduate work somewhere in something.

This initial decision met with a mixed reaction from his parents. No longer would the Archdiocese of Detroit pick up the tab for his education—a fact that drove his father nearly mad. Alphonse Groendal had never quite understood what his son saw in the priesthood. Father, mother, and son were all Catholic, but Alphonse tended to take priests for granted. Somehow, they were there when you needed them. He had just never given much thought to where they came from. Certainly not from *his* family.

As with most major domestic decisions, he had caved in to his wife's pressure. Only when his son reached the third year of college, and board and tuition were absorbed by the Church, did Alphonse Groendal begin to see the value of this vocation. And now, just after the free ride had begun, the fool kid had suddenly decided against the priest-hood. Worse, he wanted money to go away to college.

As far as Alphonse was concerned, Ridley could go out and get an honest job.

But Alphonse was soundly overruled by his wife, Mary, for whom Ridley's departure from the seminary was a source of great sorrow and concern. She it was who had planted the seed in her son's mind that the priesthood would be a most acceptable vocation. She knew her son well enough to be sure that it was not his sudden choice to quit the semi-nary. . . .

Handling Ridley more gently than she treated her husband, she prod-ded and pried, trying to uncover the truth. Whenever Ridley came close to losing patience, she backed off. In better times, he had had almost infinite patience where his mother was concerned. Now he had been worn close to the breaking point.

But no one other than Ridley himself knew just how close. And even he knew it only in a very confused way. Pressures seemed to be closing in from every side.

For the first time, he was aware of having lost an enormous security. In the seminary, one had no concern about whence meals, lodging, warmth, clothing, sustenance would come. One need have no concern over minor or even major decisions. Most of them were made for one beforehand and set forth in the rules.

It was as if, for a second time, he had left the total dependency on, and security of, the womb and had been cast out into the world to fend for himself. He was unsure of which path to pursue and he wasn't getting any practical help in solving his problem.

He had even lost his seminarian's selective service classification of 4-D. He would have to reregister and would probably become 1-A unless he could get into college and qualify for another sort of defer-ment.

Even the beauty of this May morning did nothing to lift his spirits.

It was the Groendal family habit to attend the 10:00 A.M. Sunday High Mass at Holy Redeemer. Since early April, Ridley had been on a more or less extended vacation and so the three of them religiously attended that Mass together. In this sort of routine, very little untoward ever happened. Until the final Sunday in May.

No sooner had the family exited the church's side door than someone touched Ridley on the shoulder. As he turned, his mouth dropped in surprise. "Jane!" Not only had Ridley never expected to see her, he had all but forgotten her, occupied as he was with more current and pressing problems.

"Rid, can I talk with you?"

"Wait a second."

Ridley told his parents to go on without him; he would be home shortly.

Alphonse and Mary Groendal instantly evaluated the girl, with sharply differing reactions.

Alphonse smiled. About time his son did something normal for a change. One of the many things he'd never understood about that seminary was the total abstinence from women. So they were going to be priests. They weren't priests yet. Life would be long enough without sex, let alone having nothing to do with girls while it was still legitimate to fool around at least a little.

He could not tell much about this girl. Her coat hid her figure, but she had a pretty face. All in all, it was about time. He approved.

Mary Groendal, on the other hand, was certain she had sighted The Enemy.

Ever since Ridley had come home for good during Easter Week, she had been trying, overtly and covertly, to discover the underlying reason for her son's drastic decision.

She had wondered too about his physical injuries. She could easily believe that boys' sports were rough and that injuries were common enough. However, nothing Ridley had told her satisfactorily explained the root cause of his quitting the seminary. Deep down, she had felt it was some girl. But if so, who?

She knew where her son was almost to the minute. He was safe enough from feminine wiles as long as he was at school. And he habitually accounted for his whereabouts at all times while he was home. Thus, as far as she was concerned, the puzzle was twofold: Which girl had gotten to him, and given the impossible that some girl had reached him, how?

One glance at this girl and the way Ridley had reacted to her gave Mary Groendal half the answer. All that remained was to discover how the girl had broken through all the barriers. It was with great reluctance that she complied with Ridley's request that they precede him home. She would have preferred meeting this girl. She would like to give her a thing or two. She wanted to tear her limb from limb. But . . . all in good time. For the moment, she would act the indulgent mother and go on home. But later . . . !

"So, Jane, how are you?" He had not seen her since New Year's Eve. He was at a loss at what to say to her after what had happened that night.

"Okay, I guess. Can we talk?"

"Sure. What do you want to talk about?" They were engulfed by parishioners leaving church. No one seemed to be paying them any mind. Still, it hardly qualified as a secluded place for a chat.

"Not here, Rid, It's too congested and it's too public."

Groendal became wary. He was determined not to get trapped again. The very last place he would agree to meet would be her home. "Where'd you have in mind, Jane?"

"I don't know. Someplace where we can talk in peace without being interrupted. How about Clark Park, say this afternoon?"

He couldn't have picked a better place himself. Clark was a large municipal park only a short distance from each of their homes. And very public. "Okay . . . how about, say two this afternoon?"

"Fine. I'll meet you at the corner of Vernor and Clark."

Groendal went home to breakfast and one of the most intensive interrogations he had ever undergone. To his credit, he did not break. The girl: Jane Condon. Where had they met: She was an usherette at the Stratford and everyone knew how regularly Ridley went to the Stratford to keep abreast of the film industry. See her? Just casually; she's a Redeemer grad. Don't know what she wants to talk about; will just have to go and find out. No, of course she's not the reason for leaving the seminary. Don't be silly; one doesn't make a decision that serious over a mere girl.

There was much to be said for Mrs. Groendal's perseverance. She kept up the inquisition till it was time for him to leave and meet Jane. There was much to be said for Ridley's patience. He repeatedly fended off his mother's thrusts without ever contradicting or implicating himself.

He walked down Vernor Highway lost in thought, paying no attention to the stores and bars all serried one next to the other and all respectfully closed for Sunday. He was oblivious to the Baker streetcar clanging past.

He was conscious of his surroundings only once—when he passed the Stratford—where it all had started.

If only he had not been taken in by the attention given him by the only female in his life besides his mother. If he had not put even one foot into the trap, at least that low point of his life would have been avoided.

But he had done it, there was no denying that. Now he had to face the girl.

Well, he supposed, it was the least he could do. He would listen to whatever she had to say. If there were too many questions, he would fence with her as he had with his mother. One meeting and it would be over. And none too soon; he had enough problems facing him without resurrecting this mess.

There she was, at the southeast corner of Vernor and Clark, by one of the corners of rectangular Clark Park. She looked forlorn standing there all by herself. She was still wearing her spring coat. He caught himself trying to remember what she looked like nude. But he couldn't. At that point in the evening his senses had been blurred by alcohol; now he could not dredge up even one detail. Besides, the attempt to remember embarrassed him.

As he crossed toward her, she looked up and smiled. When he reached her, she turned and began walking up one of the paved paths. He fell in step.

A wind had come up. It was beginning to get chill. He regretted having selected a light windbreaker. But there was no going back now. He jammed his hands deep into his pants pockets and tried unsuccessfully to conceal a shiver.

"Cold?" she asked.

"No, it's okay. I just didn't expect it to be this windy. I'll get used to it."

"You'd think it would be warmer by the end of May."

"Yeah. Well, that's Michigan: If you don't like the weather, just wait a minute and it'll change."

The weather! What a thing to talk about. Still, he could call to mind bits of stage business and snatches of movies where characters did just that. When people were faced with discussing some awkward subject, they frequently started with some remote, harmless topic—like the weather.

In any case, he wasn't about to bring up anything serious. After all, it was her nickel—the current price of a phone call.

"What did you think of the sermon this morning?"

Wow! That had to be further removed from whatever she wanted to talk about than the weather. "The sermon?"

"Yes. Father Buhler's sermon."

Ah, yes. Good old deaf Father Buhler. Refuge of all who wanted absolution without having the priest hear the sins. "It was okay, I guess."

"I suppose you're used to better sermons in the seminary."

Groendal smiled at the memory. "Yeah. Funny thing, though; the faculty are all diocesan priests who fear the Redemptorists."

"Fear them!"

"Well, maybe not fear them. Have an inordinate respect for them. The diocesans are probably more conscious than the Redemptorists that the order was founded by Alphonsus Liguori basically to preach and refute heresies. Sight unseen, secular priests probably would concede the preaching title to the Redemptorists without a struggle. But that would, for the most part, be wrong. Actually, they're all alike. Some are good speakers and some aren't. Some work at it and some don't. Doesn't make much difference whether they belong to a diocese or to the Redemptorist Order."

"And I take it Father Buhler doesn't fit into the good speaker category."

"I'd guess old Father Buhler stopped really preparing his sermons years ago." Groendal suddenly remembered that it was Buhler who had absolved him from his sin with Jane. And it had been Buhler specifically because he was nearly deaf but wouldn't take himself out of the confessional box. Once again, Groendal felt embarassed.

"Speaking of sermons and the seminary, you didn't go back after Easter. Is anything wrong?"

"Wrong? What could be wrong?" Groendal sensed she was nearing the heart of what she wanted to talk about. Oh, in a roundabout way, but she was getting there.

"Are you ill?"

"Ill? No. I had a slight injury. Sports. But I'm okay now." He wondered if she'd seen him moving about slowly and painfully at Easter time. Outside of lying to his parents, which, due to his mother's incessant questioning, he'd had to do repeatedly, he had not discussed the seminary with anyone.

"But you haven't gone back."

"I decided not to. At least not for now." He was strongly tempted to tell her it was none of her business. Some sense of chivalry prompted him not to.

"I thought maybe it had something to do with us."

"No, of course not." He flushed. Absolutely the last thing in the world he wanted to talk about. Especially with his partner in sin. Why else had he taken his confession to a deaf priest?

"I just thought it might have been. And I felt bad about that."

"No. No. For one thing . . . that . . . happened at New Year's. And I went back to the seminary after Christmas vacation. So . . . that . . . had nothing to do with my staying home now. Nothing!"

It was Jane's turn to feel a stab of anger. "Nothing! It was hardly 'nothing'!"

"I don't mean that. I don't mean that at all. I'm sorry. I just mean it had no bearing on my not returning to the seminary. But I don't want to talk about that."

"About what happened between us? Or about not going back to the seminary?"

"Neither one. I don't want to talk about either one."

They walked in silence for a while. It occurred to Groendal that this was not unlike the seemingly endless walks he used to take around the seminary grounds. Except of course he had never walked those sacred paths with a girl in tow.

"That was an accident, you know."

"What?"

"What happened between us."

Hadn't he just told her he didn't want to talk about that? This had to be it. This is what she simply had to talk to him about. Well, maybe if he let her get it out of her system she'd be satisfied and she wouldn't have to talk about it anymore.

That's what some of the priests out in the field had told the seminarians in conferences. The students had been told by men who were on the firing line that just listening could be an apostolate in itself. If they would just listen while some troubled soul got the problem off his or her chest, he or she might get rid of an intolerable burden.

Maybe it would work now. He certainly prayed it would. One more time. Then he would never have to think of that night again.

He sighed. "You really want to talk about it."

"I think we have to talk about it."

Why, he thought, would they have to talk about it? "Well, if you really feel you have to . . ."

"Do you suppose we could sit down? Do we have to keep walking?"

The request took him by surprise. It had never occurred to him that not everyone walked endlessly while talking. He looked about. Unlike the seminary, here benches lined the walkways. And—something he had not adverted to before—there were very few other people in the park.

"Sure. We can sit down."

They did, at the next bench, near the deserted pavilion. They were silent for a few moments.

"This whole thing started out innocently enough, Rid. I had a schoolgirl crush on you. I used to time it so I could see you when we went to school. You always left at the same time, so I did too. Of course I was younger than you, and the girls and boys almost never got together at Redeemer, so you wouldn't have noticed me."

That was true. He'd never really seen her before that night at the Stratford when something—something indefinable—had happened. But with the careful and continued surveillance she was describing, he wondered how he had managed not to notice her.

"I used to daydream about going out with you. And then you went away to the seminary, so that was that as far as a date went. But I never quite got over you. I used to watch you serve Mass when you were home on vacation. And I never missed any of your piano recitals."

Groendal felt haunted. How could he have overlooked someone who described herself as in almost constant attendance on him? Either he had instinctively avoided looking at the girl—a testimony to the custody of the eyes he'd been so carefully taught in the seminary—or it was a monumental lack of awareness.

"When I got that job at the Stratford I never thought I'd see you there. It never crossed my mind that you'd be so close to me."

She shivered. It was colder sitting on the bench than it was walking. And all she had was that thin coat. Tentatively, he put one arm across her shoulders. She settled gratefully against him. Immediately he regretted his action. But, having given the arm, he could not in good grace withdraw it.

"Something happened, didn't it? You felt it too, didn't you? When you handed me your ticket. Something happened. Didn't you notice it?"

"Yes, something. I guess I noticed you for the first time."

"It was more than that. There was no need for me to walk up and down the aisle as often as I did that night. But I could feel you looking at me. And I liked that . . . a lot."

All she was saying was true. He had felt something akin to a not unpleasant shock when their fingers touched as he'd handed her his ticket. And he had noticed her as she repeatedly walked by that night. He'd supposed—correctly, as it turned out—that she'd taken many unnecessary trips, all for his benefit. And it hadn't been wasted. He had studied her each and every trip. Unobserved, he had thought. Apparently, he hadn't gotten away with it.

"Then when you came back the next night, I knew you had come back to see me. I can't tell you how happy I was. I never expected it. I could hardly even believe it."

Well, part of the reason for his return was to see that excellent movie again. But why tell her that? She would never believe it. Besides, she was on the right track: A good part of his reason for going back had been to see her. What had the priests told the seminarians? Listen.

"Just knowing that you had come back to see me made me really happy. Then when you asked me out after the show, I was nearly delirious. But—and this is very definite, Rid—I didn't have any reason for inviting you over on New Year's Eve except just to see you again. I wanted to see you and I knew you'd have to be going back to school soon and I just figured you were in the right mood to see me again. And that if you went back to school you might forget me. I was sort of striking while the iron was hot . . . do you know what I mean, Rid?"

He shrugged. It was up for grabs. Who knew what she'd really had in mind? It was certainly possible she had just wanted an innocent date. After all, how could she have come up with such an elaborate plot when she had no way of knowing he would come back to the movie or ask her out after the show?

On the other hand, once he did return to the Stratford and asked her out, she had the entire length of the movie to make her plans for New Year's Eve. He'd put a judgment on that matter on the back burner for the moment.

"Everybody goes out to parties on New Year's Eve," she continued. "I didn't think you'd want to do that. Besides, as long as we had this date that it seemed like I'd been waiting for most of my life, I wanted you all to myself. There didn't seem to be any better place than home.

"I swear, Rid, I would have invited you over even if my parents had been home. They would have let us alone. But since they were going to a party, it seemed just perfect." She hesitated. "The very last thing in the world I wanted to happen was what happened . . . you do believe that, don't you, Rid?"

Again he shrugged. What had happened he had tried to put out of his mind. As time passed and particularly with the relationship that had grown with Charlie Hogan, Groendal had been quite successful in suppressing the memory. Now she was dusting off an old recollection that he preferred keeping buried.

He felt himself begin to flush. He tried to check his embarrassment. But the more he tried, the more he was conscious of the reddening that betrayed his emotion.

"I've thought it over many, many times. It was the whole thing, don't you think, Rid? The holiday, New Year's Eve, and the heat of the house. But most of all the liquor. Getting out that Scotch was one of the dumbest stunts I ever pulled. That's what really did it, Rid: the Scotch. . . . Rid, you're not saying anything."

"I guess you're right. It probably was the Scotch."

She moved slightly. His hand touched her breast, which was delicately outlined beneath her thin coat. He moved his hand away.

They were silent a while. She shivered and moved closer. He did not move away. After all, it was cold and she was just trying to stay warm.

"So, what are you going to do about school?" Jane asked. "I mean, in a week or so you would have graduated from college. Isn't it kind of strange not to go back after Easter? When you're about to graduate?"

He didn't answer immediately. What was the use of fooling with it? "I'm not going back, Jane. I'm not going to be a priest. Things have changed. I can't explain it to you. Things have just changed." Most times, he had found, confession was good for the soul and the psyche. But, having confessed his radically changed status to Jane, he felt not one bit better.

"You're not going back to the seminary! Not ever?" Jane pulled herself away and sat facing him from farther along the bench. She clearly had been taken by surprise.

"I'm not going back," he affirmed.

Happy, she slid back across the bench and snuggled beneath his arm. "Then things can be different for us, Rid. One of our problems before— our main problem, really—was that we had no time. Now we can back away and do it right. We can go on dates. Go to a show. Go for a ride.

Go on a picnic. We can get to know each other. We can forget what happened and start all over."

"No, we can't, Jane." He said it softly.

She felt a flash of panic. "What do you mean, we can't? What happened was a mistake—something neither of us was responsible for. It just happened. It was a special, tender holiday. We had too much to drink. It was an act of love!"

"It was an act of passion."

"Passion is love!" She moved away, facing him.

"Passion is an irrational, animal act."

"I was in love!"

"I wasn't."

"So," she had now become quite angry, "that's the type you are, after all! Just get your kicks with a girl and then leave her!"

"Jane, that's not the way it was. That's not the way it is. You know better than that."

"What makes it any different?"

"You said it yourself. It was an accident. We didn't know what we were getting into . . . at least I didn't."

"What's that supposed to mean?"

"Bringing out the Scotch and having good-sized belts of it on a nearly empty stomach wasn't my idea."

"You mean to suggest that I planned the whole thing!"

"No, that's not what I mean!" Now he was becoming angry. "Just that it was not all my idea. Or all my fault. It wasn't an act of love." (God, how he hated talking about this!) "If we must face what happened squarely, we were just getting to know each other when you brought out the liquor.

"We got intoxicated, to put it bluntly. We were no longer rational. We were animals. And we did what irrational animals do: We got carried away by our emotions. It's silly to say we were in love. We were just getting to know each other. It's silly to say it was an act of love. It was an act of drunkenness. That's all it was."

"That's all it was, was it? Then what's this?" In a few rapid motions that seemed rehearsed, she flung open her coat and raised her blouse, exposing bare midriff.

Groendal was stunned. "Jane! What are you doing? Cover yourself! People can see!" He looked around quickly; not only was no one watching, he could see no one in sight. Nevertheless, what she was doing seemed shameful. "Pull your blouse down!"

"Not until you look! Long and hard!"

He forced himself to look. If anything, she seemed to have put on a little weight. "Well?"

"It's just beginning to show!"

"Show? Show what?"

"That I'm in the family way!"

"You're what?"

"Pregnant!"

The word hit him a stunning blow. He had no reply.

"Yes, pregnant!" she repeated.

"How—"

"How else? What you did to me!"

"How do you know?"

"I haven't had a period in almost four months."

That meant little to him. Oh, he certainly knew of pregnancies. He had some vague ideas of how that was accomplished. Such information, in the seminary curriculum, was postponed until the final courses in moral theology. Good Catholic parents scarcely ever discussed such things either with their children or each other. In effect, Groendal, in his ignorance of conception, was somewhere between delivery by the stork and the flood of sexual information that would inundate society in just a few more years.

"I mean," Groendal amended, "how do you know it was me? How do you know I'm the father?"

Jane's eyes widened. She struck at him. Instinctively, he blocked the blow. First, his body was still too sore to endure another onslaught. Second, he was not as willing to accept penance for this sin. This was an affair in which they both had participated.

"It's a reasonable question," he insisted.

"Didn't you see the blood? On you? On me? On the floor? It took me hours to clean that carpet! You took my virginity!"

Another new concept. He knew that women who had never had intercourse were considered virgins. Among others, he had the Blessed Virgin Mary to thank for that information. But how one "took" virginity was another question. Whatever was involved finally seemed to explain the blood that he'd found on himself and about which he'd had all those nightmares.

Ridley said nothing. He could think of nothing to say. He felt overwhelmed, as if he were being backed into an inescapable corner.

"Well?" Jane challenged.

"Well, what?"

"What do you intend to do about this?"

Again he was silent. He could think of no practical answer. The idea that he might pray for her occurred to him. But it seemed less than sufficient, so he didn't mention it.

"What do you intend to do about my pregnancy? What do you intend to do about our child?"

The term *"our* child" grabbed his attention as nothing before had. He began to lose sight of Jane. All he could think of was that he didn't need this. Not now. He had not yet recovered from the tragic end to his relationship with Charlie Hogan and the loss of a vocation that meant the world to him. He was still reeling from those severe traumas and here was this young woman demanding that he take virtually lifelong responsibility for "our" child.

In his panic he was not conscious that the muscles in his throat were constricting. In a very short time, he would experience great difficulty in breathing.

"What about our child?" Jane sensed she had scored heavily and wanted to press home her advantage.

As if by miracle, the answer came. "Adoption! You can adopt it out!"

"Adoption! Give my baby—our child away to some stranger! Over my dead body!"

"Jane, be reasonable. There are lots of reputable agencies. Catholic Charities can do it. And you'd know it would have good Catholic parents who would give it a home. So much more than we could give it."

"Not if we get married."

"What?"

"If we got married, we could give our child everything anybody else could give. More, really, because we would have our baby. It's the only honorable thing to do."

"Jane!" Could it have suddenly gotten much warmer? He was perspiring profusely. "Jane! I just got kicked . . . I just lost . . . I have no . . . I can't . . ." He felt as if he were about to faint, although he had never before done that. He couldn't faint here in the middle of a public park! He had a weird vision of caretakers digging a hole beside his inert body, rolling him into the hole, and covering it over. He had to get out of here, and fast!

Not caring any longer what Jane might think of all this, Groendal rose and ran. It was not a graceful exit. He moved the way a desperate man would escape if, say, because he'd been tortured he couldn't run up to his full, normal capability. He more staggered than ran up Vernor. He was oblivious to stares. He assumed he'd left Jane standing in the park with her damned baby. But he could focus on only one thing: He must find sanctuary before he died. It didn't matter who offered sanctuary, the church or his home.

It was only because home lay between him and the church that he turned in when he got to his house. By the time he reached the front hallway, his clothing was sweat-drenched. He'd torn open his shirt trying to make it easier to breathe.

Mary Groendal had been waiting impatiently for her son's return. She had long since concluded that he was spending entirely too much time with that woman this afternoon. The conviction was growing, too, that her son's loss of priestly vocation was the fault of that woman. Long before Ridley lurched through the front door, she had decided to have it out with him.

However, when she saw his pallor, his sweat-covered face and drenched clothing, she gasped. Shocked, she could think of nothing to say.

Ridley felt as an elephant might upon finding the burial ground. It was now safe to collapse. So he did.

*   *   *

When he came to, he had the impression he had awakened many times since losing consciousness in the front hallway. But he couldn't remember things clearly. He couldn't remember anything clearly. Oddly, he felt rather comfortable without memory. As if there was nothing in his past worth remembering.

He was too tired to move anything but his eyes. He was in some sort of institution. He knew he'd reached that conclusion before, but he couldn't recall how or why.

It was a long, narrow room with an impossibly high ceiling. The walls were an indeterminate mixture of blue and green. Sickening. Except for the ceiling, which was too high, it could have been a room in the seminary's St. Thomas Hall. But the color was not right. And of course there was no reason why it should be St. Thomas Hall.

The overhead light was lit. He wondered if they left the light on all the time. He wondered if it was day or night. He didn't care. He was lost in a blessed void of neutrality. He couldn't remember the past and he didn't care about the future.

He became conscious of sounds somewhere in the corridor. Institutional sounds. People—more than a few—talking. Quietly, mostly. Somebody giving orders: Somebody must stay in his or her room till later. Crockery rattling.

Then the sound of a loudspeaker. He could hear that clearly. "Dr. Bartlett . . . Dr. Bartlett, please pick up line two."

No doubt about it, he was in some sort of hospital. He tried for a moment, but couldn't remember which one. Gloriously, it didn't matter.

14

It was not at all typical of Bob Koesler. But he wanted very much to see Ridley Groendal and that would require extreme measures.

When Koesler began summer vacation, he learned, first, that Groendal was in St. Joseph's Retreat, and second, that only members of his immediate family were permitted to visit him. How was a seminarian, fresh from college graduation, to pierce that defense?

The solution seemed obvious to Koesler. There was one exception to every rule in most institutions—the friendly clergyman. Spouses and relatives might be denied access to their loved one, but—particularly in a Catholic hospital—not the priest. He could go virtually unchallenged through almost any hospital at any time. The presumption was that a clergyman was always on business and that his business was "higher" than mere regulations.

In addition, the priest was identified by his uniform. Nothing more was needed. He did not need any ID or hospital garb. A black suit and Roman collar with clerical vest was all that was required. And Bob Koesler had that. Now that he was about to enter the theologate seminary, he was expected to add the clerical vest and collar to his wardrobe, and he had.

All he needed was an extraordinary measure of self-confidence, perhaps the Yiddish chutzpah. He could dress exactly like a priest out on professional calls. He looked like a priest—albeit a very young priest. Now he had to pass himself off as one. He had to tough it out. Brazenly enter through the front door as if he owned the place, walk by hospital staff in the corridors with no more than a curt nod, and march into Ridley's room as if he'd been summoned to confer a sacrament or two.

Carrying off this masquerade was precisely where Koesler anticipated the most trouble. It was not in his nature to dare anyone to call his bluff. Crossing the border between Detroit and Windsor, he never tried to smuggle anything either way. He was certain his guilty countenance would betray him.

But now he was intent on seeing his former classmate and fellow parishioner. And desperately intent people are led to desperate deeds.

Three days before, he had made his first foray into the impressive brick structure on the northeast corner of Michigan Avenue and West Outer Drive. Later it would be replaced by a car dealership. But now it was a sanitorium mostly for disturbed Catholics. Run by the Sisters of Charity—who, at that time, wore the imposing winged bonnets—St. Joseph's Retreat housed every infirmity from alcoholism to schizophrenia.

Koesler's initial adventure had been so successful that he had been emboldened to try it again. So here he was in his second attempt. He was under no delusion that this experience would qualify him to fool a border guard. Conning nuns by wearing priestly regalia was one thing; deceiving a customs agent trained to detect frauds and conditioned to expect them was quite another.

As it turned out, the second time was easier than the first. Then, some of the staff had looked at him a bit dubiously. Undoubtedly because they'd never seen him before and because he was so young—and looked it. Though his was not an impossibly youthful appearance; when he was ordained a priest four years hence, he would not look noticeably older.

But familiarity, in addition to breeding contempt, also breeds acceptance. Thus, on his second try, not only did Koesler nod to staff personnel as he passed them in the hall, several smiled as they returned the nod. A few even offered, "Good afternoon, Father." Koesler loved it. He could hardly wait for ordination when, to paraphrase the book title, everybody would call him "Father." This, then, was a foretaste of bliss.

Koesler knocked. Hearing no response, he entered Groendal's room. As had been the case the previous time, Rid, arms crossed on his chest, lay fully clothed in bed. He seemed completely passive and, all things considered, not unhappy.

Koesler removed his white straw hat, dropped it on the small table and sat in the room's only chair. Groendal regarded him for a few moments without any sign of recognition. Finally, a light seemed to go on in his eyes. "Bob! What happened? You get ordained?"

Koesler was taken aback. This was exactly the way they'd started the previous visit. "Of course not. Don't you know where you are?"

Groendal shook his head, put both hands beneath his neck on the

pillow and stretched. "It's June, isn't it? I'm not certain of the year
. . . 1950?"

"Yeah."

"Hmmm. Then why are you dressed like a priest? You're not ordained. You just graduated from college."

"Uh-huh. But we went through this before. This is the only way I can
get in to see you. If they think I'm a priest."

"You were here before?"

"Don't you remember?"

Groendal shook his head again. "Not really."

Koesler had never encountered any phenomenon to match this. He
found it unnerving. "What's happened to you, Rid?"

Groendal frowned and tried to concentrate. "I'm not sure, Bob. I
think it's electroshock. They give it to me every three days or so. It
seems to be wiping out my memory . . . at least my memory of recent
events. I can remember distant things, but the more recent things I'm
not too clear on. This is a good example. You say you've been here
before. I don't doubt you were, especially since you say you were. Since
I've forgotten all kinds of things over the past few days, your visit is
probably gone with the rest. Sorry."

"No need to be sorry. It's not your fault. But what are they doing to
you?"

"I don't know. Curing me?"

"Of what?"

"Oh, didn't they tell you? I had a nervous breakdown. The psychiatrist has a couple more technical names for it. But it comes down to a
nervous breakdown."

"Holy cow! I never knew anybody with a nervous breakdown."

"Neither did I." Groendal grinned weakly. "Yesterday I didn't know
what a nervous breakdown was; today I are one." The grin didn't last.

"What brought it on?"

"I . . . I don't know. At least I'm not sure."

"Was it that business at the seminary?"

Groendal looked at Koesler sharply. "What business?"

"Uh . . . between you and Charlie Hogan."

"What do you know about that?"

"There was talk."

"What was it? I want to know. Maybe I need to know."

Koesler recited a synopsis of the various hypotheses that had been bandied about, especially among the philosophy students. Groendal listened with more attention than he'd been able to drum up in the recent past. The theories were substantially correct. That surprised Groendal. Scuttlebutt was rarely accurate. Those details that were incorrect were not worth arguing over. Especially not in his impaired condition.

Without identifying which items in the account were right or wrong, Groendal conceded that the rumors were basically true.

Ridley pondered what he might say next. Because Koesler was a classmate; because he was a fellow parishioner, a neighbor; and for some other indefinable reason, maybe because he had proven himself trustworthy, Koesler had been privy to nearly everything that had happened to Groendal. Ridley decided to share the final secret. He told Koesler of his meeting with Jane Condon and her announcement.

"Wow!" was Koesler's comment.

"Bob, you're going to have to find some other kind of reaction to news. 'Wow!' is not going to get you all that far in the priesthood."

"Uh . . . you're right."

"Do you mind if we go out and walk the grounds for a while? I'm permitted to do that . . . I just haven't felt up to it till now."

"I don't know, Rid. I'm here under false colors. What if they challenge me?"

"They won't. If you got this far, you won't have any more trouble. Besides, if we stay in this room all the while, someone may accuse us of having a 'particular friendship.' " There was bitterness in Groendal's tone as he pronounced the last two words.

Koesler flushed. The thought that he and Ridley might have been suspected of having such a relationship had never crossed his mind. He agreed to the walk.

They started along the brick path within the grounds, slowly at first, then picking up speed. It was so like the walks they'd taken so often at the seminary. And so different. Now one was still a seminarian and one was not. One was still on his way to the priesthood. The other had no idea of what might become of him. So far, however, Groendal was correct: No one had challenged them.

"One thing puzzles me," Koesler said. "You said that . . . whatever it is they're doing to you . . ."

"Shock treatments."

". . . is affecting your memory of recent events. But you can remember what happened between you and Charlie Hogan and between you and Jane Condon."

"I know, Bob, and I can't explain it. Except that those things were so important to me. It's like I couldn't forget them even if I wanted to. Maybe these are the memories they're trying to erase."

"So Jane's going to have a baby."

"So she said."

"And you're going to be a father."

"Again, so she says."

"You don't believe her?"

"What if she told me she was going to have a baby just to get me to marry her?"

"Okay, I suppose that's possible. If you wait a little longer, you'll know. Either she'll have the baby or she won't. What if she does have the baby?"

"What if I'm not the father?"

"Don't get me wrong, Rid; I'm no expert in these things. But either you did or you didn't."

"Oh, I did all right. But what if someone else did it after me? What if he is the father?"

"Hmmm. I don't know. What can you do about it?"

"Nothing that I can think of."

"Mr. Groendal! Mr. Groendal!" An attendant was calling from the building. "Dr. Bartlett wants to see you now."

"I guess that's it, 'Father' Koesler." Groendal led the way back.

"Are they going to give you the shock treatment now?"

"No, they save that for the morning. Tomorrow morning, I think."

"What's it like?"

"I don't think you want to know. Oh, well, they put something in your mouth, then they put these electrodes on your head. I guess it's something like being electrocuted. They just don't give you enough juice to kill you."

Koesler shuddered. "That's awful!"

"You said it."

They shook hands.

"You really put yourself out, Bob. I appreciate it. I won't forget you."

Koesler hesitated. "One last thing, Rid: Have you given any thought to what's happened to you? I mean, all of it has happened to you. You don't seem to have been in control of anything. Just a thought. I don't know why I even mentioned it. Well, good luck, Rid. *Oremus pro in-vicem.*"

"Yeah, we'll pray for each other. Thanks."

Groendal watched Koesler, straw hat in place, walk away from St. Joseph's Retreat. Koesler was leaving. Groendal was confined. But what was it Bob had said? In effect, that Groendal was passive. Things happened to him. He was not in control.

These thoughts reverberated through his numbed mind as he approached Dr. Bartlett's office.

There were those who would argue that Groendal was lucky to have Dr. Roland Bartlett as his psychiatrist. He was regarded in Catholic circles as God's gift to emotionally ill priests and nuns. In addition to an extensive private practice, he made himself available almost every time a priest or a nun was committed to psychiatric care.

Bartlett himself was a devoutly religious Catholic who preferred a revisited or refreshed sacramental life to deep psychoanalysis. Everyone —priests, nuns, and laity—who came to him was queried about his or her religious condition. The next question: How active was his or her active participation in that religion? Backsliders of whatever denomination were ordered to return to their church before the esteemed doctor would treat them.

Thus, those whose problems were caused by their church got caught in psychoreligious Catch-22. It was only one of Dr. Bartlett's flaws.

"Good afternoon, Ridley. Feeling down again?" The doctor's expression suggested he was hoping for a bit of depression to work on.

It was as if the doctor's greeting awakened Groendal. "I don't think so. I was wondering when the next treatment—you know, the shock treatment—was due?"

"Tomorrow morning. Why do you ask?"

"What do I have to do . . . what has to happen for the treatments to be stopped? What would make you decide to cancel or postpone tomorrow's treatment?"

"Well, Ridley, we're in a series now. I would prefer not to interrupt the series."

"Uh-huh. I have an idea that might save us a lot of time. But I've got to work it out and I don't think I can do it while the treatment goes on. I'll need every bit of my mind and memory."

"Hmmm, I see." He pondered a moment. "Ridley, since you entered this facility, you've been in a depressed state. And we've spoken of this often. How do you feel now?"

"Actually, kind of good. I just had a visit with my . . . uh . . . priest. And it left me feeling a bit hopeful." Groendal was well aware of the stock put in religion by Bartlett and was willing to pander to the doctor's fixation, even to the point of acknowledging a priesthood that Bob Koesler did not yet possess.

"Your priest?" Even though Bartlett had left orders for no visitors, it did not surprise him that a priest had broken through. The question in a Catholic institution such as St. Joseph's was not whether a priest could see whomever he wished whenever he wished, but whether the parish priest would bother coming to visit. While Bartlett put more than ordinary stock in religious curative powers, he did not cotton to priests who dabbled in psychotherapy. There was a place for everything. Or, as St. Paul put it—We each, in the mystical body of Christ, have our gifts contributing to the good of the whole.

This deserved some investigation. "What did the two of you talk about?"

From here on, Groendal would have to deal in one long, extended lie. Since he had already lied in referring to Koesler as a priest, the remaining fabrication seemed to fall nicely into place.

"Oh, nothing much. Just about the parish . . . things going on there. But he did try to bring up the matter of what I'm going to do now that I won't be going back to the seminary.

"Father was trying to be very helpful. He promised that he would do all he could to help me get into some other field. And, you see, Doctor, that got me thinking: I've got the rest of my life ahead of me. I'm still young. I can't spend the rest of my life moping because I'm not going to be a priest. I've got to get myself organized and get started on what I'm going to do with my life."

Groendal correctly gauged the hesitation and reservation unexpressed by Bartlett over some presumptuous priest's invasion into his professional field. Ridley needed to assuage the doctor's apprehension that his area of expertise might be compromised.

"So, Doctor, it wasn't so much what Father said. It was more what he got me thinking about. He just happened to stimulate me into thinking about things that need planning. And I'll need a clear head to do it." He looked hopefully at Bartlett.

The doctor looked uncertain. Groendal needed a clincher.

"I thought," he added, "that I'd go to the chapel later today, tomorrow, every chance I get, and pray. I guess nothing can help solve a problem like this more than prayer . . . don't you think, Doctor?"

Of course he did. Maybe one more nudge.

"I wouldn't have thought about prayer being the answer to my problem if it hadn't been for you, Doctor. You've really shown me the importance of prayer. Why, I look at you as even more than my doctor —you've become my spiritual advisor."

That did it. Groendal was never more sure of anything.

Bartlett tried, not altogether successfully, to cover a self-satisfied smirk. "Well, all right, Ridley; we'll skip tomorrow's treatment. But, mind you: This means we've broken the series! And if we begin again, we'll have to start from the beginning of the series . . . you understand that, don't you, Ridley?"

Ridley understood. Completely.

"Now then," Bartlett continued, "let's take up where we left off. We were talking about your reasons for going to the seminary in the first place . . ."

Only part of Groendal stayed attentive to the doctor. That part strove to be affirmative and bright, not the type that required shock treatment. The rest of Groendal's mind rejoiced in the visit of Bob Koesler. Good old Bob. Maybe not Ridley's best friend. Perhaps not anyone's best friend. But a good friend, nonetheless. Unwittingly, Bob might just have stumbled on the core of the problem.

The remainder of that day and in the days to come, Groendal spent much of his time in the chapel. That part of his promise to Dr. Bartlett had been sincere. Groendal had long found a church, almost any church, one of the best places for deep thought as well as prayer. Well, prayerful thought, if you will.

Bob Koesler had given him the central subject of his meditation. Things happened to Groendal. He was in control of nothing. Passive. Passivity. It was true. All too true.

As the days passed, Groendal was virtually lost in the memories of his life to date. The memories, of course, were colored by his own bias. In that, he was by no means unique. Can anyone be completely objective in his or her own case?

Groendal spent little time analyzing his relationship with his parents. Without doubt, they had had an enormous impact on his life. But this was the area that appeared to most fascinate Dr. Bartlett. As they discussed it, Ridley found it interesting that in his recollections, his mother always seemed to dominate his father as well as himself. It did not occur to him that this might have set the pattern for passivity in his life. Nor did Bartlett draw such an inference.

Groendal was absorbed, rather, in what he considered the four pivotal relationships in his life. Naturally, though he affected to consider them objectively, the memories were tinged with a bountiful measure of self-interest.

First, there was David Palmer. Groendal had begun it all as a practical joke. Sophomoric, perhaps, as most practical jokes were, but harmless. Just a few bars of "Bumble Boogie" instead of "Flight of the Bumblebee." All right, so it took Palmer by surprise and made him look stupid for a moment. It was only a rehearsal. No harm.

But what massive retaliation! In performance, no less, setting an impossible tempo. On top of it all, it was done in the presence of representatives of Interlochen. No doubt about it, it had changed his life. He might have won a scholarship. He might have been able to make music his life.

No!

Groendal stopped himself. These were passive, subjunctive suppositions. He had to eliminate this tendency. He would have won that scholarship. By now he would have had the training and experience necessary to carve out a life in the music world.

But it was not to be. And all because of David Palmer, who was now pursuing what promised to be a most successful life in the music world.

And what had Groendal to show for it all? Nothing. He had settled no scores. Pointlessly, he had taken out his frustration on a blameless piano. In retrospect, he had been extremely fortunate that his symbolic gesture had not turned into a major case of arson.

He had been a passive victim, and David Palmer, far from being punished for having wronged Groendal, had been rewarded with the career Ridley had coveted.

Next there was Carroll Mitchell.

It might have been different if the seminary had not turned it into a competition. Even then, it might have been different if Mitch had not entered the contest. After all, Mitch was the closest thing the seminary had to a professional playwright. What right had he to enter such a competition? Immediately, the contest was by its very nature rigged and unfair. In such an unbalanced contest, Ridley had had every right to borrow from another professional writer. It did no more than equalize the odds.

So why had Mitch acted so self-righteous when he discovered what Ridley had done? The reason of course was that now it had been turned into an honest competition for a change. Now Mitch would have to contend with an equal. That's what had made him so angry. Not the plagiarism, which was a loose charge at best. No, that was a smoke screen. The real problem was that, for the first time, Mitch stood to lose what he had considered a lead-pipe cinch victory.

This reasoning put the whole incident into some sort of logical perspective.

God knows what would have happened if Mitch had taken his plagiarism charge to the faculty. Would the faculty have understood that Ridley was just trying to turn a rigged competition into a fair contest? Not likely. If Mitch had told and Groendal had presented his legitimate defense, it simply would have highlighted how unjust and foolish it had been for the faculty to have made this a contest in the first place. And the faculty never would have admitted that. They would have been forced to make a scapegoat of Groendal.

No, Ridley had turned to the only option available when he applied the rule of "fraternal correction" and reported Mitchell's foolhardy violation of the rule.

Carroll Mitchell had created the impression that he was the wronged party—that Groendal had betrayed a friend who trusted him. Nothing could have been further from the truth, as Groendal viewed the facts he had twisted. Groendal was the offended party. He had been the victim of an unfair competition. Both the faculty and Mitchell had been playing with loaded dice and Groendal was the victim.

And once more, he had been passive. Things had happened to him. He had been in control of nothing.

Then there was the affair of Jane Condon.

Of all that had happened to him, Jane Condon had indisputably been the most manipulative force. He could see it all so clearly now in the quiet, meditative atmosphere of the chapel.

At one time, he had considered them both victims of a series of unfortunate accidents. But now that his rationalization was working so well, he saw clearly through to the cause of the whole mess. It was Jane Condon alone. The only thing left to chance would be on which night he might have decided to go to a movie at the Stratford. But attend a movie during vacation he would. Anybody who knew him knew that.

Jane herself confessed that she had placed him practically under personal surveillance for many years. She would know how devoted he was to the arts. She had to know that he would attend a movie during Christmas break just as he had during vacations of the past—Easter, Christmas, summer, whatever. From that knowledge, all she had to do was choose her time.

His final year in college—a good choice, coming before the greater commitment of the theologate. She got the job as usherette and just waited for him. Why did she not throw herself at Koesler? No; she had preset her sights on Ridley.

He had to admit that he had played right into her hands when he returned the next night. But, for someone who had studied him as thoroughly as Jane said she had, it was not a bad gamble. It was his first flirtation, which she undoubtedly knew. Once he had slipped into her trap and returned to the theater, the rest was child's play.

An innocent invitation to a New Year's Eve party. Arrange to have her parents out for the evening. Get him to play the piano until he was fatigued. And then the liquor. In this case the coup de grâce. Overheat the house. Set the whole thing up so it all comes together at exactly midnight. What more natural than to share a kiss at midnight on New Year's Eve? And then, intoxicated or nearly so, let one thing follow another. Get pregnant then—or later with somebody else; it doesn't matter so long as you trap the man you're after. And that's it.

On reflection, never had he been more passive. The whole thing had just happened to him. He was in control of nothing.

Finally, Charlie Hogan.

With the shock of Ridley's first act of intercourse and subsequent retreat from his first sex partner, Charlie Hogan had played the object of that syndrome called the rebound.

And don't ever try to tell Ridley C. Groendal that Charlie Hogan was unaware of what was going on! Not after Ridley's prayerful meditation in the chapel told him otherwise. Of course Charlie knew. He would have to have been stupid not to know that he and Ridley were more than just friends. There were young men in the seminary who were friends with one another—lots of them. But how many shared all the confidences, the mutual joy of learning from one another, the nearly exclusive companionship, as Ridley and Charlie?

Groendal could think of no one who had shared as much as he and Charlie.

Hogan would have had to be stupid not to see that. And Hogan was by no means stupid. Being the younger of the two, Charlie probably knew where their relationship was heading better than Ridley did. So why then the violent reaction when the climax was reached? Why the beating? Why the betrayal?

Once again, Groendal had been used. And most shamefully so. At least Jane Condon had wanted no less than Ridley himself. She wanted to force Ridley to marry her.

As obnoxious as that was, it wasn't as contemptible as Charlie's motive. He did not want Groendal. He just wanted to destroy Groendal. And he had. He had demolished Ridley's vocation to the priesthood.

Ridley had been passive. All this had happened to him. He had been in control of nothing.

It took Groendal several days to reach all these conclusions. All of them arrived at by prayerful meditation.

As he reached each solution he felt an increasingly greater inner peace. It was as if he were able to lay to rest one ghost of his past after another. This tranquil attitude was communicated in his sessions with Dr. Bartlett, who grew ever more satisfied with Groendal's progress. No longer was there any immediate threat of shock therapy. Regression, of course, was always possible, but unlikely as long as this promising progress continued.

Obviously, Dr. Bartlett and Ridley Groendal were operating on different wavelengths. Bartlett continued to explore Ridley's motivations in the various choices he had made. Meanwhile, Groendal was putting his life into subjective order by examining those—four, it turned out—who had shabbily and shamefully manipulated him.

Once he had his house of cards in final order, the question was what he was going to do about it all. What was he to do about his passivity? What could he do about his apparent lack of control over his life? Particularly, what could he do about all this in a Christian context? This is what puzzled Groendal more than anything else. Because, above all, he was a Christian. His entire life bespoke that. My God, he'd almost become a priest! In fact, it was, his prayerful meditation had clearly indicated, certainly not his fault that he had not gone on to the priesthood.

At this point, enter Bob Koesler for the third time, again masquerading as a priest. This time he made a hurried vow never to try it again. Henceforth, he would dress as a priest only if he really were one or if the seminary rule called for that garb.

The first two times had been so easy. Today, he couldn't quite put his finger on what had gone wrong. Now, instead of deferential if not reverential greetings, he got skeptically raised eyebrows. One nurse actually challenged him, asking with which parish he was affiliated. Why had he not given any thought to the possibility of that logical question?

On the spur of the moment, he had blurted out that he was on special assignment. She accepted with obvious reservations. Unlike the FBI or CIA, the Archdiocese of Detroit gave out no unspecified "special assignments." Fortunately, the nurse was not au courant.

So it was with a good bit more perspiration than was called for even by the warm weather that Koesler greeted Ridley Groendal.

"Bob Koesler—just the man I was looking for!" Groendal welcomed him effusively and offered him a tissue. "Here, wipe off. Is that getup that warm?"

Koesler dabbed at neck and face. "No, I was almost found out. This is the last time I try this masquerade."

"That's okay. It's providential that you came just now."

"You mean you remember my coming to see you before?"

"What? Oh, I see: You mean the shock treatments. When I couldn't remember things. Well, I haven't had a treatment since then . . . thanks to you."

Koesler would never guess what it might be that he had contributed to ending the treatments. "Well, I'm overwhelmed. I just came to visit and find out how you're doing. I didn't expect to be greeted like the Prodigal Son."

"Speaking of the Prodigal Son, I've been trying to puzzle something out and you may be able to help. Put it this way: I need to plumb these ideas and you're the best sounding board I can think of."

"Not your doctor?"

"The last one! No, not the doctor. He and I are off exploring motives and distant relationships. Mostly I'm trying to keep him away from the electricity so he won't give me any more treatments. No, this is something Biblical I've got to figure out."

"Biblical, eh? Well, what the hell, shoot."

"Okay. Do you think Jesus was aggressive?"

"Huh?"

"Do you think Jesus was assertive? Do you think he was in control of things?"

Koesler thought a while. "Sure."

"Then you don't think Christ was passive . . . that he let things happen to him?"

Koesler thought again. "Well, if you put it that way, I guess he was."

Ridley sighed. "Make up your mind."

"I don't know, Rid. Is anybody one way all the time? Isn't everybody passive sometimes and aggressive others?"

"I suppose so. But what am I looking for?" Groendal appeared to be genuinely searching. "I'm looking for the dominant feature in life. You know: Granted, in some situations, common sense tells you to be submissive, sort of flexible; other times you have to be aggressive. Still, a person is dominantly one or the other . . . know what I mean?"

"I think so. Okay then, let's see: I guess you'd have to say that Jesus Christ basically was in control, wouldn't you?"

"I think I would. But how do you figure it? At the end of His life, He certainly didn't seem in control. He was captured and tortured and executed. That certainly doesn't seem like He was in charge. It's almost the ultimate in submissiveness. And that was the most important part of His life—the end."

"Yeah, but there was something else going on." Koesler rummaged for the right Scripture. "Sure—didn't He say something like, "No one takes my life. I have the power to lay it down and I have the power to take it up again?"

"That's it! That's it!"

"Rid, mind telling me what all this is about?" Koesler had the impression this was less a search for truth than a quiz to which there was only one correct answer. And he had just guessed that answer.

"Oh, nothing." Then Groendal added softly, "And everything." He paused. "You know, I tended to think of Christ as a very passive character. The meek will inherit the earth, and all that. Turn the other cheek. Put away your sword. All those things.

"The last time you were here and you said that things were always happening to me, that I wasn't in control of my life—it really hit a chord inside. You were absolutely right. But my first thought was that that's the way to be a Christian. Christ was passive. Things were always happening to him. He wasn't in control.

"But that's not logical. I guess I had been at least subconsciously modeling my life on what I thought was the imitation of Christ. But it's not that way. Christ was assertive. God! St. Paul was aggressive, wasn't he? I mean taking it to the Gentiles and all that. Standing up to St. Peter. And it was Christ who started them all off. Go and teach all nations, he said. You can't say that and then want a bunch of passive, submissive people on your side, can you?"

The two young men spent more than an hour in a similar vein. Koesler wondered about the origin of this conversation. Ridley gave every indication that somehow, somewhere, he had found a fresh enthusiasm.

In the two earlier visits, Koesler had been moved by Ridley's depression, inertia, and passivity. This, today, was a new Ridley Groendal. Koesler found the change in Ridley's attitude refreshing. So he encouraged Ridley with more examples of positive, confident, assertive Christians through the centuries. It was not difficult to find illustrations.

Koesler had no way of knowing that on that warm June afternoon in St Joseph's Retreat, he was present at the rebirth, the literal metamorphosis of Ridley C. Groendal. Their conversation was innocuous enough. To Koesler it seemed no more than an exercise in selective Church history. A sort of pious pep talk.

It was much more than that for Ridley Groendal. It did indeed mark the emergence of a radical change in his personality. Groendal was by no means the first nor the last to twist the Christian ethic to suit his own purpose. But he did it.

What had begun as an emphasis on Christian assertiveness quickly translated into a profound selfishness. His creed became, "Do unto others, then split."

As he applied his newfound ethic to his life, past and future, he solemnly vowed he would never again be vulnerable. As Christ had been in control of His life, even when He did not seem to be, so Groendal would be in control. It meant a 180 degree turn, but it had to be done. It had to be done if he would be master of his fate as Christ had been.

Groendal had already pinpointed the four people who had most manipulated him. He held them responsible for, among other things, his double loss of vocation: life as a professional musician, then life as a Catholic priest. In the end, they were responsible for putting him here, in a sanitorium.

Nor was there any reason to believe they were done with him now.

They, and others like them, would try to gain control of him again. But, just as Jesus Christ took control of His life and was always at least one jump ahead of His enemies, so would Groendal manipulate before being manipulated.

He had a lot of planning to do. This change in his lifestyle could not occur overnight. He'd spent twenty-one years building this passive compliant character. He could not tear it apart and rebuild it instantly. But with the fierce determination now motivating him, it surely would not take much time to turn things around.

* * *

Bob Koesler was not to see Ridley Groendal again for almost thirty-five years. Koesler would follow Ridley's career as would almost every other literate American. But the two would not talk again until, a little more than a year before his premature death, Groendal would move back to the Detroit area and into St. Anselm's parish. There the two would meet again. They would have periodic conversations lasting well into the night.

And always, inevitably, Ridley Groendal would expound on his peculiar philosophy. A righteous morality that had earned him many, many enemies. A theology that Groendal equated with Christianity but which, in reality, was a stark mockery of the values that Christ taught.

It was only gradually that Father Koesler realized that this bizarre lifestyle of which Groendal boasted had begun on a day in June 1950. Not only had Koesler been present at the beginning, he had assisted in the birth. Even presented with all the evidence, he could scarcely believe it.

Part Five

The Canon

15

The gifts of bread and wine had been prepared. The altar, the Paschal Candle and the casket had been incensed. Clouds of incense had dissipated and spread throughout the church. Hours later, members of the congregation would still be able to detect its distinctive odor on their clothing.

The Funeral Mass, now called the Mass of Resurrection, proceeded into its most solemn stage. During the Canon—so called because it contained the standard, never-varying words of consecration—the same words spoken by Christ at the Last Supper are spoken by the priest over the bread and wine. According to Catholic faith, at the consecration Jesus Christ becomes present under the appearance of bread and wine.

With more than one priest present at Mass, it became a common post-Vatican II custom for all the priests present to concelebrate. All the priests would, as one, speak aloud the words of consecration. Several of the priests standing at the altar with the principal concelebrant —in this case Father Koesler—would take turns reading the various other prayers of the Canon.

With that sort of activity, Koesler could have predicted that his mind would wander again while others were reading. And he was correct.

His first distraction centered on Charlie Hogan. Koesler wondered whether Charlie would join in the concelebration. Even though, in the words of Church law, he had been "reduced to the lay state," doctrine held that "once a priest, always a priest." Technically, Koesler thought, Charlie had the power to consecrate, though formally he was forbidden, under ordinary circumstances, to exercise that power. So if Charlie concelebrated quietly from his pew, Koesler guessed it would be valid but illicit. He also guessed that Charlie wouldn't give much of a damn about liceity.

Charlie Hogan had plowed ahead a steady four years behind Koesler in the seminary. So that when Koesler was ordained a priest in 1954, Hogan was graduating from Sacred Heart Seminary College. Just where Koesler and Groendal had been when "the incident" had occurred.

In time, almost everyone forgot what had happened between Groendal and Hogan. As far as other seminarians were concerned, punishment had been administered and the matter was finished. Hogan had been grounded from Easter until summer vacation began. And Groendal had been expelled. Officially, he had resigned. But everyone knew.

At least three people never forgot: Groendal, Hogan, and Koesler.

For Groendal, the incident was one of the straws that had broken his emotional back and helped beget his new philosophy and lifestyle.

It had an intense effect on Hogan. The most significant manifestation was his withdrawal. He continued to participate in intramural sports, but only for exercise. Athletics no longer seemed to attract him. And winning was no longer either the most important or the only thing. Most of all, he distanced himself from the other students. He seemed to fear that any friendship could or would be construed as a "particular friendship." And he was determined that would never again happen.

Koesler remained part of this living memory simply because he was a friend of both principals. He had been a confidant of Ridley Groendal. He was to become a confidant of Charlie Hogan.

Hogan was ordained in June of 1958. He invited Koesler to preach at his first Mass the day after his ordination. The invitation was intended and taken as a great honor. Those invited to play a part in a first solemn Mass were among the priest's closest friends.

Thereafter, while they were by no means inseparable or even the closest of friends, Hogan and Koesler would be partners in an occasional round of golf or join the same group of clerical diners at the close of an invigorating day off.

What happened to Charlie Hogan and so many other priests of his vintage and younger was, as much as anything else, an accident of chronology. At least that was Bob Koesler's opinion.

Six months after Charlie's ordination Pope John XXIII ordered that two things be done. He called for a worldwide council of the Church. It would be known as the Second Vatican Council or simply, Vatican II. He also ordered a reform of Canon Law, which had been codified for the first and, to that date, only time in 1917. In 1983, twenty-five years after Pope John's mandate, Church law was finally recodified, though basically unaltered from its former content.

A phenomenon called "The Spirit of Vatican II" emerged just before the first session of the Council was convened. It swelled during the duration of the Council and continued well after the Council was con-

cluded. The "spirit" was not necessarily identical with the Council itself.

At the Council's close, the conclusions of the bishop-participants
were spelled out in sixteen officially promulgated texts. In them the
liturgy was dramatically changed. Ancillary documents contained
heady language, such as defining the Church as "the people of God"—
creating the impression that there was an element of democracy at the
root of the Church.

But, as time passed, practice proved that the functioning Church was
still that same old triangle with the Pope on top, the bishops well below
him, the priests making up the next inferior level, and the good old
"people of God" constituting the ground floor.

Of somewhat greater impact and of greater interest was the elusive
"spirit" of the Council. It was an emotion. It was an attitude. It was
self-startingly motivational. It paralleled the "spirit of change" that
marked relevant youth and adults in America in the sixties and seventies. It swept up, among others, Charlie Hogan. Charlie became a statis-
tic, one of the thousands to leave the priesthood.

Neither Pope John, who convened the Council, nor Pope Paul VI,
who concluded it, nor the bishops, who wrote the conciliar documents,
could have foreseen this unique worldwide exodus—so many priests
and nuns leaving their religious vocations.

They could not foresee it because it was not a logical conclusion of
the Council, but of the "spirit" of the Council, which came to expect of
the Council much more than it delivered. No sooner was the Council
concluded than did the official Church begin digging in its heels trying
to resist the changes promised by the "spirit" of the Council.

This official demand for obedience and retention of the status quo
flew in the face of a spirit of adventure, experimentation, and freedom.
This dilemma was the main contributing factor that helped propel thousands of priests and nuns into the lay job market.

Shortly after Hogan made his decision to leave, he phoned Koesler
and made an appointment to meet him for dinner. The priest was more
than a little surprised when Hogan arrived with a female companion.
Koesler and Hogan had dined together often, especially in the six years
Charlie had been a priest. Sometimes they had dined alone, sometimes
with others. But never with anyone other than priests and almost always all had worn clerical garb. Koesler felt a little awkward seeing
Charlie in civvies and with a woman in tow.

Hogan introduced her as Lil Schulte. As the evening progressed, it became evident to Koesler that she soon would be Lil Hogan. They were not unlike other engaged couples Koesler had known. But he was unfamiliar with an engaged couple one of whom was a priest.

Over drinks, salad, and entree, they told Koesler how they'd met and fallen in love. As they conversed, Koesler at first toyed with, then totally discarded, the idea of talking them out of marriage. It was obviously too late for that.

Both Charlie and Lil were activists. Drop a social problem area and they were involved in it. Racial justice, housing, the poor and elderly, peace, the environment, and so on. The "spirit" of Vatican II had led both into the active life. Their common interests had brought them together so often they had become friends. The questioning "spirit" of the Council had led them to wonder what was so exalted about the single life, particularly when two people loved each other.

Push came to shove as Charlie's pastor first objected to, then flatly forbade Hogan to get involved in extra-parochial matters. According to the pastor, there were plenty of problems in the parish—"and this *is* your assignment, Father"—without going all over kingdom come looking for trouble.

The Chancery was reluctant to act on Charlie's request for an assignment that would free him to get involved in larger questions. In those days, it was still a seller's market and priests were pretty well expected to go where they were sent and not go looking for anything extraneous. Much later, and as a direct result of the departing Charlie Hogans, priestly assignments would slip into a buyer's market. And priests would have much more to say about their own duties.

"So," said Hogan over dessert, "that's about how it stands."

"And you and Lil?" Koesler stirred his coffee, trying to cool it.

"We plan on getting married. But God knows when."

"What's the problem?"

"Problems!" Hogan corrected. "First off, I've still got this obligation of celibacy. I've applied for laicization, but that's a chancey procedure. It almost depends on how Pope Paul happens to feel on any given day whether Rome grants these requests to return to the lay state."

Koesler was pleased that Hogan was going through the laicization process. A goodly number of departing priests were not bothering with it. Later, dispensations would be delayed or denied seemingly as a matter of whim. Much later, under another Pope, dispensations would be virtually eliminated.

"What about the other 'problem'?"

Hogan winced. "Finances! Life gets mighty tough when Holy Mother Church removes her breast from your mouth."

Koesler glanced at Lil. She wasn't blushing. He wondered if he was. "That's right. You've got to get a job, don't you?"

"Only if we want to eat."

"How about you, Lil: Are you working?"

"Only as a volunteer, and at that not very often, Bob."

Ordinarily, Koesler preferred the use of his title, "Father," with the obvious exception of family, extremely close friends, and of course, his colleagues in the priesthood. Although it was new to him, another obvious exception would be the wife, or future wife, of a priest.

"She's working on her master's in social work in graduate school," Hogan explained. "Her parents are financing her education. At least they have been until now. We haven't told them about us. They're pretty traditional Catholics. I'm afraid if they knew, they'd disown Lil. It's got to happen sometime, but it'd be better later than sooner."

"Even if you get laicized? If they knew you were trying to follow Church law . . ."

"I don't think it would make much difference. We've heard them talk about it before. According to them, if the Church doesn't let people get unmarried, it shouldn't let priests get unpriested."

"But," Koesler objected, "the indissolubility of marriage is divine law. Celibacy is Church law. If there's a real marriage, the Church can't do anything about dissolving it because that's God's law. But the Church can do anything it wants about its own laws. If the Pope decides to dispense you from your obligations as a priest, he can certainly do it. Why would any Catholic object to that? Especially traditional Catholics; they, above all, should rubber-stamp whatever the Pope does."

"You're right, of course, Bob," Lil said. "And I don't know what it is with my parents. Just a blind spot, I guess. But they come down hard on priests who leave. That's just the way it is."

"Well, then," Koesler said, "how far away are you from your degree?"

"I've got most of my hours in. It's mostly the practicum that's left."

"And then you'll have an income. Won't that begin to take care of the financial problem?"

"Bob," Hogan said, "I'm not going to live off my wife's earnings! Besides, we want a family. When that happens, there'll be only one income, and it'll be mine."

After a moment's silence, Koesler said, "If you could use a loan, Charlie . . ."

Hogan grinned. "Thanks, Bob, that's real thoughtful of you. But what you could afford to loan us would be a hardship on you and wouldn't begin to take care of our needs. No, I've got some savings; that should tide me over till I get steady work. We're not in desperate straits. It's just that for a couple of good reasons, we're not able to get married yet."

"Well, isn't there anything I can do? How about your job hunt? How's that going?"

"I guess as well as can be expected. All those years in the seminary didn't prepare me for the job market. Well, to be fair, they weren't supposed to. It's just that neither business nor industry has any great need for a theology major. I didn't even bother trying an employment agency. I'd feel foolish. What would I say when they asked what I could do? 'Baptize'? 'Preach'? 'Anoint'? More likely I'd have to say, 'Nothing.' "

"Don't be so down on yourself, Charlie. You've had six years of experience in management of, in effect, a small business. You've got great organizational and leadership abilities. And, beyond that, you've got a fine liberal arts education. And you always liked to write. If you need a letter of recommendation . . ."

"I might, Bob. Especially from you as editor of the *Detroit Catholic.* 'Course I already applied at the *Free Press.*"

"You did? That's great! What'd they tell you?"

"That I'm not ready for the major leagues. It didn't surprise me. There's no reason to expect to walk out of a parish and right into a publication like the *Free Press.*"

"How about the *Detroit News?*"

"I'm not real fond of rejection. If I'm not ready for the *Free Press,* I'm in no better shape for the *News.* Anyway, the *Free Press* wasn't that discouraging. The guy in charge of their hiring told me I needed seasoning. He said I should try to get a job on one of the smaller papers. Get some experience. Build up a portfolio. It makes sense."

"Then maybe I can help you land a job at one of the suburban dailies," Koesler offered. "I do have some contacts with some of them."

"That I'd appreciate, Bob. What's discouraging is starting at the bottom of the job ladder at age thirty-one. I'm a solid ten or more years behind everyone else."

"Maybe, honey," Lil said. "But you've got experience the younger guys don't have. That's got to count for something." She turned to Koesler. "Charlie's going to write a book! He's told me the plot and I think it's terrific. It's got a Catholic background. How's that for using his experience!"

"That's great!" Koesler tried to catch her enthusiasm, but with some experience in the literary field, he had an inkling of the enormous obstacles that would confront Charlie.

"I'm not kidding myself," Hogan said. "It'll be rough. But I know what I'm up against and I'm going to give it everything I've got."

"We're going to make it!" Lil echoed his confidence. "And when we put it all together, Bob, we'd like you to marry us—if you don't mind."

"If I don't mind! Don't be silly. It would be an honor. You've got me so excited with your enthusiasm that I can hardly wait till you make it really big, Charlie. I can hardly wait to tell everybody that I knew you when."

They all laughed. But Koesler was the one who picked up the tab. As he did so, it occurred to him it might be a long while before these two loving people would be able to afford a night on the town.

16

Charlie Hogan left the priesthood and embarked on a new life. Meanwhile, Father Koesler had no way of knowing that a dark eminence would cast a relentless shadow over the lives of those perceived as archenemies.

Not long after Bob Koesler made his bogus visits to St. Joseph's Retreat, Ridley Groendal was discharged from the sanitorium. Groendal emerged from that institution changed almost antithetically. He had entered beaten, submissive, passive, defeated, and profoundly depressed. He emerged confident, assertive, controlled, crafty, and planning his resurgence.

Never again would he blunder, never again enter into any situation without careful preparation. Not if he could help it. And so he took a series of carefully calculated steps.

He cemented several previously casual friendships. While he would be leaving the Detroit area to establish an entirely new life, he did not want to lose touch. Specifically, he wanted to know precisely what was happening in the lives of the four people who, according to his lights, had brought him down. Soon, as offhandedly as possible, he commissioned his newly established friends as informants.

He was careful not to create the impression that his informants were spies. They were simply friends who would keep Groendal informed about the doings of other friends he would necessarily leave behind.

Greg Larson was a good case in point.

Larson: So, you're off to Minnesota. That's a big jump.

Groendal: I know, Greg, but it's a chance I can't turn down. A partial scholarship at the University of Minnesota and a job that'll take care of the rest of my expenses. It's just too good to pass up.

Larson: I guess. But we'll miss you. I was just getting to know you.

Groendal: If I could do it any other way . . . But . . . Anyway, I know I'm going to miss Detroit.

Larson: Geez, yeah. You've lived here all your life, haven't you?

Groendal: Uh-huh. Mostly around our parish, good old Holy Redeemer. That and Sacred Heart Seminary, of course. Golly! When I think of how much of me is wrapped up in those places!

Larson: It's a shame, just a rotten shame that you've got to go. But you'll be back, of course.

Groendal: I don't know, Greg. It just depends. It depends on where destiny leads. I'll just have to rely on God. But who better?

Larson: Jeez! Is there anything I can do to help?

Groendal: I don't think so, Greg. At least I can't think of anything. Except, maybe . . .

Larson: What, Rid? Anything . . . you name it.

Groendal: Well, if it's not asking too much, do you think you could send me copies of the parish bulletin? Just so I can keep up with what's going on. Golly, it'd be fun even reading the altar boy assignments. Always nice to read those familiar names. Then, as the years go by, I'll be able to keep up with the marriages . . . who's having babies. There's no end to what a parish bulletin can tell you.

Larson: Sure, Rid; won't be any trouble at all. And if I see anything in the papers about the seminary, I'll include that too.

Groendal: Are you sure, Greg? Are you sure this isn't too much trouble . . . I mean, the postage and all . . .

Larson: Good grief, Rid, if I can't spend a few pennies a week for a friend, what kind of world is it?

Groendal: Well, old pal, I'm grateful. I just can't tell you how grateful. I can really depend on you. That's really something.

Larson: Jeez, Rid; think nothing of it.

Groendal: But I do think about it, Greg. I can't help it. I'm really depending on you, boy. Oh, and Greg, by the way, speaking of who's having babies, there's one in particular I'd be interested in. Remember Jane Condon? Redeemer, class of '50? You know her?

Larson: Well, not till recently, Rid (grinning mischievously). She would have just gotten lost in the shuffle if it hadn't been for . . . well, the rumors. You heard them too, eh? Well, I guess it must be so then. Jeez! Having a baby out of wedlock! Not many Catholic girls do that, eh? What about her, Rid?

Groendal: Well, she used to be a friend of the family. We kind of lost touch with her lately. But I learned about her condition. And . . . well, I tried to get in touch with her, but there was no response. I can understand it, of course. She's pretty embarrassed. I don't blame her. But I'm still concerned about her. Even though we haven't had much contact lately, I still care what happens to her. I mean, she was a family friend and all. I'd just like to know how she's doing . . . how this pregnancy comes out and all. Would it be too much trouble to keep me informed as to what happens with her? I'd really appreciate it. Of course, if it's too much trouble . . .

Larson: Don't be silly, Rid. (Soberly, since the girl turns out to be a friend of the Groendal family), I'll let you know exactly what happens.

Groendal: Thanks a lot, Greg. I'd ask my parents to do that, but they don't want to have anything to do with her. Now that she's in disgrace and all. You know how these traditional Catholics can be. It's not their fault . . . the way they were brought up. So, I'd just as soon my parents weren't involved in this. Just between you and me, buddy.

Larson: Of course, Rid, just between you and me.

And so it went. Jane Condon, Carroll Mitchell, David Palmer, and Charlie Hogan. Four enemies, four informants. It was not easy to firm four hitherto random relationships into four fast friendships. Nor was it easy introducing the underlying reason why Groendal wished to stay in touch with his newfound friends. But Ridley pulled it off.

Over the years, it was an unrelieved drag keeping up correspondence with the informants. They were, as far as Groendal was concerned, not especially interesting or witty people. But they were faithful. They wrote regularly with news of the city, or the parish, or the seminary, or other classmates. All of which they thought was where Groendal's primary interest lay. Almost as an aside, they would include news of their assigned person: Jane, Mitch, Dave, or Charlie.

One reason the informants were faithful was due to Ridley's careful selection of people whose prime virtue was fidelity. Another reason was Ridley's pained but faithful response to their letters. Still another reason was that as the years passed, Groendal progressed from student to successful journalist to celebrity. It was gratifying to the egos of four lackluster citizens of Detroit to correspond with a famous personality.

But fame did not come to Groendal quickly or easily. It came as the result of a combination of talent, hard work, and meticulous planning.

Groendal began at the University of Minnesota trusting no one and using everyone. He was not by any means always justified in suspecting the motives of others. But it didn't matter, not to him. For Groendal, it was cause and effect: a steady progression from one goal to another.

It did not take Groendal long to secure his bachelor's degree. Many of the credits he'd accumulated at the seminary college were recognized by the university. He went on from there to graduate school, majoring in English and journalism. Finally, he won his doctorate in English.

Along the way, he free-lanced for all four St. Paul and Minneapolis papers. After graduation, he was offered a teaching position at the university. It was an opportunity most would have seized immediately. But teaching had no place in his scheme of things.

Instead, he applied at the *Minneapolis Tribune,* one of the papers for which he had been a stringer. Because of the very satisfactory work he'd done in the past as well as the prestigious degree from Minnesota, he was given his own column outright, without having to go through apprenticeship as a reporter or staff writer. In no time, he turned his column into a commentary on the arts, concentrating on stage, music, and books. This, also, was part of his grand plan.

Fortune smiled on him in a special way when the Guthrie Theater opened in May of 1963, with George Grizzard in *Hamlet.* Much of America had been hoping that the illustrious Tyrone Guthrie would open his proposed theater in their community. He surprised nearly everyone by opening in the unlikely minimetropolis of Minneapolis.

It was not considered an unlikely site by Minneapolitans, who knew they had an extremely livable city but, lest they be inundated, were keeping it a secret. Drawn by the Guthrie, theater buffs throughout the country converged on Minneapolis. In the middle of all the hullaballoo was Ridley C. Groendal as the renowned local critic.

It didn't hurt. It helped him begin climbing the ladder to bigger newspapers and bigger cities. Not necessarily better, but always larger.

It was during the summer of 1965 that he learned from one of his Detroit informants that Charlie Hogan had quit the priesthood and applied for a job at the *Free Press.* It so happened that at that very time he was working at one of the Knight newspapers. The *Free Press* belonged to the Knight chain.

Most people would term that a chance occurrence; at most, fate. Groendal knew it was divine providence.

Inquiries revealed that the *Free Press* had recommended that Hogan gather experience before they would consider hiring him. This hiatus afforded Groendal the opportunity to sow seeds of doubt in the minds of the *Free Press* management.

It was done in subtle but judiciously repeated ways. It was so laughably simple: All he had to do was grab every reasonable opportunity to mention some fictitious flaw in the character or performance of one

Charles Hogan. After all, who would know Hogan better than a one-time schoolmate? And who better able to judge his journalistic talent than a fine arts critic with a now-respected track record?

As a result, Groendal effectively scotched Hogan's chances not only at the *Free Press,* but throughout the entire Knight chain as well.

Hogan, of course, knew nothing of Ridley's machinations. Hogan thought he was serving his time at the *Oakland Weekender.* He considered the months spent at that suburban weekly a purgatorial preparation. He completed assigned stories and initiated others with professionalism. He did not badger the *Free Press* to rescue him from veritable oblivion. He was patient. And confident that in God's good time he would move onward and upward.

In a little more than six months, Hogan's petition for laicization was granted. One obstacle overcome. He was not earning anywhere near the amount he considered necessary to support a wife, let alone children. Nevertheless, it was time. So, preparations were made for a modest wedding at St. Mel's parish where Father Koesler had helped on weekends while he was editor of the *Detroit Catholic.*

Koesler felt some misgivings about this wedding. He had had similar presentiments about scores of other weddings at which he had officiated.

It seemed that seldom was any wedding free of all anxiety. Sometimes a bride and/or a groom had a problem, such as immaturity or marrying on the rebound. At other times there was in-law trouble. Over the years, Koesler learned there could be as many problems affecting a marriage as there were people entering the institution. Rarely could a wedding be described as trouble-free.

At the same time, one could be, and frequently was, fooled. Some unions that promised doom survived quite well. While some that seemed made in heaven quickly became hell on earth.

Charlie and Lil admittedly had a lot going for them. They very definitely were in love and maturely so. They were a good age, not too young or too old. Granted, Lil's parents weren't crazy about having an ex-priest for a son-in-law, but at least they weren't making a fuss about it. However, neither set of parents was able to help financially. And that was the sore spot.

Lil was very close to getting her master's degree, after which she anticipated no serious problem getting a job. But that wasn't the plan. The scenario called for a family supported not by a social worker wife but by a journalist husband. Except that Charlie's salary needed a second opinion. If he lived frugally, he might have survived alone. In the school of hard knocks, he learned that two could not live as cheaply as one. Their combined incomes provided enough for themselves with little as a buffer.

To afford children, both Charlie and Lil would both have to keep working. But if they both worked, they did not think it fair to have children they could not personally care for. A dilemma.

There was no escaping it: Unless Charlie accumulated so many merit increases that he approximated the income of the publisher of the *Oakland Weekender,* or until he landed that job with the *Free Press,* there could be no children.

That was reality, and reality was Koesler's long suit. The money was not there to provide for a child, let alone children. And since Charlie and Lil plainly wanted a family, that was a problem.

However, neither bride nor groom, at the time of their marriage, viewed their future as problematical. Charlie was as certain as one could be that there would be a place at the *Free Press* for him.

Little did he know.

Little did he know that the tentacles of Ridley Groendal's vengeance had already touched him and would continue to close about him. Short of death, Groendal was determined never to let up. Already his clout was considerable. It was growing and would continue to grow. Feeding Ridley's ambition was the insatiable drive to destroy the hopes of those who had brought him to the nadir of his life at St. Joseph's Retreat.

Not long after the wedding Charlie decided it was time to bring the matter of the *Free Press* to a boil. By mutual agreement, the ball had been in his court. But he was certain the *Free Press* had had enough time to evaluate his work.

So, carrying his now swollen portfolio, he applied once more.

His application was accepted and he was told it would be carefully considered. And it was. It was, indeed, one of the more hotly contested applications in the memory of many in management.

In the end, it was not so much that Hogan lost as it was that Groendal had won. After all, how could the *Free Press* be expected to know that Groendal was lying?

The assistant personnel manager tried to let Hogan down as gently as possible. The man was motivated by the best of intentions. There was no opening "at this time." Maybe "sometime in the future." Excellent credentials. Perhaps a bit "overqualified" in some respects. Have you tried any other publications? Maybe that would be a good avenue to pursue . . .

In the end it would have been kinder to have dealt in the naked truth: Short of a miracle, Charlie Hogan would never land a job with a major journalistic publication if Ridley Groendal had anything to say about it. And insidiously, of course, he did.

As it was, tranquilized by the groundless hope engendered by the personnel department, Hogan continued to nurse the prospect of an eventual job with the *Free Press*. By the time Hogan was disabused of the possibility and began widening his job search, Groendal had become sufficiently powerful in the profession to, in effect, blackball Hogan's every attempt.

*   *   *

It happened shortly after what was to be Charlie's final encounter with the *Free Press*. While Lil was preparing an after-the-movie snack, Charlie picked up a paperback crime novel she had been reading.

A few evenings later, he finished it, then announced: "I could do better than that."

"Than what?"

"Than that book. I could develop a better plot and better characters than that guy did."

Lil smiled encouragingly. "Sure you could, Charlie."

"I'd have to change the setting. Give it a religious twist. Put some priests and nuns in it. Something like that."

"That's what they say: Go with what you know. Why don't you do it?"

Charlie shrugged and grinned. "Oh, I was just talking off the top of my head. I've never seriously thought of writing a book. Besides, I haven't got the time."

"This might be the best time for you to do it, dear. You're always saying that you're not working up to full capacity at the *Weekender*. So a book shouldn't be a major distraction. You could work on it little by little, in your free time. And the idea of giving it a religious background is neat. Not many could do it . . . not and carry it off. But you could."

"I don't know." He smiled self-consciously. In reality he was buoyed by her confidence. "That's a pretty gigantic task . . . I mean, a book!"

"Every book starts with the first word." Hey, thought Liz, I just might have coined a cliché.

So Hogan began writing a book, a mystery-adventure whose characters were mainly people he knew, and with a plot he thought had some unique twists.

A few weeks later, after Sunday Mass, Hogan bumped into Dr. Payne, a dentist and prominent member of the parish.

After an exchange of pleasantries, Hogan said, "By the way, Doc, guess what? I'm working on a Catholic murder mystery."

Payne pondered a moment. "You mean you think Catholics murder people differently than other murderers?"

Taken by surprise, it was Hogan's turn to ponder a moment. "No, it's not that, Doc. It's . . . well, there's a reason why it's a Catholic murder mystery, but I can't think how to explain it. . . . Wait, I've got it! Remember that old cop series on radio and then TV . . . the LAPD . . . Jack Webb . . . ?"

"Sergeant Joe Friday. 'Dragnet,'" Payne supplied.

"That's it! Very good, Doc. Well, there was this episode—maybe you remember it—where there was a theft of some drugs from a Catholic hospital?"

Payne shook his head.

"Well, Joe Friday was there to get 'just the facts, ma'am.' Except that the 'ma'am' he was getting the facts from was, of course, a nun, since it was a Catholic hospital.

"Sergeant Friday is interrogating the nun.

"Who might have had a motive for taking the drugs? A key? Access to the cabinet? Who was on duty? Were there any security precautions? Questions like that.

"The nun answers all Friday's questions. And when he's done getting all the facts, ma'am, she says, 'Have you solved this case yet?'"

"Friday says, 'Well, no, ma'am. We've just begun the investigation.'

"And the nun says, 'Father Brown would have solved it by now.'"

Payne laughed.

"And then," Hogan continued, "Friday's sidekick nudges him and says, 'Joe, I didn't know they had their own police force!'"

Payne laughed a bit harder.

"That's it, Doc," Hogan said. "That's why I'm working on a Catholic murder mystery: I've got my own police force. And it's a Catholic priest."

"Like Chesterton's 'Father Brown.' "

"And that's all I've got in common with Chesterton."

"That's enough," Payne said. "You're serious about this, aren't you, Charlie?"

"Un-huh. I'm running mostly on Lil's encouragement. But, I must admit, it's sort of Walter Mitty-ish to think that I might actually get this thing published. It's exciting to think I might be able to earn a living writing."

"Charlie, what do you think you're doing now?"

"Doc, I'm not 'writing' at the *Weekender*. I'm pushing words. And it's not a 'living.' This is different. Oh, I try not to get my hopes up, but it's hard not to. If I could make enough from books, Lil could quit her job and a lot of our dreams could come true. I'm trying not to count on this. But if it works . . .

"By the way, Doc, I haven't told anyone else. Let's keep it between the two of us. I don't want a bunch of people asking me all the time how it's coming."

Dr. Payne agreed, with a silent reservation. Surely Charlie Hogan wouldn't want his news kept from his good friend and one-time schoolmate Ridley Groendal.

Before leaving town, Groendal had entrusted the responsibility of keeping him informed about all that was happening in Hogan's life to Dr. William Payne. Groendal had taken great pains to explain his abiding interest in Hogan. Since Payne was a mutual friend, he could understand why Groendal would ask the favor. He could also understand the rather complex reasoning which demanded that this news-gathering be kept secret.

Dr. Payne took pride in his commission. He was doing a favor for both Groendal and for the man Groendal had promised to help in every possible way, Charlie Hogan.

Payne had faithfully reported to Groendal Hogan's overtures to the *Free Press*. The doctor attributed that vague promise of a future job at the paper to the good offices of Ridley Groendal. Someday, Payne hoped, Charlie Hogan would know what a friend he had in Groendal.

For now, the doctor could hardly wait to get home and write Groendal about Hogan's new venture into literature. Surely Ridley would want to be alerted. A budding author could use all the help he can get.

Payne shook his head as he walked briskly home. No doubt about it: There were very few people like Ridley Groendal.

17

Among those things that could be said of Ridley Groendal was that he did not wait around for opportunity to knock. At least he had not since he'd left the Detroit area and entered the University of Minnesota. From that time on, he was the master of his fate, the captain of his soul.

A significant number of men and women dragging their shredded careers behind them could testify to that. Some had befriended him at the university, some there had fought him. It didn't matter. Groendal had manipulated them all, trusted none of them, and used them indiscriminately as stepping stones to advance his academic life.

Once he had wrung out and discarded them, he scarcely ever thought of them again. They, however, never forgot him.

But while many plotted vengeance, none succeeded. Groendal left nothing to chance. He trusted none of his victims, before or after exploiting them. Ever vigilant, he was prepared for them at all times.

After all, hadn't Jesus been ever alert? How many times his enemies, the Pharisees, had tried to entrap him, but never successfully. Just one example of so many: when they challenged him on whether it was right to pay a tax to Caesar.

It was a source of constant frustration to the Jews that they were obliged to pay a tax to a foreign power. So, with their question, the enemies had Jesus on the horns of a dilemma. If he approved of the tax, he would needlessly have lost most of his following. Needlessly because it was not a relevant question, since the presence or absence of Caesar had nothing to do with his mission.

On the other hand, to oppose the tax would put him on a collision course with civil authorities—again needlessly. But he was ready for them. He asked to see the coin Caesar claimed as a tax. He demanded to know of his enemies whose image and inscription was on the coin. They could answer nothing but "Caesar's." "Then," he told them, "render to Caesar the things that are Caesar's. And to God the things that are God's."

Magnificent! But hardly something done in the heat of the moment.

Jesus consistently outsmarted his enemies because he was prepared for them. He anticipated them. He was ready for them at whatever time, theirs or his.

And so would Ridley Groendal be ready for his enemies. He would anticipate and defeat them. Just as Jesus had.

His enemies might find it hard to believe, but Groendal prayed regularly and frequently. However, his meditations were subconsciously programmed to fit his new lifestyle. In effect, he was not trying to conform his life to that of Jesus. Rather, he was "prayerfully" twisting the life of Christ to fit the new theology of Ridley Groendal.

Thus, Groendal climbed over the torpedoed careers of reporters, columnists, here and there an editor, staff writers, authors, playwrights, actors, musicians, musical directors, and such, across the nation.

The higher he climbed, the more human debris he left in his wake. And the more angry people he left behind, the more he was forced to keep looking over his shoulder. For his newly made enemies, sorely wounded, would not forget. Almost to a person, they sought revenge. While churning ahead toward the pinnacle of success, Groendal also needed to protect his rear.

Constant vigilance took its toll. Groendal began to suffer from high blood pressure. It would get worse. He comforted himself with the thought that Jesus probably had high blood pressure too, what with all the enemies he had.

Eventually, all this skulduggery won him the highest status of all, a place as one of the *New York Herald*'s fine arts critics. Ostensibly, his responsibility was to review the stage and serious music. But he was also a book reviewer. And though he was not in charge of the book section, due largely to his burgeoning reputation in the other arts, he quickly became the most influential of all critics—theater, music, or literature.

Along the way, he also learned that he was homosexual.

Until he left Detroit for the University of Minnesota, he'd had but two overt sexual experiences, one hetero-, the other homosexual. At that time, he'd been confused as to his own sexual preference.

At the university, it did not take long for him to establish that preference. At first, he had begun to date girls. He had the tentative attitude of sitting back to see what might develop. Some coeds found his gentlemanly passive behavior oddly stimulating. Some sought to fill the sexual void by initiating physical foreplay. He found that repulsive. They found his disgust contagious.

Briefly, Groendal considered the possibility that he might be asexual. That was what the seminary system of his day was programmed to produce. Was it possible his peculiar Catholic upbringing had accomplished in him what it aimed for in its priests—the assembly of a macho asexual?

No. He was gay. He had to conclude that his single episode with Jane Condon was a fluke. He had been passionately overcome by accident exacerbated by some mind-numbing alcohol. Once he gave the homosexual style a chance, it did not take long to know he belonged there.

But it was depressing. Oh, not the sexual expression. No, the impermanence, the ephemeral, little more than one-night stands. Something in him demanded permanence, indissolubility—a quality that was most elusive in the gay community.

When he finally made it to New York, he was determined things were going to change. Either he was going to find a stable relationship, or be continent.

Thanks to his superlative *Herald* salary, he was able to afford a sumptuous apartment in the heart of Manhattan. He was not far from St. Patrick's Cathedral. Although proximity was not a factor in choosing the Cathedral to be his parish. For Catholics, St. Patrick's was *the* prestigious church of New York City. A lot of time could be passed just in counting the deceased Cardinals' red hats hanging from the high ceiling. (One could count on it: Whoever was Archbishop of New York was pretty sure to be a Cardinal.)

The length of the nave of St. Pat's was one of those famous-but-smaller churches measured against St. Peter's in Rome. At one spectacular funeral Francis Cardinal Spellman was celebrant, Bishop Fulton J. Sheen preached, and Jim Farley and Fred Allen were two of the ushers . . . leading a Jewish gentleman present to whisper, "What a cast!"

St. Pat's always had lots of visitors. As far as tourists were concerned, there was only one Catholic church in all of Manhattan. Anyone could find it right across Fifth Avenue from Rockefeller Center.

One could go on and on . . . but St. Patrick's Cathedral was the one and only parish for the infinitely upwardly mobile Ridley C. Groendal.

He favored the early Sunday morning Mass—less crowded. Of course he never got the Cardinal at that time, usually just a monsignor or a bishop, but it was sufficient. The routine was early Mass, then one of the attractive, pricey brunches.

Attending the same Mass week after week, one gradually becomes at least casually familiar with the other regulars. There were many couples, a great number of young, middle-aged and elderly unaccompanied women, but not that many single men. Not as regulars.

Something about one solitary regular attracted Groendal's interest. Not only could he not help studying the man from time to time, occasionally he caught the stranger studying him.

Without words, with no conscious sense of purpose, the two began taking pews closer to each other. Thus, just before Communion, eventually they were able to shake hands during the greeting of peace. Groendal did not know what it was, maybe something in the man's eyes, that communicated tenderness and interest.

It began one Sunday, months after they had first noticed each other in church. They were leaving after Mass when the stranger dipped his hand in the holy water font and offered some to Groendal.

"I don't mean to be forward," Groendal said, "but would you care to join me for brunch?"

A look of extreme relief passed over the other's face. "I thought you would never ask."

They brunched at a nearby hotel. It was Groendal's choice. He sensed the conversation would be more important than the food. It was.

As they settled in and the waiter brought coffee, Groendal began. "I'm—"

"Ridley C. Groendal, fine arts critic of the *New York Herald*."

"How—?"

"Your picture is with your column, and I read you faithfully."

Groendal was pleased. "I regret I can't return the courtesy. You are . . . ?"

"Peter Harison. No reason you should know me. I too used to be a critic—for a chain of papers on the West Coast."

"And now?"

"Now, I'm vice-president of the Art Guild Book Club."

"Of course. Peter Harison. I've heard of you. I hope none of my reviews have compromised any of your selections."

"Oh, no, dear boy. We generally select books before they're published and reviewed. Although there have been times when we've taken a book and have gotten burned by your review later. Fortunately we can always find somebody's favorable review to add to our hype."

Groendal laughed. "I suppose that's so true."

"I think," Harison continued, "what I like most about your opinions is that they're so original. Ridley—may I call you Ridley . . . ?"

"Rid. And please do."

"Rid, a case in point is your review last month of the *Brigadoon* revival."

"Oh, yes."

"I can't remember any other critic that took the musical itself apart. The only thing one ever gets from a presentation of a war horse like *Brigadoon* or *Oklahoma!* or *Carousel* or any of that ilk is that the voices were good or bad, the staging was inventive or inadequate, the sets were imaginative or pedestrian, and so forth. Nobody, but nobody looks at the vehicle itself. That's what I find exciting about your reviews."

Groendal beamed. "Well, it's true. The music is second-rate, sometimes third-rate . . . and has been vastly overrated through the years. Simplistic melodic lines and no development at all. One of those things where if Freddie Loewe hadn't had his name on it, no one would ever have heard of it. And the story line . . . incredibly unbelievable!

"I suppose it is possible to want us to imagine, in an excess of fictional credulity, that there could be a little village in Scotland that sleeps away a hundred years between each working day. But to think a modern-day New Yorker would choose to enter that never-never land is just preposterous!

"And it's not even a matter of being swept up in the emotion of the moment. The hero makes his mature decision to come back to the real world and let Brigadoon sleep away the next century. Then Lerner asks us to believe that after returning to civilization for a while, he would, after plenty of time for mature deliberation, return to Scotland and voluntarily lose himself in the village forever—never to see civilization again! Well, really! Every time I'm subjected to that drivel I feel like yelling out, 'Don't do it, Tommy Albright! Think it over! It's not worth it!' "

They laughed.

"You're right, of course, Rid. But most critics wouldn't have the nerve to write it. You did!"

"And I paid for it. Peter, you have no idea how many idiots there are out there who are willing to accept something as senseless as *Brigadoon.* But I heard from them . . . all of them, I think."

They laughed together and enjoyed their time together. By Groendal's gourmet standards, several dishes were unforgivable. But in honor of this occasion, he forgave.

Before parting, Harison eagerly accepted Groendal's invitation to accompany him to the Met's new staging of *La Bohème* that week. Groendal would not like it. But then, Groendal did not like *La Bohème* itself. In honor of Harison's being with him and sharing his dislike of the opera, Groendal wrote a particularly scathing review. So biting, indeed, was the critique, that it was all the company could do to prevent "Rodolfo" from going down to the *Herald* and punching Groendal in the nose.

The following Sunday, Groendal and Harison sat next to each other at the Cathedral. It took no time for their mutual discovery that each was gay. And not much more time to be convinced they were in love. Blessedly for both, it was evident from the outset that this was no ephemeral fling. It was the real thing, permanent and indissoluble.

If any law would have recognized their marriage, they would have entered into that solemn contract. Since no law would legitimize their union, they exchanged vows quietly and privately in a side chapel of the Cathedral with no one but God in attendance.

They became conversant with each other's history. There were no secrets between them.

Unlike Groendal, Peter Harison had learned early on that he was gay, and had suffered accordingly, especially since he was a Catholic. After being humiliated, ostracized, and beaten, Peter opted for the closet approach.

In fear for his very life, he stayed in that closet, venturing out only most infrequently and guardedly. Occasionally, he would try a gay bar. But his experience in that milieu was no different from Ridley's. One-night stands, brief encounters, guilt, disappointment, and danger.

As a result, he, like Groendal, had virtually retreated from social contact. Peter was quite positive that no one at work was aware of his sexual preference. He had never before had the happiness he now shared with Ridley Groendal.

Groendal, on his part, held nothing back of his life's experience. As a lad, Peter had thought long and hard about the priesthood. But just about the time he would have entered the seminary high school he discovered his homosexuality. With that knowledge he decided—and correctly so at that time—that a religious vocation was doomed.

Harison got to know the four pivotal characters in Ridley's life about as well as Groendal himself knew them. Not unlike couples anywhere, Ridley's friends became Peter's and vice versa—and the same could be said for enemies.

Together, they decided that Peter could be a help in Ridley's insatiable drive to square things with Charlie Hogan, just in case Charlie managed to produce a manuscript.

Granted, neither of them could control the various editors at the various publishing companies directly. But it was not difficult to pass the word that Charlie Hogan was an ungrateful wretch, difficult to deal with, a problem to edit, and more trouble than his work was worth. There were even aspersions regarding his honesty, and someone—no one ever knew who—even started the rumor that he was (a) a Marxist, and (b) a pederast, and (c) a wife-beater.

Unfortunately, Harison could be of little more than moral support in the case of Groendal's vendetta against Mitchell, Palmer, and Condon. But Peter was assured by Ridley that he could handle the stage and musical fronts by himself.

Revenge against Jane Condon was problematical, since Jane had not gone on to any professional platform. Yes, Jane was a problem. But then, she always had been.

*   *   *

If Ridley Groendal had not left Detroit to establish himself in Minnesota during the summer of 1950, he might well have become part of the ugly scene in the Condon house when Jane could no longer hide her pregnancy.

The altercation between Jane and her father was loud, acrimonious, and the subject of subsequent gossip. It was reported to Groendal by Greg Larson, the scribe Ridley had appointed to keep him apprised of Jane and her delicate condition.

The explosion came in July. Jane, who had passed off her weight gain as being caused by compulsive eating because of the school load, confessed to her mother what she already fearfully suspected. Jane had counted on her mother's discretion. It was a misplaced trust.

When informed of the situation, Mr. Condon cursed and yelled and threw things, as Jane cowered.

"I ask you, Martha," Condon ranted at his wife, "what the hell good did it do to send this girl to a parochial school? Did it do any good? Well?"

"Now, John, don't be too hard on Jane." Mrs. Condon immediately regretted having told her husband, though even in hindsight she could think of no alternative. "She's had to carry this secret by herself all these months."

"She's not only been carrying a secret all these months. She's also been carrying somebody's bastard kid! You were the one who insisted we send her to Holy Redeemer. I wanted to send her to McKinstry . . . pay for it already with my taxes; why not use the goddam school? But no; she's gotta have a *Catholic* education! Paid for her goddam education twice and look what it got me: A goddam bastard kid!"

"John, watch your language. The neighbors can hear."

"Watch my language? Watch my language! Your slut of a daughter is the whore of the block, and now everybody will know it, and you tell me to watch my language! Ha!"

"John, we've got to be sensible about this. We've got to be rational. We've got to decide what we're going to do. No, please be calm."

"Calm, is it! When did you do it, whore?" Condon addressed his daughter. "When did it happen?"

Jane did not answer. She curled up more tightly on the sofa where she had retreated at the beginning of the tirade.

"No answer! I'll tell you when it happened: It happened New Year's Eve. It's the only time we left you alone in the house. And you said you were gonna have someone over. Boy, you sure had someone over! Remember, Martha, I pointed out some stains right there on the carpet New Year's Day. But you passed them off as nothing. Nothing! That's the spot right there where our bastard grandchild was conceived."

He waited, but neither his wife nor his daughter said a word.

"You wanta know what we're gonna do about it, Martha? I'll tell you what we're gonna do about it: We're gonna find out just who the father of this bastard is. We're gonna find him and we're gonna make him pay! That's what we're gonna do!"

At this point, Jane was grateful for any small favor. She had gone numb when her father pinpointed New Year's Eve as the time of conception. He was correct, of course. She couldn't believe her luck that he didn't know who the father was.

She had expected Ridley to do the honorable thing. But when he baldly refused and then, on top of everything else, had that nervous breakdown . . . well, she had determined that as messy as this situation was, she was not going to further roil it. She had no intention of dragging Ridley into a knockdown battle. That would be a confrontation doomed to failure.

She had absolutely no intention whatsoever of telling her parents who had fathered her baby.

However, as determined as Jane was not to tell, so resolute was her father to find out.

"Who was it?" he shouted.

"I won't tell you! I can't tell you!"

"You can tell me as long as you can talk. Which is not gonna be much longer if you don't tell me! Who was it?"

"No!"

"Goddamit, yes! Who was it?"

Jane clutched herself tighter and said nothing. If she could have, she would have become a small ball of fluff and blown away.

"Who?" Condon grabbed a table lamp, yanking the plug out of its socket. He threw the lamp. It glanced off Jane's shoulder and pitched over, shattering on the floor behind the couch.

"John!" Mrs. Condon shrieked.

But John was quite beside himself. Mouth foaming, he hovered over his daughter. "Who was it? Answer me, whore! Who was it? Who? Who? Who?" He began striking Jane about the shoulders and back, the only areas she'd left exposed.

Martha Condon leaped on her husband's back in an attempt to wrestle him away. The two fell in a heap to the floor. She used all her strength to hold him down.

"Then get out!" he shouted from his prone position. "Get out! Take your bastard baby and get out! I paid my good money so you could go to a Catholic school. And what did you learn there? How to make a bastard baby! If you think I'm gonna spend a nickel so you can give birth to that thing while the father gets off scot-free, you got another thing coming! Get out! Get out! Get out! You got an hour, and then I don't ever want to see you again!"

Condon struggled to his feet and stormed out of the house.

Jane and Mrs. Condon spent some time sobbing in each other's arms. At last there was no alternative. They packed as many necessaries as Jane could carry, and she left. But not before her mother made her promise to keep in touch. Mrs. Condon in her turn promised that she would try to help in every way she could. In tears, they parted.

From that point, it would have been difficult for Greg Larson to follow Jane Condon's story. However, as luck would have it, Jane's mother, in dire need of a confidante, unburdened herself to a sympathetic neighbor, who, though close, was not close-mouthed. The news, having reached one ear, soon reached many—including that of Ridley Groendal's faithful correspondent.

Jane thought it would be a good idea to leave town. The priest she consulted agreed. He put her in touch with the Department of Catholic Charities for the Archdiocese of Chicago. They arranged for her to stay with a family there until birth. It was not a pleasant experience, but then, nothing in this entire affair had been.

At about the time school started for Ridley Groendal in September, Jane delivered a baby boy. She would never forget the shock when first she saw and held him. He had slanting eyes, a short broad skull, and broad fingers. He was a Mongoloid . . . a Down's Syndrome baby.

That was enough for Ridley Groendal. It couldn't have been his child. If there had been any doubt, and there certainly wasn't in Ridley's mind, all uncertainty was dispelled when Jane produced a defective child. Groendal, without the need for corroborating evidence, knew he never would have fathered a deformed child.

That could well have been the end of his vendetta against Jane. There was no question that she had suffered and that she continued to hurt.

She was cut off from her parents. Her father would have nothing to do with her. When he learned of the condition of her child, he drew a strange satisfaction from the tragedy. It was God's punishment. John Condon was not a religious man. But he could tell divine retribution when he saw it, by God!

Mrs. Condon was distraught. But she was helpless. Her husband forbade her to help her daughter or her grandchild. And so, in a show of obedience, she did nothing overtly. Secretly, she sent as much money as she could scrape up to Jane as the girl moved from place to place trying to survive.

Even for one bent on vengeance, this suffering surely should have been enough.

It wasn't enough for Groendal. That the child was Mongoloid was God's hand. He had punished her for having a child out of wedlock. That was clear enough. Groendal had no idea whether the child's father was likewise punished. He of course had no idea who the father was. But if Jane had set her trap for the unlucky fellow as she had for Groendal, it probably wasn't the real father's fault.

The point was that whether or not the father of the child had been punished, the mother—Jane—had been chastised by God, but not by Groendal. And since Jane had done her part to ruin Groendal's life, he owed her. And he would repay.

But how?

He was at a loss to invent a retribution that would reach Jane. She seemed to be at the bottom of a barrel. In disgrace, in poverty, with no employment, nowhere to turn, and a Mongoloid infant to care for.

It seemed that fate had foiled Groendal. Even if Jane were able somehow to reach a level of survival, she still would not fall under his sphere of influence. She was not a professional and showed no promise of ever becoming one. She was no actress. She was no playwright. She would never be on the stage or contribute to it. She was not literary. She would write nothing that he might be able to destroy. And if she did come up with some story, it would have to be an "as-told-to" book. And to whom would she tell her story? No one would be interested.

Finally, she was no musician. So there would be no musical career for him to shoot down.

Beyond these boundaries, what could he do? Supposing she got a job as a clerk in a department store. What could he do—complain to her supervisor that when they had been considerably younger, she had seduced him? So what?

Frustrating.

But among Ridley's strong points were patience and perseverance.

Actually, his most difficult task at this time was to keep Greg Larson on the case. There just wasn't much to report. And what news there was was so depressing that Larson was tempted to write only happy news to Groendal.

Ridley was in no position to argue against whatever Larson chose to write. The idea was to keep him going until something broke, as Groendal hoped, prayed, and knew it would.

As it turned out, Jane did exactly what Groendal supposed she might. She returned to Detroit and got a job as a salesclerk in Hudson's department store. With this and the little her mother was able to pass on surreptitiously, Jane made ends meet. There was almost nothing else in her life. She rarely splurged on entertainment of any sort. She couldn't afford it.

She was still attractive, but she never dated. Her life revolved around her son. Outstandingly lovable and sweet, as many Down's Syndrome children are, he needed Jane constantly. And so, outside of the times she had to leave him with a sitter while she worked, Jane spent nearly every free moment with him.

Down's Syndrome children frequently have health problems that reduce the normal life span. Jane's little boy, Billy, lived ten years. And then he broke her heart once more and died.

Billy's death did not move Groendal one way or the other. He was interested only in what might happen next.

According to Greg Larson's infrequent but faithful letters, nothing much happened next. Jane kept her sales position at Hudson's. Her social life remained a cipher. She went out infrequently, as far as Larson could tell, usually with "the girls."

Groendal found maintaining the correspondence with Larson more and more taxing. Jane's life—Ridley's sole genuine interest in this communication—seemed to be going nowhere.

It happened in March of 1964. Jane was thirty-three. She got married. In old St. Mary's downtown, near the apartment complex where she lived. Somehow the courtship had escaped Larson's notice.

The event piqued Ridley's curiosity. At first blush, the marriage did not appear to lend itself to any purpose Groendal had in mind. Jane's husband, William Cahill, was a skilled worker at a Ford automotive plant. Groendal could not wreak revenge on Jane through her husband. Jane as a sales clerk, and William, as an automotive worker, were outside the sphere of Ridley's influence.

But once more Groendal's patience and preseverance paid off. A little more than a year after their marriage, a daughter was born to Mr. and Mrs. William Cahill. She was to be their only child.

Here was a distinct prospect. How better to get revenge against Jane than through her daughter, her only child. The potential increased when Larson was finally able to send a photo of Valerie Cahill, age seven, on the occasion of her First Holy Communion.

She was, by anyone's standards, an outstandingly beautiful girl. With her childish yet evident comeliness and charm, there was a possibility that she might choose to be an actress.

Ridley's prayers paid off. Through her high school years, Valerie was not only the most desirable girl on the Redford High campus, she was the staple star of virtually all the plays staged by the school. In three out of four major stage presentations—*Arsenic and Old Lace, Meet Me in St. Louis,* and *Annie, Get Your Gun!*—Valerie played a female lead.

Annie, Get Your Gun! was the annual school play during Valerie's senior year. For that, Ridley Groendal actually returned to Detroit. He attended one performance of the musical, taking care not to be noticed or recognized.

From far back in the crowd, Groendal was able to spot Jane. Her hair was now entirely gray. But she'd kept her figure. Groendal had not seen her since that Sunday afternoon in the park those many years ago. From the distance that separated them, he could see no great change in her. A more mature way of walking and moving, perhaps, but he would have recognized her anywhere. And, my God, he thought, it had been more than thirty years!

If he had seen her at close range, which he would never again do, he would have seen the difference. It was in her eyes. They reflected the suffering, sorrow, and hard times she had undergone.

The man with her had to be her husband. They took each other for granted after the fashion of long-married couples. He certainly was nondescript.

Groendal had no fear of being recognized. Though his photo appeared frequently enough in New York and national publications, who would expect him to be attending a high school presentation in Michigan? And even if any present thought they might know him, they would dismiss the idea out of hand. What would a nationally famous critic be doing *there?*

The only one who could undoubtedly recognize him—and perhaps even guess why he was there—was Jane. But she and her husband were occupied greeting friends and acquaintances.

The lights dimmed; those still in the aisles scrambled for their seats.

The "orchestra"—piano, drums, and bass—struck up an abbreviated version of the overture. Groendal sighed and slumped in his seat. He was going to have to endure the tortures of purgatory. But he had already determined that it was worth the discomfort to see and hear his next victim. And there was always the chance that it might be a better than average performance.

Alas, it was what one would expect based on the age of the actors. Blown cues, misread lines, vibratoless voices, awkward interaction. Scenery and costumes obviously made by the loving and unprofessional hands of proud parents, relatives, and classmates.

With one glowing exception: the lead—Annie Oakley—Valerie Cahill. She was good. Not just the promise of developing into an adequate actress. She was good right now. If she had been Jane's first child, Groendal might have considered himself the girl's father. But that little mistake of nature? Forget it.

At intermission, Groendal buried himself in the program. Carefully, he studied the brief biography of Valerie Cahill. Unlike classmates headed toward college, Valerie intended to get right into show business while working on a college degree in her spare time.

Right into show business, eh? Delightful. We'll see about that!

Part Six

Communion

18

Mass is, essentially, a reenactment of the Last Supper. As that event is narrated in the three synoptic Gospels, the setting is the ceremonial Passover meal. After that dinner had been completed, Jesus took bread and wine and told his Apostles to eat and drink. *"Take this and eat it, this is my body."* And, *"All of you must drink from [this cup], for this is my blood, the blood of the covenant, to be poured out in behalf of many for the forgiveness of sins."*

The reenactment is set not at a dinner but in a liturgical rite that has evolved very slowly over the centuries. At the Last Supper, the words of consecration were followed immediately by the eating and drinking of the bread and wine. In the Mass, the two rites are separated by many prayers.

The Communion Rite begins with the Lord's Prayer, which is followed by the greeting of peace. Members of the congregation are urged to turn toward each other, shake hands, and offer a prayerful greeting, ostensibly wishing each other the peace of Christ.

At the appropriate time in this Mass of Resurrection, Father Koesler announced the greeting of peace. This was taken up with enthusiasm by the priests in attendance, and with restraint by the laity.

Koesler shook hands with several of the priests concelebrating with him in the sanctuary. Then he walked down into the nave of the church to greet some of the laity, certainly Peter Harison.

Koesler paused momentarily at Ridley Groendal's coffin. Briefly he visualized Ridley's mortal remains as last seen before the casket was closed. Koesler remembered Ridley as he had lived. The two of them as young boys sharing their secret hope of becoming priests. Koesler's dream unalloyed; Ridley torn between becoming a professional musician and a priest. That dilemma solved for him when Dave Palmer sabotaged the musical career with a deliberate, if childish, trick. Then his seminary progress seriously threatened when Carroll Mitchell discovered Groendal to be a plagiarist, even though, in Ridley's view, Mitch was the cause of the incident. Groendal's priestly vocation finally ending with a one-sided homosexual "relationship" with Charlie Hogan. Again, Groendal managed to blame Hogan for that disaster.

Finally, what Groendal considered the disgrace of a nervous breakdown, triggered by Jane Condon's pregnancy. Once more, as far as Ridley was concerned, it was somebody else's fault, even though in actuality Groendal was undoubtedly the father of Jane's child.

A strange man, thought Koesler. If there was any consistency to his life it was that he seemed constantly prone to shift the responsibility and blame for his own actions to others. Maybe it made him a happier person. Certainly it was not a realistic way to go through life.

In point of fact, such behavior was Koesler's pet peeve. He had long since been disenchanted with those who refused to accept responsibility for their own actions.

Well, whatever. It was over. Ridley was gone. According to Koesler's belief, Groendal had been judged. But Koesler was of two minds about that judgment. He liked to believe that when we die we will be judged by Love.

It was a consoling theology offering almost infinite understanding and forgiveness. On the other hand, there was that admonition by Christ that on earth we should judge others with understanding and forgiveness—for we will finally be judged in the same way we judge others.

In all truth, Groendal had left no legacy of understanding, forgiveness, or even fair judgment. In any case, whatever judgment Groendal deserved from God had already been given to him. What more could Koesler do than remember Ridley and pray for him for whatever good that might do.

"May Christ's peace be in your heart today, Peter," Koesler said as he shook hands with Harison.

Harison could not speak. He merely nodded as tears—unique at this funeral—streamed down his cheeks.

As Koesler finished greeting as many in the congregation as possible in a brief time, his eyes swept the rest of the people. Smiling, he tried to communicate a peaceful wish to all. His gaze was arrested by the face of Carroll Mitchell. Koesler flashed the "V" for peace sign. Mitchell smiled and nodded, as if to say, "Yes, I am indeed at peace . . . now."

Koesler's mind returned to the seminary of his day. Then, the greeting was called "the kiss of peace." But it was about as removed from a "kiss" as possible. The "giver" placed his hands on the shoulders of the "receiver," who supported the other's elbows. The greeting was, *"pax tecum"*—"peace be with you." The response was, *"et cum spiritu tuo"* — "and with your spirit." Koesler, Mitchell, and Groendal had exchanged this greeting many, many times.

Koesler now wondered what might be on Mitchell's mind. Would Mitch be generous enough to wish that Groendal be at peace now in death? Koesler was fairly sure that Mitch himself felt a greater sense of peace. If there were any doubt whatsoever in Koesler's mind, that doubt would have been dispelled by a conversation the two had had recently.

Koesler and Mitchell had not crossed paths for many years. That was to be expected; they traveled in vastly different circles. It was difficult enough for Koesler to keep in touch with all his priest friends without keeping in contact with someone he once knew in the seminary—even if they had been, at that time, good friends.

Then, one day about two months before Ridley's death, they chanced to meet in downtown Detroit. Mitchell's wife was with him. It was midafternoon. The three found a quiet cafeteria where they could sit and visit over coffee.

It did not take them long to review their histories since last they had met. Mitchell was far more familiar with what had been going on in Koesler's life than vice versa. Koesler had been editor of the *Detroit Catholic* and had been involved in helping the police in several criminal investigations. So he had had some measure of publicity.

"Well, I've read about you, too," Koesler said. "Something about Hollywood?"

"Something about Hollywood," Mitchell repeated as if Hollywood had been a disease instead of a place. "Yeah, I go there from time to time. Screenplays. I go to L.A. either to write them or fix something somebody else wrote. It's a living."

"It's better than that," Lynn Mitchell amended. "It's a darn good living." She spoke with an unmistakable sense of pride in her husband.

Mitch chuckled. "At least we don't have to live there."

"You don't?" Koesler had no idea what screenwriting involved, but he was not uninterested in learning something about it.

"No. Generally, if I'm commissioned to write a screenplay, I do my research here or, if where the story takes place is vital, I go to the location. Whatever, I don't write in L.A.—unless of course that's the location of the story."

"But you must go to Hollywood sometime."

Mitch nodded. "When I finish the script. To present it to the producer and director. Once they read it and okay it, I get out of town until they start shooting."

"You've got to go back?"

"It changes."

"It does?"

"Once they begin filming, the script is likely to change by the day."

"After the producer and director already approved it?"

"Yeah, that's right. But that's a problem right there. I figure not only can't they write, they don't read very well, either. So when they get together with the actors, it gets kind of existential. The actor isn't comfortable with a scene. He or she wants a change in dialogue. Or the director wants to throw his weight around. So he calls in the writer and tells him to change everything."

"Why doesn't he change it himself?"

"Like I said, he can't write."

"So what do you do then?"

"I usually take the script he's hacked to pieces and let it rest a while. Then I retype it just the way it was and give it back to him. And," Mitch gestured offhandedly, "this time he loves it."

"But it's the same material."

"I told you: He can't read either."

"I'm beginning to see why you want to spend as little time there as possible."

"And," Lynn added, "Mitch is considerate enough not to insist that I go along . . . unless I feel I need a vacation, that is."

"A vacation from the kids?" Koesler asked.

"Thank you very much, Father." Lynn smiled. "From the grandkids."

Koesler was thankful he had erred on the diplomatic side of flattery. But he was also taken back. This couple was his age, almost exactly. They were grandparents. With no children and thus no grandchildren he never consciously thought of himself being of a grandfatherly age. Maybe it was because everyone—whether they were much older or much younger than he—called him "Father."

Or, perhaps because he had no family of his own, he could not appraise himself as most other people. In the mainstream of life, human beings begin as children, then they marry, have children, watch those children mature and marry. Soon there are grandchildren; perhaps great-grandchildren.

Seeing oneself reproduced through generations probably is nature's way of reminding one of the aging process—and a preparation for one's own death. The priest found that a rich thought. He would have to develop it in meditation sometime soon.

"What I can't quite understand," Koesler said, "is why with all your screenplays, I haven't seen your name in the papers more often?"

Mitchell shook his head. "That's something else, Bob. For one thing, a lot of the scripts I work on never see the light of day. I'm given the assignment to work up something original, maybe adapt something from a book somebody else wrote. So I do the job and nothing happens. Maybe they run out of money before or during shooting. Or maybe they get the whole thing in the can and can't find a distributor. Lots of things can happen."

He shook his head. "I know. I know. You thought every movie made gets shown. But no: Lots of times it stays in the can on the shelf of some producer's home or in some studio."

Afternoon drive-time rush hour was approaching. Koesler wanted to start for his suburb before the majority of downtown workers joined him. Too, he sensed that Mitch and Lynn had other things planned besides talking to him. He crumpled his paper napkin and dropped it in his empty cup. The others caught the signal and began preparations for leaving.

"Oh, by the way," Koesler said. "I meant to ask you about the stage —the legitimate theater. You must be involved in that."

Though the question had been uppermost in Koesler's mind from the moment he first recognized the Mitchells, it had slipped to the back with all the talk about movies. He would not have forgiven himself had he not asked about the stage. God only knew how long before he might bump into the Mitchells again.

From the look that crossed Mitch's face, Koesler realized he had broached a painful subject.

Lynn cleared her throat. "It's his first love, Father. It just hasn't worked out the way we wanted."

Koesler felt awkward. He shouldn't have introduced the matter. But how could he have known? "Well, that is too bad, Mitch. But then, you've got the movies. And from all you and Lynn have said, that pays pretty well."

Mitchell shrugged. "It's not the same. It's just not the same. The stage is where it's at. For one thing, the playwright is in command in almost the same way the author is in command of a book. You're reasonably sure going into it that if it's performed, some halfwit isn't going to mutilate it. On the stage, the director and actors usually enhance what you've written.

"And best of all, it's an act that lives. You make a movie and it's in a can—or these days in a videocassette. But it's like a body in a casket: It may deteriorate, but it isn't going to change. Ever been in a movie house after a particularly good picture ends and the audience applauds?"

Koesler nodded.

"Well, what for?" Mitchell continued. "The applause is instinctive. It's also futile. Nobody who had anything to do with making the movie is there to receive the audience's appreciation. The writer, the producer, the director, the actors, the technicians; they're nothing now but credits on the screen. The audience's reaction—good or bad—has no effect on the performance. It's all in the can. It can't change. It'll be the same performance yesterday, today, and forever."

"I think I see what you mean," Koesler said.

"Sure you do. On the stage, everything is just the opposite. It's why actors can get up there and play the same role day after day and scarcely ever get tired of it. Each audience is different. Each night is like opening night. The audience and the actors derive nourishment from each other. If the actors are tired or not giving everything, the audience senses that and reacts. It works every which way. An especially enthusiastic audience can inspire the actors. And the playwright—the playwright can know that every time the work is performed, a little unpredictable magic can happen."

"Not unlike a sermon," Koesler observed. "You give a lot and the congregation responds. Within the first few minutes, you know whether you've got them or not."

"Exactly! A live performance. A living thing."

"So," Koesler paused, "then, what happened? It's so obvious—just as I expected—that you're in love with the stage. What goes?"

Mitchell opened his hands on the tabletop. "A funny thing happened on the way to the theater."

"He has written plays, Father," Lynn said. "He's written excellent plays. It's just . . ."

"It's just that they haven't gone anywhere." Mitchell completed her sentence.

"Nowhere?"

"He means, Father, that none of them have made it to Broadway. Not even to Off-Broadway."

"Is Broadway that important?"

Since the previous move had proven a false departure, Lynn went for more coffee.

"It's heaven, Bob," Mitchell explained. "I've been in limbo, sometimes purgatory. But not heaven. Some of my stuff has been put on here —Wayne State, the Institute of Arts, U.M., M.S.U., places like that."

"I'm going to have to pay closer attention."

"Not your fault, Bob. Very low-budget stagings. Little quality publicity . . . with even less mention of the author.

"I've even gotten as far as some of the better places—outside of Manhattan, of course. Like the Long Wharf, the Studio Arena in Buffalo; Yale and the Goodman, and Steppenwolf in Chicago. But they barely get there. And when they do, they close quite promptly. Usually due to, or partially due to, poor to extremely bad notices."

"And they absolutely do not deserve those bad reviews." Lynn was back with coffee. "It all comes down to the Actors Theatre of Louisville!"

Mitchell snorted. "Lynn's got this thing—"

"Because it's true!"

"Well," Mitchell said, "we had been wondering over the years. You know, nothing was making any sense. Here I was with a successful, if rather anonymous, career doing screenplays. I mean, I guess that indicated I had some talent for writing . . . you know what I'm getting at?"

"I think so," Koesler said. "It isn't as if you were merely an aspiring writer. Good Lord, I've known so many of them. Some defensive, some aggressive—all out to prove that they can write. And some write very well. But they need somebody to affirm it for them. They need to be published. And with all those screenplays behind you, you don't need anybody to tell you you can write. You make a good living. You're a pro."

"Exactly. I've known all along I could write. Even in school—and stage writing is not all that different from screenwriting. I mean, it's virtually all dialogue—almost nothing *but* dialogue—stage or camera directions, no narrative.

"So, the question that's been hounding us is: If I'm as successful as I am with screenwriting, what's happening to playwriting?"

"And the answer, Father, was at the Humana Festival in Louisville!" It was evident that Lynn felt very keenly about this.

"I don't understand," Koesler confessed. "I'm afraid I'm not familiar with this . . . Humana Festival?"

"It's the new mecca for an entree to the theater," Mitchell explained. "It's run by Victor Jory's son . . . you remember Victor Jory, the character actor?"

Koesler nodded.

"The festival is just a little more than ten years old, but it's big, Bob. About eight hundred people attend—a good part of them critics and producers. The producers especially are looking for another *Agnes of God* or *Crimes of the Heart* or *The Gin Game*. And the critics are sharpening their stilettos. For the playwrights—none of them untried or unrepresented amateurs—it could be the start of something big.

"Well, last spring I entered the festival for the first time. You see, I've grown kind of content with life the way it's worked out. I'm satisfied to earn my living with screenplays and just dabble with the stage."

"I ask you, Father," Lynn protested, "isn't that a crime? This man normally couldn't care less about Hollywood. He lives for the stage. And he's talking about it as if it were an avocation. I mean!"

Mitchell smiled at his wife. "Anyway, my agent talked me into it—to enter a play I wrote last year. It's been staged a few places—one of the new requirements of the Humana. I didn't really expect that much from it. But, on the other hand, there's always hope."

"What he didn't expect, Father, was to be screwed!"

"Now . . ."

"What do you mean, Lynn?" Koesler asked. "What happened?"

"One of the critics there," Mitchell clarified, "was Ridley Groendal."

"Ridley!" Things suddenly began to get a lot clearer for Koesler.

"Yeah, Ridley. Lynn came up with a scenario that I'm afraid is stranger than fiction."

"It is not my imagination! That Groendal did everything he could to destroy you at that festival. And from what I learned, he's been doing the same thing for years, every chance he gets."

"Lynn . . ."

"It's true! I was the one who went around to the various producers, after I found out what he was up to in Louisville. Face it, Mitch, it hasn't been you all these years. It's been Ridley Groendal. Your plays have been good. It's been Groendal working hard and wielding all of his clout."

"I can't believe that, Lynn. Could you believe it, Bob? You know Ridley; hell, the three of us were classmates once!"

Koesler hesitated. "I don't know, Mitch."

"I can't bring myself to believe such a thing," Mitchell said. "To me, the biggest argument against it is motive: Rid would have absolutely no reason to do anything like this . . . I mean, what reason could he have? I've never done anything to him. If anything, on the surface at least, I owe him: After all, he got me booted out of the seminary."

Koesler betrayed a surprised look.

Mitchell laughed. "Oh, it's all right, Bob. I told Lynn all about my most daring escapade in the sem. In fact, when things are glum, we laugh about it.

"But I don't even hold a grudge about that anymore. Hell, I ought to be grateful to Rid, the way it worked out. If I hadn't been booted and told never to darken the seminary's door again, I would have missed out on Lynn and the kids and the grandchildren. And I owe all this to Rid and his scheming mind.

"And that's what it comes down to, Bob. I long ago forgave what he did to me. And I didn't do anything to him." Mitchell looked reflective. "And God knows I could have."

Catching Mitch's eye and directing his gaze briefly at Lynn, Koesler asked, "Have you ever told—?"

Mitchell shook his head. "No reason to. It's between Rid and me."

Interesting, thought Koesler. Mitchell had freely shared with his wife a most embarrassing and compromising incident that had happened to him. If he had been in Mitchell's shoes, he might have hesitated many times before telling his wife about having been in bed with another woman, no matter how innocent it might have been or how long ago it had happened.

Yet Mitchell told Lynn that, but hadn't revealed to her that the man she so heartily disliked, the celebrated critic, had once been guilty of a most deliberate and flagrant plagiarism.

Koesler's respect for Mitchell increased; he had done very well, indeed, at keeping secrets.

"What it comes down to, dear," Lynn said, "is that you can't think of a reason why that creep has done this to you. So, because you can't come up with a motive, you deny a proven fact. I talked to them! I talked to producers, directors, even other critics. Some of them weren't even all that aware of what had been going on until I came right out and asked. Then, almost all of them could recall times when Groendal had put you down, denigrated you, both personally and as a writer; made it evident that they would be fools or jackasses to stage any of your work, or even to be kind—much less fair—to you.

"He let it be known—made it very clear—that were they to ignore his advice, his future reviews—not only of your plays, but of all their productions in general—would be critical and belittling. And because he wielded a long pen—and a long memory—it would have taken a very gutsy—foolishly gutsy—director to cross him."

She turned to her husband. "These are the facts, whether you can find a motive for them or not!"

Mitchell didn't reply, though the conversational ball was definitely in his court. Finally, he said, "I can't help it. It just doesn't make sense . . . oh, don't get me wrong, Lynn; I don't doubt for a moment that the people you talked to said what you say they said. And I'm not ungrateful for all your legwork. But it just doesn't make sense. Maybe they're confused. Or maybe they've got an axe to grind with regard to Rid. Maybe that's it. I don't know." He looked at Koesler. "What do you think, Bob?"

"I don't know. It's hard to say. Rid always had a . . . different mind. It's just hard to tell."

"Hmmm. Well, you know him better than I do. Hell, you both came from Redeemer parish, didn't you? And now . . . God, now he's your parishioner! But I just can't see it."

"Well, it's very interesting," Koesler said. "Tell me, Mitch: Suppose it were true. Suppose what Lynn discovered is absolutely true. Supposing Rid has effectively blocked your whole career as a playwright. Just suppose, for whatever reason it's true. Then what?"

A long period of extended silence followed while all three pondered the question, What if . . .

"What if, eh?" Mitch said, finally. "What if Rid has actually blocked me from what I love most next to Lynn and the kids? What if he's done that?

"I'd kill him!"

Lynn laughed, a bit nervously. "Well, that just proves that Mitch can keep up his sense of humor."

They all laughed.

But Carroll Mitchell and Father Koesler both knew the laughter was not genuine.

19

"The body of Christ."
"Amen."

Father Koesler had been distributing Communion for slightly more than thirty years. Unlike many other priests, he never tired of it.

The distribution of Holy Communion had gone through many stages, as had almost every other ritual in the liturgy since the Second Vatican Council.

At the time Koesler was ordained, and for hundreds of years prior to that, Communion was given by the consecrated hands of a priest alone. Outside of the most dire emergency, no lay person ever touched a consecrated host. That was a time when there were, proportionately, more priests and fewer communicants than today. When the balance tipped in the other direction, the laity was urged to exercise the "priesthood of baptism" and become "extraordinary ministers" of the Sacrament. It was, Koesler believed, a variation of Parkinson's Law. In this case, lay sacramental functioning tends to multiply in direct proportion as there are fewer priests around to perform sacramental tasks.

The pre-Vatican II formula for distributing Communion was a comparatively long Latin invocatory prayer. Now, the minister of the Sacrament merely held aloft the consecrated host and announced, *"The body of Christ."* And the recipient responded with the affirmation, *"Amen."*

Koesler remembered well when that formula was in transition and the current form was in vogue but still in Latin. He recalled a Sunday when he presented the host to a young lady, saying *"Corpus Christi."* To which she responded, "Texas."

Gaffes like that could be expected but not foreseen. But it added a measure of innocent humor to what could easily become stuffy repetition.

The line of communicants kept coming. Evidently, there were a surprising number of Catholics at this funeral. Even though several priests were helping with the distribution, the time for giving Communion was proving to be unexpectedly long. Of course, it took longer now since communicants had the option of receiving under the form of wine as well as bread, and the chalice had to be wiped after each person sipped.

Koesler selected another wafer, held it over the brim of the ciborium and looked at the next communicant. It was Charles Hogan.

"Charlie, the body of Christ."

"Amen."

While he continued the distribution of Communion, Koesler's thoughts, as usual, wandered. Jogged by the memory of his conversation with Carroll and Lynn Mitchell, Koesler recalled a similar talk he had recently with Charlie Hogan.

That Hogan and Koesler had remained active friends was a little out of the ordinary. Generally, after leaving the priesthood, a man quite naturally traveled in different circles, made new friends. No longer sharing common interests, the resigned priest usually drifted away from former comrades. It was an understandable phenomenon. But with Koesler and Hogan it had been different.

That Koesler had been selected and invited to witness Charlie's marriage to Lil was evidence of the depth of this friendship. Seldom does a bride or groom know a priest well enough to request him to witness their wedding. But when such a request is made, it usually signifies some degree of friendship along with a good measure of respect.

This demonstration of friendship by no means ended with the Hogan's wedding. Koesler and Charlie met periodically. Occasionally Koesler would dine with the Hogans. The priest was aware that Charlie and Lil were far from wealthy. The fact that they were meticulous in keeping up their house and that they ate simple though nourishing meals did not conceal their comparatively spartan existence.

As far as Koesler could tell, Charlie's membership in a local health club was his sole "extravagance."

Several months ago, Koesler had joined Hogan at the club. On the agenda were a few games of racquetball, a swim and sauna. Not slated was a conversation about Hogan's material status, his work, his income, his prospects. The conversation did not take place until the sauna. The swim and particularly the racquetball had pretty well wiped out Father Koesler, who was breathing heavily while perspiring freely.

Hogan grinned. "Winded?"

Koesler barely nodded as, head bowed, he watched droplets fall from his face to his lap.

"You ought to do this more often, you know," Hogan said.

"What are you trying to do, kill me?" Koesler panted.

"It's good for you."

"Like the relatives of Don Quixote in *Man of La Mancha,* you're only thinking of me!"

"You're not fat, Bob. But you could lose ten pounds or so. And the exercise is good for you."

"I'm too old for this sort of nonsense."

"You're only four years older than I am; don't go pleading old age on me."

Koesler thought about that. He was determined not to add this much activity to his regimen. He just had to find some acceptable excuse. "We're gearing up for the Fall Festival. I've got too many things going on in the parish now." He glanced at Hogan to gauge the effect of his words.

Hogan shook his head. He would not accept the priest's attempted evasion. "Come on; I know you better than that. Other pastors may worry themselves sick about how much money the festival will make. Not you. If anything, you'll be concerned about whether the folks are having enough fun with the games and rides."

Koesler shrugged. He couldn't argue the point.

"It's a nice attitude," Hogan continued, "and I admire you, I guess. I also envy you."

"Envy me?"

"It's a healthy attitude. Other pastors are nursing ulcers and worrying themselves sick over finances. They've got to keep the damn school open or keep the church heated, or air conditioned. They've got to pay for a religious education coordinator. And on and on and on."

"Those are realistic concerns," Koesler said.

"But they're not yours," Hogan insisted. "Oh, I'm not saying you're not concerned about all those things. But they don't eat you up. If the people want a school, they'll support it; otherwise, it'll close. It's their school; it's their choice. No?"

"Well, isn't that realistic? It *is* their school. The parishioners built it long before I got there. It may be there long after I'm gone . . . maybe. But my job is to make sure we offer a quality Christian education. It's not my job to finance the thing. No?"

"Maybe," Hogan said. "But you'd never know that by the way other pastors do it. When it comes to finances, you are about the most laid-back person I know."

"Really!"

"And that's what I envy. I think you're correct in your basic approach to finances. Priests, generally, don't have to be terribly concerned about personal income. Not unless they have to support an indigent relative, or unless they're living way over their heads.

"Maybe the ones who worry themselves sick over collections and festivals are concerned about their parishioners' finances. Who knows? The thing is, they don't have to get all worked up about their own income."

"Aren't you generalizing, Charlie?"

"Bob, I've lived both lives. I know. Let me tell you, the overpowering feeling you get when you leave the priesthood is that you are letting go of maybe the greatest security in the world. And you're trading it for maybe the greatest insecurity in the world."

"Is your experience typical?" Koesler spoke hesitantly.

"Maybe, maybe not. I know a lot of guys who quit the priesthood who are doing a lot better than I am. I also know some who aren't doing nearly as well. But if it weren't for Lil and her job at the clinic . . ." Hogan added more water to the hot coals, decreasing visibility to near zero.

Koesler was too tired for more than token objection. "But you're working, Charlie. I see your byline all the time. That's pretty steady."

"It just seems as if I get published a lot because you're aware of my name on articles. And, fortunately, I do get a lot of assignments in local publications. But that's partly because they like the luxury of using freelance writers. Then they're not stuck with a union wage and they also get out of paying the fringes."

"But you do get paid."

"They pay me." Hogan sounded as if he were smiling. Koesler couldn't tell; the steam was too intense.

"But not enough?"

"It's not so much a case of enough or not enough. It's not consistent, not dependable, not predictable. That's it. There's no foretelling what I'll be able to scrounge up. Some years it's pretty good, sometimes not. Sometimes I earn more than Lil. But one thing's for sure: We wouldn't survive without her health care package that covers both of us."

"But you are surviving—and a bit better than that." Koesler was still trying to find a silver lining. "You do get your assignments. And Lil's insurance takes care of the both of you."

"You don't understand. Or maybe I'm just not making myself clear.

"When a guy leaves the priesthood, he isn't prepared for much of anything else. Just remember our education. Plenty of the classics. An excellent liberal arts program. Very good so far. A nice broad base on which to build.

"But, after that, we began to separate ourselves from the rest of humanity. Along about college, certainly postgrad, the others began zeroing in on a career: law, premed, accounting, journalism, mechanics —you name it.

"Well, so did we prepare for a career, but a unique career, administering sacraments, preaching, instructing in the Catholic faith. Nothing the world is interested in. But then, we weren't preparing for life in the mainstream. See, when you leave the priesthood, necessarily you enter the mainstream—the very place that has no room for you. So you begin to scramble. You've got to make a living in a hostile environment."

Another spa member entered the sauna. He moved toward the far end, so as not to inhibit their conversation. But, as he passed the hot coals, he dumped a large supply of water on them. The steam rose immediately. It took Koesler's breath away for a moment. He waited till he was sure his lungs were not seared before speaking again.

"Charlie, you make it sound like it's Us against Them—that everybody outside the priesthood is lined up, waiting for one of us to leave so they can pounce on us."

Hogan coughed. Apparently the steam had gotten even to him. "Okay, that's a bit melodramatic. But look at it this way: I left in my mid-thirties. At that age, my peers, with a few exceptions, were already working away at whatever they were going to do for a living for the rest of their working lives. Guys in business were up to middle management —or higher.

"They've got their homes, maybe their second or third home. They've got their families, maybe all the kids they're ever going to have. All of a sudden, here I come. I join them, only I've got nothing. I'm starting where they did when they were in their late teens, early twenties. Except that I'm in my mid-thirties. And starting on the bottom, I'm competing against guys in their teens and twenties.

"So I had to scramble, see? I figured I'd never catch up if I started in something based on strict seniority like the postal service or some other civil service job. On the other hand, I'm no good at selling. So that cancels something like insurance. I chose newspapering because it takes only four to five years to reach top scale in a union wage and also because I knew I could do it."

"But that's a crowded field, Charlie."

"But I knew I could make it. I still know that. Hell, I'm making it right now. My pieces are getting published regularly. Seldom do I get any rejections.

"Oh, I can do it, all right. It's just that I can't do it where I want to do it—working steady at a major newspaper, where I could bank on a regular paycheck and good income. Where I could support Lil without her having to work. Where we could have a family. That's what we wanted from the beginning, Bob; you know that. We wanted a family. We never had one. Probably we'll never have one. Lil has to keep working. Together, we just get by. And without her insurance coverage, neither of us could afford to get sick."

Koesler, well remembering how much Charlie and Lil had wanted children, was painfully aware that, on the one hand, they would have made excellent parents and on the other, in all likelihood, they never would be.

"If you don't mind—" Koesler stood, "—let's get out of here before I turn into a lobster."

They showered and started dressing.

"I've never talked to you about this—" Koesler had feared he might be prying, "—but what about your books? It's not everybody who's a published author. I've got all three of them—autographed, of course." Koesler smiled.

"Yeah, you and not enough others."

"Not enough others?"

"None of them sold more than 5,000 copies."

"That's bad?"

"Think of Michener with well over 100,000 hardcover copies, book clubs, paperback, foreign sales, big screen movies or a TV miniseries. That's success."

"That's a bit extreme, isn't it?"

"Granted. But if I were going to make a living at this sort of thing, my books would have to sell at least 25,000 copies in hardcover, along with some of those auxiliary sales. And, as you can see, I'm a long way from that."

"But they were good books."

"I thought so. And so did a couple of thousand readers. But that's just not enough."

Koesler pondered for a few moments. "I don't understand. They were good books. Why didn't they sell?"

Hogan shrugged.

"If memory serves," Koesler continued, "they got good reviews in the *News* and the *Free Press* . . . didn't they?"

"As a matter of fact, the reviews were mixed. Actually, I guess I was lucky to have them reviewed at all."

"You were?"

"Bob, there are about 400,000 book manuscripts submitted every year. About, roughly, 40,000 of them get published. And only a very small percentage of that number are even reviewed, let alone get a favorable review. Take a look at the *Free Press* and the *News*. Each paper uses a single page on Sundays for books, with, once in a while, another review or two during the week."

"You're right . . . I guess I never gave it much thought. When you consider the number published, I guess comparatively few do even get reviewed."

"It doesn't really matter that much. Most authors seem to feel that reviews neither sell books nor discourage people from buying them. A few readers, maybe, but not many . . . certainly not enough to make a difference.

"From my relatively narrow experience, I didn't mind so much when a reviewer simply didn't like my book. What bugs me—and I suppose most other writers—is when the reviewer is just flat-out wrong—incorrect. It happens. You knock yourself cold researching—and you're accurate. You have experts in the field read and okay your manuscript. Then some reviewer, based on nothing but his or her own ignorance, right off the top of his or her head, says you're wrong." He grinned ironically. "If I had my way, reviewers would have to be licensed."

"Licensed?"

"Use whatever criteria you want. But insist they have licenses. And, as in driving points, once they make X number of factual errors in reviews, they lose their license. "What do you think?"

"You're kidding?"

"No."

"Okay, but you said reviews are not all that important in selling books. So what happened to you? How come your books haven't done better?"

Hogan bit his lip, seeming to weigh explanation. Finally, he said, "There's a word for it—actually, two words . . ." He paused. "Ridley Groendal."

Koesler felt he should not be surprised. Still, he was. "Rid? But, how—?"

"He's powerful, Bob . . . at least he was. Especially when he was at the *New York Herald.* He reviewed my first book—although by his criteria he shouldn't have. My publisher wasn't that significant. Anyway, he went way out of his way to rip hell out of it. He even went so far as to question the motives and intelligence of my publisher. I think it was easily the worst review of anything I've ever seen."

"But I thought you said reviews were not all that important when it came to book sales?"

"His carried more clout than maybe any other. Besides, the review was not only grossly negative; it was symbolic. The review predated publication by several weeks. So he was sending a message to other reviewers.

"But much more importantly, he was going out of his way to influence the bookstores . . ." Hogan stood before the mirror combing his hair. He smiled, but there was no joy in it. "I'll have to give him that: He went to one helluva lot of trouble."

"Trouble? What—?"

"This wasn't just any ordinary vendetta. He went way out of his way to get me. He made sure his review was seen by influential editors.

"The thing that really gets me is the job he did in the stores. He managed to get his negative review reprinted in a publication influential on booksellers—that sort of thing. He really did a job!"

"This is all Greek to me. I thought all you had to do was write a good book."

"Ha! Even without the determined opposition of a Ridley Groendal, that's not even in the ballpark. If you're a nobody like me, in addition to a damn good book you've gotta have promotion, publicity, packaging, marketing, distribution—and a helluva lot of luck."

"Holy crow!"

"People like me don't get big advances. So the publisher is not going to lose a lot of sleep trying to recover the millions he didn't advance me.

If he runs into a big enough brick wall—in this case one built by Rid—he's just not going to bother. And word gets around."

Koesler had difficulty getting his shoes on. Not unexpectedly for him, with all the exercise and steam, his feet had swollen. "How long have you known about this, Charlie?"

"How long have I suspected is a better question. A long time. It was a combination of strange happenings. Why couldn't I get a job at one of the metropolitan papers? Why did I have so much trouble—at least in the beginning, selling my stuff as a free-lancer? And most of all, why all this determined opposition from critics and editors and book chains?

"Of course the initial supposition is: It's my fault; I can't cut it; I should be out digging ditches. But it just didn't wash. I knew I was better than that. I knew it. And some friends I could rely on—including you—reinforced my confidence.

"No, it was something else, some third person or force or something. I must confess I didn't suspect Rid until fairly recently. And then only because I had investigated and dismissed almost every other possibility."

"But you did find out, Charlie. From what you said, you know it's Rid now."

"Yeah, I know." Again the joyless smile.

"Then, how . . . ?"

"It happened a few months ago. I was doing a piece for the *Suburban Reporter.* I've done lots of stuff for them."

"That's the same paper Rid writes for, isn't it?"

"Yeah, only he's never there. Or he's there so infrequently he might just as well never be there. I don't know how many times I've been in that editorial office, but lots. He's hardly ever there. It's like a throne the king never sits in. It's just there. And he isn't."

"I didn't know that."

"Not many do. He mails most of his stuff in. About the only time he ever comes in is when he's covering something like a concert and he's on deadline. Then there's almost no way out; he has to come in and bat out the copy. But he doesn't stick around . . . just goes through his mail and leaves."

"You seem to know an uncommon amount about Ridley's comings and goings."

Hogan shook his head. "Bob, everybody does. Everybody but you. Almost everybody's done at least one feature on Rid, especially since he came back from New York. You're just not keeping up on local gossip columns. Besides, in effect, I work at least part-time at the *Reporter* free-lancing. I'm there lots more often than Rid. And I talk to the staffers."

"Okay, but how did you find out about Rid . . . I mean about his negative influence on your career?"

"As I was saying, a few months ago I brought in one of the pieces I'd done for the *Reporter.* It just so happened that Rid was making one of his rare appearances there at the time. As I was handing my article to the editor, I glanced over—and there he was. I guess my chin hit the floor. I never expected to see him. In fact, I hadn't seen him since the seminary. And what was that . . . more than thirty years ago?

"Anyway, I decided I'd challenge him . . . why not?"

"And . . . ?"

"It was incredible. It just spewed out of him. His friend—uh, Harison, is it?—was there. He tried to stop Rid, but he couldn't. Rid was citing chapter and verse. How he had reached the "right people" at the *Free Press* and the *News.* How he'd programmed and manipulated and poisoned so many of the reviewers, book editors, bookstores, chains, against me. How he had singlehandedly screwed my career."

"He admitted all that?"

"Admitted? He bragged about it! It was as if he'd been storing it all up, just dying to let me have it."

"Then why did he keep it a secret all these years?"

"That was the only way it would work. If I'd known what he was doing, I might have been able to head him off. No, it worked only too well."

"So what did you do?" Koesler was well aware that Hogan had always operated on a notoriously short fuse.

"It's what I almost did. And you can guess that. I almost beat the shit out of him. I think I would have if he hadn't taunted me about that very thing. I was on the verge of hitting him when he seemed to read my mind. 'What are you going to do about it,' he said, 'hit me? Like you did the last time? Go ahead . . . go ahead, then. Only I can tell you: No matter what you do to me now, what I've done to you was worth it. Go ahead! Go ahead!' He was shouting. Everybody in the office stopped work to listen.

"Somehow, it took the spontaneity off the moment. I don't know; I suppose I would have passed up most of the fights I've had if I'd ever stopped a minute to think about it. It certainly worked this time: All he had to do was invite me to do exactly what I was about to do, and I lost the urge.

"God, now that I think of it, maybe that's what the bastard had in mind . . . do you suppose the son-of-a-bitch was programming me right to the last?"

"I don't know, Charlie. I doubt it."

"But that was it? It ended like that? With Rid daring you to hit him?"

"Not exactly. I cooled off enough so I no longer felt like belting the hell out of him. But I was still damn mad. And . . . well . . . I warned him that if our paths ever crossed again, I'd . . ."

"You'd . . . ?"

"I'd kill him."

"You said that?"

"Uh-huh."

"Did the others hear you? The others in the office?"

"I guess—I hadn't thought about that—but, yes, I suppose so. They all heard Rid challenge me. And I wasn't exactly whispering my threat. Yeah, they heard me. They had to."

Koesler shook his head. "Not good. What if something were to happen to Rid?"

"Something like death? Then we celebrate."

"Seriously, Charlie: What if Rid were to get hurt—or actually die under suspicious circumstances. All those people heard you threaten him."

"So?"

"So, if I were you, I'd hope I had a really good alibi for the time in question."

"Come on, Bob, you don't think anyone would actually think I would kill somebody!"

Briefly, Koesler envisioned a prosecuting attorney describing for a jury the brutal beating Hogan had given Groendal years before, reminding them of the damage Rid had caused to Hogan's career, and bringing up examples of Charlie's quick temper.

If their paths did, indeed, cross again, Koesler could not predict the consequences. But he could well imagine a Hogan beyond anyone's control.

"Just the same," Koesler wrapped the familiar clerical collar around his neck and snapped it shut in the back, "let's hope that Rid lives a long life and passes away quietly in his sleep."

"You can't expect me to drink to that, Bob." Hogan completed knotting his tie, and slipped on his jacket. "I know only the good are supposed to die young, and, while we are not all that young, God could make an exception for this bastard. He's screwed up too many people's lives. I'd be doing mankind a favor if I were to . . . well . . ." Again his laugh held no mirth.

They parted in the parking lot, promising to get together again soon, although, privately, Koesler resolved not to meet at the spa again. Entering his car, he quickly started the engine and turned the heat on full. He was intolerant of the time that it took for the forced air to heat up. He was tired and shivering. He hoped this would not mark the beginning of one of those lingering Michigan colds. He had escaped both the flu and a cold for several winters. And he'd accomplished this without benefit of a "health" spa. No use ruining a proven formula. If it ain't broke, don't fix it, he thought grimly.

As the air warmed and he started feeling more comfortable, he thought about the just-completed scene when he had donned his clerical collar and Hogan his tie. Koesler recalled the time of Hogan's momentous decision that would take him out of the world of the Roman collar and put him in the world of the tie.

What would have happened to Hogan if he had not made that drastic change? If he had remained a priest, undoubtedly Rid would never have been able to reach him. Charlie would have been not only secure in the priesthood; he would have been safe. Safe from Ridley Groendal.

Among the elements Hogan had considered in his decision to leave the priesthood, he had not figured on Groendal. There was no reason to include the all-but-forgotton Groendal in his plans. But once Charlie left the comparative shelter of the priesthood, he had become unknowingly vulnerable. And, silently, behind the scenes, Groendal had struck —again and again.

And what had this cost Hogan? Only the work for which he was qualified and which he so desired. Plus a possible and even more desirable career as an author. And finally, the children he and Lil had planned for and wanted.

Quite a bit, all in all.

And Charlie knew it, of course. He knew it in far greater detail than Koesler could ever realize.

With all of this in mind, was it possible to totally disregard Hogan's death threat against Groendal? Koesler wondered about that.

*   *   *

The time of Communion was over. The communicants had returned to their places as had the visiting priests who had helped in the distribution. Optional at this point was a period of silent prayer. The option was favored by Koesler, who regularly observed this period of quiet. All were seated; the silence was unusually profound.

A beautiful sound wafted over the congregation, as a rich mellow violin began a solo of the "Meditation" from Massenet's opera, *Thais.* Appropriate, thought Koesler.

His next thought was of the presence in the church of another musician, Dave Palmer, a violinist of rank. Koesler wondered what Dave thought of the performance of the "Meditation." As far as Koesler was concerned, it sounded great. But he suspected that a gifted musician was equipped with a special ear that could discern a level of perfection —or lack of it—denied to the ears of the general public.

Could it really be more than forty years! Koesler did not want to admit it had been that long since they had graduated from elementary school. But the arithmetic didn't lie. Palmer off to Interlochen and a priceless musical education, training and performance opportunities. Groendal leaving his heart at Interlochen and going instead to a seminary.

Dave Palmer and his ulcer. Of course the cause could have been any number of things. Privately, Koesler had named the ulcer "The Groendal Connection." God and the reading public knew that Ridley had been harsh—many would say vicious—to any number of performers. But no one would dispute that for frequency and intensity of attack, Dave Palmer was certainly one of his favorite targets.

Strange; as far as Koesler could tell, Palmer and Groendal had not exchanged a word face to face in these past forty years. Yet, in peculiar ways, they had been virtually in constant communication. When Groendal was not writing snide and bitter comments about Palmer's performances, Rid frequently could be found badmouthing Dave to other critics, impresarios, and symphony directors, as well as those of the general public who were interested in serious music.

As for Palmer, he spent a generous amount of his time complaining and griping about fate in general and Groendal in particular. For those close to Dave, it was moot which had come first: Groendal's unrelenting persecution or Palmer's grouchy and offensive disposition. In time they seemed to feed on each other.

Much of the problem, as far as Palmer himself was concerned, stemmed from the quality of his talent. How much talent did he possess? Still more basic, how could talent be measured?

In the seminary attended by Koesler and Groendal had been a young man of great athletic ability. Of all the sports in which he participated, clearly he was most outstanding at hockey. Consensus had it that he was of professional caliber, not merely big-league but superstar. In time, the young man dropped out of the seminary and later won a tryout with the Detroit Red Wings. By his own admission, the Wings, led at that time by Sid Abel, Ted Lindsay, and Gordie Howe, had skated circles around him. Thus was the young man's talent measured: not against fair-to-middling amateurs, but in the league of gifted professionals.

In some such way were Dave Palmer's musical abilities weighed.

In the setting of a parochial grade school, little David Palmer was looked on as a child prodigy. And perhaps he was. But he was being measured against mediocre-to-good musical students. For the final concert of his primary school presentation, Palmer was paired with Ridley Groendal. The billing alone created the impression there was some element of equality between the two. That simply was not true. Groendal was paired with Palmer solely because Ridley was a good pianist, not because he was a gifted musician destined, as was Dave, to become a professional.

So, when it came to oneupmanship, Palmer left Groendal in the dust —an inevitability that everyone but Groendal would have recognized. However, no one told Groendal. No one could have. And there was the rub.

Groendal believed—as it turned out, to his dying day—that he might have had a magnificent musical career had it not been for Palmer's "cheap trick." Thus, Palmer went on to get his specialized musical training and Groendal did not.

No one, with the exception of Ridley and his parents, in any way expected Groendal to attend a school such as Interlochen. People were not at all surprised when Ridley went off to the seminary. He was a religious young lad and lots of religious young lads of that vintage routinely at least gave seminary a try.

Few besides Ridley knew that the seminary was his second choice.

Even Groendal did not know at that time that his hatred for Palmer would endure to the very end of Ridley's life.

Dave Palmer went blithely off to Interlochen and immediately suffered a severe case of specialized culture shock. Though his talent was considerable, it no longer placed him head-and-shoulders above his campmates. He was now merely one of many gifted young people.

Nonetheless he was good, very good. And he worked hard. A combination that won him honors and predictions by at least a few of his teachers that he would achieve great things.

Then he left academe. Like all who do so, Palmer found a cold, challenging world that dared him to find his place in it.

The first place he wanted was a chair in the Detroit Symphony Orchestra.

That was understandable. If he had been an athlete it would have been quite natural for him to have wanted to play for the Detroit Tigers, or Lions, or Red Wings. Of course, if he'd been an athlete he would most likely have been subjected to a draft or a bidding war between teams. As a musician, he didn't have to worry about anything like that. So long as there was a vacancy and he qualified for an audition, he could try for his boyhood dream: to become a member of the DSO.

As luck would have it, shortly after graduation, there was a vacancy; he qualified, auditioned, and was chosen.

That was about the last bit of unmixed good luck he was to have for many, many years.

A few months before graduation, Palmer had married Anna Krause, an art student he'd met at Interlochen. Anna was not nearly as talented an artist as Dave. But they did share at least two qualities: Both were extremely fertile and both were—for that day—exemplary Catholics, which led to a family of formidable proportions.

A few of their nine children were baptized by Father Koesler. The Palmers and Koesler kept in contact only sporadically. When not distracted by his family, Palmer was kept busy at the DSO. He had time for little else.

Even though they saw each other infrequently, Koesler was proud of his former classmate and bragged to anyone who seemed interested about his friend—his one and only acquaintance in the DSO.

Koesler was not particularly surprised at the number of children produced by Dave and Anna. Those were the days when faithful Catholics were grateful Pope Pius XII had discovered the rhythm system of family planning . . . even though it didn't work for some—among that number, Dave and Anna.

Anna, like so many other wives of that era, hardly ever got out of her "eternity" clothes.

The peculiar fact that Dave was both a musician and father of a considerable number of children reminded Koesler of a true story then passing through clerical circles. It involved a suburban parish's music director who was father to thirteen children. At a parish meeting, the music director complained about the quality of instrument he was forced to use, and he pleaded for a new and better organ. This prompted one of the ladies of the Altar Society to comment rather loudly that he seemed to be doing pretty well with the organ he had.

In any case, upon acceptance, Dave Palmer was assigned a seat in the second violin section. As far as Dave was concerned, this was a satisfactory beginning. But he had plans.

In that, he was not alone. While many members of symphony orchestras are content to remain at that professional level for the length of their professional lives—occasionally making lateral arabesques from one orchestra to another—some considered their orchestras mere springboards to further musical heights. Among the latter was Dave Palmer.

Palmer's plan, not infeasible, considering his talent and education, was to move up: to the first violin section, to concertmaster, to featured soloist, to director of his own orchestra. Eventually, like Toscanini, Stokowski, Beecham, Koussevitsky, von Karajan, Munch, Bernstein, Solti, Reiner, Leinsdorf, Giulini, and Dorati, to become a household word. At least in the better houses.

However, he had not counted on Ridley C. Groendal. Palmer had no reason to do so. He should have.

Realistically, Groendal had no way of blocking Palmer's entry to the DSO. That had happened much too early in Ridley's career, long before his power had emerged to any degree. Besides, there really was little argument that Palmer was good enough to be a member of a major symphony orchestra. The only question was how far his talent might take him. It was to this question that Groendal effectively addressed himself.

In a sense, it was Ridley's easiest victory. Groendal was powerfully motivated to make Palmer a victim. As far as Groendal was concerned,

Dave ranked first, at least chronologically, as an instrument that had changed and ruined Ridley's life.

Further, Palmer existed for the world of music, the strongest of Ridley's critical fields and the one for which he would become best known.

Once Groendal was completely established at the *New York Herald,* it had been almost child's play to torpedo Palmer's musical career. Harshly negative reviews, ignoring important concerts, the almost unique instance of singling out Palmer as the cause of a failed orchestral performance; anticipating Palmer's occasional auditions for other orchestras and reminding the pertinent music directors of Palmer's many "failings."

Added to all of this was Ridley's enormous sway with not a few other critics. All in all, Groendal enjoyed being able to keep much of his clout in reserve and still make Palmer run in tight, frustrating circles within the DSO's structure.

A few weeks before Ridley's death, Koesler had been invited to the Palmers' for dinner. It was not the sort of invitation that Koesler welcomed. He'd been through it occasionally and invariably had endured an evening of the couple's petty bickering, recriminations, arguments, and sullenness.

From time to time he wondered why the Palmers did not simply divorce. Their brood had grown up and moved away. The two were left grousing and generally dissecting each other. He wondered if they might be the embodiment of that fictional couple who filed for a divorce in their nineties. The judge, at a loss, asked how long they'd been married. Seventy-five years, they said. Then why had they waited so long for this action? They had been waiting, they replied, for their children to die.

If the Palmers were waiting to bury their nine children, they had many years of connubial misery ahead of them.

"Would Father like more spaghetti and meatballs?" Anna Palmer asked Koesler, preparatory to clearing the table for dessert.

"No, no, that's fine, Anna." Koesler was grateful he'd gotten through the single serving Anna had heaped on his plate. The overcooked spaghetti had been dry. He knew he would have trouble digesting it. And the meatballs reminded him of that old TV commercial: " 'Atsa some spicy meataball."

He wondered how Palmer, with his ulcer, could stomach all that spice. Having experienced Anna's cooking many times in the past,

Koesler had downed his glass of Chianti before taking a first bite of anything, hoping the dry red would make more palatable what would follow. He thought it had helped.

"You want more, honey?" Anna asked her husband.

"No. And why the hell do you put so much spice in those meatballs? You know I've got an ulcer!"

"You and your 'hell' with a priest in the house! Besides, if you didn't baby that ulcer so much, it wouldn't bother you so much."

Dave tossed his napkin on the table in disgust. "I'm not in a contest with the damn ulcer. I'm not trying to conquer it. It won a long time ago. I'm just trying to live with it. And all that spice isn't helping."

It seemed that Anna did not hear all that he'd said. While he was speaking, she was rattling the dishes in the sink. They both finished at about the same time. She took from the refrigerator three servings of red Jello and put them on the table. For the first time Koesler wondered about the truth of the motto, "There's always room for Jello." Perhaps not, he thought, after one of Anna's meals. But, out of politeness, he would try.

"Will you be coming to the concert, Bob?" Dave asked.

"Which one?"

"The Midwest Chamber Players." Dave seemed miffed that there was any doubt as to which concert was under consideration.

"Oh, yes." Koesler acknowledged he should have known Dave had to be referring to his baby rather than the DSO. "I remember now. It's going to be right after Christmas. Gee, I don't know, Dave. Even if I'm not busy that night, I'm sure I'll be beat. That's a very busy season for Santa and for me. But I'll try."

"I wish you would, Bob. Chamber music needs all the support it can get. After all, this isn't Minneapolis. Chamber never caught on here in Detroit as it should have."

"There you go," Anna cut in, "nagging our guest. Can't you let the man eat in peace?"

"I'm not nagging! I just asked Bob if he planned on going to our concert."

"That's nagging. And what's with this 'Bob'? The man's a holy priest of God. Why don't you call Father 'Father'?"

"For God's sake, Anna, we grew up together! He's a classmate, for God's sake!"

"There you go, taking God's name in vain. Breaking the Second Commandment. And a priest right here in the same room!"

"Good! Then he'll be able to give me absolution!"

"You have no fear of the Lord!"

"I'm more afraid of your spicy meatballs!"

"So, Dave," Koesler, who was beginning to develop a nervous stomach, interrupted, "what are you going to play in your concert?" Experience had taught that his efforts at peacemaking could be little more than stopgap measures.

Dave smiled at the thought. "Beethoven, Mendelssohn, and Schubert."

"See?" Anna said. "All the old-timers. Dear, you're going to make everybody think you never heard of the twentieth century."

"There she goes again!" Dave countered. "An art student—and not a very good one at that—and she wants to be my program director!"

"Leave my art alone!"

"Why not? Everyone else has. But tell me, my lovely, whom would you have on the program?"

"Somebody. Anybody. At least from this century. Stravinsky maybe."

"Good! Excellent! Superb! Then we could be certain that if someone fired a cannon during the concert, no one would get hurt."

"Okay. All right, André Previn. Stick to your 'masters' and see where it gets you."

"A few more people. Maybe a full house, my pet!"

"And the usual negative reviews. Ridley Groendal is not going to like that program."

"Ridley Groendal can go to hell!"

"Forgive him, Father!"

"Forgive me, Father."

Koesler shook his head.

Anna rose in a huff and went to the sink to scrape dishes and stack them in the dishwasher. Though it was a little noisy, it enabled Palmer and Koesler to talk without interruption.

"She's wrong, you know," Palmer said. "God knows I understand the atonals as well as anybody. And I like a lot of them. But we've got to face it: The general public has resisted them. With the Symphony, we'll tuck one or another of them in among the classics, hoping that the audience will come to hear, say, Mozart, and learn to like Cage. But, to date, it hasn't really worked; they'll give Beethoven a standing ovation and sit on their hands for Prokofiev."

"And you don't fear Rid?"

Palmer shrugged. "I never feared Rid. I alternate between not understanding him, pitying him, and despising him."

"An odd mixture."

Palmer rose and motioned Koesler to follow him into the living room where the kitchen sounds would be muted and they could talk more confortably. "I suppose. But that's the way it worked out."

"Care to explain?"

Palmer registered doubt. "Rid's in your parish now. The two of you talk from time to time?"

"Yes, but I'm not the type to betray a confidence. You know that."

"God, yes. I know that. Well, I pity the man because he's a shell. There's no substance. Performers, the artists know that. The trouble with Rid is he thinks he knows everything. He doesn't. Nobody does. But, there he is, maybe the premier critic in America, certainly the most influential—or at least he was when he was with the *Herald*.

"He passes himself off as the expert in theater, music, and literature. And what does he know? Jargon! Outside of artsy phrases, he doesn't know any more than the average patron of the arts. And he's insecure."

Koesler lifted a questioning eyebrow.

"Oh, he's insecure, all right. Like insecure people, he has to namedrop. Like, 'When I was talking to Lennie last . . .' or 'Pinky prefers the pizzicato played this way . . .'

"No, Ridley never really knew what he was talking or writing about. What he knows is how to intimidate people. People in middle and upper management. That's where his power lies. But when he acts the critic, he just plain doesn't know his rear end from a hole in the ground.

"So, part of me pities him." Palmer stopped to light his pipe.

Koesler took up the slack. "You pity Rid, but you also mentioned you don't understand him?"

Palmer puffed several times to kindle the tobacco. "I don't understand why he hates me. I haven't done anything to him."

"There was that time when we were all kids . . ." Koesler well knew how unforgetting and unforgiving Ridley could be.

"You mean the eighth-grade concert?"

"Uh-huh."

"You really think it could be that! I've thought about it many, many times. It's the only conflict we ever had. But it was so childish. And so many years ago. It seems impossible. If memory serves, all I did was pay him back for what he did to me. A couple of adolescent tricks. Do you think that could be it?"

"It's possible." Actually, Koesler was certain it was so.

"I suppose you're right. Yeah, it's the only thing. But, so many years ago . . . so long ago . . . and such an insignificant incident . . . it seems incredible." Palmer puffed, contemplatively.

"One man's insignificant is another man's mountain." Koesler regretted the words no sooner than they left his lips; he sounded like a pop-psych guru. Fortunately, Palmer seemed still deep in thought. Koesler picked up another thread. "And your hatred for him?"

"Huh! Oh, well, that's the clearest of all. He's ruined my career quite singlehandedly. I won't go into chapter and verse, but he's gone out of his way to screw me at every turn. And he's been good at it. As I said, he has a knack for influencing the powers that be. And he's certainly done it where I'm concerned." Palmer puffed for a few moments. "I can't help thinking every once in a while what my life would have been if not for Ridley Groendal. By this time—God!—I would have had my own organization . . . a guest soloist . . ." He was lost in reverie.

Not for the world would Koesler have suggested that Palmer might well have contributed to his own limitations. As his career sank ever more inextricably into the DSO, his temperament and behavior had deteriorated in tempo.

At Symphony parties to which Palmer had invited him, Koesler sometimes overheard other orchestra members complaining about Dave —picayune things, such as when it was Palmer's responsibility to turn pages, he would flip a page just far enough so he could read the music, forcing his partner to complete the chore. Little things—but sometimes the rabbit punches were life's most difficult afflictions.

Anna came in with coffee.

"So," Koesler summed up, "pity, bewilderment, and hate. An odd combination."

"Oh, good grief!" Anna exclaimed. "You've been talking about that Groendal person again."

Koesler was not surprised that Anna was familiar with Dave's feelings toward Ridley.

"Yes," Palmer said, "Groendal once more."

He set the pipe in an ashtray, where the dottle smoldered. "Funny thing, if I ever stopped feeling pity—for even one brief second . . ."

"You'd what?" Anna prompted.

"I'd . . . I'd kill him. Yes, I really would."

"Dave!" Anna exclaimed. "That's a sin! Now you really are going to have to ask for absolution!"

"Instead of that, I think I'll play something." Palmer tried to create the impression that his threat had not been serious. But Father Koesler wondered.

Palmer picked up his violin, tuned it, and began the gentle opening theme from Beethoven's Sixth Symphony.

For Koesler, the beauty of the music more than made up for Anna's spaghetti and meatballs. As he listened, he could not help but reflect on Dave's threat. That completed the circle of all three men who had been so crippled by Ridley's revenge. Three men who, otherwise, were essentially nonviolent. Yet, in Koesler's hearing, all three had threatened to kill Ridley Groendal.

That left Jane Condon, now Jane Cahill, and her daughter, Valerie Cahill, now Valerie Walsh, as the only victims who had not threatened to kill Groendal—at least not in Koesler's hearing.

Koesler would have known very little of either woman in recent years had he not heard from third parties, and, finally, from Valerie herself.

20

"Let us pray." Koesler intoned the prayer after Communion. *"O Almighty God, may this sacrifice purify the soul of your servant, Ridley, which has departed from the world. Grant that once delivered from his sins, he may receive forgiveness and eternal rest. Through Christ our Lord."*

Koesler doubted that Valerie joined in the sentiments of that prayer. Of all those marked for vengeance by Ridley, Valerie had perhaps the strongest motive for striking back.

Palmer, Mitchell and Hogan each had been personally hurt by Groendal. As for Valerie, not only she but, much more, her mother had been deeply wronged. It is ofttimes easier to forgive or at least live with an injury done to oneself than to overlook some evil done to a loved one. Groendal had hurt Val. She might have risen above that. She could never ever forget or forgive what he had done to the one person she loved most next to her husband.

If Valerie had not gotten an aisle seat, Koesler might not have located her in the crowd. Quite obviously, Red Walsh was not in attendance, otherwise Koesler would have easily spotted the human skyscraper. Koesler did not closely follow the comings and goings of the Detroit Pistons, but, he thought, probably Walsh was at practice.

In fact, Valerie was accompanied by her mother. Koesler did not remember ever having seen the two together.

The first time he could recall seeing Jane was at the Stratford movie theater nearly forty years before. He might not have paid much attention to her then if that had not been the start of something big, however brief, between Jane and Ridley. After Groendal had related what had taken place between himself and Jane, Koesler hadn't known quite what to do. So he had spent that summer praying fervently for Jane.

After he was ordained four years later, he occasionally visited Jane. Again, there was not much he could do. While it was a heartrending situation, for whatever her reasons Jane wanted to handle it alone. So she worked at Hudson's, hired a babysitter, and brought home what bacon she could. After her boy, Billy, died, Koesler had lost touch with Jane.

He had not met Valerie until she returned from New York with her husband. She felt she needed to talk to a priest. But nearly all the young priests she'd known in high school were now former priests. As far as Valerie—and most other Catholics—was concerned, the magic was over. One might have great confidence in a priest. But once he left the priesthood, though he was the same person, the old confidence in him seemed to evaporate.

Jane recommended Father Koesler to her daughter as a kind and helpful priest and, even more to the point, one who knew Ridley Groendal very well.

Koesler listened to Valerie's life story, which was not much different from any other Catholic girl's. Peculiar to Valerie was her enormous theatrical talent, along with her extraordinary beauty. Unlike some similarly endowed girls, Valerie had let none of her gifts go to her head. Through the difficult high school years, she had remained in control of herself and her destiny. But, aside from her talent, beauty, and self-containment, her life through high school was not markedly different from others with a parochial education.

All that of course changed when she went off to New York after high school graduation. Her parents had no money for college. In addition, Valerie could see no point in college. By consensus and her own conviction, she was ready for the stage. She was aware she had lots to learn. But she knew the next lessons would have to be in the school of hard knocks. She had no idea how hard those knocks were destined to be.

She told Koesler of arriving bright-eyed and eager in Queens, where she would stay with cousins on her father's side. Of visiting one theatrical agency after another. She was convinced she was unsinkable. She was talented, beautiful and—if inexperienced—at least young, healthy, and willing to knock on endless doors until something inevitably opened.

She did not know until much later that almost every time a door began to open, someone was on the other side slamming it shut. That someone, she would eventually learn, was Ridley Groendal.

Valerie visited Koesler several times, each time pouring out more of her story. In the beginning, he could not tell where this was leading. But, in time, the dark shadow of Groendal was evident.

Though her cousins were gracious and kind, her presence shortly became awkward. The modest rent and board she paid, plus the sheer cost of travel in Manhattan, soon exhausted her small savings. Then it grew embarrassing. The cousins were encouraging and sympathetic, but she knew they were operating on a tight budget. They could not carry her indefinitely.

There was no alternative; she had to get a job.

The job was not long in coming. But then, Groendal was not blocking her job hunt—only because he could not. After a two-week search, Valerie was hired by Sports Gear International. The New York store was headquarters for a chain of sporting goods stores in the U.S. and Canada. The job combined clerking with occasional modeling.

In what spare time she could squeeze from her work, she continued to audition for Broadway and Off-Broadway shows. Among her attempts to break into show biz: *A Chorus Line, Joseph and the Amazing Technicolor Dream Coat, Fiddler on the Roof, Marco Polo,* and *Foot Falls.*

Although she invariably tried for the chorus or an understudy part, she never came close. It was a combination of her youth and comparative inexperience along with the pervasive behind-the-scenes presence of Ridley Groendal.

Meanwhile, her modeling career continued to prosper. Sports Gear International used her increasingly in display ads for everything from tennis outfits to golf equipment. It was not the theater; it was not what she had come to New York to do. But it was income she desperately needed.

Learning to live in New York City is an art and Valerie was a quick study. She was actually able to contribute a little more than was expected for her room and board. She was even able to put aside small amounts after coping with the city's substantial cost of living.

A milestone in her life occurred when SGI selected her as a model for their Christmas catalog. Not only did this bring far wider exposure and considerably more money, but it set the occasion for her meeting William Xavier Walsh.

As Valerie told Koesler about Red Walsh, she glowed. It was easily the most significant happening of her life.

"I was putting on my makeup and I saw in the mirror this image come up behind me. Whoever it was just stood there. That makes me angry—people fooling around. So I turned. I was ready to cuss out whoever it was. And I just kept looking up, and up, and up. At the top of this towering body was this grinning face with freckles and a mop of red hair. It seemed as if he was the biggest thing I'd ever seen. I guess my mouth dropped open—like Annie Oakley's when she meets Frank Butler."

Koesler well remembered *Annie, Get Your Gun!*

"Still, I was sore at him. I don't know why. He was just standing there grinning at me. Anyway, I started yelling at him. It was our first fight. And it was at first sight. And it was very one-sided."

She told Koesler that it was a long time after their first meeting before she and Walsh became friends, let alone fell in love. Walsh, at that time, was a senior at Notre Dame. After he modeled gym shoes and other athletic gear for the Christmas catalog, he returned to college and the completion of the basketball season. He was a consensus All-American in both his junior and senior years.

They dated a few times. Unfortunately, Walsh cared little for the theater, while Valerie found basketball the least interesting of major league sports. But an indefinable something drew them together. Over the months during which Walsh closed out a rather distinguished academic career, he and Valerie corresponded with increasing frequency.

She found it difficult writing him about her professional life, which had improved and disintegrated simultaneously. As a result of the Christmas catalog and the inspired activity of her agent, she had begun free-lance modeling. This new career, plus her continuing auditions for the theater, left increasingly less time for her work at SGI. Reluctantly, she left her job, sacrificing a regular and reliable paycheck for the hope of much more, if unguaranteed, money.

And so Valerie began showing up for the morning casting calls, better known by the young hopefuls who suffer through them as cattle calls. After considerable thought and prayer, she had decided against signing an agency contract. She correctly deemed such an arrangement too binding for a young person with limitless confidence in her own ability. The cattle call was the unfortunate alternative.

She actually shuddered when she recounted for Koesler the interminable months as one of New York's most frequently photographed models. In most cases, the models knew beforehand what type of shooting each day held. If the character was going to be a housewife, the models would come dressed appropriately. Frequently it would be a beach scene. So the young women would wear bikinis under street clothing.

When it was their turn, they had no more shield for changing than a curtain.

Whatever they wore to model, they would be screened, usually by a panel, usually composed of three men: a producer, a director, and someone from the ad agency. Perhaps a sponsor might be thrown in. The women would be ogled. The process was, Valerie attested, degrading. It resembled, she told Koesler, a singles bar—another area of expertise in which he was lacking. But he got the idea. And he wondered how an admittedly talented person like Valerie could have gone through it.

The answer of course was The Theater. Unlike most other women in the profession, modeling was not Val's goal. It was a means of employment and exposure while she continued to pursue the stage.

During the 1977 theater season, among many other shows, she auditioned for *Breathless, Otherwise Engaged, Ashes,* and *Stop the Parade.*

Stop the Parade, in effect, stopped Valerie's parade. It was the first major production in which she'd won a part—albeit that of understudy.

When he learned of her—however slight—success, Groendal was livid. His lackey, who should have been monitoring that area of Broadway, had been asleep at the switch. That worthy pleaded too vast an area of responsibility to pay attention to every broad who was hired as an understudy. Groendal reminded him that Valerie Cahill was his priority responsibility. Ridley reminded him of this just before firing him.

Until *Stop the Parade,* Valerie had not been aware that Ridley Groendal even knew she existed. Even then, if not for a bewildering set of circumstances, she would not have known of Groendal's malevolent machinations.

Night after night and matinee after matinee, Valerie kept her vigil in the wings in case she might be called on to take over for an indisposed star. Of course, her keenest desire was to appear on stage. Yet the rigors of free-lance modeling so exhausted her that she was almost grateful for the star's seemingly cast-iron constitution.

Then, one night it happened. Pauline O'Kennedy came down with the flu. Diagnosed as the twenty-four-hour variety, still it was potent enough to take her out of the show for one night. It was Val's big opportunity. She put everything she was capable of into that performance.

It is difficult to gauge one's own endeavor, but she honestly thought she'd done well. The audience was generous in its applause. And the other performers were lavish with praise. She was so "up" she had a difficult time sleeping that night.

Next morning she could scarcely control her trembling hands as she paged through the *New York Herald*. The play had been reviewed weeks prior to this, just after opening. So there wasn't much chance anyone would comment on it again, especially since there was little prior notice that an understudy would be appearing.

Her eyes widened when she found a single column item regarding the performance. She reread it several times before fully comprehending its viciousness.

The review centered solely on her performance, which it described as "amateurish, degrading to the other performers, who should not be forced to share a stage with someone who shows neither ability nor promise . . . One would hope," it went on, "she finds her niche in life —perhaps modeling in Peoria. Seeking solace somewhere, it can be said that Valerie Cahill is a mere study—Deo gratias—and she will mercifully sink slowly in the West."

There was more, most of it as bad or worse. Her eyes were so filled with tears that she had a difficult time making out the byline. Ridley C. Groendal.

At that time that meant nothing in particular. Only that he was *the* Broadway reviewer and this was her first Broadway performance, her golden opportunity, and she had failed. She had blown herself out of the water. Not for a moment did she think to question the review.

There would be no cattle call today. She could not possibly endure that degradation in addition to suffering through the end of her world.

She told Koesler of going as quickly as possible to the hotel where Pauline O'Kennedy was staying. Miss O'Kennedy was almost completely recovered from her brief bout with the flu. She was healthy enough, indeed, to be concerned about the distraught young woman who sat on her couch, alternating between sobbing and abjectly apologizing for ruining her play.

"Come on, now, you didn't ruin any play." Pauline patted Valerie's shoulder, trying to console her.

"You weren't there," Valerie sobbed.

"Of course I wasn't there. That's why you were. But I've talked with the others. There wasn't a dissenting voice: You were very good . . . great!"

"But the review . . . ?" Val offered the column, clipped out and so heavily fingered it had almost reverted to pulp state.

Pauline pushed it back toward Val. "I've read it."

"It's so bad. So negative."

"Just pay attention to the good ones, dear." Pauline did not sound convincing.

"This is different. No one would take a chance on me after this."

Pauline hesitated, as if weighing carefully what she would next say. "But it was written by Ridley Groendal."

Clearly, Val did not comprehend what Pauline was trying to tell her. "But," Val protested in an unbelieving tone, "but, he's . . ."

"He's your enemy."

"My what?"

"Your enemy. I don't know what you ever did to him, but it must have been a doozy. I've never seen anything like it. It's the talk of the business, at least here in New York." She broke off, at the sight of Val's uncomprehending look. "You didn't know?"

"I . . . I don't know what you're talking about."

"Groendal. For the past year and more he's been making sure you're blackballed up and down the street."

"I don't understand. I've never . . . well, I've never even met the guy."

"Then I don't understand it either. Nobody can recall anything quite like this. Oh, there've been feuds and vendettas. But nothing like this. He's been busy with owners, producers, directors—even angels. I don't know how you even got into our show. Tom was taking some chance letting you on—even as a study."

"But, what could he do?"

Pauline rose, walked across the room, got a cigarette, lit it, coughed violently, and stubbed it out. "How many shows will it cost Tom?"

"What?"

"Groendal can and has shut down shows with just one review. He's done it for lots less reason than this."

"But, why . . . ?"

"I haven't a clue. You tell me."

"No, why didn't anyone tell *me* about this before . . . I mean, if so many people in the business know about it?"

Pauline returned and sat on the couch. "You remember McCarthy . . . Senator Joe McCarthy?"

"The Army hearings? The Communist witch-hunt? I read about it."

"How many people stood up to Joe McCarthy? Damn few. For very good reason. At worst, you could go to jail. At best, you could become unemployable. Something to think about. Why didn't anybody tell you, honey? Because they like putting on plays, that's why. Because they like acting."

Val was thoughtful. "So why did you tell me now?"

Pauline tried another cigarette, did not inhale so deeply, and managed to suppress the cough. "It was the right time, honey. Oh, I'm not that brave. It is the perfect time. You can go straighten it all out with Groendal. All you have to know is one fact that you could have learned from nearly anyone and you can go settle this once and for all."

"One fact? If I know one fact? What fact? What are you talking about?"

"Ridley Groendal wasn't there last night."

"But he wrote—"

"He wrote off the top of his head. He wrote out of hatred for you. How the hell do I know why he did it? All I know is that he wasn't there. He didn't even see your performance!"

Pauline stubbed out the cigarette. "You could, of course, complain to the *Herald* that Groendal panned your performance without seeing it. But that's like going to the dead-letter department without going through the post office. They'll never call him on it. When it comes to the world of critics, he's like God.

"Besides, if he condescended to respond to your complaint, he'd probably say he dropped in after intermission for the last act. Or that he had one of his bird dogs cover it. But, believe me, honey, it didn't happen. He just wanted to kill your career."

*   *   *

At this point in her story, Valerie stopped speaking and seemed to drift off in the memory of the event, immersed in the enormity of an act that cried to heaven for vengeance. Imagine panning a performance without having witnessed it, motivated by hatred alone.

At length, Koesler spoke. "So what did you do then?"

Val returned to the moment with a start. "Oh! Sorry . . .

"Well, I didn't know how to deal with that. There was just no reason. I mean, I'd never even met the man. Why would he do a thing like that? It just wiped me out. Fortunately, I had a pretty good-sized nest egg put aside . . . from the modeling. So I didn't need to work—for awhile at least. I came back to Detroit and stayed with my parents. I just wanted time to think and put my life back together."

"You didn't tell your folks what happened?"

"I didn't want to trouble them. Especially I didn't want to dump a problem on them when I didn't even know what had caused it, let alone how to handle it."

"Then . . . ?"

"My mother, of course, figured that something was wrong. What's more, even without my telling her, she more or less guessed what had happened. Finally, we talked. When I got to the part where Ridley Groendal had pretty well killed my career with his offstage power brokering and then delivered the coup de gráce with that review, Mom nodded.

"Then she told me the story. It was such a shock . . . I'll never forget her words."

*　　*　　*

"We never talked about this, Val. Maybe we should have. I never lied to you. I just never told you everything."

"Mother?"

"You had a brother once."

"What?"

"Before I met your father."

"Before—"

"Wait, Val; let me finish. I was your age, only I didn't know what you know. I had a crush on a young man. On our first and only date we had too much to drink and got carried away."

"You mean that was it? One time and you were pregnant?"

Jane nodded. "I told you I didn't know then what you do now. Even if I had, I had no intention of even necking or petting, let alone actual intercourse. But, it happened, and I was pregnant."

"What happened to the guy? He didn't marry you?"

Jane shook her head. "It gets complicated. But, to make a long story short, he left town."

"Left town! And left you with a baby? But what became of him? What happened to my brother . . . my half-brother?"

"He . . . he had Down's Syndrome."

Valerie gasped.

"The dearest, sweetest child you'd ever want to know," her mother continued. "I was with him as much as I possibly could be. But, you know about kids with Down's. Frequently, they don't have a normal life span. Your brother, Billy, died when he was ten. It was about four years before I met and married your father, about five years before you were born."

"A brother! Billy! Retarded! I wish I could have known him. I wish I could have taken care of him. I wish . . . but . . . why are you telling me this now?"

"Because . . . because of what happened to you in New York. And because you want a career in the theater."

"What's that got to do with it?"

"The father of your half-brother has everything to do with it. His name is Ridley Groendal."

"Ridley Groendal? Ridley Groendal! It's almost impossible to imagine. Besides, he's gay, isn't he? How—?"

"For a few moments, a long time ago, aided by some whisky, he wasn't gay. And those few moments changed my whole life. And, I suppose, to be perfectly fair, they changed his life too."

It was clear Valerie was stunned. "Groendal and you! I can't believe it! The father of my half-brother . . . God!

"But what's this got to do with me? It all happened long before I was born. Why would he sabotage my career? I never had anything to do with him. I don't even know him. So, again: What's this got to do with me?"

"It's hard to say, baby. It's a feeling. A feeling I've had all along. That he was out to get me. It's like a scale that was left unbalanced."

"But why? God knows you've had a tough enough life."

"I know. I know. But he hasn't done anything to me personally. I feel as if he thinks I made him leave home and that he deserves some sort of revenge for that. But he's never gotten it. He couldn't, I guess. For most of the time, I was so low he couldn't kick me. But he still 'owes' me. That I feel. And if he can't reach me directly, I feel he'll try to get at me through someone I love—you."

"Mom!"

"This is all hindsight, baby. It never entered my head for a moment that he would take it out on you. That's one reason I never told you. But now . . . well, it seems that's the only explanation for what he's done."

Val clenched her jaw. "Mom, I'm going to get the bastard for you. I swear it."

Jane shook her head. "Val, don't lower yourself to his level. Just take special care of yourself. I don't know what I'd do if anything happened to you."

"Don't worry about me, Mom. Thanks for telling me all this. It couldn't have been easy for you. But . . . does he know about all this —about Billy?"

"I don't know. I only saw him once after . . . that night. He didn't seem to believe the baby I was carrying was his. Maybe he never knew about Billy. Or, if he did, he still probably wouldn't have admitted his responsibility."

"Then that's my ace in the hole. I may never have to play it. I hope I don't. But one thing: Whatever it takes, I'll get the bastard for you. I really will."

*　　*　　*

Again, Valerie seemed to be lost in a private fantasy.

It was as if someone had added color to a black-and-white photo, clarifying it. Koesler had lived through the original events of Valerie's story with the principals. He'd been there when Jane and Ridley met. Later, he had felt constrained to listen to Ridley recount the details of his sexual encounter with Jane. Subsequently, Koesler had witnessed the aftermath of Ridley's breakdown after learning of Jane's pregnancy. Finally, Koesler had attempted to aid Jane in her struggle to raise a handicapped child.

But Koesler had been unaware of Ridley's attempt to revenge himself against Jane through Valerie.

The priest thought of all this for a few moments before nudging Valerie on. "And then . . . ?"

"And then I returned to New York, did some more modeling. Even the modeling began to suffer. It may surprise you, Father, but you can't have a blank mind while you're modeling. It takes a lot of concentration."

"I never thought about that."

"Well, it does," she said pointedly. "And I was preoccupied with Ridley Groendal. I had a lot of trouble concentrating on my modeling. I also had a lot of trouble sleeping. It was one thing to say I was going to avenge my mother and myself, and another thing to actually do it.

"A guy like Ridley Groendal leads a pretty insulated life. Physically, it's hard to get near him. The *New York Herald* is like an armed camp. You can't get beyond the lobby without an appointment. And even then, there's no entry until the person you're going to see comes and gets you.

"It's very much the same with Groendal's apartment building. The security is excellent. And anyway what are you going to do even if you do get next to him?

"The whole thing was very frustrating. And then something else happened."

"Huh?"

"Red Walsh graduated. He was drafted number one by the Detroit Pistons. It wasn't the team he wanted. He wanted to go to the Knicks because he thought I was going to stay in New York and he wanted to be close to me."

She did not state this at all self-consciously, which gave Koesler pause. He concluded she must be a most self-assured young woman.

"And that's where he came, right after the draft. Then he came after me. Boy, did he ever! He gave the full-court press a new definition. We were together almost all the time. He got to like the theater. And I promised I would get interested in basketball.

"Well, we got engaged. By now I was so happy I had darn near forgotten about Groendal. Then it happened."

Valerie got up and began to pace. She stopped and hunted through her purse until she found some cigarettes. She lit one. "Excuse me, Father. I rarely smoke, but I'm kind of nervous." She looked around for an ashtray; finding none she wondered if this might be a "no-smoking" section of the rectory.

Koesler calmed her fear by finding an ashtray in one of the drawers and placing it on the desk. From her manner, he assumed she was nearing the heart of her story—the reason she had come to see him in the first place. "What happened?"

He brought her back to the point.

"Okay." She inhaled deeply, then let the smoke drift from her nostrils. As she continued speaking, she exhaled smoke from her mouth, punctuating her words. "We were walking down Fifth Avenue near St. Patrick's Cathedral, Red and I. We had just picked out our wedding rings at Cartier's.

"You know how when you're in New York and you see somebody

who looks like some celebrity, it usually turns out to be not a look-alike but the real celebrity?"

Koesler nodded. He'd had the experience.

"Well, we were walking, very happy together, when who should be coming toward us but Ridley Groendal. That other guy—his home companion—Harison—was with him. But I didn't even notice him till later. All I could see was that face—that cocky, self-satisfied face.

"I'd never done anything like this before, but something inside me snapped. I just rushed over, blocked his path, and started yelling at him.

"At first, he looked startled. But then, when he recognized me, he got this smirk. It just made me more furious. I was shouting, shrieking, demanding to know how he could rate my performance when he wasn't even at the theater.

"I called him every name I could think of, most of them words I'd never used before. The street was crowded and people started to gather 'round.

"But it was obvious that I wasn't getting anywhere. His smirk never wavered. He was really reaching me. So, I started hitting him."

"You what?" Koesler could not imagine a diminutive person like Valerie causing much damage to one as big as Rid. On the other hand, intense emotion can confer incredible strength.

"Yes, I started hitting him. At first, Harison tried to stop me. So I hit *him*. He would have come back at me but Groendal pushed him aside.

"That was what was so odd, looking back at it: Groendal just stood there taking it, with a little smile on his face, like he was enjoying it. And I was getting in some pretty good licks."

Koesler was momentarily distracted. He recalled the beating Charlie Hogan had given Rid in the shower room at the seminary. Then too, Rid had just stood and taken it. Did he never in any way try to defend himself? Was there a masochistic streak in him?

"Anyway, it didn't last long. It takes longer to tell it than it did to do it. Once I got physical, Red moved in, grabbed me around the waist from behind, lifted me clear off my feet and carried me away. I think he acted just before a cop arrived on the scene to put me away."

"And then?"

"And then I started swinging at Red. At that point I would have hit anybody or anything. But, of course, he didn't take it like Groendal did. Thank God he didn't hit me back. He just pinned my arms and talked to me quietly till I calmed down." She ground out the cigarette and resumed her chair.

"That was it?"

"Pretty much, Father. But one thing still bothers me."

Ah, thought Koesler, here it comes. Valerie waited a moment. But when Koesler did not ask, she went on. "About the time Red pulled me away from Groendal, I was shouting that I would kill him. I shouted it over and over."

"Hmmm."

"Well, isn't that a sin? Murder certainly is a sin. And we were taught that a thought about committing something like murder could be a sin too . . . Father?"

"Maybe. It depends. Thoughts are kind of tricky."

"Tricky?"

"We're capable of thinking anything. A thought all by itself probably doesn't have any morality to it at all. Nor do words, if they have no real intent. Remember the story Jesus told about a father who sent his two sons into the fields to work? Son number one says, 'Sure I'll go, Pop'— or words to that effect. Son number two says, 'Not on your life.'

"But son one ends up going fishing while son two rethinks the whole thing and gets down to work.

"The point Jesus was making is that some of our thoughts and words are effective and some are empty and meaningless. Part of the proof, at least sometimes, is what a person will actually do about what she thinks or says.

"Make any sense?"

"Well, I haven't killed him—yet. But I don't know if that's only because of what's happened since.

"Very shortly after my encounter with Groendal, Red and I got married. Of course we moved back to Detroit. Red's been with the Pistons ever since he broke into the league and, as a result, his best business connections, endorsements, commercials are here. And there wasn't any point to my remaining in New York. Groendal had effectively shot down my stage career—and he was still on guard in case I continued to try. Red makes good money . . . real good money."

Koesler nodded. "I know."

"So, I've been able to do a little community and semipro theater here in Michigan. We enjoy our kids. And thank God there are no more cattle calls or hanging myself out on a line like a piece of meat.

"So, what I mean is, I haven't killed him. But to be honest, I don't know why I haven't. I guess maybe because I've got 'the good life.' I certainly wouldn't want to go to jail . . . not with a good and loving husband and a fulfilled life.

"But . . . what if I could get away with it? Just between you and me, Father, I honestly don't know whether I'd do it. After what he's done to me and my poor mother . . . I just don't know. I've got a lot of getting even to do before we're quits."

" 'Vengeance is mine, saith the Lord.' " Koesler threw the Biblical quote out reflexively. It fit. But he had never known it to be effective in the face of a genuine, deep desire for revenge.

"Well, if it's His, He'd better get cracking. No. I'm sorry, Father. I'm sorry, God. That's flip."

"Would you feel better about it if you went to confession? If you confessed it—sin or not—as it is in the sight of God?"

"I don't think I can do that, Father."

"Why not?"

" 'Cause I'm not sorry. I don't know whether it's a sin or not. But I know I'm not sorry. And you gotta be sorry to go to confession . . . don't you?"

"That's true."

"It helped. It really helped, Father. Just saying it out loud. I feel better just having told you about it. Honest, it helped. But I've still got to wrestle with this. Do I really want to kill him? Do I have to get revenge?" She sighed, then smiled tiredly. "I guess I'll see you again. But thanks for taking all this time with me, Father."

Koesler showed her out of the rectory. He poured a light Scotch and water, turned on the classical music station, and thought.

The "talking cure"—it never failed to amaze him. There comes a time in most people's lives that some secret and/or shameful thought or deed demands verbalization. And if it doesn't get aired, it may drive the person mad. But saying it, speaking it, telling it to someone, acts as a release valve. That's where Catholics have traditionally had an advantage—in confession. Not only do they have the opportunity of telling the secret either in the anonymity that the confessional provides—or, lately, face to face—but they can walk away feeling that they have been forgiven.

*   *   *

And this pretty well wrapped up the strange case of Ridley C. Groendal. During his relatively brief life he had managed to make many enemies and very few friends. Of the enemies, four were literally mortal enemies in that each had stated in Koesler's presence the intention of killing Rid.

And now he was dead. Nature and Rid's abuse of nature had contributed. Diabetes, high blood pressure, and heart problems were exacerbated by high living, thoughtless consumption of food and alcohol, and —finally—AIDS. Rid's was a condition programmed to explode. It had been detonated by four letters—one from each antagonist. After an evening of particularly heedless gastric abandon, Ridley had read the letters. All was in readiness for the explosion, and the letters had done it. Groendal read them and became apoplectic. His blood pressure shot up to the ceiling. He went into a convulsion and died.

Each of the letter writers had threatened to kill him. Which of them had succeeded—or was it a collaborative effort?

Shortly after leading the recitation of the rosary for Groendal, Father Koesler thought he knew the answer to that question. Of all the people in this drama, his position was unique in that he knew each of the dramatis personae and their interrelationships.

He needed to ask only one question and, depending on the answer, his solution would prove to be either right or wrong.

Part Seven

In Paradisum

21

The Gregorian Chant was so reassuring and beautiful. Ridley would have wanted the choir to offer this final commendation of his soul to heaven. Father Koesler wanted to think that he would have suggested it even if Peter Harison had not requested it. But why quibble over credit for so inspired a thought?

Koesler stood at the foot of the casket to conduct the final church rites before leaving for the cemetery. He let his mind wander through the familiar Latin. *"In paradisum deducant te Angeli . . ."*

May the angels lead you into paradise; may the martyrs come to welcome you and take you to the holy city, the new and eternal Jerusalem. May the choir of angels welcome you. Where Lazarus is poor no longer, may you have eternal rest.

The police had been most cooperative last night. Of course, things might not have gone so smoothly had it not been for Inspector Walter Koznicki.

Koznicki and Koesler had been friends for many years. The Inspector was head of Detroit's busy homicide department. It happened that Father Koesler had been of some help, by contributing his religious expertise, in solving some police investigations that had Catholic overtones. While their relationship had begun on a completely professional basis, over the years it had grown into a close and abiding friendship.

It was Koznicki who, after being contacted at home by Father Koesler, had gotten the ball rolling. David Palmer, Carroll Mitchell, Charles Hogan, Valerie Walsh, and Peter Harison were summoned to police headquarters at 1300 Beaubien.

While they waited for the principals to arrive, Koznicki showed Koesler the letters that Ridley Groendal had read just prior to expiring.

Koesler was quite sure he knew essentially what each letter would contain, but he read them nonetheless. There was nothing better to do while awaiting the others.

The letters had been smoothed out and flattened in clear plastic binders. But Koesler could tell by the creases in the papers that Ridley had crushed them rather forcefully before casting them in the wastebasket or on the floor. His final fury was almost palpable.

Later, Koesler would remember only salient segments of the four letters.

David Palmer:

. . . Groendal, I find it hard to believe that any adult could hang onto and nuture a childhood grudge the way you have. You played a trick on me. I played one on you. We were kids, for God's sake! All these years, you've imagined that I took something away from you—Interlochen.

Nothing could be further from the truth. You had no talent. You were a fourth-rate musician. You turned into a fifth-rate human being. But because of our childish pranks you have shit on my career over these many years. And I've taken it. All I've done is gripe and grouse over your unfair treatment. It occurs to me that you've done all you can to me. The time has come to return the favor. You've been sitting in the critic's chair untouched and untouchable for too long.

I wonder how artistic America would react to the fact that its premier critic is an unpunished and, to date, undetected arsonist. You were not alone when you set that fire in the auditorium. I was there with my camera. I've got the photograph. You and the fire.

It happened a long, long time ago. But not long enough for your ego to be free of the shame of it. I know you, Groendal. You've built the irreproachable image of the impeccable commentator who feels free to tear everyone else apart, confident that your seamless garment will never be rent or soiled.

I promise you this, Groendal: Beginning with arson, I will find out all your evil, from peccadillos to capital sins, and make sure the artistic world, especially your many victims, knows what a prick you are. Groendal, the world lost one of its great assholes when God decided to put teeth in your mouth. . . .

It continued in the same vein. Koesler shook his head. He wondered how Dave would feel if the media got hold of his letter. Undoubtedly he had never thought of that when he sent it. Koesler went on.

Carroll Mitchell:

. . . It seems to me that your function is to be the constant judge of competition. Actors competing with each other, competing with actors of the past. Playwrights in competition with each other. Which is the best play on Broadway; which is the worst? Constant competition. And you are

the judge, the acknowledged chief judge. The judge of all this competition.

You have judged my work over all these years and always found me sadly wanting. You have been a harsh and cruel judge of many other adequate to fine playwrights. You have been the supreme judge for all these years. Yet, the only time you were in actual competition with me, you were so frightened by that competition that you committed the most heinous crime possible to any writer: You stole. You plagiarized!

The time has come for the public to know what sort of individual has been setting standards for America. Fortunately, you won that contest. Or rather, Emmet Lavery won it with his "The First Legion." So your "winning" entry was published in The Gothic. I have had several copies made of that and will offer it as proof when I give this story to literary publications.

I hope you know, Rid, how dearly everyone out there wants to "get" you. Needless to say, they will have a field day with this story. Your credibility is all you have going for you. Say goodbye to it. In a little while, it will be gone. . . .

Koesler did not know in which order Groendal had read these letters, but he himself was beginning to experience the cumulative effect they must have had. He continued.

Charlie Hogan:

. . . Some people know you're gay, others don't. I've got to hand this much to you, you've been discreet. You've been living with this Peter Harison for years now. And yet you've never come completely out of the closet. Nor has anyone made a publicized statement about your homosexuality. That seems to be the way with you gays. You either flaunt it or keep it decently quiet.

I don't know why the hell you've bothered, but you evidently want to keep it private. Well, the time has come to let people know what kind of a bastard you are. I think the public would relish knowing that not only are you gay, but that you were kicked out of the seminary not just for being gay but for a homosexual attack.

At this point, you probably think I can't prove this, because, in return for your leaving quietly, Monsignor Cronyn allowed you to quit. What you didn't know is that, so you could never go back on your decision, Cronyn made the notation in your permanent record, along with the reason for your dismissal.

I'm sure the gossip columnists—dung beetles that they are—will appre-

ciate clearing up the mystery of your sexual preference along with that juicy tidbit from your younger days.

Further, no one could have been so vengeful against me all these years without slipping up himself. That much meanness can't have been contained. So I pledge myself to finding and exposing every fault and failing of yours I can uncover. And I'm confident I can find plenty. . . .

Koesler had a quizzical look. There was something in these three letters that disquieted and at the same time intrigued him. At the moment, he couldn't put his finger on it. Instead of going back to find the source of this feeling, he decided to complete the cycle.

Valerie Walsh:

I think I will never forgive or forget what you did to me. What baffled me was why you'd do it. You worked overtime keeping me off the stage. You were grossly unfair, cruel, and rotten. I would never have discovered the reason if I had not confided in my mother. She clarified it all. Why would you sabotage my career when we had never met? To get even with my mother. Even with my mother! You certainly had reason to get even! You left her pregnant, homeless, and unemployed. She certainly treated you shabbily! She didn't give you away, or take you to court for child support, but stayed out of your life.

Over the years, you've built a reputation of being above and beyond any sort of disgraceful affair. You've been welcomed into the homes and parties of the movers and shakers. You are above all criticism.

Well, the time has come to burst your pretentious bubble. Mother is making an affidavit concerning your responsibility. Just imagine how titillating all your former friends will find the delicious gossip about you and your one-nighter. Yours is not the conduct of a noble critic. Yours is the behavior of a scoundrel and a fraud.

I know, from being on the New York scene, that people laugh behind your back at the combination of your gay lifestyle and your thin reputation of self-righteousness. Think of the fun they're going to have with this new scandal. It will be a marvelous season for the critics of the critic. We're going to enjoy it. We are all going to enjoy very much seeing the modern-day Grendel monster skewered. . . .

While Koesler had been reading the letters, Sergeants Charles Papkin and Ray Ewing, the investigating officers, had been speaking quietly with Inspector Koznicki. As Koesler completed his reading, the first of the five summoned people arrived. The others appeared within minutes.

Lynn Mitchell and Red Walsh, who had accompanied their respective spouses, were asked to wait in an adjoining room.

There were more than enough chairs around the several tables in the squad room. After all were seated there was an awkward silence. No one seemed to know who should begin. The guests looked expectantly at the police, who, in turn, gazed at Father Koesler. Following the officers' lead, the others began to stare at Koesler. It was he, after all, who had requested this gathering.

The first thought that crossed the priest's mind was the bromide, "Well, I suppose you're wondering why I asked you here?" He dismissed that. Instead, he said, "I may be wrong, but if a couple of hypotheses are correct, I think we may be able to clear up the matter of Ridley Groendal's death."

Sergeant Papkin failed to suppress a sardonic smile. He could recall a few times this priest had been wrong. He would not be at all surprised if Koesler were wrong again.

Sergeant Ewing, on the other hand, kept an open mind. Confident and self-assured, he was willing to take a chance on an amateur. He did not feel at all threatened by Koesler's hypotheses.

"I'll try," Koesler proceeded, "to approach this logically, more for my own benefit than anyone else's." Not far from him on the table was a legal pad with a few unused sheets. He pulled it to him and began making notes. It would help keep him on track.

"The status of Ridley's health, particularly over the past year, was no great secret," Koesler continued. "Partly in the gossip columns and partly on the entertainment pages of the newspapers, we could read both rumors and facts about Ridley. So, anyone interested in knowing how he was doing—or, more pointedly, how badly off he was—could find out easily.

"All of us, for varying reasons, were linked to Rid. All of us, particularly you five, were affected by him. So, it is quite likely—probable?—certain?—that we all knew his health was delicate and deteriorating.

"We knew he was a diabetic, that he had high blood pressure, that he had suffered heart attacks and was prone to having more. We might have known—or guessed—that he had contracted AIDS. There was a popular rumor to that effect.

"In any case, it would have been simple for any of us to guess that he would not likely survive a serious emotional strain." Koesler continued to make notes. And he spoke more slowly, seeming to choose his words ever more carefully.

"Now," Koesler continued, "before he died just a few days ago, Rid had gone to Orchestra Hall. Afterward, he went to his office, where he wrote a review of the evening's concert. Then he went through his mail. And in that particular batch of mail were letters from four of you—Mitch, Charlie, Dave, and Valerie.

"Ridley read each letter, one after the other, growing more furious and agitated as he did so.

"Now I read these letters just before you came tonight, and I must admit they are provocative. The information you threatened to make public was no secret to Ridley. In fact, due to my association with Rid and the rest of you, it was no surprise to me.

"But these were all old, old skeletons. Why would you all pick this particular time to threaten Rid with their revelations? For there is no doubt—am I correct, Inspector?—that Rid died of a massive coronary as a result of reading those letters?"

Koesler looked toward Koznicki for corroboration. The Inspector nodded.

"By no stretch of the imagination," Koesler continued, "could this be a coincidence. All these letters dredging up the very worst of Rid's past at the same time. Either you all got together and agreed to do this now —in which case you would have counted on the cumulative effect of your letters to cause Rid's death. Or—and I tend to think this is the case—some outside agent prompted each of you individually to get it off your chest. Did you all, indeed, get some sort of invitation to strike back at Rid? Did you get some sort of letter that prompted you to write?"

He looked expectantly from one to the other and was more than mildly surprised that each of them readily nodded. Koesler was even more startled that each likewise wore a combined bewildered and bemused expression.

"We've already been through this, Father," Papkin said.

Koesler knew he had blundered. He tried not to blush. But the more effort he put into it, the more he reddened.

"Each of these four claims to have received a letter inviting him or her to threaten to reveal their charges against Groendal." Sarcasm was evident in Papkin's voice. He began to pace restlessly, one hand deep in his pocket rattling change.

"We've got the letters these people received, Father." Ewing's tone was conciliatory. "Each of them is identical with the others. They don't appear to be copies; each seems to be a typed original. And, of course, there's no signature. The letters just end with the words *from another victim of Ridley Groendal.*

"The presumption is that one of these four sent the invitation to all four, including himself—or herself." Papkin's tone clearly implied that they were wasting valuable time that might have been used in the continuing police investigation.

"The type in the invitation doesn't match the type in any of the hate letters sent to Groendal. So whoever wrote the invitational letter used another typewriter. We haven't found it yet. But we're looking." Again the implication that the police would find "the smoking gun" if only they were left to do their job.

"Well . . . I'm sorry," Koesler fumbled. "I should have known that you would have investigated that. How stupid of me!"

"Not at all, Father. You were only trying to be helpful," Koznicki said. "But I'm curious; tell me: What made you think there had been an invitation? It might just as easily have been the result of an agreement between the letter writers."

"Well . . ." Koesler pushed the legal pad away; from now on he would wing it. ". . . A number of things, really. I kind of had my suspicion bolstered tonight when I had a chance to read the letters sent to Rid.

"There was a recurring phrase in each of the letters. Something about 'the time has come.' Each letter contained that phrase. As if someone had suggested that Ridley had overstayed his welcome and was overdue for revenge. As if someone had programmed the response 'the time has come' by stating forcefully that the time, indeed, had come.

"If these four had conspired among themselves in sending their letters to Ridley, they surely would have taken pains to make sure each letter was entirely different from the others. Editors, politicians, and I'm sure, the police, when they get more than one letter regarding a specific issue, are on the lookout for repeated phrases that indicate a form letter or, at the very least, collusion. These are intelligent people. If they had conspired, they certainly wouldn't have let that phrase—'the time has come'—appear in each and every letter. No, somebody had to have invited them to write."

"Interesting, Father." The Inspector nodded. "And that's exactly the conclusion we ourselves had reached." Ewing's face registered no emotion; Papkin seemed bored. "However," the Inspector went on, "you said that reading the letters sent to Groendal merely bolstered a suspicion . . . a suspicion that you already held. Is that not correct?"

"Yes, Inspector."

There was a good deal of shifting about in chairs. Koesler knew he'd better get to the point soon. "Well," he said, "I was sort of subconsciously aware of that suspicion when I selected the first Scripture lesson that will be read at the funeral Mass tomorrow."

"Go on, Father." By now, Koznicki was playing straight man for his friend, who seemed to be zeroing in on his target at his usual, gradual, systematic pace.

"When I selected the reading," Koesler continued, "it seemed appropriate. But I didn't know why it felt so right. It must have been something deep inside me dictating. Actually, it wasn't until after we recited the rosary tonight for Ridley that everything sort of fell into place. And the first thing to tumble was my less-than-conscious reason for selecting that first reading."

"What was—or rather—what is that first reading going to be?" Was the normally placid Inspector becoming impatient?

"I was getting to that. The reading is from the Second Book of Samuel in the Old Testament. I scarcely ever select that reading for a funeral Mass. It seldom seems appropriate. But for some, as I say, subconscious motive, I picked it for tomorrow.

"It tells the story of how King David mourned at the loss of his son Absalom. Now, even though David was reluctant to admit it, Absalom had to be killed. Even so, David became inconsolable when he was finally informed that his son had been killed. And David says, "If only I had died instead of you.' "

Koesler paused. The others looked from one to another. No one seemed to be able to make any sense out of what the priest had said.

Koesler looked intently at each of the guests seated in this barren squad room and very deliberately repeated the quotation, directing it at each of them in turn: "If only I had died instead of you."

There followed a painful silence.

"Well, don't look at me," Charlie Hogan said. "He ruined my life. I wouldn't have died instead of him."

"Same here," Carroll Mitchell said. "He did everything he could to to block me from what I deserved. Honestly, I'm glad the bastard's dead."

"To borrow from Rhett Butler," Dave Palmer said, "frankly I don't give a damn. If anything, I'd have to agree with Mr. Mitchell here. I'm glad he's dead."

Last but by no means least, Valerie chimed in. "I'm afraid, to be brutally honest, I go a bit beyond these gentlemen. I had rather hoped it was my letter that killed the asshole!"

"Well," said Koesler, "that accounts for almost everyone."

"Whaddya mean *almost*? That *is* everyone," Sergeant Papkin said brusquely.

"Not quite," Koesler replied. "Not quite." He looked steadily at Peter Harison.

"What?" Harison seemed to be waking from a shallow slumber. "What? You can't . . . you can't mean me! Why, I was Rid's dearest friend. I was . . . well, you simply can't mean me. Of all the people here—of all the people in the world—I have got to be the least likely suspect. I say! This is ridiculous! I loved Ridley Groendal!"

"Yes, you did," Koesler affirmed. "In fact, you were the one I was subconsciously thinking of when I selected that reading. Of you alone might it be said, 'If only I had died instead of you.' "

"Look here: If you are referring to AIDS, I did not give that disease to Rid. I took a test for AIDS—after Rid's death. It came out negative." He looked to Koznicki for corroboration.

The Inspector nodded. "That is correct; Mr. Harison underwent testing at our request."

"I told you how Rid got that disease," Harison continued. "And," he almost spat the words at the priest, "I told you in confidence!"

"It has nothing to do with how Rid got AIDS, Peter. And nothing you or Ridley told me in confidence has anything to do with this."

"Then what in God's name are you talking about?"

"I'm talking about the other night, when Ridley Groendal died. If you could have died in his stead, I'm sure you would have."

Harison loosened his tie and undid the top button of his shirt. "Well, Father , that's very nice of you to say. But it has no relevance here. The police are trying to discover which of these people invited the others to vent their spleen, as it were, on Ridley. That has nothing to do with me."

"Well, I don't know about that." Koesler pulled the legal pad back and began making notations again. "I think everybody has wondered about the fact that Ridley opened and read all four letters on the same evening and consecutively—even though they had not all been mailed on the same day.

"Now, from your own statements in the papers and on radio and TV, you maintained that you were the one who prepared and presented his mail to Rid."

"And what is that supposed to mean?"

"That Rid did not suffer his fatal seizure until he had opened and read all four letters. It was the cumulative effect that brought on his death. And, although the letters were mailed at different times—even on different days—they were presented to Rid at one and the same time, all together, one after another, by you—you who were the only one who knew the part all four of the others had played in Ridley's past life."

The four looked at each oher as if in tacit assurance of ignorance as to each other's past role in Ridley Groendal's life.

Harison, however, seemed to gain a measure of assurance. As if he suddenly had become aware that he had betrayed some anxiety a few moments before, he quickly rebuttoned his shirt and slipped his tie taut to his neck.

"Well, I don't know who knows what—and I don't see how you could prove whether they did or didn't. As for the letters being presented all at once, here's nothing greatly unusual about that. Really! I mean, you know the post office, particularly around Christmastime. They're swamped. It's notorious that mail is delivered helter-skelter at this time of year.

"Besides, we only dropped in at Rid's office periodically. By no means did we get to his mail on a regular basis. It was quite ordinary for it to back up so that we had to go through quite a pile. It was the rule, not the exception, for us to open mail that had been delivered over the course of many days—sometimes a week or more.

"As to the fact that he opened the letters from these four people consecutively, well, yes, that's the order in which I gave them to him, I suppose. But routinely, I always stack the junk mail, notices, releases, announcements together. I always put the first class mail at the end. And there seldom is much first class mail at the office. So it's easily understandable that Rid would have letters that could very well have been delivered at different times. And that they would be together in the first class mail." Harison appeared quite self-assured.

"Indeed." Koesler seemed to have expected Harison's explanation. "But the coincidences go on.

"We all know that Rid's health was failing. Even for those of us who don't read gossip columns, we could see it for ourselves in his dramatic weight loss and in just his general appearance and demeanor. His condition, particularly the diabetes and high blood pressure, was common knowledge. But far from being in any sort of fit or even adequate condition for the onslaught he would absorb from the threats in those letters, he was in the worst condition of his life.

"Now, according to what I read, the medical examiner stated that Ridley had ingested large quantities of extremely rich food and, in fact, had had enough alcohol to be legally drunk. Peter, you were his only companion at dinner that evening. The same person who presented him with what turned out to be lethal mail also undoubtedly encouraged him to eat and drink things that would help measurably to prepare the way for a fatal seizure."

"That's not true! That simply is not true!" Harison tugged at his tie, but did not loosen it. "You can ask the waiter—what's his name?— Ramon. Ridley ordered his own food. If anything, I tried to discourage him from abusing himself with all that food, and those drinks."

Harison turned to face the three officers, who, seated near the door of the squad room, were paying careful attention to this exchange. "Do I have to go through this?" Harison was almost pleading. "Do I have to answer these charges? The imaginings of some priest?"

No one replied for a moment. Then Inspector Koznicki said, "Not really, Mr. Harison. You are under no obligation to continue this conversation with Father Koesler. However, if he stops asking questions of you, we will begin. Of course, if you would prefer an attorney be present . . . ?"

"Uh, no. No, of course not. I have no need of an attorney."

Harison turned back to Koesler with a defiant look. All three officers silently agreed that Harison should have opted for an attorney.

"All right," Harison challenged, "you who think you are Father Brown, you have brought up the fact that it was I who handed the letters to Ridley and it was I who dined with him. Both of those things we always did together. But it is obvious, is it now? Somehow, in your fatuous clerical mind you have made me responsible for the death of Ridley Groendal. If that isn't the most ridiculous supposition! Why on earth would I do such a thing? We were not having any sort of 'lovers' quarrel.' We were the best of friends. He was—" his voice faltered— "my best friend."

"Of course he was." Koesler's sympathy was evident. "And that's why you did what you thought you had to do. Because he was your best friend."

"That's ridiculous! It's silly! It's absurd! I don't have to listen to this!" Harison was close to panic.

"Calm down, Peter. I'm sure the police would eventually have checked your typewriter and found that it was the one used to type the letters all four of these people received."

It lasted only an instant, but Koesler noted despair flit behind Harison's eyes. "It's impossible! Why would I do such a thing?" Still Harison struggled.

"You told me all about it this evening at the funeral home, Peter. But it was only after I left, after we said the rosary, that it all fell into place. That was when I called Inspector Koznicki. He called Sergeants Papkin and Ewing and they called the other four."

"But, how . . . ?"

"For all your avant-garde ways, Peter, you and Rid were very traditional Catholics," Koesler explained. "For instance, the liturgy you and I worked out for tomorrow's funeral Mass is as traditional as it could be short of it all being in Latin. Even then, you requested the "In Paradisum" be sung in Latin and in plainchant.

"And this traditional penchant of yours also prompted you to ask me this evening whether I might get in trouble by granting Rid a Catholic burial given the fact he had AIDS. It was very thoughtful of you, Peter. You were concerned that once the Chancery became aware of that condition of Rid's that they might come down hard on me because of . . . what? Because I gave Catholic burial to a public sinner?

"Well, as I explained to you, it doesn't work that way. But you were deeply concerned that for some publicly known sin, Rid might have been denied Catholic burial.

"Now granted, every once in a while, the Church does deny burial rites to someone such as a notorious criminal because of the scandal it might cause. But that never happens merely in a case such as AIDS.

"However, there is a more ancient and historic reason for denial of Christian burial. It is so famous that it is seemingly well known by everyone, and referred to in fiction and in fact. The one sin that has been traditionally associated with the denial of Christian burial . . ."

"Suicide." Charlie Hogan, who had been intently following Koesler's reasoning, barely whispered it.

"Indeed," Koesler said. "Suicide."

"Remember, Peter? It was just after we had talked about the AIDS business. You were telling me, at some length, about Rid's atrocious dining habits. You said something like, 'He's been killing himself lately. And then, this AIDS! Well, it was just a matter of time.'

"When I thought back on it, Peter, that's when it all fell into place. It was just a matter of time. Rid's condition was bad enough with the heart and the diabetes. When AIDS was added to that and he lost his immune defense system, he was doomed to practically disintegrate before our eyes.

"But, rather than let these diseases ravage him, he was, with his gorging and guzzling and his lifestyle, doing exactly what you said—he was killing himself. And he was doing it quite deliberately.

"If he had continued—if he had succeeded—it would have amounted to, at least in traditional Christian thought, the 'unforgivable' sin. In that view, he was condemning himself to hell.

"And you, Peter, his best friend—the one who would have died for him had you been able—could not let that happen. You could not let your friend condemn himself to hell.

"Yet you could not stop him. He was determined. You could find only one alternative. You had to intervene. It was the kindest thing you could think of doing for your friend.

"In a way, he was already under a death sentence. If one or another of his illnesses did not kill him, in all probability AIDS would have. But anything would have been better than the death he was preparing for himself—suicide.

"As Rid's closest friend, you, of course, knew of the virtual war that had gone on between him and these four people. You knew all the details. So you invited them to play their trump cards. You were certain the cumulative effect of the threats would be a burden his system could not sustain.

"Either you hoped or you presumed that all four would leap at the opportunity—and that their letters would all be delivered to the office on the night in question, or that you could hold the earlier ones until all were there. You wanted your weapon to be potent enough. You made sure he ate and drank all the wrong things. After the concert, he wrote his review, you gave him the letters—and waited.

22

Inspector Koznicki followed Koesler out to Norman's Eton Street Station in his own car, so they arrived at about the same time. Norman's was a restaurant in what had once been a railroad station. Koesler had selected it because it was managed by a parishioner, so they would be able to order very little, enjoy privacy and, at the same time, not vex the staff.

Once inside, Koesler introduced the inspector to James McIntyre and explained the purpose of their visit. The personable manager showed them to an out-of-the-way alcove table and gave instructions to their waiter.

Both Koesler and Koznicki ordered decaffeinated coffee. The waiter promptly brought the coffee and a basket of breadsticks. He would return periodically to refill their cups.

It had been longer than usual since the two had last met, so initially they filled each other in on what had been happening in their lives. Koesler spoke of Christmas, always an especially joyful event in his parish, with the crêche, the decorated evergreens, the sanctuary filled to overflowing with poinsettias. The choir had done exceptionally well this year.

Koznicki spoke of Christmas with his wife and, for a change, all of his children, their spouses, and their children. It was rare that all were free to gather together for the holidays. After a few minutes, the Inspector paused. He sensed his friend was distracted by what had occurred earlier.

"Troubled, Father?"

"Oh, I guess so. A bit."

Koznicki waved a massive hand. The waiter approached to fill their cups. He checked the breadbasket, but it was still nearly full.

"You should not be troubled, Father. A case is solved and you were pivotal in its solution. That should give you a feeling of satisfaction."

"Huh? Oh, I suppose so . . ."

"Yet there is something. What is it?"

"Would you police actually have checked Peter Harison's typewriter? Would you have discovered who really invited those others to write to Ridley? Would you have found 'the smoking gun' without my lucky guess?"

Koznicki smiled briefly. "You do yourself a disservice, Father. It was not a lucky guess. It was an excellent piece of deduction. As for whether we could have checked and found Mr. Harison's typewriter," Koznicki spread his hands, "well, that is a matter of pure speculation."

"Then, would you mind speculating?"

"Difficult." Koznicki sipped the coffee. "I suspect we would have gotten around to it, providing we spent enough time on the case. We were trying to cover every angle. There was the syringe under the desk —which, as far as we could ascertain, turned out to be quite innocuous; there was nothing in it but traces of insulin. Then there was the AIDS question; we asked Mr. Harison to undergo a test for that—which, as you now know, turned out negative. As for the 'smoking gun,' as you term it, in all likelihood, we would have first tried to exhaust the possibility that any of the original four might have used a typewriter other than their own. While that would have taken many man hours, we already had several detectives on the case besides Sergeants Papkin and Ewing.

"Failing that, I suspect we would have searched among those who hated Groendal—and I take it there were many."

Koesler exhaled audibly. "As the stars in the sky or the sands of the desert."

"Perhaps out of sheer desperation we would eventually have come to Mr. Harison. But, of course, we were looking for an enemy—of which, as you state, there were many—not a friend."

"Then I misled Peter when I told him the police would have discovered that his typewriter was the one they were looking for."

"Not necessarily. It was a fair assumption. And, in the end, probably was true."

"There's something nagging at me, though," Koesler said. "Why didn't Peter just destroy those four letters, I wonder? I mean after Rid had his fatal seizure? Then everyone would just have thought Ridley had merely suffered a heart attack. With his medical history, it certainly would come as no surprise to anyone that Rid would go that way without any outside provocation."

"It is a good point." The Inspector pondered as he sipped more coffee. "Why did Nixon not destroy the tapes? Probably because enough people knew the tapes existed that, had they been destroyed, and had their existence been subsequently revealed, their destruction would have aroused suspicions. Even more so in this case. Each of four people knew that he or she had sent a most inflammatory and threatening letter to Groendal. It would be only natural for one—or all, for that matter—to wonder what had happened to his or her letter. All that needed to happen was for one of them to raise the question—to poke around the *Suburban Reporter's* newsroom, to ask someone in the news media. Just to become inquisitive about what had happened to the letter. If one questioned the matter, certainly the others would join in. At that point, Harison, as the one who sorted and presented all Groendal's mail, would be hard-pressed to explain the absence of these letters.

"Better to let the letters alone and let them point to the writers as the probable guilty parties.

"Harison simply could not know that the instigation of the letters would be traced back to him. Or, he took the chance they would not be."

Koznicki caught Koesler gazing longingly as a diner some tables away lit a cigarette. It had been many years since the priest had given up smoking. If he was being tempted at this late date, Koznicki concluded his friend must be in a very distraught state. Koznicki leaned forward. "It is Peter Harison, is it not? You are concerned over what is happening to him."

Koesler looked intensely at Koznicki and nodded.

The Inspector glanced at his watch. "He should be processed by now. It may be time enough to check on what is happening. Would you excuse me, Father?"

"For that? Gladly."

During the approximately fifteen minutes Koznicki was gone, Koesler absently gazed at the Christmas decorations. In addition to the basic green and red, there was a generous sprinkling of attractions for children, including a Santa. All in keeping with the restaurant's merited claim to be a "family" dining establishment. Because his parishioner managed the place, Koesler felt especially pleased by its success.

So lost in thought was he that he was taken by surprise when Koznicki resumed his chair. The inspector wore just the hint of a smile.

"Good news?" Koesler was eager.

"Tentative, but, yes, good news. At least as good as the news could be at this stage."

"You've talked to Peter."

"No, to Sergeant Ewing. After he processed Mr. Harison and put him in a holding cell, he phoned the chief deputy prosecutor and explained the case. It was the prosecutor's opinion that we have here a most rare, if not unique, case and that he would have to check it out first thing in the morning."

"Excuse me, but check what?"

"Various statutes and cases, to determine what, if any, charge to bring. He will, after all, be the one to prosecute the case."

"What happens to Peter in the meantime?"

"That is the part I think you will like. The prosecutor asked Sergeant Ewing if he thought Mr. Harison would try to escape if he were released overnight."

"And?"

"And the sergeant said he thought not. And, in very truth, I must agree. So, Mr. Harison was 'released to appear.' That is a term we use to indicate that when we get a warrant, the prisoner must return to our custody."

"That means that Peter will at least be able to attend the funeral tomorrow morning?"

"I would think so, yes. It probably will take several hours to formulate the case against him. So it should be at least midmorning before a determination is made."

"Thank God." Koesler was genuinely relieved. "At least he'll be able to attend the funeral. And then?"

"And then we shall see what we shall see."

Part Eight

At the Grave

Father Koesler could remember—long, long ago—when he had been an altar boy. Especially on school days, it had been most desirable to accompany the priest to the cemetery. That way one could miss an entire morning of school.

In those days, priests usually ate breakfast—their first nourishment of the day—immediately following the funeral Mass. Then the priest and his altar boys were chauffeured to the cemetery by the mortician. Mourners usually were kept waiting in their cars until the priest finally arrived. All in all, the process consumed considerable time.

Like everything else, these things had changed. Now it was permissible as well as sensible to eat before Mass. Nor did the priest usually take altar boys with him to the cemetery.

Thus, Koesler arrived at Holy Sepulchre Cemetery alone and well in advance of the cortege. None of the visiting priests who had attended the Mass would be at the cemetery. The cemetery, Koesler thought sardonically, was for diehards. Only the most committed mourners accompanied the body to the grave. And literally no one this day would go all the way to the grave. In winter the final rites were held in the mausoleum. That was as close to the frozen ground as the funeral party could get.

There was no point in staying in his car and running the motor to keep warm. So Koesler entered the mausoleum as soon as he arrived. He was greeted by the cemetery's manager. Over the years and through hundreds of burials, priests and cemetery personnel became acquaintances, if not friends.

"Cold enough for you, Father?"

"Plenty. And we've still got all of winter to go."

"Got the burial permit with you, Father?" The manager carried a pad of permit certificates just in case a priest forgot. It happened.

"Sure, here."

"Ridley C. Groendal. Must have been kind of famous. Got a big obit in the paper." The manager studied the certificate.

"Yeah, he was kind of famous." Koesler had long since ceased to be surprised when a celebrity in an artistic field was not generally known. About the only ones widely famous were motion picture and television personalities.

"Really peculiar middle name, eh, Father?"

"Huh? Peculiar?" Koesler tried to recall Ridley's middle name. At one time he'd known it but, never having a use for it, he'd forgotten it. "It's . . . it's . . . oh . . . Charles, isn't it?"

"Maybe according to the baptismal certificate, but not according to the birth or death certificate. Got it right off the county records. It's Caligula."

"Caligula! Are you sure?"

"Yep. Never seen that one before. I mean outside a history book."

Caligula! Koesler had no reason to disbelieve the man. Rid had managed to keep it a secret all these years, if, indeed, he had ever known what his real name was. What kind of parent would give a name like that to a child? Thinking back on Ridley's parents, Koesler could only guess it must have been Rid's father. Some sort of ultimate joke played on a child the father never wanted. The name, now revealed, spoke volumes on what Ridley's early life must have been.

Well, no more time for speculation. The cortege had arrived and was being organized by the funeral directors.

The metal casket was carried carefully up the few steps and set on the wheeled cart. A mortician guided it into the mausoleum. The mourners filed in and were directed to stand near either side wall. The crowd had thinned drastically. Only a few of those who had attended the Mass had come to the cemetery.

Once again, and for the final time, Koesler stood at the foot of Ridley Groendal's casket. Although the entire cemetery had been consecrated, and although they were not standing at the open grave, it was customary to read the prayer:

"Lord God, through your mercy those who have lived in faith find eternal peace. Bless this grave and send your angel to watch over it. Forgive the sins of our brother whose body we bury here. Welcome him into your presence, and with your saints let him rejoice in you forever. We ask this through Christ our Lord. Amen."

Koesler sprinkled the casket with holy water again. As he continued the familiar prayers, he scanned the little group. Peter Harison, present by the grace of the prosecutor's office. Dave, Mitch, Charlie, and Valerie were not there. Evidently, they were satisfied that Ridley would no longer be around to foul their lives. They trusted Koesler and the few remaining faithful to plant Ridley.

*　　*　　*

Peter Harison felt the tension ease. Why, he did not know. Perhaps because the burial service was near its conclusion. Perhaps because so few of those in the church had come to the cemetery. That was it, probably. Especially with the four—Palmer, Mitchell, Hogan, and Walsh—gone. Truthfully, they made him at least slightly uneasy. It was like being confined in a room with one's own murder weapon—a club, a knife, a gun. And yet, the four were not really his weapons; he had merely orchestrated their assault of Ridley. The determination to kill Ridley had been theirs.

Harison—familiar as he was with his friend's private life—knew well their animosity toward Ridley. Even though found out last night, it had been a damned clever plan—as uncomplicated as uncapping an active volcano. All he'd had to do was write them—posing as a fellow victim of Ridley's venom—assuring them the time was ripe, and urging them to an act of revenge. In actuality, the time was more ripe than any of them could have suspected.

After that, it had been easy. So intent was Rid on killing himself that almost any occasion would have served. All Harison had to do was wait —and he was reasonably sure they all would write—until all the letters had been delivered; then, at an appropriate moment, set them up for Rid.

The way Rid was abusing his health, Harison knew that almost any moment would be appropriate. And so it had been. That evening had been a classic. Rid had perfectly set himself up with his gluttony, guz-zling, and attitude. All Harison needed to do was to stack the letters with their predictable contents and let nature take its course.

Soon, he felt sure, he would have to pay the price for what he had done. But, at most, it would be an earthly penalty. Before God, he'd done nothing wrong. Of that he was certain. They—Rid's enemies— had killed him. Harison, at most, had let them do so. And, in any case, he had saved his friend from suicide and the eternal fires of hell. Let civil law do its damnedest. He was ready. He would not whimper.

*　　*　　*

As he neared the end of the Prayers at Graveside, Koesler noticed an additional person enter the mausoleum and take a place at the rear. It was Sergeant Ewing. He wore the same somber expression as the others. If one did not know he was a police officer, there would be no way of telling he was not one with the other mourners.

Koesler concluded the rite:

"We command our brother, Ridley, to you, Lord. Now that he has passed from this life, may he live on in your presence. In your mercy and love, forgive whatever sins he may have committed through human weakness. We ask this through Christ our Lord. Amen."

Koesler intoned, *"Eternal rest grant unto him, O Lord."*

And all responded, *"And may perpetual light shine upon him."*

"May his soul and the souls of all the faithful departed, through the mercy of God, rest in peace."

"Amen."

The funeral director spoke briefly, thanking all for attending, and directing them back to their cars. After many funerals, at least those who had taken the trouble of going to the cemetery were invited to return to some location where a luncheon would be served. Not at this funeral. Everything ended at this point.

In silence, those present began to depart.

Peter Harison seemed at a loss. He appeared uncertain as to whether to go or stay. He moved as if to approach Father Koesler, then thought better of it and turned to leave.

When he was stopped by Ewing at the door, Harison seemed startled. The officer spoke earnestly to him for several minutes. From time to time, Harison nodded. Finally, when Ewing had finished, Harison made an abortive gesture, half turned as if to return to Koesler, decided against it, and hurriedly left the mausoleum.

Only Ewing and Koesler remained. The priest inclined his head slightly and looked inquiringly at the officer.

Ewing, smiling benignly, approached Koesler. "I suppose you're wondering what happened."

"I certainly am."

"Well, you broke this case. There's no reason why you shouldn't be among the first to know. My friend the prosecuting attorney got out his law books first thing this morning.

"And, briefly, the prosecutor has denied our request for the issuance of a warrant."

"That means . . . ?"

"Harison walks. He skates. For all intents and purposes, he's free."

"They're not going to prosecute?"

"The determination is that, at most, it's a civil cause of action. The charge would be Intentional Infliction of Mental Distress. So, in theory, Harison could be sued for soliciting those letters. But there's no one left to sue him. Groendal is dead, survived by no one. No one close. No one who cares. The only one who cared was Harison and he killed the guy."

"Then Peter will not be tried?"

"Without a warrant—no. There is no criminal charge."

"But those letters did it. Reading them, as Rid did, killed him."

"Father, I guess the moral is, If you've got a weak heart—diabetes, whatever—and you're expecting some inflammatory mail, you'd better get someone to open your mail for you."

"Well, I must say, nothing much surprises me anymore. But this is surprising."

"It sure as hell is. The most the prosecutor said was that he'd have to face a higher judge. But I don't operate on that level. If they get by a judge and jury in the city of Detroit, they're by me." Ewing turned and walked away.

"Thanks," Koesler called after him. "Thanks for taking the trouble to explain it for me."

Without turning, Ewing nodded and shrugged.

Koesler was alone in the marble vault. Alone with the mortal remains of Ridley C. Groendal.

The priest returned to the casket. He placed his hand against the metal. It was wet. Beads of holy water still clung to it.

As if a videotape was played at fast-forward, Ridley's life, as Koesler knew it, passed before his memory. He and Ridley were children making their way through Holy Redeemer grade school in the good old days. There was the ill-fated concert when Rid took on Dave Palmer and lost. The treasured days of the seminary during which Rid tried to compete against a more talented playwright, Carroll Mitchell, and felt himself compelled to plagiarize. The friendship with Charlie Hogan that turned into a different lifestyle for Rid and got him expelled from the seminary. His awkward and fateful evening with Jane Condon that produced a doomed child and, eventually, an unexpected enemy in Valerie Walsh. His lasting love of Peter Harison and the one infidelity that cost Rid what little health he had left.

Koesler thought of what Sergeant Ewing had said: that the prosecutor had left those involved in Rid's death to a higher than earthly judge. The matter now rested between God—the just judge—and the consciences of five people.

It was impossible for Koesler to crawl inside those consciences and learn what their individual judgments might be. But, if he had to bet on it, he would have wagered that their consciences would have told them that they had done God's will at best or a good deed at worst. Peter Harison was convinced he had saved his friend from suicide and the fires of hell; the others that they had righted the scales of justice and insured that Ridley would ruin no more lives.

Koesler was brought back to the present with a start when the casket moved. He had been so lost in reverie, he had not noticed the attendant who came to take the coffin into a holding room. "Done here, Father?" The attendant was surprised the priest was still there. Usually, everyone cleared out immediately after the final rites.

"Oh . . . oh . . . yes. Sorry."

"Gotta get ready for the next funeral. Just turned in the gate. Gonna be here in just a couple of minutes. Life goes on, y'know."

Koesler watched as the casket was wheeled from the room. Life goes on? For some of us, yes. For others, no. You did not fit too well into this life, Rid. Be at rest now, Rid. Be at peace.